Praise for Jennifer McMahon and *Dismantled*

"One of the brightest new stars of literary suspense."
—*Los Angeles Times*

"A failed marriage. A long-buried secret. A lonely child's imaginary friend. From these simple ingredients, Jennifer McMahon has constructed a fun, twisty thriller. Expect *Dismantled* to earn comparisons to *The Secret History*."
—Stewart O'Nan, author of *Songs for the Missing*

"A prank gone wrong drives this outstanding novel from bestseller McMahon. . . . By alternating the present-day lives of Henry, Tess, and Emma with the origins of the Dismantlers, McMahon allows the inexorable sense of dread to build incrementally. Perhaps most memorable are not the young artists but Emma, a child whose intense imagination only adds fuel to the slow-burning fire." —*Publishers Weekly* (starred review)

"[A] disturbing, darkly hypnotic novel . . . McMahon's deftly creepy prose creates a world of chaos and abuse; the book brims with unexpected and often startling plot twists, taking the reader on a strange journey that never disappoints . . . beautifully written and extraordinarily imaginative."
—*Kirkus Reviews*

"[A]n eerie an⟨...⟩ ⟨...⟩nd Emma is a triumph of cha⟨...⟩ ⟨...⟩ an author who can so compe⟨...⟩ ⟨...⟩view.

—*Boston Globe*

"In her third, elegantly spooky mystery revolving around the vulnerability of a young girl and a haunting past, McMahon fashions a fresh and entrancing ghost-in-the-woods tale replete with startling psychoses, delectable Hitchcockian motifs, and dangerous attractions." —*Booklist*

"McMahon builds the suspense well, using several creepy fake-outs as she muddies the waters with a private detective, a mysterious art patron, and most potent of all, Emma's imaginary friend, Danner. But is Danner imaginary? A sign of mental imbalance? Or is she something more . . . ghostly? . . . McMahon's skill keeps the reader wondering just what happened that night at the lake and what form revenge will take." —*Library Journal*

"McMahon has once again written a suspenseful and smart novel that weaves past and present seamlessly, slowly opening the minds of her characters in such a way that they almost feel like part of your real life long after you put the book down. . . . Plan to read Ms. McMahon's novel in one sitting and to nibble your fingernails to the nub." —*The Chronicle* (Vermont)

"A word of advice when picking up Jennifer McMahon's latest thriller, *Dismantled*. Hold on tight. McMahon launches her third adult novel with a present-day suicide and the hint of a decade-old murder. She adds a handful of white-knuckled scares and the suggestion of a ghost story, much of it seen through the eyes of an imaginative, adorable nine-year-old named Emma, making it hard to put the book down—right to the final page." —*Times Argus* (Vermont)

"McMahon's latest is surely her best. It's gripping and scary in so many ways." —*Curve*

© DREA THEW

ABOUT THE AUTHOR

JENNIFER MCMAHON is the author of *Island of Lost Girls* and *Promise Not to Tell*. She lives in Vermont with her partner, Drea, and their daughter, Zella.

www.Jennifer-McMahon.com

Also by Jennifer McMahon

Island of Lost Girls
Promise Not to Tell

DISMANTLED

a novel

Jennifer McMahon

HARPER

NEW YORK • LONDON • TORONTO • SYDNEY

For Michael, who knows how to take things apart

HARPER

A hardcover edition of this book was published in 2009
by HarperCollins Publishers.

HarperCollins books may be purchased for educational, business, or sales
promotional use. For information please write: Special Markets Department,
HarperCollins Publishers, 10 East 53rd Street, New York, NY 10022.

FIRST HARPER PAPERBACK PUBLISHED 2010.

Designed by Pat Flanagan

Library of Congress Cataloging-in-Publication Data is available upon request.

ISBN 978-0-06-168934-5 (pbk.)

10 11 12 13 14 OV/RRD 10 9 8 7 6 5 4 3 2 1

Present Day

"DISMANTLEMENT EQUALS FREEDOM."

Suz is there, whispering the words in his ear, each syllable hot and twisted. She's glowing, radiant, still twenty-one and burning with the fierce need to fuck up the world.

The dead don't age.

He finishes the knot, his hands steady, without the slightest tremble, then climbs onto the chair and throws the rope up over one of the beams in the kitchen. Old, hand-hewn beams his builder rescued from a salvage yard. They'd reminded him of Vermont. Of the cabin near the lake.

In his mind, he goes back ten years, sees Suz coming up the path, stepping into the clearing, pole in one hand, string of fish in the other: bass, sunfish, trout. They glisten like jewels, strung on the braided nylon rope she's carefully looped through their mouths and gills.

Suz's walk is a dance, her movements fluid, the silk tunic she wears flutters around her, making it seem as if the wind itself is carrying her, buoying her along like a kite.

She winks at him.

He loves her.

He hates her.

He doesn't want to be here, but there's no way he could ever leave. Once you're in her orbit, it's impossible to pull yourself away.

The others gather around as she lays the fish out on the table to clean them. She pulls the trout off the braided rope, lays it flat on newspaper, and slides the knife in, slitting it open along its belly from gills to vent. The fish opens its mouth, sucking at air. Suz smiles, showing crooked teeth, pushes her fingers gently inside the fish, widening the opening with her hand. The skin stretches; the movement of her fingers produces a wet, tearing sound.

"To understand the nature of a thing, it must be taken apart," Suz says, tugging out a string of entrails, sticky and shimmering with rainbows, like oil on a puddle.

"You never really got it, did you, babycakes?" he hears her whisper in his ear.

"No," he tells her, slipping the rope around his neck, pulling the postcard from his pocket to look at one last time. "But I do now."

He steps off the chair.

The postcard falls from his hand, drifts to the floor in slow motion, turning: moose, words, moose, words—until it lands, the carefully printed words facing up, the last thing he sees before losing consciousness:

DISMANTLEMENT = FREEDOM

THE COMPASSIONATE DISMANTLERS WERE HERE

Nine Years Ago

WHEN TESS'S WATER BROKE, she was staring into the long-forgotten aquarium, her eyes fixed on the bodies of the frogs floating like lost astronauts in oversize spacesuits, something clearly not of this world. They were pale and spongy, having frozen and thawed with the cruel cycles of winter and spring. It was, somehow, to Tess, as if they were stuck in limbo, waiting to be rescued, to rise singing from their own tiny galaxy of stagnant water; calling out in deep, vengeful bullfrog voices, *How could you leave us here? How could you forget?*

And they stank. God, how they stank. They reeked of cruel abandonment. Of things gone terribly wrong.

It was the first of May and Tess and Henry had hiked up to the cabin to *take a look around*. What they were looking for exactly, neither of them could say. And even if they could have named it, this thing that they hoped to find, they wouldn't have dared utter it out loud.

They were a week away from Tess's due date and the trip had been her idea. She thought they should visit the place one last time—the cabin where they had conceived their child, where so much of their lives had both begun and ended. The building, and everything in it, had been abandoned nearly eight months before—the night Suz died—just left as it was, nothing taken with them but the clothes on their backs, the summer of the Compassionate Dismantlers left entombed within the cabin walls.

The building was a hunting camp built sometime in the late sixties and the only access was up an old logging road, impassable by car most of the year. Henry and Tess opted to walk up, as the road was still soft and muddy from snowmelt and spring rains. The cabin itself sat in a clearing at the top of a steep hill—a simple single-story box twenty-four by thirty feet, with a gable roof that made room for a sleeping loft. The outside was sheathed in plywood once painted red, now warped and faded by years of snow and rain, chewed through in places by porcupines with a taste for wood, glue, and the sweat of human effort. The roof was rust-splotched tin, layered with years of pine needles and maple leaves that had formed a rich compost where baby maples sprouted and grew, stunted, with no hope of ever fully developing.

They arrived in the clearing out of breath, their shoes caked with mud, blackflies buzzing around their heads like angry halos. Several times on the way up, Henry had suggested they turn back. He was worried about the strain on Tess, who had a difficult enough time traversing flat surfaces with her large belly, much less mountain climbing. Surely it couldn't be good for her or the baby. But Tess was determined to stick to the plan, to make it to the top.

To the right of the clearing was the path that led down to the water. The lake and the land around it was a protected watershed area and threatening TRESSPASSERS WILL BE PROSECUTED signs were nailed to trees every twenty-five feet or so. The lake, referred to on maps only as Number 10 Lake, was not accessible by the main road and theirs was the only cabin even close. About fifty feet up the driveway to the cabin, there was a turnoff leading to the little beach they used, but the brush and weeds made it almost impossible to recognize it as a road. In any case, you'd never make it to the water without four-wheel drive and a lot of clearance. They'd never attempted it in Henry's van, sure they'd lose the exhaust system or put a hole in the gas tank. The entire summer they spent there, they never saw a single person anywhere near the lake.

TWO TRASH CANS LAY tipped over outside the cabin, their contents scattered in a wide swath: rusted cans, wine bottles, plastic containers torn to shreds. Henry picked up a ripped-open Hershey's syrup can.

"Bears," he said.

Tess nodded, gave a little shiver as she scanned the treeline at the edge of the clearing. Henry dropped the ruined can and touched his wife's shoulder in what he hoped was a reassuring way. She wasn't expecting it, and jumped, startled. As if his hand was a thick brown paw with razor-sharp claws.

"Sorry," he muttered, knowing already that he'd been right all along: they shouldn't have come.

Above the rough-hewn door (which Henry found to be un-locked, just as they'd left it at the end of August) were the words THE COMPASSIONATE DISMANTLERS WERE HERE. It had been painted in dripping black letters the week they'd moved in, mid-June of last year, when they were all sure they were going to have the most exciting, important summer of their lives. The words were a way of marking the building as theirs, the way gangs tagged their home turf with graffiti. Henry couldn't remember who had painted them—him, Tess, Winnie, or Suz—and this surprised him; he had already forgotten a piece of their puzzle.

Circling the cabin, like alligators in a moat, were the cats. Yes, he'd forgotten the cats too; they both had. Not forgotten them exactly, but just assumed they'd gone elsewhere, found some other home. They now seemed more wild than tame—mangy, skin and bones, their fur dingy, their eyes weeping, ears torn. At first, just a few, then more gathered, until Henry and Tess were surrounded by ten or twelve feral cats, half starved, who seemed to remember that these were the people who'd once fed them. The cats mewed and screeched, their voices ragged and pleading as they circled Henry and Tess, followed them inside, hopeful, insistent. Henry kicked at them, while Tess hurried to the kitchen.

"Maybe we left some cat food. Friskies. If there's water, I could mix up some powdered milk," she said.

Henry bit the inside of his cheek, knowing it was hopeless to try and stop her.

The air in the cabin was stale and smelled like mice: a sour stink came from the ceiling and walls, where Henry imagined the insulation torn into nests, pockets, cities of hidden condos, dampened by the urine of generations of its residents. Behind the mouse smell was something more sinister: the damp smell of rot and decay.

"There might be a dead animal in here," Henry called from his spot near the front door. "Maybe one of the cats got stuck."

Tess only grunted, focused on her search through the kitchen cabinets.

The cabin's downstairs was one large room divided into living room, kitchen, and dining area. In the far corner of the living room, tapestries hung from the ceiling to separate off the space where Suz and Winnie had slept. Henry did not pull back the curtain and look in, unable to violate their privacy even then. Instead, he focused on the chair by the window, just to the left of their curtain, and felt slightly queasy when he saw the pieces of rope still looped around the arms and legs. He remembered the feel of the rope in his hands, stiff and bristly, like an unwieldy animal, as he made the knots.

Tighter, Henry, Suz had told him. *Tie it tighter.*

"Tuna!" Tess exclaimed, holding two cans in her hand and

turning back to lean into the cabinet, her enormous belly bumping against the counter, to pull out a can of condensed milk. She gave a little cry of triumph. The cats screamed. Henry drew in a breath and surveyed the inside of the cabin while Tess got down bowls and began pulling open swollen, reluctant drawers, rattling silverware, in search of a can opener.

Nothing had been touched. No vandals had come. No kids looking for a place to get stoned and screw around. Everything was just as they'd left it, frozen in time like some museum diorama. Henry half-expected Suz to come flitting in, gesturing madly as she went off on some new tangent, the sleeves of her silk tunic like butterfly wings.

On the table was half a bottle of tequila, and five empty glasses. Inside the bottle was a dead mouse. *Lucky fucker,* thought Henry, staring down at the drowned rodent, a wave of nausea washing over him.

There were five plates out, dirty silverware, used napkins. The mice had taken whatever crumbs remained from their last supper, licked the plates clean.

In the corner of the table was the ransom note, never sent, a jigsaw of letters and words cut carefully from newspapers and magazines. Henry read the last line: *If you do not follow our instructions, we will kill your son.*

On the coffee table in front of the couch, Henry found Winnie's old Polaroid camera and a handful of snapshots, scattered like tarot cards spread out to tell not what will come, but what had been. Henry glanced over at Tess, who was too busy with the cats to notice what he was doing. Without looking through the photos, he scooped them into his knapsack. Underneath the photos was Suz's journal: a heavy hardcover black notebook with the words DISMANTLEMENT = FREEDOM painted on the cover in red nail polish. He traced the glossy words with a trembling finger, then the journal went into the bag too, unopened. He shouldered the knapsack, impossibly heavy already, and looked longingly at the open door. He fought the urge to run from the cabin, lungs gasping for fresh air. Cold sweat prickled between his shoulder blades. *Wing bones,* Tess called them.

Wings.

Suz always wore those tunics, long and flowing, in muted earthy colors. Black leggings beneath. And beat-up combat boots. Standard Suz uniform.

"We shouldn't stay long," he mumbled, more to himself than to his wife. *Shouldn't have come at all.* This wasn't part of the deal. They promised, that last night, to never speak of what had happened. To never return. And if anyone should ever contact them about Suz, they were supposed to say that at the end of the summer, last anyone saw her, she was headed west, for California. She was always talking about California. And wasn't it Suz herself who told them that the secret to telling a really good lie is to make sure there's a shiny pearl of truth hidden deep inside?

Henry glanced over at Tess, who was setting down bowls of tuna and canned milk. She bent at the knees to get down to the floor, and hoisted herself back up with both hands on the counter. The cats fought for places at the bowls.

"Careful," Henry warned. "They don't know you anymore." He had always hated the cats, could never keep track of their names and little histories. Now he had reason to believe they could be dangerous, and Henry saw his biggest job as husband and soon-to-be father as making things safe. He couldn't control what happened, but he did his best to be prepared. Hope for the best, but prepare for the worst. A good Vermonter's motto.

They had been married four months, out of college not even a year, and Henry still found himself staring dumbly at the gold wedding band on his finger. Tess. The girl he never meant to end up with who now stood in a wrecked kitchen feeding starving cats, a matching gold band around her own swollen finger, some physical, tangible thing that linked her to him. Proof. As if the baby wasn't proof enough.

His father paid for the small wedding, persuaded them to move in with him afterward. Henry's mother had died the year before and the large, rambling farmhouse left his father lonely. There was plenty of room for all of them, plenty of room for privacy. And there was the inground pool Henry's mother, Ruth, had insisted on years before. Tess loved the idea of having a pool.

"Babies come out of the womb knowing how to swim," she told Henry. "It's instinct. We'll get her right in the water and our baby will be swimming before she can crawl."

Henry cringed, silently thinking, *We'll see about that.* Henry hated the pool. An inground pool was an extravagance in and of itself, but to have one in Vermont where it could only be used three months out of the year seemed like pure foolishness. Not to mention the fact that it was just plain dangerous.

Henry worked full-time with his father at DeForge Painting, saving money for the baby. He kept busy. He went out on crews all day, wearing a crisp DeForge Painting T-shirt tucked into white painter's pants, and came home in the evening to work on the house. He got a nursery ready for the baby and cleaned up one of the small sheds out back for Tess to use as a painting studio. He baby-proofed every room, putting safety covers on all the outlets, installing plastic locks on the cabinets that contained medications and household cleansers, placing foam padding over the sharp corners of furniture. He drained the pool. He even cooked dinner most nights for his father and wife. When he finally got to bed, he slept a hard, dreamless sleep and woke up rested and ready for whatever the day before him held. There was no time in Henry's life for looking back, for thinking about what had happened at the cabin. He lived in a world ruled by the present and immediate future. So when Tess had insisted they go back to the cabin once the snow melted, he put up a fight.

"Why would you want to do that? We swore we'd never go back," he told her.

"I want to take one last look around, before the baby comes. It's something I need to do, Henry."

"But we made a pact," he reminded her.

"I'm going with or without you."

Henry knew better than to argue with Tess, especially now that she was pregnant. If she said she wanted fettuccine carbonara at three in the morning, she would damn well find a way to get it, even when it meant sending Henry to the all-night grocery store and cooking the meal herself.

Henry had no choice but to join the pilgrimage. To do his best to make things safe. But here, in the cabin, that felt like an impossible task.

He climbed up to the loft where he and Tess had slept, where they'd made a baby together. Their bed was an old futon laid out on the floor, piled high with sleeping bags, now chewed through by mice. Like a thief in a hurry, he quickly sorted through their things: clothes stacked in milk crates, mildewed books, Tess's paints and brushes, his wood-carving tools. He grabbed the canvas roll of chisels, gouges, and knives and stuffed it into his pack along with some of Tess's better brushes. The paints he left.

The loft felt small and airless. Henry made his way back to the ladder and down, going straight for the hanging tapestries this time, pushing his way through quickly as if he half-expected to catch Winnie and Suz there if he moved fast enough. Privacy be damned. But their bed was empty. Clothes lay scattered on the floor. Combat boots and white canvas sneakers with intricate designs hand-drawn on them. A spilled box of crayons. A bong made from a plastic bear that once held honey. An empty wine bottle with a candle shoved in its neck, red wax drips covering the glass like coagulated blood. And there, taking up the entire wall behind their makeshift bed, was the moose. Not the wooden sculpture that Henry knew lay in pieces behind the cabin, but the paintings: nine canvases put together to make one large moose, a study Suz did before tackling the real project: the sculpture, which would be the ruin of them.

TESS STOOD OVER THE cats, watching them choke the food down, listening to the low drone of their purring. She contemplated ways to convince Henry to take the cats home with them. Maybe not all of them. She'd just start with a couple. Surely Henry's father wouldn't object. And though Henry was allergic, there were medications available, right? It wasn't too much to ask—just one or two of the cats. Carrot definitely, because he had been the first. And maybe little Tasha with no tail. The rest they could at least take back to town. But how would they get the cats down the hill? She didn't believe the animals would follow them, even if they led with open cans of tuna, fishy Pied Pipers. She began searching around for something to put them in—a large box or crate. That's when she noticed the aquarium, set up just where they'd left it, on the counter to the left of the sink. She immediately understood that was where the dead animal smell was coming from.

She remembered the day she and Winnie brought home from the lake an old peanut butter jar full of dark eggs in a gelatinous mass. It was the beginning of summer. Anything seemed possible.

"Oh," was all she could say as she stood before the glass tank now, the stench overtaking her.

How many were there? Fifteen? Twenty? It was hard to make a guess. The aquarium was thick with partially decayed frogs, trapped in the sickening green gel that had once been water and now more closely resembled primordial ooze.

It was there, standing before the tank, that Tess remembered the way Suz had said the word *met-a-morph-o-sis*, emphasizing each syllable, promising the same fate lay in store for the four of them, the Compassionate Dismantlers, that they too would each be irrevocably changed and there would be no going back.

It was at that moment that Tess's water broke, the stink of the frogs filling her nostrils, Suz's voice filling her head. *Met-a-morph-o-sis.*

"Oh!" Tess cried again, louder this time, more of a moan really. Like a heartsick child crying for home.

AS HIS WIFE'S WATER broke, the liquid pouring down through her cotton panties, down through the tented opening of her skirt and onto the worn kitchen floorboards, Henry regarded the moose.

He had locked eyes with the animal in the painting and believed the moose pinned him there. He dared not move for fear of startling the creature to life. He noticed for the first time how the shape and color of its iris was not unlike Suz's own eyes—light amber flecked with gold—and only then did he imagine that it was Suz looking down, judging him, asking why he had come back, what it was that he had hoped to find.

"You," he told her in a whisper, speaking to the moose directly, saying the word at the same moment his wife began to moan.

Henry stepped forward and removed the upper-left-most painting—the close-up of the moose's left eye and raggedy brown ear. Then he pushed through the curtain and went to find Tess, clutching the painting under his arm. He moved through the sea of cats in the kitchen and found his wife standing in a puddle before the aquarium. At first, he thought that she'd been trying to rescue the frogs (though it was clear to him at once they were long past the point of rescuing). He imagined that she'd been bailing out the green stinking water with her hands and the very idea terrified him to the point of paralysis.

"I think the baby's coming," Tess said, hands over her belly.

It took long moments, even after Tess's explanation, for him to understand what had happened, and plan his next move. He carefully orchestrated their escape from the cabin, the slow walk down the hill to the car, painting jammed under his arm at an awkward angle, that big brown eye glancing up in his direction, seeming to ask, *What were you hoping to find?*

PART ONE

TO UNDERSTAND THE NATURE OF A THING, IT MUST BE TAKEN APART

Chapter 1
Present Day

THE MOOSE, OR RATHER, the left eye, ear, antlers, and snout of the moose, hangs from a nail gone rusty in the front hall of their home—the brick farmhouse Henry himself grew up in—watching their comings and goings, greeting each visitor over the years, sizing them up. Sentry moose. Give him the password and enter. But who knows the password? Not Tess. Not Henry, who moved out of the house and into the barn nearly a year ago. Not Franklin DeForge, Henry's old father who has been dead now four years—brain aneurysm. The moose takes pity on all of them and lets them pass, day in and day out. Watches with curiosity as uncountable bags of groceries, boxes of pizza, handfuls of mail, and loads of firewood come in. As snow is shaken off coats, mud scraped off boots, umbrellas left to dry.

Finally, it is their daughter, Emma, who thinks up the password. It is Emma who names the moose Francis, and knows you have to look straight into its one turbulent eye and whisper, *Nine,* just as you come in. Nine is the magic number. Francis, Emma knows from her parents, was nine paintings big. Eight are missing. Nine would make him whole.

Francis was painted *A Long Time Ago* by a friend they knew in college. Suz, her name was. Whenever Emma asks questions about Suz or the moose—like, "How long did it take Suz to make Francis?" or "What happened to the other eight paintings?"—her parents shake their heads. Their eyes go blank as dolls' and they say only, *That was A Long Time Ago*.

A Long Time Ago is its own country, a place Emma doesn't have a passport for and can only imagine. It's the time before time; the world without her in it.

Emma sometimes stands in the hall and tries to imagine the other paintings, the full effect of Francis in his entirety. He'd take over the wall, the room, be large as life, and yes, maybe if he were whole, maybe then his entire body would move—not just his eye, as Emma swears she's seen. Maybe he'd step off the wall and onto the floor, leaving great muddy hoofprints next to their own predictable shoes.

Nine. A lucky number. And just last month, Emma herself turned nine. They had a little party, just Emma, her parents, and her best friend Mel. Her parents had been eager for her to invite more friends, but the truth of it was that Emma didn't really have any other friends. Most of the other kids in school made fun of her, called her a mental case. And even if she'd had another friend, she probably wouldn't invite her to her house. Especially not now that her dad was living in the barn. That was not something she wanted going around school.

Mel's the only one she trusts. The only one who doesn't make a big deal about her counting under her breath or having to go through the trays at lunch until she finds a blue one without scratches.

On her birthday, Emma, Mel, and her parents went candle-pin bowling, then came home and ate red velvet cake, which was Emma's absolute favorite because it's both chocolatey and a strange Mars red color. The other thing she loved about it was that when her mom was growing up, this was the *exact same cake* Grandma Bev baked for her each year. Emma loved the words *Family Recipe,* and each birthday, when she took her first bite of the cake, so sweet it made her teeth ache, she'd imagine her mother at the same age—seven, eight, nine—taking her first bite, and for those few brief seconds each year, she felt linked to her mother in this fleeting, sugary way.

Emma closed her eyes as she blew out the nine candles on her cake, sure that when she opened them, something miraculous would have happened. She would discover she'd sprouted wings, or find herself living underwater with the starfish. Francis the moose would have come to life—not just a little twitch of the eye, a little wink, but a full-fledged, living, breathing, smelly moose.

But this is not what she wished for. What she wants most, what she concentrated on with all her might as she blew out the candles, was that her parents would get back together again. They would realize they love each other and her father would move out of the barn and back into the farmhouse with them.

Maybe, she decided, as she watched them grinning at her over the cake with its smoking candles, they just needed a little help. A little push in the right direction.

I T ' S M E L , W H O I S ten, one whole year older, who suggests they start snooping.

"We can't do that!" Emma complains. It's Monday, the ninth of June, the first full day of summer vacation, and they're bored already.

"You're the one who wants to get them back together so bad," Mel says, then she starts picking at her cuticles, a sure sign that she's on the verge of losing interest in the problem altogether. Mel is smart, but she hates to be shot down and it doesn't take much for her to get bored and move on to something else. If Emma's not careful, Mel might even hop on her bike and ride home, leaving Emma alone and bored, nothing to do but watch bad reruns. It's the first day of summer vacation. The first day of freedom. This one day could set the tone for the whole summer and Emma doesn't want to blow it.

"But how's that going to help? What would we even be looking for?" Emma asks, hesitant, knowing that what Mel suggested is wrong, bad, it is not RESPECTFUL, and respecting one another is the biggest, maybe the only, rule of their house.

"Evidence," Mel says, her face twisting into a concentrated scowl.

Mel's father is a police officer. Her mother's a librarian at the high school. And Mel always gets 100 percent on the weekly vocabulary tests in school, which means Mel *knows* things. Things like the definitions of abdicate and fortuitous, how to lift fingerprints off a drinking glass with Scotch tape and talcum powder, and maybe even how to get two broken people to love each other again.

"Okay," Emma agrees. "But if we get caught, they'll kill us."

Mel loops her arm around Emma's neck, pulling her tight in what could be a hug or the beginning of a headlock, and says, "You won't regret it." Mel's words are hot, sour puffs against Emma's cheek, whispered in a fiery excitement that immediately makes Emma wonder if she should have agreed to this after all.

Their search (now officially dubbed Operation Reunite—OR for short—by Mel) begins with Tess's bedroom. Henry's at work. Tess is in the basement working out—Emma can hear the thunk of her mother's gloved hands on the huge black punching bag hung by chains from the floor joist. *Everlast,* the bag says. Thump. Ka-*chang.* Thump. Ka-*chang.*

Emma stands guard in the hall, shifting nervously from one foot to the other, while Mel pokes through all of her mother's things. A closet full of clothes from Land's End and L.L.Bean.

Practical shoes. In the drawer of the bedside table Mel finds only a flashlight and a paperback mystery with a noose on the cover.

Emma plays with the brass knob on her mother's bedroom door, turning it to the left nine times, then nine to the right, for luck.

"Nothing here," Mel says, dejected. "Let's try the office."

They tramp down the stairs, through the living room and into the tiny room that serves as the office. Mel sits in the old leather swivel chair and goes through the desk. Emma gets the file cabinet. All they come up with are monthly budgets, bills, old coupons, and dust bunnies. Emma hates dust. She read once that household dust is 80 percent flaked-off human skin. Gross. People are like snakes, they just shed differently. Emma vacuums her room every day. She ties a bandanna around her nose and mouth, bandit style, while she cleans, to keep from breathing in all those sloughed-off skin cells.

"I don't know how you got to be so fastidious," her mom always says.

"You're a super freak," Mel tells her.

"No," Emma says. "I'm just fastidious."

Mel laughs. "Like you even know what that means!"

But Emma does know. She looked it up. And it has nothing to do with being either fast or hideous. It just means she's careful and particular. Nothing freakish about that. Emma believes in order. In putting things together in exactly the right way so that the universe makes sense. Which is why she wants her parents back together. If things are out of order, bad stuff can happen. Storms, car accidents, brain aneurysms. Right after Emma's dad moved out, a huge tree fell in the yard, almost crushing the house. If that wasn't proof, what was?

Emma closes the door to the file cabinet. Then, worried she forgot to straighten the hanging folders inside, she opens it again to check. All straight. She closes the metal drawer, resists the urge to open it and check again.

Fastidious.

Sometimes, she hates these feelings. This need to make sure things are put together just right. She can get stuck in one spot forever fixing something, then checking it again and again.

She gives in, opens the drawer, runs her fingers over the perfectly straight files, feels her body relax.

"There's nothing here," Mel says, scratching her head. Mel cuts her own hair, so it's shaggy, with brown bangs at a funny angle across her forehead. She needs a shower. Sometimes Mel gets so caught up in inventing her own secret language or figuring out how to make cupcakes explode that she forgets about details like eating and taking a bath. Her dad works a lot of extra hours and her mom's kind of a hippie, so Mel gets away with stuff most kids wouldn't.

Thump, thump goes Emma's mom in the basement. Left, right. Jabs and hooks.

"Now what?" Emma asks.

Mel looks out the window, across the yard, her blue eyes glimmering. "Your dad's barn."

"I'm not allowed in there when he's not home." Emma's voice comes out as a near whine and she's a little embarrassed.

"Do you want your parents back together or not?" Mel asks, pushing her glasses with the heavy square plastic frames up her nose. Mel doesn't even need glasses—these are from a costume shop. She thinks they make her look smarter. Emma thinks they make her look like Velma from Scooby-Doo—who is, she admits, the smart one.

"Yes. Of course." *Thump, thump, thump, thump. Ka-CHANG!* Emma can feel through her feet the vibrations of her mother pounding the bag, feels the fury and is sure that one of these days, her mother's punching is going to knock the entire house off its old granite foundation. Her mother swears the boxing isn't about anger, it's about exercise.

"Then quit being a dumbass," Mel says. "Come on."

Mel makes her way out of the house and to the barn, Emma behind her, stopping in the front hall to whisper *nine* when Mel's out of earshot—smart as she is, there are some things Mel just doesn't get. Like the importance of Francis. And Danner. Mel doesn't get Danner at all. If Danner shows up when Mel is over, Emma just has to pretend Danner's not there. Sometimes this makes Danner mad—she doesn't like to be ignored.

It takes Emma eighty-one steps to get to her father's barn. Very lucky. Nine goes into eighty-one nine times, which makes it the square root. Trees have roots and so do numbers.

It doesn't get much luckier than eighty-one.

When Emma gets to the barn, she sees Mel has lit up one of her homemade cigarettes. Mel uses Wrigley chewing gum wrappers and dried herbs from her kitchen: oregano, basil, thyme.

"You can't smoke that inside," Emma says.

Mel rolls her eyes, licks her thumb and forefinger, and pinches the burning end of the Juicy Fruit cigarette until it's out. Then she puts the remains into the Altoid tin she keeps her smokes and pack of matches in.

Mel and Emma start with the south side of the barn, the part converted into living quarters. It's a studio apartment—one compact room for cooking, eating, and sleeping, and a bathroom tucked into a corner. Emma's grandpa had it built as a little retirement cottage for himself. He didn't want to be "in the way" in the main house and felt he didn't need much space of his own. He was ready to downsize. To simplify.

It doesn't take Emma and Mel long to search the small living area. Her dad doesn't have much stuff: a daybed, a desk, some shelves, and a table with two chairs. It feels more like a motel room than a home, and this gives Emma hope. Like somehow he knows it's only temporary, that he'll move back into the house one day, so it's best not to get too settled in the barn.

They move through the kitchenette and open the door to the other side, where her dad has his workshop. It's an old horse barn, but the stalls and loft were taken out. Now it's just one huge cavernous space, big enough for a small airplane, Emma guesses. The workshop smells like sawdust and grease. There are metal shelves, workbenches, and tools from three generations of DeForge men: a lathe, drill press, band saw, table saw, seemingly endless hand tools. Her dad also keeps some company equipment in the barn: an extra power washer, scaffolding, broken ladders.

Mel steps through. Emma's heart is pounding. She knows she's not allowed in there. She has this sense that if she passes through the doorway without her father's permission, something terrible is sure to happen. She hesitates at the threshold, turns the doorknob nine times each way, but the feeling doesn't go away.

"Sometimes my dad comes home for lunch," she says.

Mel checks her watch. "Please! It's ten thirty, Em." She flips on the lights. "Now get in here and help me."

Emma holds her breath and steps through. Nothing terrible happens. Not yet. But the truly horrible things take time.

"Global warming," she whispers. "Cancer." She imagines one little cell somewhere in her body going bad, dividing into another.

"What?" Mel barks.

"Nothing."

There, in the center of the cathedral-size room, raised up on its own specially constructed frame, is the dugout canoe Emma's dad is making. He's installed bright track lighting above it, leaving the rest of the workshop in shadow. Large and pale, with graceful curves, the canoe reminds Emma of a long, white dolphin. It makes her nervous, seeing something so obviously meant for water stuck on land. Not just stuck, but held with wooden clamps and braces. Imprisoned.

"You look over there," Mel orders, pointing to the metal

shelves and cabinets that line the east wall of the workshop. Mel goes to the old wooden workbench, starts picking up tools.

"My dad doesn't like people to touch his stuff," Emma complains. It's not RESPECTFUL.

"He'll never know," Mel promises, dropping a large metal rasp back down on the bench with a clang.

Emma scans the shelves: chain saw, pruning shears, a burned-out headlight. Mostly what she finds is row after row of half-empty paint cans. She picks one up, reads the top: Bone White. She counts the letters in the name: nine. Emma hears from up above what sounds like a cat sneeze.

There, sitting on the edge of the top shelf, with her long legs dangling over, is Danner, smiling down.

Danner is a girl with dirty blond hair, just like Emma's. She's around Emma's age. In fact, she could almost be Emma's twin. Her nose is a little different, her chin a little more pointy, but every now and then, Emma catches a glimpse of herself in a mirror or shop window, and thinks it's Danner she's seeing.

Sometimes Danner shows up in Emma's clothes, which Emma can't stand, but Danner always puts them back, clean and folded. Sometimes Danner arrives in some outfit of her mom's or dad's. For some reason, she never puts back the clothes she borrows from Emma's mom. If Danner shows up in Emma's mom's new running shorts, you can bet that they'll either disappear forever or turn up ruined. One time, she borrowed Emma's mom's cashmere coat and the next day, it showed up at the bottom of the pool.

Today, Danner's wearing Emma's dad's old fishing vest.

Danner gives a little snicker, which is what makes the cat-sneeze noise.

Emma puts her finger to her lips: *hush*. Danner puts her own finger to her lips, smile growing wider. Then she takes the finger from her mouth, and rests it on one of the paint cans on the top shelf. Emma shakes her head *no!* but it's too late. The paint can crashes down on the floor, the lid pops off, and a thick, dark green paint splatters everywhere.

Emma's whole body vibrates with panic. How is she ever going to clean up this mess? If there's paint on the floor, her dad will know she's been in his workshop. She should never have come. What was she thinking? She grabs some rags from the shelf. Danner snickers. Emma's too mad to even look up at her.

"I've got something!" Mel yells. She's hunched over an old red metal toolbox.

Emma's skin gets prickly. She drops the rags into the center of the forest green puddle, leaves Danner and the spilled paint, and moves in for a closer look. There, stuffed into the rusty bottom of the toolbox, is a stack of Polaroids and a heavy black book with the words DISMANTLEMENT = FREEDOM painted across the front.

"No way!" Mel squeals, picking up the photos and looking at the one on top. "It's your parents. Look!"

Emma snatches the photo. Her mom and dad are in the picture, but even though Emma knows it's her mom and dad, everything about them is different, wrong somehow. Mom's hair is long and tangly, and Daddy looks like he's growing a beard. And they're smiling! They actually look genuinely happy. He has his arm around her. Emma can barely remember the last time her parents touched, with the exception of bumping into each other accidentally, which is always followed by a very awkward *Excuse me*.

Beside her parents are two ladies Emma doesn't recognize. The lady at the far right has short dark hair and is holding a gun. A rifle, like for hunting. The other lady, a blonde, has her head on the shoulder of the gun lady. And the blond lady is showing her middle finger to whoever is taking the photo, which is a dirty thing to do. Like swearing.

"Check it out!" Mel says, snickering. "She's giving someone the bird."

Emma looks for a bird, but just sees the gun, the girl holding up her middle finger, her mother leaning in to her father, her head on his shoulder.

Emma stares at the picture so long and hard that she starts to feel dizzy. She knows she's seeing her parents *A Long Time Ago*. She hardly hears Mel speaking, and when she does, it takes her a minute to remember where she is, how she got here, who it is who's speaking to her.

"It's a journal by someone named Suz," Mel says, holding the heavy black book. "You're not gonna believe this, Em! Your parents were part of some group called 'the Compassionate Dismantlers.' They had a manifesto and everything!"

"Manifesto," Emma repeats, not 100 percent sure what the word means, but thinking it sure doesn't sound like anything her parents would ever be involved with.

Emma looks back across the workshop to Danner, still perched on the top of the shelves, to see if she's catching all this. Danner gives her a wink.

"Listen to this," Mel reads, "'*To understand the nature of a thing, it must be taken apart.*'"

Emma just nods. She thinks of Francis the moose. "Nine," she whispers without thinking, looking back down at the photo in her hand. Suz is the lady who painted Francis. Is she the one with the gun or the one giving the camera the finger? And who had taken the picture?

"What'd you say, super freak?" Mel asks.

"Nothing."

Emma tucks the photo into the back pocket of her shorts, then looks up again, searching for Danner, but she's gone. Danner's like that. Here one minute. Gone the next.

"Holy crap!" Mel says, holding the journal out to Emma. "Check it out: there are addresses in the front for all the group members. We've gotta write to them!"

"And say what?" Emma asks.

Mel studies the names and addresses, thinking. Then, she smiles so big that all her teeth are showing. "Oh my god!" she howls. "This is it!"

"What?" Emma asks.

Mel holds the book out in front of her in both hands, shaking it like a tambourine. "Don't you get it? We've gotta write to these people and find a way to make them come back. Maybe if we can remind your parents of their old college days, they'll like go back in time and be all gaga for each other again. This is our answer." She shakes the book again. "Right here. It's exactly what we've been looking for!"

"But these addresses are like ten years old," Emma says.

Mel nods. "They were in college. Which means these are probably their parents' addresses. And parents can stay in the same house forever. Trust me." Mel pulls a small spiral notebook and pen from the back pocket of her grungy army fatigues and copies the addresses from the journal. When she's done, she puts the journal and photos back into the toolbox. "I'll get the bikes and meet you out front. Go tell your mom we're going to D.J.'s for Cokes. And get some money."

Emma shakes her head. "I've got to clean up the spilled paint first."

Mel looks over at the huge green mess on the floor. "Great going, super freak," she says, shaking her head. Then Mel goes over, grabs a bunch of rags, and starts wiping it up.

AT D.J.'S GENERAL STORE, they choose three cheesy Vermont postcards from the spinning rack (each with a moose, in honor of Francis) and stamps. Bernice sells them to the girls, and says, "Doing a little correspondence this morning, huh?"

Bernice has run the store forever. Even Emma's grandpa couldn't remember there ever having been a D.J.

"Yes, ma'am," Mel says with a proud smile. "We're writing to our friends at summer camp."

Mel says that Bernice is a textbook case of split-personality disorder. Sometimes, you walk in and she's all smiles, and gives you a free piece of licorice. Other days, she snarls, "This ain't the place to window-shop. If you don't have money, go on home."

"Maybe it's menopause," Mel guesses, and Emma nods, but has no idea what she means.

The best part is, you can always tell which Bernice you're up against by her face: on the days when she's evil Bernice, she's got on makeup—little circles of pink rouge, orange frosted lipstick put on all wrong.

This morning, she's just plain old friendly Bernice with her gray hair in a ponytail, her pale liver-spotted skin scrubbed clean.

"Good girls," she says. "Kids can get homesick at camp. A postcard from a friend will put a smile on their faces. You each take a root beer barrel. On the house."

"Thanks, Bernice," they both chime, reaching into the plastic bin on the counter.

Mel rolls her eyes, unwraps her candy, mouths the words *mental case,* and Emma steps hard on Mel's foot to shut her up. They both start laughing.

Emma is sure she can still see a trace of green just under her fingernails even though she scrubbed her hands with hot water and a brush. It took them almost forty-five minutes to clean up the paint. Mel kept saying it was good enough, but Emma was sure her dad would be able to tell.

"This floor is a mess," Mel said. "It's already covered with paint splatters and grease and Christ knows what all. Trust me, Em, the only one who's going to notice whatever little smudge of green we left is you."

ON THE POSTCARDS, THEY write down words carefully copied from Suz's journal: DISMANTLEMENT = FREEDOM. *To understand the nature of a thing, it must be taken apart.* They address the postcards to Spencer Styles, Valerie (Winnie) Delmarco, and Suz Pierce with *PLEASE FORWARD* in big letters beneath each address.

"If you write that, whoever lives there will send it to the right address," Mel explains. "My dad showed me. His sister, my aunt Linda, she moves around a lot, and whenever we write her, we put that on the envelope."

Emma nods, watches Mel drop the cards in the out-of-town mailbox outside.

"Now what?" Emma asks.

"Now we wait for something wonderful to happen," Mel says.

"NINE," EMMA WHISPERS ONCE they're back at home, Mel already halfway to the kitchen where Emma's mom is making the girls their favorite: grilled cheese and bologna sandwiches. Mel says bologna is made from the lips and buttholes of pigs, which is totally gross, but makes eating it kind of like a double-dog-dare, which is why it's their favorite.

Emma lingers in the front hall, stares into the great unblinking eye of the moose, and realizes for the first time (how could she never have noticed it before?) that Francis's eye, the iris a rich brown flecked with sparkling gold, is exactly like Danner's. Then, she's sure she sees it: the lid closing for a mere fraction of a second, the moose giving her the tiniest of winks.

Chapter 2

"LOOK, DADDY, I'M A frog!"

Dog paddle. Frog kick. Splash. Legs bent. Extended. Pretzel-thin limbs. Her face goes under. Henry holds his breath too. His heart beats double time in his chest. His breath goes whistley. He knows she'll drown. He's seen it in his nightmares a thousand times.

Since summer vacation started ten days ago, Emma's been in the pool every day, sometimes with Mel, which he can't bear. Too much horseplay. They pull each other under. Pretend to drown. He yells at them and they yell back, laugh, call him the *Fuddy Duddy Daddy*. Mel says he needs to *Take a chill pill,* and Emma only laughs harder at that, which makes his chest ache.

Emma swims to the side of the pool, touches the white ce-ment wall, bobs up, smiling, blond hair slicked back. She has Tess's small, elfish nose and Henry's deep brown eyes.

"Dad! Did you see me? I'm a frog!"

He lets himself breathe. Bites his tongue to keep from saying the words: *Are not. Now get the hell out of the water.*

His jaw hurts from keeping it clenched tight. He opens it wide, like he's yawning, trying to get the muscles to relax.

He watches Emma go under, holding her breath, her lime green bathing suit shimmering through the water. She has a special waterproof watch she uses to time herself. Tess gave it to her on her birthday. He gave her a camera. A nice one. Digital. For taking pictures on land. Safe old solid ground.

Emma pops up, gasping, her eyes bright red from chlorine. "One minute, nine seconds, Dad!"

He gives her a smile, nods wearily. "You're the champ," he says. "Where are your goggles?"

But she's already underwater again and doesn't hear him.

She starts doing laps. Nine times back and forth across the pool, touching the edge, counting out loud.

He should have filled in the pool when his father died. Put in a tennis court or a greenhouse for Tess. Anything but this. He knows one day his daughter will drown. Feels it in his bones. In his shaking muscles each time she jumps in. Swan dive. Belly flop. Sinking down, down, nearly to the bottom while he gnaws the insides of his cheeks like a desperate animal, until he tastes blood.

In his dreams she's there in the water, reaching for him, calling, *Daddy!* as she goes under, sinking down, down, down.

HENRY LOOKS MUCH THE same as he did when he graduated from college. Same close-to-the-skull haircut, same way of walking with his hands shoved deep in his pockets. Only he wears chinos these days more than ripped jeans. The scruffy beard is gone. And there are faint wrinkles around his eyes. He's still very boyish. Fidgety. A stranger would look at him and call him handsome. Would say he was a lucky man with a beautiful wife and daughter, a successful business, a swimming pool. A stranger would look at him and think Henry would be a fool not to be in love with his life.

But a stranger wouldn't know that Henry actually lives in a

converted barn out back beyond the pool and hasn't slept in bed with his wife for nearly a year. And as far as sleeping with his wife in the conjugal sense, it had been a year and a half. Sex had become increasingly unsatisfying and more of a trial than anything else. Tess put more of an effort into reviving it than he did. She bought books, sensual massage oils (including one that was supposed to be arousingly warming but caused an allergic reaction, burning his penis), but in the end, he just didn't feel all that interested. Passion, Henry told himself, was for young lovers, poets and artists. None of which he was or would be ever again.

But a stranger would not know any of this. They would have no idea that Henry sees every part of his life as a miserable failure. True, he loves Emma profoundly, painfully—yet surely he is failing her too.

Fuddy Duddy Daddy. Take a chill pill.

Fuck.

Henry chews the inside of his cheeks. Feels a headache coming on. It always starts with a little tickle just behind his eye. Then the tickle turns to a pinprick and Henry imagines his skull, like the body of a pinhole camera: that little pinprick lets in the pain and magnifies it; projects it onto the wall of his skull where it vibrates until even his jaw and teeth are sore. He carries aspirin around in his pocket the way some people carry breath mints. He shakes the bottle with his fingers, hears it rattle. There's comfort in that. He pulls it out, pries off the lid, lets three tablets fall into his open palm, tosses them into his mouth and chews. The aspirin burns the cuts on the inside of his cheeks. Eats away at the exposed flesh there—wounds that never heal.

AT FIRST, HE'D MADE Emma wear a bright orange life jacket. Then water wings. Eventually, Tess argued that Emma was too old, too strong a swimmer, that the flotation devices did more harm than good. Into the garage they went, any hope of saving his daughter piled up with the mildewed camping gear and bald tires.

Henry doesn't even own swimming trunks. Doesn't take baths, just three-minute showers. Lather, rinse, out. Tess calls it a phobia.

"Survival instinct," Henry says. "We were not born with fins."

Sometimes, though neither of them says it, when they look out at the pool, they remember the dark water of the lake.

Tess remembers out loud what a good swimmer Henry used to be. How he and Suz would race out to the rocks from their beach at the lake. They'd have contests to see who could go farthest underwater, who could hold their breath longest. Suz usually won but Tess suspected that Henry let her.

"You used to love the water," Tess says, shaking her head mournfully.

Secretly, Henry now wonders if he'll have the courage to save his daughter when the time comes. In his nightmares, his feet are concrete blocks and he has no hands. When he dives in to save her, he goes straight to the bottom, trying to picture Tess's face when she finds them both there—waterlogged on the cement floor of the pool—and he's sorry he won't be able to come back to life for an instant to deliver his final words, sound traveling up in bubbles escaping his blue lips: *I told you so.*

EMMA'S TOWELING OFF WHEN the phone rings. The sliding glass doors leading from the patio to the kitchen are open, and he hears it through the screen. Tess will never hear the phone in the basement, iPod buds in her ears as she works out.

"Stay out of the pool," he tells Emma. She just rolls her eyes. He stops, rolls his own back at her, which gets a laugh. He jogs into the house, through the sliding screen door, picks up the phone just before the answering machine kicks in. Technically, this phone is now Tess and Emma's, although there is still an extension in the barn.

When the office can't reach him on his line in the apartment side of the barn, they call the other house line. People at work have no idea he lives apart from his wife and daughter—he tells them the first line is for his workshop and to always try there before calling the home number. Somehow, his entire life has come to be about deceit.

"Hello," he stammers, out of breath.

"Is this Henry? Henry DeForge?" A woman's voice. Young. The words carefully enunciated and crisp as pressed linen.

"Yes." None other. The Fuddy Duddy Daddy himself.

"My name is Samantha Styles."

Henry draws a blank. A client? He doesn't think so. But there's something familiar about the name. Something that tells him he *should* recognize it. He searches his brain, but the headache is coming on strong now and not leaving room for much else.

"Yes?" he says, not willing to give away that he has no idea who she is. He just wants to get rid of her and take some more aspirin. Or maybe he'll head for the medicine cabinet and steal one of Tess's codeine tablets. She's got some old Percocet in there too. That might take the edge off.

"I believe you were a friend of my brother, Spencer?"

Henry feels the pain in his eye go off like a firework, blossoming into the rest of his face.

"How did you get this number?" he asks.

"I found it in an old address book of Spencer's. My brother . . ." Her voice falters. "Spencer killed himself two days ago." The words come fast, a nearly inaudible blur, no longer careful and crisp.

Henry falls back against the wall, covers with the sweaty palm of his hand the eye that feels as if it has an ice pick going into it. "I'm sorry," he murmurs into the plastic phone. Really, he's more terrified than sorry. He hasn't thought of Spencer Styles in ages. He just put a wall around that part of his brain. Caged the Spencer memories in. Or, more appropriately, tied them up.

He remembers the feel of the rope in his hands—rough, unyielding hemp—and Suz's voice, *Tighter, Henry. Tie it tighter.*

He blinks the memory away. Mustn't start down that path. No sir-ee.

"He didn't leave a note," Samantha Styles tells him. "But he was found with a postcard from Vermont. All it says is, '*Dismantlement Equals Freedom*' and . . ." She pauses, and he imagines her peering at the postcard to read it carefully. "And '*In order to understand the nature of a thing, it must be taken apart.*' Does that mean anything to you, Henry?"

Oh Jesus. Does it ever.

"Not a thing." His voice is just above a whisper. He's pressing his hand into his eye, trying to quell the pain as he wonders why Spencer would have kept an old postcard and why, in God's name, he was holding it when he offed himself. It's been ten years.

"The postmark says that it was sent from Vermont last week," she tells him.

"Last week?" Impossible. The only remaining members of the Dismantlers in Vermont are he and Tess. It must be a mistake. A card lost in the mail all these years. That kind of thing happened now and then, didn't it?

Shit, Henry thinks. Suz would have loved this. He actually smiles at the thought of it. Can't help himself.

"My father's hired a man, a private investigator, to look into Spencer's death. Whatever the words on the postcard mean, he'll get to the bottom of it. He's planning a trip out to Vermont. I'm sure he'll want to talk to you."

The smile turns back into a grimace of pain. Suz would *not* love this part.

Fuck. If some private investigator shows up and starts sniffing around . . .

"I don't know how much help I'll be." Henry hears the words leave his mouth, but he's hardly aware of having formed them.

He's down on his knees now. The lines of grout in the tiled floor are wavering, making the floor seem to ripple. The light is impossibly bright. His mouth has the salty iron taste of blood.

"The memorial service is next week," she says. "Here in Chicago. It would be great if you could make it."

"I'm afraid I can't get away. I run a painting business. This is our busy season."

There's a long pause. He resists the urge to just hang up. Get rid of this woman the quickest way he can.

"You know," she says, "I don't think Spencer had many friends after college. Not like the friends he had then. It would mean a lot if you could come."

Tighter, Suz said. *Tie it tighter.* By then Spencer had given up fighting.

Henry's palming his eyeball, trying to keep it from popping out from the pain, the pressure of the explosion happening inside his head. He listens as Samantha Styles rattles off the address, date, and time of the memorial service, pretends to write it down, just in case he's able to get away. He hangs up just in time to get to the sink and throw up. There's blood in his vomit from his bleeding cheek. He runs water, turns on the garbage disposal. *The Electric Pig,* Emma calls it. He peeks out the window. She's lying down in a chair beside the pool, her skin streaked ghostly white from the sunblock she's applied. Good girl.

He takes the stairs to the basement slowly, gripping the rail, his legs rubbery. He hears the sound of Tess's gloves on the bag, the rattle of the chains. Her grunts, gasps, heavy breathing. It's incredibly sexy, the boxing. Sometimes when he's alone in his bed at night he plays little movies in his head of Tess boxing. In his fantasies, he's holding the bag, feeling the force of each punch until he can't take any more, then she guides him to the floor, he slides her shorts down and she climbs on top of him, her padded gloves pushing down on his shoulders as she rises and falls with him inside her. His fantasy sex life is much more exciting, more vivid than the real thing had ever been.

It was her idea that he move out of the house last April.

"It's not working," she said. "I'm tired of just settling."

Her decision wasn't based on any one thing, rather the accumulated years of struggling, just getting by. One day she woke up and decided she'd had enough.

"Don't you ever want more, Henry?"

"No," he'd told her.

She shook her head mournfully. "You used to."

"But I love you," Henry said. He'd been saying those three words for so long. They were the three magic words that were always supposed to make everything better.

And it wasn't a lie. He *did* love her. Maybe it hadn't ever been this bright, passionate thing that she imagined it should be, but it was solid. It had a strong foundation. He firmly believed that he and Tess were bound in some deep way by the things they'd shared. They were meant for each other. No one else would have them. No one else would ever understand who they each truly were, where they'd been. When he looked at Tess, he saw all of her: the college student, the Compassionate Dismantler, the mother, the artist, and now, the boxer. How could he help but love someone he saw so completely?

And they'd been happy together, hadn't they? It was true that their marriage hadn't been picture perfect every moment, but it was good, it was fine. It was enough. Or it should have been. But Tess always seemed to want more; that ever elusive more that Henry could never manage to get his head around.

"I love you," he repeated again. A mantra. An incantation.

She shook her head. "I'll never be her, Henry. And I know that every morning, you wake up from your dreams, open your eyes, and some part of you is always a little disappointed. Isn't that right?"

He packed his clothes and moved into the barn that night. All his father's old widower furniture was still there: the dusty daybed, the small table and desk.

Only later, tossing and turning under his father's duck-decoy-print sheets, did he realize he should have said something more to her (something along the lines of *But you're real, you're alive*); he should have put up a fight. But by then, it seemed too late.

HE GETS TO THE bottom of the stairs and turns to the left, there she is, her back to him, pounding the shit out of the hanging bag under a flickering fluorescent light. She's a small-framed woman. Barely five feet tall and ninety-five pounds, nearly all of it muscle. She's wearing a sports bra and running shorts. Her body is soaked with sweat. It flies from her closely cropped brown hair as she lunges at the bag, going in for the full assault, grunting with the effort of it.

Henry circles around his dancing, punching wife so that he's in her line of sight. She gives a surprised little shriek.

"Jesus, Henry! I had no idea you were there!"

He smiles apologetically. He sees her tremble a little and imagines being able to lay a reassuring hand on her arm, say, "Sorry, love," maybe even take her in his arms. He'd like that. To take her in his arms again. Feel her damp body against him, the heat radiating, warming him in the deepest way.

In the early years of their marriage, when they slept together, she fit so neatly, so perfectly against him, filling all his empty spaces. And she was always warm, even on the coldest winter nights when she'd shriek at the feel of his frozen hands and feet on her bare skin.

She'd take his hands, tuck them under her body, then, once they were no longer painfully cold, she'd guide them to her warmest places, and soon, he'd be hot, sweating, throwing the covers off.

He clears his throat. "Didn't mean to startle you. I just got a phone call."

She uses her teeth to un-Velcro the thick boxing glove, pulls it off, then removes the other. Underneath, her hands are wrapped in what looks to Henry like black bandages for extra support and protection. Once the gloves are off, she removes the earbuds. He can hear the music thumping out of them. One of the snarling women Tess listens to when she exercises.

"From whom?" she asks, reaching for a towel to mop the sweat off her face. Tess looks worried, her damp brow creased. She knows he wouldn't have interrupted her if it wasn't important.

Henry closes his left eye to keep the pain at bay.

"Another headache?" she asks, her voice soft.

She used to take her thumb and rub this spot just under his eyebrow. She'd start out soft, then press hard against the ridge of bone, the pain almost excruciating, and just when he thought he couldn't stand it anymore, she'd stop and the headache would be gone.

He nods, then, one eyed, he tells her about the phone call from Spencer's sister: Spencer's suicide, the postcard, the private investigator coming to Vermont.

"If the truth comes out . . . ," he starts to say, looking at her through one eye, Cyclops eye.

Tess nods. Her shoulders slouch, her knees bend, her head drops down, and she closes her eyes tight, as if she's making a wish.

"But maybe," Henry says, desperate to make things okay again, to stick to his role as protector, "maybe it doesn't have to. It's been this long, right? We'll practice our stories before the investigator gets here. I'll go up to the cabin and make sure there's nothing incriminating there."

Tess looks up at him, her eyes glassy. "Henry," she says. "What would happen to Emma? If we went to jail?"

"We'll get through this," he tells her, letting himself take her wrapped-up hand in his. She gives his fingers a gentle squeeze.

"Henry, do you ever think about what would have happened if . . ." Her voice trails off.

"Everything's going to be all right," he promises, remembering that they were the same words he told her the night Suz died. Empty, hollow words.

Chapter 3

HER RHYTHM IS OFF. Her concentration, gone. Spencer is dead. Their past is surfacing, like she somehow always knew it would.

Dismantlement = Freedom.

"Christ," she mumbles, stepping away from the bag to get her water bottle. Holding it clumsily between her two boxing gloves, she takes a long swallow.

Henry got right up to her without her having any idea he was in the room. She hates being sneaked up on, knowing someone has been watching her without her awareness. Even harmless Henry.

She's been feeling like that a lot lately: as if someone's watching her. Spying. She feels eyes on her when she's working in her studio, buying flowers at the farmers' market. Last Saturday morning the feeling was so strong she had to stop herself from running across the town green back to her car, weaving between card tables and vendors set up with white umbrellas; everything felt sinister, right down to the bluegrass trio, whose music, as she race-walked past, made her almost scream—the notes brushing her skin like feelers from some hideous, invisible insect.

"Paranoia, the destroyer," she says, remembering the old Kinks song.

But what if it's not her imagination? What if someone—something, even—is watching her?

It's crazy to even think of.

And what about the vermilion paint? she asks herself. *Explain that one, will ya?*

She gets a chill, puts down the water bottle, goes back to the bag, but it's no good. Today's workout is ruined.

The whole reason she started boxing was because it was the one thing she'd tried that made everything else go away: the summer of the Dismantlers, the complicated mess her marriage had become. When she practices boxing, she's that focused. There's her, the gloves, and the bag. There's no room for anything else.

She's done it all: yoga (God, she hated lying there on the mat, concentrating on her breath, trying to be calm and centered and one with the universe. *Please.*), aerobics, even Jazzercise where a pert blond instructor kept everyone in step in a room that smelled distinctly like bad clams. Henry had chuckled when she told him this detail.

"I swear," she'd said. "Rotten seafood. But no one else seemed to notice."

"How could they not?" he'd asked. "Maybe they were just being polite."

"Polite?"

"Yeah," Henry said. "Maybe they all knew the smell was coming from the instructor."

They laughed harder.

They used to be a couple like that: they'd tell each other little stories from their days and laugh. Fill the space and silence with these small details, but rarely would they delve into anything deeper, more meaningful.

Tess thinks of those water bugs, striders, who skate across the surface, but never dive. That's what their conversations used to be like.

TWO YEARS AGO, WHEN Tess was feeling particularly unsatisfied, she tried therapy, where she'd gone over and over her childhood and her dead-end marriage. She knew better than to expect any sense of resolution, of ever feeling whole again. She knew there were too many things she'd never tell any stranger—a therapist, a priest, anyone.

Tess sidestepped carefully around the real issues, her secret Dismantler history. She got close sometimes, but never told. Instead, she talked about her dreams. Dreams where she discovered some forgotten pet tucked away in a closet or basement: a starving puppy who's chewed off his own tail, a box of mice who have eaten each other's eyes out.

"And I pick the box up and the mice are all banging against the sides of it, their feet are bloody stumps from trying to dig their way out."

Her poor therapist gave an involuntary shiver and this left Tess feeling strangely satisfied. But that small satisfaction aside, therapy was going nowhere.

"What do you think the mice represent?" the sweet New Age woman with hennaed hair had asked.

Tess shrugged.

Therapy was just another mistake in a long series of mistakes, lined up like tumbling dominos, leading her right there to that place: blubbering to a near stranger about her unsatisfying life with a husband who didn't love her the way she longed to be loved. Pathetic.

"But then there's Emma," Tess was careful to mention at the end of each therapy session, a reminder to herself and her therapist that not every part of her life was empty and unfulfilling. Emma was her greatest accomplishment—the one good thing she had to show for the last ten years.

When things between Tess and Henry were going badly, on days when they couldn't even muster the energy for small talk, they had Emma. Their bright jewel of a girl who gave their relationship focus and meaning. She'd waltz into the room and they'd be a happy family again—laughing at knock-knock jokes, tripping over words, talking over each other, because suddenly, they all had so much to say.

IT WAS ONE OF the trainers at the health club, Joe, a tiny man with Brylcreem hair, who turned her on to boxing. He showed her the heavy bag and some basic moves. He taught her the proper way to wrap her hands, the importance of the right gloves. At first, they just worked on her stance and he had her circle the bag, chin tucked in, face protected by her hands, silly and cartoonish in bright red gloves.

"You have to learn the footwork first," he told her. "It's the foundation you're going to base everything else on. If you don't have a solid stance, you're through."

Then came the punches. The straight left, the jab and the hook. The cross. The uppercut.

She'd master one and he'd teach her another.

"Beautiful!" he'd shout. "Watch your feet. Eye on the bag. Chin down. Gloves up. That's right. Circle to the left. Hit it again. Picture your hand going through the bag, out the other side. Nothing can stop you!"

And as her fists connected with all eighty pounds of the hanging leather bag, she felt something she hadn't in a long, long time. Not from her art, her life, her marriage. She felt *satisfied*.

HER GLOVES AND WRAPS off, she moves to the weight bench, lies back, and does ten presses.

If the truth comes out . . .

Ten years. Ten years spent avoiding it, circling around it, not daring to look it in the eye. Talk about fancy footwork.

"You've gotta look, Tess," Suz told her, blowing sweet, resiny smoke in her face. They were getting stoned on the roof of a parking garage in Burlington. They had just finished going carefully down the rows, dumping sugar in the gas tank of every SUV. They left little typewritten, photocopied notes tucked under the windshield wiper of each one: *Gas-guzzling motherfuckers get dismantled!*

Winnie and Henry were off scoping out the construction site of a new bank around the corner to see if it was a good target for a late-night dismantling mission.

Suz passed the joint to Tess and continued. "Really look at things without all the bullshit filters you've been taught to look through your whole life." Suz's amber eyes were bloodshot, but glittering. She tucked her hair back behind her ear. "That's what this is all about. Waking people up from the consumer-culture coma. That's the compassionate part, you know? We're showing people the truth, and even if it hurts, even if the shit they think they love gets destroyed, they're *awake*. Truly living, maybe for the first time in their lives."

At the time, it seemed true, felt true. Suz believed it so passionately, and her passion was contagious. But Tess always wondered—maybe people were better off with the watered-down version of life, life with blinders, filters, cars that ran and buildings that went up on time, simple, stupid, mindless jobs. Maybe they were happy.

It was something Tess still struggled with—it was why she'd insisted that she and Henry separate, wasn't it? Because the watered-down version of life had left her profoundly unsatisfied. But she wasn't an idealistic kid anymore. Maybe she was wrong to expect more.

Tess looks up at the bar resting above her, the rings of round silver weights clamped on. She reaches up to do another repetition, but finds she can't. She's somehow exhausted. Her arms are shaking.

Nothing can stop you.

Bullshit.

Every superhero has his weakness, his own kryptonite. The summer of the Compassionate Dismantlers is hers. Apparently, it was Spencer's too. Powerful enough to make him take his own life, even after ten years.

"Fuck," she mumbles.

She sits up, grabs her towel.

She's strong. Fast. Has developed a hell of a right hook, the power of her whole body behind it. She can run five miles and feel great, barely winded. But none of that matters. It's been a year since she started boxing and only now does she understand that in the end, it won't protect her.

She turns to look in the large mirror she installed along the paneled wall, for shadowboxing, and is startled by what she sees: fear. *I know what you did,* the face in the mirror tells her. *And soon, the rest of the world will know too.*

You can sink a thing deep, weight it down with stones, but eventually, it will surface.

Chapter 4

THEY'RE ON THEIR WAY home from the supermarket, Henry at the wheel, the back of the Blazer full of grocery bags, Emma strapped in the backseat.

"Mel gets to ride in the front seat," she complains, thumping her foot against the back of his headrest because she knows it drives him crazy.

"The backseat is safest," he tells her, for what must be the thousandth time. "Now quit kicking my seat."

Tess wanted to work on the latest installment in her sculpture garden and Henry offered to do the shopping. He thought it would calm his mind after the phone call with Spencer's sister earlier that afternoon. He finds comfort in the mundane tasks of everyday life—pushing the shopping cart with the wobbly wheel through the all too bright Price Chopper; scratching the items off Tess's carefully penned list: lemons, dish soap, bran cereal; giving in easily when Emma asks for a Butterfinger in the checkout line. It makes him feel almost normal. Just a man out shopping with his daughter, guided by his loving wife's thoughtful list.

It's all about deception.

Seven miles from home now, they've just passed the blind corner beyond Halloway's Used Furniture, the place where every few years some kid gets killed. The trees beside the road are lined with wooden crosses, sometimes decorated with plastic flowers and Mylar balloons. On the left ahead is the old Seven Bridges Egg Farm with the giant wooden chicken cutout in front. Someone painted it purple with pink spots a few years back, on April Fools' Day, and no one ever fixed it. The egg farm is now owned by a guy who calls himself Muskrat and sells handmade drums, rattles, and didgeridoos. The chickens are long gone, but sometimes after a summer thunderstorm the acrid scent of chicken shit still haunts the road.

Henry is listening to the Red Sox on the radio when he glances in the rearview mirror to see that Emma's talking to Danner again. Nonstop talking in a low, deliberate voice. Her hands are flapping, head bobbing as if her talk is a dance, a secret dance done for her secret friend no one else can see.

He catches only a few words and phrases: "If you could see . . . only . . . and then I wonder . . ."

He thought Emma would grow out of it, but it seems the older she gets, the more important Danner becomes. Tess says it's not cause for concern. "Emma's imagination is so vivid," she tells him. "We should be grateful, not worried."

The Red Sox are behind, five to two. Henry's chewing the insides of his cheeks again, sucking on the scars he's made there. What must his dentist think?

It's stuffy in the Blazer. He turns up the AC. They pass Burt's Texaco. He spots one of his DeForge Painting pickups gassing up, gives a beep and a wave to the kid filling the tank. A new kid. College boy. David. David gives him a salute.

Henry's mind circles back around to the phone call from Spencer's sister. It isn't Spencer's death that bothers him. Or even so much the sad fact that his sister is under the illusion that Spencer had his closest friendships in college. No, what worries Henry is the fucking postcard. *Dismantlement = Freedom.*

Hearing the words again had torn something open inside him, a tear too jagged and unexpected to close neatly.

He tries to tell himself that it's possible the postcard had been lost, stuffed at the bottom of some forgotten mailbag for ten years.

But what if it wasn't?

He feels the tear inside him widen. Where had the card come from? There were only five people who had ever used that phrase: himself, Tess, Winnie, Spencer, and Suz. Surely Spencer didn't send the card to himself. And neither he nor Tess would do such a thing. Winnie? After that summer, she returned home to Boston and they hadn't heard from her since. In some ways, she'd lost the most that summer and would be the last person to go poking around in the past. If it was her, why would she have sent the card to Spencer? It just didn't make sense. That left Suz. And Suz—well, she was down at the bottom of Number 10 Lake.

To understand the nature of a thing, it must be taken apart.

Was there another possibility? Someone else who knew the secrets of that summer?

Henry looks up into the rearview mirror, sees Emma talking with Danner. She's nodding her head. Saying, "I know. I don't think so either."

He drums his fingers on the wheel.

Damn it. She's too old for this. She needs more real friends. She spends too much time alone. There's Mel, but Mel's a little off herself with her fake glasses and hacked-up hair. He and Tess should have found a good summer camp for Emma. Something with crafts and horses and cute little campfire songs. But no lake. God, no lake.

Maybe they should have planned a camping trip themselves, like they did when she was little. They had a big old cabin tent that they'd throw in the back of the pickup with sleeping bags, and a cooler full of hot dogs, soda pop, and beer. Tess had a rainbow-striped woven hammock she'd bring, and tie it between two trees at the campground. They'd all three get into it, the sides curling up around them. *Cocooning,* Tess called it. Sometimes they'd fall asleep there. Mostly they wouldn't. They'd just swing gently, wrapped in each other's arms, sticky with sunscreen and bug spray, playing the game where you looked up at the clouds and said what you saw there: *hammer, walrus, banana.*

"A troll, Daddy! I see a troll. He's watching us."

"Want me to make him disappear?" Henry asked, and Emma, sweaty, fearful, nodded. Henry puffed out his cheeks and blew a loud, hissing breath into the sky just as the wind picked up, distorting the clouds, carrying the troll away.

Emma cheered.

"Daddy's magic," Tess said, smiling wistfully. "He makes all the bad things go away."

HENRY CAN'T BE SURE when Danner first showed up. It's almost as if she's been around since Emma was born. Since she learned to talk, at least. In the beginning, the invisible girl wasn't called anything, then, when she was first learning to read, Emma named her.

Henry had an old pair of hiking boots, something he'd bought just before graduating from college, visions of trekking around the world in his head: Ireland, Wales, Australia, the Alps. They'd all four go—"The Compassionate Dismantlers take on the world!" Suz had shouted, delighted by the idea. But then Suz died and Tess got pregnant, and that put an end not just to the Dismantlers, but to his wanderlust. The boots were relegated to yard work and the occasional hike through the woods behind his house. And these days, the only dismantling he did was taking apart the trap under the bathroom sink to retrieve whatever small artifact

Emma dropped down the drain. Earrings. A little Eeyore pin she got when Tess's parents took her to Disney World.

"Daddy, what do your boots say?" Emma asked one afternoon as she lay on the kitchen floor staring at the boots abandoned by the door. The company name was pressed into the leather across the heel of each boot.

"Danner."

"Why?"

"Because that's who makes them."

"Like the elf?"

"What elf, honey?"

"The elf who makes the shoes."

"Something like that, I guess."

Emma gave a nod and went back to staring dreamily at the boots. The next day, the invisible girl had a name. Named for a shoe-making elf, and a pair of heavy boots that spoke to Henry not of regret exactly, but simply of what might have been.

Henry grips the Blazer's wheel tightly, worrying over the base-ball game, the origin of the postcard that drove Spencer to suicide, and now, over whether or not Danner is going to be a permanent fixture in their lives. Emma gets quiet. He glances in the rearview mirror, sees she's still talking, but in a low, quiet voice. Subdued. He turns down the radio.

"How did you die?" Emma asks. Then, in the mirror, he watches her nod, her face as serious as it gets, all pinched up. *I've got a splinter* kind of serious. *I think my hamster's sick* kind of serious.

On the low murmur of the radio, Henry hears the crack of a bat. The announcers go wild. Home run. Bases loaded. The Sox have taken the lead. It's a new ball game.

Chapter 5

WHAT IS A GHOST? Danner says it's not always the way people think. A ghost doesn't have to be someone dead, rattling chains, stuck between two worlds. A ghost is a spirit and everyone has a spirit, living or dead. Animals, plants, people.

They're bumping along in Emma's dad's Blazer. Her dad is always saying this stretch of road is the worst and wondering where the hell his tax dollars go.

"Potholes the size of Rhode Island," he says.

He's watching Emma in the rearview mirror, his eyes all worried and strange, which is the way he looked at her each time she coughed when she had pneumonia last year.

"Imagine," Danner tells Emma, as she sits beside her on the crumb-covered, juice-stained backseat, "that the world is like those layers of clear pages in encyclopedias and biology books: put them all together, and you get a whole image, like a frog or a person. But making that up is layer after layer: sheets with heart and lungs, the nerves, the muscles, the skeleton, the skin. This is what the world is like. Do you understand?"

"No," Emma admits. She doesn't get it at all. If Mel were here, Mel might get it.

Danner looks out the window at the world going by: a barn with a broken back; a woman watering the pansies around her mailbox; the Heigh-Ho Cabins, which promise satellite TV and have a glowing red VACANCY sign. Danner's wearing an old faded green college sweatshirt of Emma's dad's. SEXTON, it says, in big white letters.

Emma's never been to Sexton College, even though it's less than an hour away from their house. She knows it's where her parents met. Where they studied art *A Long Time Ago*. Sometimes, Emma says, "I'm going to go to Sexton when I grow up," and her parents talk in their irritated-but-trying-to-sound-calm voices, and tell her there are plenty of schools out there and we'll just have to wait and see, and besides, Sexton might not even be around by then.

Emma's dad turns down the radio, which is fine by Emma. She doesn't get baseball at all. B–O–R–I–N–G. Emma shifts in her seat, puts her hand on the worn green sleeve of Danner's shirt and asks the question again.

"How did you die?"

Danner turns back toward her, shakes her head. "Who says I did die? Who says I'm not some future version of you, or the daughter you'll have one day, peeking in from the transparency all the way on the bottom?"

"You're not me," Emma says. Her head is starting to hurt. She wishes they'd hurry up and get home.

"Your parents think so. They think you invented me," Danner tells her.

Is it Emma's imagination, or has Danner's face changed a little now? She looks a lot more like Emma. A grown-up-girl version of Emma wearing a Sexton College sweatshirt. Emma closes her eyes tight. She doesn't like it when Danner plays these games.

"But I didn't."

"Are you sure?" Danner asks.

"Yes," Emma answers. "You're real." To prove her point she reaches out and touches the sleeve of the sweatshirt again.

"So you can't invent something real, imagine it to life?" Danner pinches the thin skin on the top of Emma's hand.

"Ow!" Emma cries, pulling her hand away. "Whose side are you on anyway?" Emma asks, annoyed.

Danner laughs. It's that quiet, cat-sneeze-sounding laugh.

"Yours," she says, smiling a sly smile. Her face is her own again. "I'm always on yours."

Chapter 6

TESS HAS WORKED LATE into the night to finish the grotto. Coleman lanterns hiss around her. Her fingers have holes burned in them from the cement. At some point or other she always takes off the thick, clumsy rubber gloves, needing to feel the sculpture take shape against her skin, forgetting, in the moment, the acid-burn pain that contact will bring.

The grotto is the latest addition to her ferrocement sculpture garden. *The Island of Doctor Moreau* is Henry's name for it—he jokes, but the truth is, great artwork or not, she knows he finds the whole thing unsettling.

Emma, on the other hand, has always loved the garden. She's spent hours, whole summer days, playing out here, imagining it to be its own country, a land she's named Freesia. She even made up a little song, a sort of national anthem:

Everyone's free in Freesia
The lions, the dodos and me
We wear what we like, we go swimming at night
Everyone's free in Freesia!

The garden began, eight years ago, with the sculpture of Henry and Tess themselves, stuck in the middle of a long-abandoned, overgrown flower garden just between the house and Tess's painting studio. She created a form with rebar and chicken wire, then covered it with layers of carefully sculpted cement.

Tess named that first piece *The Wedding Dance*. It's a life-size sculpture of the two of them dancing, his arm around her waist, her right hand clasped tightly in his left. From the waist down, they have the bodies of lions, tufted tails held gracefully. Their human faces seem frightened, a little horrified even, like they've just glanced down for this first time and discovered what's happened to them. They understand there's no going back. They're stuck this way forever.

"Why lions?" Henry asked. "Lions are supposed to represent strength, right? Power? So why do we look so scared?"

"Lions are killers, Henry."

His face went pale. He never asked about the sculpture again.

After *The Wedding Dance* came the dodos, a parade of them, each wearing a sign around its neck telling its name. There's Faith, Hope, and Charity. Honor, Wisdom, and Obedience. Flightless birds, all long extinct. Some people don't get the joke. Others, like Henry, call it too obvious, but Tess finds it amusing, which is good enough for her.

The next project was a cement-and-stone goldfish pond with a fountain in the center in the form of a spitting frog.

Met-a-morph-o-sis, babycakes.

Along the east and west side of the small pond, Tess built curved benches shaped like a mermaid and merman, the concrete rough and inlaid with stones and shells. Landlocked, they eye each other across the water with serious faces, cross eyebrows, as goldfish jump and the frog spits on and on.

Beyond the pond, a pair of five-foot-tall owls loom, facing each other in menacing poses: wings open, claws reaching as if a fight is about to begin. *Who?* they seem to ask out loud, the un-answered existential question that feathers will be torn over, beaks broken. *Who? Who? Who?*

Here and there, a scattering of flowers Henry's mother planted years ago: foxglove, bee balm, jack-in-the-pulpit squatting in the shade of the owls, clematis clambering across the merman bench. Tess has been thinning, moving, nursing the garden to life. She brings home new perennials from the farmers' market, planting them here and there; she has no plan.

Then, last week, at the north edge of the garden, which is bor-dered by trees leading into the woods, Tess dug up a patch of hostas and started the grotto. She constructed an arch made from stone and cement, embedded with a mosaic of broken glass, beer bottle caps, and assorted things from the junk drawer: springs, dials, wash-ers, cog wheels from an old bicycle—a tribute to the broken and neglected, to things taken apart and never reassembled. And now, in the center of the grotto, in the niche, behind the row of votives in glass jars, sits a photo of Suz encased in a clear plastic box, protected from the elements. Our Lady of Compassionate Dismantling.

The picture was taken just weeks before she died. Suz sits on a chair outside the barn, whittling a piece of wood that would be-come part of an antler. Henry had caught her by surprise with his camera. In the picture, Suz is looking up, startled almost, raggedy blond hair falling into her eyes, which are amber flecked with gold. Her face is a question mark, a *who goes there*?

It is Tess's favorite picture of Suz because the camera captured this sense of vulnerability. Of being both startled and startling. It is the one thing Tess saved from that summer.

Tess has been in a frenzy to get the grotto done—spending every free moment on it for a week now, mixing cement by flash-light in the dented wheelbarrow. Soaking her aching wrists in a mixing bowl full of ice water before bed so she won't be too sore to work out with the heavy bag in the morning.

"What's the hurry?" Henry has asked, but how can she explain the fierce necessity she feels? The burning need to work faster, to have it done. And today, now that she's heard about Spencer's death, the postcard he was found with, she's more driven than ever.

Tess does not believe in signs. Or curses. Above all, she does not believe in ghosts.

But she has no explanation for the vermilion-paint incident that precipitated the building of the grotto.

Last Tuesday, Tess had been in her studio, a small barn that sits at the eastern edge of the sculpture garden, between it and the house. Behind the barn lay the quarter mile or so of thick woods that act as a barrier between their yard and the road. Tess had been working on a painting (one she doubts she'll ever finish now) of a bunch of sweet peas in a rusted watering can. She was squeezing a dab of vermilion paint from the nearly new tube to the piece of thick glass she uses as a palette when she had the now familiar sensation of being watched. But it was stronger this time, and soon accompanied by a noise. A crashing in the bushes outside.

Tess dropped the tube of paint and hurried outside to investigate. She jogged a ways into the woods in the direction she'd thought the sound had come from.

"Hello?" she yelled. There was definitely someone out there, running through the woods.

"This is posted land!" she called out. "We prosecute trespassers!"

She continued zigzagging through the trees, unable to hear any footsteps but her own.

"I own a gun!" she threatened, though the only weapon in the house was Emma's water pistol.

She stopped every few steps, held her breath, listened. She heard a car going by on the road. A hermit thrush. Her own heartbeat in her ears, loud as club music, a rhythmic throbbing she

felt from her hair to her toenails, but nothing she would dance to.
It was dusk. The shadows played tricks in the woods. She returned
to the studio unnerved, and went back to her painting.

Only she couldn't.

The tube of paint she'd been using, Winsor & Newton vermilion hue, was missing. When she'd heard the noise in the woods,
she'd dropped the tube onto the top of the little rolling cart she
stored her paints in. She'd left it right next to the thick glass palette.

Now, impossibly, it was gone. She pushed the cart away, got
down on her hands and knees, searching the floor, but it wasn't
there.

All that afternoon and evening she told herself she must have
had it in her hand when she ran into the woods, must have lost it
there without somehow realizing. She even went back, trying to
retrace her steps, searching the forest floor, but there was no tube
of paint.

The next day, she returned to her studio after lunch to find
the tube of vermilion paint set next to her easel, crumpled and
almost empty.

"What the fuck?" she mumbled, reaching for the paint, her
hand trembling a little.

Emma was outside, playing in the garden. Tess could hear her
talking to someone—Danner? the cement owls?—and saying,
"Ready the army! Freesia's been invaded!"

So it had. Tess resisted the urge to open the door to her studio,
scream for her daughter to come quickly, run inside, where it was
safe.

But clearly the studio was not safe. Maybe there was nowhere
to hide from whoever, whatever, was stalking them.

"It's your imagination," Tess tried to tell herself. Paranoia, the
destroyer.

But what about the paint, Tess?

It was then, at that moment, as Tess held the nearly spent tube of vermilion hue in her hand while her daughter fought imagined enemies with a stick sword outside, the idea of the grotto came to her, a vision of perfect clarity, a solution.

And she thought . . . what? That maybe the feeling of being watched might go away? That no other tricks might be played on her—no noises in the woods, no missing tubes of paint? That by this one simple act, she could protect her daughter?

If she named the ghost, built an altar for her, faced her in this way that bordered on worship, then, maybe then, she'd be left alone?

It was crazy. Superstitious. Maybe even a little dangerous. Hadn't they promised to never again speak of Suz or that summer? Made a pact that their very lives depended on them keeping? And yet here she was now, a week later, placing a photo of Suz front and center in the niche of the altar. Flaunting the one piece of evidence she'd kept.

How could she ever explain this to Henry? She was supposed to be the skeptical one, the levelheaded adult who always laughed at the idea of ghosts and curses and bogeymen.

"It's just art," she told him when he wandered over after getting back from the grocery store and let out an audible gasp at the sight of the photo of Suz. Surely, she thought, he'd remember what it was like, being guided by the muse, feeling like you had nothing much to do with it.

"The photo has to go," he told her. "Evidence," he said.

"It's a snapshot, Henry. Putting up a photo doesn't make me guilty of a damn thing but being sentimental."

"So that's what this is about?" Henry asked. "Being sentimental?"

Tess shook her head. "I shouldn't have to explain my art. Not to you."

She'd been furious. Furious with herself for not being able to explain the true reason for the grotto, furious with Henry for being such an asshole about it even though she knew he was just trying to protect her, to keep their family safe.

Ironic. That's just what she's trying to do too.

Chapter 7

LAST SPRING, JUST DAYS after Henry moved into the barn, the great white pine fell in a windstorm, missing the farmhouse by mere feet.

Henry himself, as a young boy, built a tree house between this pine and two other smaller trees. He pretended it was a pirate ship and spent hours sailing the seas, telescope pressed to his eye, yelling, *Ahoy!* and *Thar she blows!* Making countless invisible pirates, traitors one and all, walk the plank.

One hundred and twelve. Henry's counted the rings. The white pine had lived through 112 winters and springs. It had seen drought, floods, terrible blizzards, and ice storms that must have sent its branches cracking, snapping off, unable to bear the weight. The farmhouse was built in 1906 and this tree was older than that. This tree had seen the house built; watched the passing lives move through it. Henry imagined relations of this tree who stood beside it, felled to clear the land. Lumber was milled for the house and barn. Beams were hewn by hand. And the little tree watched as people toiled in the soil. Crops were planted. Horses raised. Gardens grown. Though countless trees had died, this one survived, and thrived.

Tess, Henry, and Emma stood over the fallen tree once the storm passed.

"We could have been crushed alive," Emma said, face twisted with worry as she glanced around the yard, eyes moving from tree to tree, wondering which was likely to come crashing down on them next.

Tess put her arm around Emma, kissed the top of her head, and said, "No, sweetie. We were safe."

"That's right," Henry said. "This house is old, but sturdy. It's built like a fortress."

He eyed the distance from the tree to the house, the roof above Emma's bedroom, and said a silent prayer.

"Maybe it's a sign," Emma said.

Henry gnawed the inside of his cheek.

Tess nodded, a smile forming. "I think so, Emma. I do. I think it means it's time for your father to do some artwork again."

"Artwork?" Henry asked, toeing the massive trunk with his work boot.

"A sculpture. Look at the size of this thing! Think what you could do!" She was almost giddy, and for the briefest instant, he let himself get caught up in it, imagining the possibilities. He leaned down to touch the surface of the trunk, thinking the tree might speak to him, as it had in the old days.

He hadn't picked up his tools since college, the summer after college—the summer of the Compassionate Dismantlers, and Tess, he knew, was disappointed in him. She'd encouraged him over the years to carve something, anything. A few Christmases ago, she'd bought him a duck-decoy kit that included a block of wood, templates, basic carving tools, a set of paints, and an instruction booklet. It was a male mallard that Tess said would look perfect on the mantel.

The gift was condescending as hell—it was like giving Picasso a fucking paint-by-numbers kit from the hobby shop. Another example of how Tess didn't understand him at all. If she was content to make tame paintings to sell to old people who came through Vermont on bus tours, wearing socks with sandals and carrying fanny packs—more power to her. But he wasn't going to go that route.

The kit, never built, was put on a shelf in the workshop. A *someday* project that both of them knew would end up in one of Tess's yearly yard sales with a tag that said *Brand New! Never been opened!*

In spite of their seemingly doomed marriage, her opinion of him stung. He was supposed to be a sculptor, an *artist,* not a house-painting contractor. He had this hope then, standing over the enormous downed tree that had miraculously missed the house by mere feet, that if he could somehow go back in some small way to the Henry he used to be, Tess might ask him to move back in. And maybe if he returned to the house, he could go back to his role as protector, and somehow his very presence would ward off falling trees and whatever other natural disasters were looming.

Daddy's magic. He makes all the bad things go away.

Maybe, as Emma had suggested, it really was a sign.

So, grudgingly, he had some of the guys who worked for him at the painting company come and help him haul a fifteen-foot section of the thick trunk into the unfinished side of the barn he used as a workshop, where each night, the massive tree waited.

Henry began by debarking the tree. He tucked the blade of his ax under a free edge of bark and drew it toward himself—the bark came off in slick strips, satisfying as peeling the dead skin off a sunburn. Then he found his long abandoned woodworking tools and got started. Or at least tried to.

What he did, those first few days, was spend his evenings after dinner walking in circles around the great tree, hoping for inspiration. He tried looking at it from various angles. Considered how naked and pale it looked without its dark, rough bark. He lay down next to it, sat on top of it, ran his hands over its surface, once finding a deeply buried nail he himself had put into the tree decades earlier, when he'd built the tree house.

Emma came into the barn to see the great sculptor at work.

"It still looks like just a tree trunk, Dad," she said, squinting at it, as if she was missing something.

"These things take time," he told her. "You can't rush into it. The wood guides the sculpture. The wood alone knows what it wants to become."

"So, what—you're waiting for the tree to start talking to you?" she asked.

He nodded. "Exactly."

Emma shook her head. "Good luck with that," she said, leaving the barn.

Henry would come stumbling out of his workshop at daybreak and make his way into the kitchen at the main house for coffee and breakfast with Tess and Emma; a semblance of normalcy that Henry clung to but at the same time found rather pathetic. He could pretend all he wanted, but in the end, he'd still have to go slinking off to the barn to shave, shower, and dress. And inevitably, each morning, Tess would gaze at him over her steaming mug of French roast and ask how the sculpture was going.

"Great," he would tell her.

"So the tree started talking?" Emma asked one morning.

"Blabbing away," he told her. "Can't get a word in edgewise."

"Can I come see?" she asked.

"Let's wait awhile, huh? Until I get it roughed out. Then you and your mom can come take a look."

"It must feel good to be working again," Tess said, and he gave her a little mousy smile.

He was a fraud and he knew it. A poseur. He'd never been a real artist. Real artists didn't quit.

He took to opening a bottle of wine each night in his barn. He'd tune the radio to a classic-rock station and drink merlot from a coffee mug while he pondered the tree. Great beached whale of a thing. He remembered the sculptures he'd done in college: rough forms carved from tree trunks—humans, wolves, bears, and fish—never finished enough so that you'd forget where they'd come from. He wanted the spirit of the tree to shine through.

The wood guides the sculpture.

The wood alone knows what it wants to become.

These were the things he believed in back in college, this naive notion of ethereal messages that it was up to him to pick up on, to spell out with his mallet and chisels.

"Sometimes I think we're just conduits," Tess told him once, years ago, when she sat in his studio space in the corner of the sculpture building at Sexton. "Like the art we make can't possibly come from us. Do you know what I mean?"

She was sitting cross-legged on the floor, cradling a mug of coffee in both hands. A small-framed, compact girl who hardly took up any space at all, yet she'd say these things with such fierce intensity in her eyes that they came out like the words of a giant.

Henry nodded. Yes. He felt that way all the time. He was just a pair of hands—someone, *something*, else was doing the real work.

Tess wore denim overalls splattered with paint and a charcoal-colored chunky wool cardigan with heavy wooden buttons. Her brown hair was twisted back in an untidy bun, held in place with a pencil.

The painting building was next door to the sculpture building, connected by a tubelike suspended walkway. The Habitrail, they called it. Tess and Henry would often be the only two working there at night. The buildings were supposed to be locked and unoccupied after ten, but every now and then they'd share a joint or a beer with Duane, the security guard, and he'd let them stay as late as they wanted.

There was a kitchenette in the painting building, and Tess had a copper pot for making Turkish coffee. She'd fill a thermos with it, then carry the hot, thick, sweet coffee through the tube to the sculpture building, and call out, "Break time!" Sometimes, Henry was too caught up in what he was doing to stop, and Tess would sit, sipping her coffee, watching him work.

"When I watch you sculpt," she told him, over a steaming cup, "I feel like there's three of us in the room: you, me, and the piece. You make the wood come alive, Henry. That's what I love about your art."

Sometimes, she'd come right up and caress the wood, running her fingers over whatever sharply angled face he was carving: wolf, bear, old man. He had this strange sense, in those moments, that the sculpture was more real to her than he was.

TESS BEGAN REFERRING TO the north side of the barn as his studio. *Going to your studio tonight, Henry?* or *How's the light in your studio?*

Even Emma started: "When can I come see you in your studio? I want to see if I can hear the tree."

"Soon," he promised. "Soon."

Henry bought more bottles of wine. He sharpened his chisels, knives, and gouges. He walked around the tree. He waited for it to speak to him. On the radio, the Rolling Stones sang about getting no satisfaction, Aerosmith told him to dream on. He poured himself cup after cup of wine and prayed Tess and Emma wouldn't show up at the door determined to see his progress.

And then, one night, it came to him. Not inspiration exactly, but more a moment of desperation. He had to do something. Anything. So he grabbed a small hatchet and began the long process of bringing one of the ends of the log to a point, like whittling the end of a giant pencil. He worked for four days at this and then he saw it. A canoe. He was going to carve a canoe! He smiled to think how pleased Tess and Emma would be to see him taking sculpture to this whole new, practical level. He was making something they could all climb inside and take out on the water. If the land ever flooded, they'd be safe. They'd have Henry's canoe, their own private DeForge family ark, to save them.

He was so happy that he did a little canoe-building dance around the log, hatchet in one hand, mug in the other, sloshing wine onto the floor, staining the front of his old work khakis.

"A canoe?" Tess's brow was furrowed, her lips pursed. The sigh that came out from between them was a low, disappointed whistle. She had, he imagined, expected a person or an animal. A face she could caress. But this was the postcollege Henry, the grown-up, fatherly, business-owner Henry. The practical Henry with tiny wrinkles around his eyes.

"But what are you going to do with it?" she asked.

"See if it floats, I guess. Maybe teach Emma to row?"

Emma was dancing around the canoe. "I think it's so cool, Dad!" she said. "Will you make paddles too?"

"Of course, sweetie."

"But you're afraid of the water, Henry," Tess said.

She had him there. So much for Practical Henry.

But he continued to go through the door in his tiny kitchen and into the workshop each night, to turn on the radio, pour himself some wine, and hack away at the giant log. He used a chain saw to cut a crisscross pattern in the belly of the log, then used an ax, an adze, and chisels to chop out the little pieces, hollowing the canoe. He had been at this for over a year now, and it was finally close to being finished. The inside was hollowed, the ends and bottom shaped. He was just doing the final smoothing, taking away the rough edges.

It was a large canoe, big enough for three or four people. Some nights, when he was done working on it, he'd crawl inside and stretch out, his body perfectly cradled by the scooped sides.

More than once, he fell asleep there, only to wake up hours later and make his way stiffly to the daybed on the other side of the barn.

He's done this again tonight. He wakes and looks at his watch. It's nearly 1 A.M. He goes to the window, sees Tess still working on the new grotto, a mere shadow in lantern light.

It's unlike Tess to be this obsessed with a project, to work so many hours. But then again, there's never been a project quite like this one, has there?

For ten years, she's mentioned Suz maybe half a dozen times. Now, suddenly, Tess seems consumed.

Henry's afraid that if anyone sees the grotto, like the private investigator Spencer's father is sending, for instance, it could be viewed as evidence. People don't build shrines for the living, do they? Surely Tess realizes this. He tried talking to her about it earlier this evening when he returned from the grocery store.

"Do you think it's a good idea? The grotto? I mean, having the photo of Suz stuck in there like that. It's kind of a red flag, don't you think?"

"You don't understand," she told him.

"What, Tess? What is it I don't get? Christ, it's practically a signed confession! And what do you think Emma makes of it?"

"Emma thinks it's a tribute to a friend. A friend who made the moose she loves so much."

Henry shook his head. "The photo of Suz needs to go, Tess. The private investigator might show up any day now—"

"I don't tell you how to carve your ridiculous canoe. And what do you think Emma thinks of that? What will she think when she learns the canoe is never actually going to go anywhere near the water, but just sit gathering dust in the barn?"

He turned and walked away.

Now, as he watches her out the window, he remembers her twenty-year-old self sitting cross-legged in a pile of wood chips on the sculpture-studio floor. The sweet, earthy scent of dark coffee and cardamom a swirling aura around her.

Sometimes I think we're just conduits.

Shit.

If Tess doesn't get rid of the photo, he'll have to. He's sure she'll see it as an act of hostility rather than an attempt to protect their family. How is it that whenever Henry tries to do the right thing, he ends up as a villain?

Henry turns from watching Tess at the grotto, looks at his own senseless project, all lit up with halogen spotlights. He doesn't let himself think about what he'll do with it once it's finished. He doesn't admit to the probability that Tess is right: the landlocked canoe will stay in his workshop, there to forever remind him of his own futility, of how he failed his wife and daughter. The boat will taunt and tease, call out to him, whispering its deepest desire, which happens to be his greatest fear—*Water,* it will whisper in its low, woody voice; garbled, thick with pitch: *Water.*

PART TWO

WE OPPOSE TECHNOLOGY, HIERARCHY, RULES AND LAWS, AND ALL FORMS OF GOVERNMENT

MORAL

MAYOR CRYSTALS

Chapter 8

IT'S A FORTY-MINUTE DRIVE from Henry's office to Alden. Route 2 all the way, traveling east, toward Maine, following the twists and hairpin turns that take you past Sexton College and then to the turnoff onto Curtis Road ten miles beyond. The blacktop ends shortly, and the woods get thicker, and the houses get fewer, and then the road signs end too. If you know the way— if you can follow the maze of forks and four-corners that look increasingly the same—eventually between the red pines there's a narrow dirt turnoff that leads up the hill to the cabin. He hasn't made the trip since Emma was born, but the way feels familiar, as if he just drove it yesterday. He blinks. Looks around at the inside of his Blazer just to remind himself that it's not the rattling old orange Dodge van he drove in college. The Love Machine, Suz called it.

Sometimes he thinks about how odd it is that the cabin has been so close—only an hour's drive from their house—all these years. So close and yet universes away. They never come out this way. When Henry, Tess, and Emma used to go to Maine in the summer, they'd loop around, take the interstate, claiming it got them to the beaches and lobster pounds faster. Alden was a big, black hole in the map, a danger zone to be avoided at all costs.

"THINK OF WHAT WE could accomplish—no classes, no jobs, not even a fucking telephone," Suz said, eyes wide as she surveyed the cabin. "We could devote ourselves to the cause full time. Eat, sleep, and breathe dismantlement."

It was the week before graduation and Winnie was showing them the hunting camp her grandfather had built back in the late sixties. They'd parked Henry's van at the foot of the driveway and hiked up the hill, arriving sweaty and winded but exhilarated.

"My grandfather owns it outright," Winnie explained. "Forty acres. Hasn't used it since his arthritis got bad. No one's been here in years."

The cabin was only a twenty-minute drive from Sexton and was in magnificent shape. Henry, who had worked for his father since his early teens, was used to assessing the condition of buildings—the level of rot, the structural integrity—and was pleased to see the old frame carrying the weight of the cabin perfectly. He got on his belly and slithered under the crawl space: the cement posts the building sat on were straight and true, despite years of frost heaves. Winnie's grandfather had understood the importance of a good foundation and had dug deep.

"It's in great shape!" he called to the others. He wiggled out from underneath the building, dusted cobwebs out of his hair, and walked around the outside. "The plywood's a little buckled here and there, and it could use a new coat of paint, but overall it's pretty excellent."

Suz opened the front door and danced through the cabin.

"Right here, in front of this window, this will be our studio space! And Winnie and I can sleep down here, near the kitchen. We'll hang up some tapestries or something for walls—do the hippie thing. Henry and Tess can have the loft." Suz was talking a mile a minute, the sleeves of her tunic flapping like frantic wings. The dust in the cabin swirled around her, lit up by the light from the window, making it look as if she had her own excited force field. "We've gotta get a camp stove. One of those little propane things. We can bring sleeping bags, clothes, art supplies, a few flashlights and oil lamps. We don't need much really."

"We'll have to haul water from town," Henry said.

"It's no biggie," Suz said. "We can get a bunch of containers and make weekly runs to Sexton if we don't find a closer source. Shit, we can just take it from people's hoses at night! Water liberation!"

"What about a bathroom?" Tess asked.

"There's a lovely outhouse in back," Winnie said. "Just gotta watch out for the porcupines."

"Ouch!" said Henry.

Tess gave a little shiver.

"And we can take baths in the lake!" Suz exclaimed. "Oh, Winnie, it's perfect!" She threw her arms around Winnie and kissed her cheek.

"What do you think?" Henry asked Tess. She was the only one of them who'd applied to grad school, and had been accepted at the Rhode Island School of Design. She was planning to move to Providence after graduation. Tess bit her lip, looked around the cabin, then back at Henry. "Fuck grad school," she said.

Suz cheered. "Dismantlement equals freedom!"

NOW, AS HENRY ROUNDS the last bend, passing the stand of red pine, straight and tall as telephone poles, he reaches the old logging road that leads a mile or so up the hill to the cabin. He slows, puts on his turn signal.

Does he really want to see it again?

The cabin, where, last time he visited, Tess's water broke.

Where they found the frogs.

He chews his cheek harder. A dread as thick and green as the ooze from that tank of frogs seeps through him.

Henry thinks of the mayhem. The photos. The ransom note and chair looped with rope. Suz's things. So many of her things lying around the cabin. Evidence. What if it's still there? And what happens when that private investigator shows up, starts snooping around and finds the cabin?

Someone's got to go check it out, clean it up. He promised Tess that someone would be him.

Henry the brave. Henry who makes the bad things go away.

"Tomorrow," he mumbles, his hands shaking a little as he shuts off the turn signal, does a U-turn in the road because he can't bring himself to even go take a look. "I'll come back tomorrow," he whispers, then he turns the radio up all the way so he won't have to hear himself think.

Chapter 9

DON'T GO OUT OF sight. Stay where I can see you. See you. See you. See you.

See who?

She has gone out of sight now but her ears are good as a rabbit's—she listens carefully for the sound of her mother calling her name. Her mother in gardening gloves with purple flowers printed on them, tending bunches of plants that Emma can never remember the names of. She'll run back when her mother calls her, her legs are fast, it won't take long.

And it's stupid, really. Emma is old enough to be on her own in the woods. Something's gotten into both her parents these past few days. They're jumpy. Overprotective.

Today, her mom said she couldn't ride her bike to D.J.'s to meet Mel for a creemee.

"I'll drive you," she said.

"But I always ride my bike! It's ten minutes away."

"Not today," her mom said, as if there was some escaped convict on the loose or something.

And her dad, who's always been a little nutty about the pool, made up some story about how she couldn't go in it because the chemicals were all out of balance.

"I have to shock it," he told her.

"But I can go in tomorrow, right?"

He shook his head. "It might take a few days. We'll see."

And now she's supposed to stay in the garden, not go out of her mother's sight. But her mom is busy with a new flat of flowers she just picked up at Agway. She's planting the area around the new grotto.

"Who's that?" Emma asked when she saw the photo of the blond girl with the knife that her mom had put in a plastic frame on a little shelf in the grotto. It was the same girl who was giving the camera the finger in the photo she and Mel had found in her dad's toolbox.

"Suz," her mother told her. "The lady who painted Francis."

"Where is she now?" Emma asked.

Her mother got that glassy, far-off look in her eyes. "Out west, I think. California, maybe. That's where she was headed last I knew. But that was a long time ago."

EMMA HEADS DEEPER INTO the woods, toward the road. The closer you get to Route 2, the thicker the woods become. The part along the side of the road, the very edge of the forest, is almost impenetrable in places. Prickly cucumber vines cover the trees in a thick blanket. Emma loves them and calls them porcupine eggs. They have spiny, oval, two-inch fruit that's hollow inside, and kind of fibrous and webby looking, like a loofah. Emma's mom says they're members of the gourd family. Her dad calls them cactus balls. Mel calls them *alien testicles,* which Emma thinks is really gross. Whatever you call them, they're bizarre and are most definitely Emma's favorite plant, except for maybe the Venus flytrap.

Emma's not near the road now, though she can hear the

cars and trucks going by, tires bumping over potholes and frost heaves that the road crews haven't gotten around to fixing yet.

In the leaf litter on the ground in front of her is a ring of toadstools, which Mel says is a magic place where fairies gather. She says if you stand in the middle of one on Midsummer Eve, they'll take you over into the fairy world. Emma doesn't believe in stuff like fairies, but then again she probably wouldn't believe in Danner if she couldn't see her with her own eyes. If she could just see a fairy once, then it would be a different story.

Seeing is believing.

Emma counts the toadstools (seven, which uninformed people think is lucky, but really isn't at all—in fact, it's most decidedly unlucky) and pokes at the largest one with a thin stick. Poison black ink seeps from the gills underneath. Fish have gills and so do mushrooms. She thinks it's nice that mushrooms have to breathe just like everybody else.

Just then, just as she's wishing she had someone with her to tell this to, she hears her name called, but it's not her mother calling. No, this is a voice from the other direction, from deeper in the woods.

Danner.

Danner's magic too. Emma just has to think of her, and she's there.

Emma runs toward the sound of Danner's voice, into where the trees grow thick together, shading out all light.

"Where *are* you?" she whisper-yells, afraid her mother might hear.

Out on the road, a car blows its horn.

"This way," Danner says. She's close by. Hiding. Playing a game, maybe. Hide-and-seek. Sometimes Danner never shows herself at all—just keeps moving farther away, calling Emma from what sounds like every direction at once.

Emma tiptoes around the trees, trying not to make too much noise. She wants to catch Danner by surprise. Emma holds still and listens. She hears only the cars going by on the road beyond the trees. Faraway crickets. Birds. She steps forward, slowly, carefully, then turns around.

There they are: the words she and Mel painted on the tree trunks last week. Words in red letters on the smooth gray bark of the beech trees.

The words are painted one per trunk, lengthwise down the trees in blocky capital letters, spelling out a message that was supposed to be the next step in reuniting her parents.

It had been Mel's idea, naturally. The day after she and Emma sent the postcards, they'd been sneaking around in the woods beside Emma's mother's studio, spying in windows, trying to catch her doing something interesting. But all she did was paint flowers, which was, in Mel's words, B-O-R-I-N-G and L-A-M-E. This was not the outlaw artist they'd read about in Suz's notebook.

"No wonder your dad moved out," Mel whispered as they crept away from the studio. Emma gave Mel a pissed-off shove and Mel tripped on a root and went noisily crashing into a small stand of striped maples.

"Who's there?" Emma's mother called from the studio.

Mel got back on her feet and hissed, "Run!"

Emma raced all the way through the woods to the road, her mother shouting threats about guns and prosecuting trespassers behind her. What Emma didn't know was that Mel had doubled back and gone into the studio. When they met up later, back by the pool, Mel took a tube of paint from her pocket and said, "I have a plan. We'll use the paint to—"

"He didn't move out on his own," Emma said.

"What?" Mel hated to be interrupted.

"My dad. My mom asked him to leave."

Mel tucked the tube of paint back in her pocket and shrugged. "Whatever. Do you want to hear about phase two of Operation Reunite, or what?"

"I'VE GOT A RIDDLE for you," Danner says. She's leaning against the tree with the last word painted down it in big, bold letters. She's wearing jeans and a T-shirt, but over it is the red robe Emma got at Christmas.

"Okay," Emma says.

"What is dark but made out of light?"

Emma thinks. Danner drums her fingers on the trunk of the tree, going faster and faster, showing time is running out. She never gives Emma long to answer.

"A shadow," Danner says, grinning. Danner loves riddles.

"I should go back," Emma says. "Closer to the house. So I can hear my mom if she calls."

Danner makes a little tsk-tsk sound. "This was a complete waste of time," Danner says, stepping forward so she can look at the tree she was leaning against.

"But I liked the riddle," Emma asks.

"Not the riddle. I'm talking about painting the trees. Do you think your parents are ever going to come out here? Have they yet?"

"No," Emma admits.

"And even if they do, a few words in the trees aren't going to change anything. You think that just because you found them in that journal, they mean something, but you don't even get what they really mean." Danner spreads her arms and the robe looks like wings. Emma half-expects to see her take off flying.

"My parents will tell me. I'll figure out a way to get them out here and they'll explain it."

Danner snorts. "When are you going to get it, Emma? Henry

and Tess don't tell you anything. If there's something you want to know, you've got to figure it out yourself."

"But how am I supposed to do that?" Emma asks.

"Relax," Danner tells her with a smile. "That's what you've got me for."

Chapter 10

"YOU'RE LATE," TESS ANNOUNCES when he walks in the door.

Fuck. He forgot all about her appointment at the gallery and that he'd promised to be back early to watch Em.

Henry has spent a lot of time standing around in galleries with Tess over the years, drinking shitty boxed wine, smiling like a good husband during openings and parties. He always nodded patiently as some earth-mother type said, "You used to do some sculpture, didn't you? Tess tells me your work was ah-*ma*zing!"

Henry could never stand all those pseudo-artsy women with their flowing clothing made from organic cotton and hemp, their necklaces and bracelets with clunky beads and words in Sanskrit. The art they make and sell sucks. It's all the same. Wishy-washy watercolors. Tired nature photographs. Simple little vessels made from clay that are supposed to represent the birth of the goddess within. If you're going to make crap, why bother?

"Got caught up at the office," Henry says, biting the inside of his cheek.

In his pocket, he carries an unopened pack of cigarettes he

picked up at D.J.'s (he hasn't smoked since college) and the mysterious paper he just found when he stopped at the mailbox at the end of the driveway. It was there, on top of the bills and junk mail, sealed in a plain white envelope with only his first name written on the outside. Once he opened it, he found a carefully folded sheet of matching notepaper with a phone number written out neatly. It looks like a cell number, but one he doesn't recognize. There was nothing else in the envelope.

"I called the office and they told me you left two hours ago. I tried to get you on your cell, but you didn't answer." She stares, waiting for further explanation, but he just stands in silence, takes the bottle of aspirin from his pocket and pops three into his mouth. "Sorry," he says, chomping down on the bitter tablets.

He can't tell her where he's been, how he couldn't even bring himself to go up the damn driveway and take a look at the old cabin.

"I've got to go," Tess says, shouldering her big leather purse. "Emma's in the pool."

In. The. Pool.

The words are bubbles of sound reaching him.

"She shouldn't be swimming without anyone watching her," Henry says, already crossing the kitchen to check on Emma. How could Tess be so careless?

Henry races out the sliding glass doors, across the patio to the pool, where he sees Emma practicing her butterfly. Her arms move in perfect circles, her face bobs in and out of the water.

Fine. She's fine. This time.

Her swimsuit has one of those backs that go between the shoulder blades—Tess would know what they're called. The muscles of her upper back and arms ripple as she slices through the water. Strong already, like her mother. Emma gets to the deep end and stops, smiling broadly at him as she catches her breath.

He hears the Volvo start in the driveway.

"Mom said it was okay," Emma tells him as she treads water. "The chemicals, I mean. She said when you shock it, it just has to sit overnight."

Henry nods. Lets himself breathe. "Nice butterfly," he tells her.

"I'm not sure I've got the leg part right," she says, then pushes off for another lap.

He watches Emma swim, and when he's sure he can't take any more, he hurries her out of the pool by saying the clouds are threatening.

"Thunder," he tells her. "Lightning."

"The sky is blue!" Emma whines. Henry points to the small, but dark, clouds in the western sky.

"They're coming this way," he lies. The lie feels thick in his throat, and once again, he imagines his lungs full of water, imagines himself sinking to the bottom of the pool trying to save her. What having no air might feel like. He imagines what he'd see if he looked up, through the water at the sky—if the blue in the sky would make it seem like the pool went on forever, impossibly deep.

Emma gets out, complaining. She towels off then goes to her room to change.

Henry makes shish kebabs on the grill: chicken, red peppers, and pineapple covered in a gooey sweet-and-sour sauce. He serves them with Minute rice and the world is good.

He touches the folded paper in the pocket of his pants, puzzling over it before sitting down to eat, decides to call after dinner. He gives the bottle of aspirin next to it a shake.

Emma's sitting at the table in a T-shirt that has a seahorse adorned with sparkling sequins. Her towel-dried hair is pulled back in a loose ponytail.

"Daddy!" she shrieks, already bordering on hysteria. "You forgot to set a place for Danner!"

Henry bites his cheek, takes a long sip of wine. "I didn't know she was coming."

Emma stamps her foot. "I told you! I told you! You never listen!"

"I thought maybe you and I could have dinner alone. Maybe Danner can come for dessert."

Emma pushes her plate away without touching a bite, folds her arms tight across her chest and gives him the silent treatment. The if-you-can't-acknowledge-Danner-then-I-won't-acknowledge-you treatment.

Knowing he's as good as beat, not wanting to ruin the evening, Henry stands up, gets out the extra plate and silverware, and sets a place beside his daughter, across from him, for their guest of honor.

"Wine, Daddy. Danner needs wine."

"Of course. Of course she does. I imagine Danner is quite the connoisseur." Henry opens the cabinet, gets a glass and sets it down on the table, grateful that at least he doesn't need to fill it. In the beginning, he did. Platefuls of untouched food had been wasted by Danner. Finally, Tess managed to convince Emma that an invisible girl must need to eat invisible food.

"If she ate our food," Tess explained, "it would show through and wouldn't it be embarrassing for her to be walking around fully invisible but for a stomach full of chewed peas and baked chicken?"

Emma fell for it. Henry kissed Tess on the nose, leaned in and whispered, "Brilliant," in her ear.

"DANNER SAYS SHE DOESN'T like that word."

"What word is that, sweetie?"

"Connoisseur. She says it's pretentious." She pulls her plate back in front of her and uses a fork to carefully take the chicken, peppers, and pineapple off the skewer, arranging them in neat, segregated piles.

"Sorry to have offended." The words are stiff. He's trying to be patient, to not snap at his little girl, give her a good shake, and tell her he's had it up to here with all this Danner bullshit.

When, he asks himself, did I turn into such a prick? He remembers how he passed the turnoff for the cabin only hours ago, tossing away any chance at destroying whatever evidence might be left in spite of his promise to Tess. A prick *and* a coward.

"That's all right." Emma stabs a chunk of pineapple, pops it into her mouth and begins chewing, stopping from time to time to turn to her left and laugh at whatever terribly witty thing Danner happens to be saying.

Whenever Henry asks his daughter about where Danner came from, she's vague.

"She must have a home," Henry says.

"She lives here, with us."

"What about when she's not with you, where does she go?"

Emma smiles. "She's never far. She always sees me. Danner sees everything."

After the *how did you die* conversation in the car, Henry has resolved to redouble his efforts. He hears himself sounding like a grim late-night cop-drama detective.

"What does Danner look like?"

Emma pushes rice around on her plate. "Like me, only different."

"Is she your age?"

"Almost exactly. Her birthday is just before mine. But she doesn't get red velvet cake."

"Do you think she was once a real girl?"

Emma makes a frustrated growling sound. "She *is* a real girl, Daddy."

"I mean, do you think other people could see her?"

"Everyone could see her if she wanted them to."

"So she doesn't want us to see her? Your mother and me?"

"Not yet."

When Henry had gone to Tess with his concerns this morning, she told him he was overreacting. Emma was still in bed and Tess was busy in the kitchen.

"She's an imaginative girl, Henry. An only child who's invented the perfect playmate." She turned her back to him to start grinding the coffee. Henry waited for the noise to stop before continuing.

"But what about the whole death thing? Don't you find that the slightest bit disturbing?"

Tess dumped the ground coffee into the basket and flipped on the pot.

"She's a young girl trying to make sense of the world. That's it. Her hamster died last fall. Her grandfather before that. She's just working it all out in her own way. Stop being so freaked out. And for God's sake, stop asking her all those questions. You're going to ruin the game for her."

Some fucking game.

Tess turned away again, started getting cups and bowls down from the cabinets.

"So what am I supposed to do when she's talking away to Danner about being dead?"

Tess turned back to face him, cradling the three bowls and two coffee cups.

"Play along. Believe it or not, you were once creative and whimsical too, Henry. See if you can call on that part of yourself, hmm? For Emma?"

So that's what Henry tries to do now. He takes his well-adjusted, child-psychology-reading wife's advice and plays along.

"Shish kebabs are Danner's favorite," Emma tells him, her mouth full of red pepper.

"I'm glad. I aim to please."

Maybe Tess is right. Maybe Danner is just an extension of

Emma, a creative way of testing out one's place in the world, of always having someone to talk to, someone to reaffirm her thoughts and feelings.

Emma sets down her fork. "Danner has a secret."

"Oh yeah?" Danner and her secrets. She's always telling Emma things she isn't supposed to reveal. Henry takes another gulp of wine, glances over at the clock, wonders how late Tess will be. He imagines her walking in now, breezing into the kitchen. He prays for it. His eye ticks. An involuntary contraction that begins with a feeling like a tickle in the outside corner of his right eye. It usually means another headache's coming on.

"She says I can tell." Emma wipes her mouth with a napkin, dabbing at the corners daintily, like a lady at a tea party worried about ruining her lipstick.

"Well then, what's the big secret?" Another tick. He rubs at the eye, keeps his fingers there, trying to soothe it.

"She knows your friend."

"What friend is that, honey?"

Play along, he thinks to himself. Play along.

"The lady who made Francis." Emma looks so casual as she says this, like a little girl who's just asked if you could please pass the rice.

Henry sets his fork down with a noticeable tremor in his hand, opens his mouth to say something, but only a hollow gasp escapes, an empty bubble of sound, and there he is again, at the bottom of the pool, unable to save anyone, especially not himself.

Chapter 11

DRIVING HOME FROM HER appointment with Julia, owner of the Golden Apple gallery, Tess is elated. Julia sold three of her new paintings this week, all to one woman—a summer person, Julia explained.

"She wants to know if you'd be interested in doing some commissioned work," Julia said and handed over a folded piece of paper. Tess opened it up and in neat script was the name *Claire Novak* and a cell phone number.

"She asked all about you," Julia continued. "Where you studied. Who your influences are."

They'd left Julia's office and were standing in the bright white gallery, where another painting of Tess's hung—daisies in a cobalt vase—along with an eclectic selection of other artists' work: collages; still lifes; photos of insects; landscapes painted on old pressed-tin ceiling squares; and a few pieces by Georgia Steiger, who did tapestrylike portraits using felt and yarn. Georgia was eighty and had been using a walker since her hip operation last fall. Her work was the best thing in the gallery and she was the most successful of all the local artists, her pieces hanging in a couple of folk-art museums. A local filmmaker had even done a documentary about her—*Woven Lives: The Art of Georgia Steiger.*

"What's she like? This Claire Novak?" Tess asked, studying a new piece of Georgia's: an old man in a wheelchair, yarn face twisted into a toothy grin. Whenever she looks at Georgia's art, Tess can't help but wonder what she herself might be producing at eighty. Will she still be painting? Or will she have given it up, realizing, at last, that she'll never come to greatness?

Julia hesitated, then, smiling, answered, "Intriguing."

Tess couldn't remember the last time she had caught the interest of someone intriguing. Well, she could remember, but it was a long time ago. Back in college. She wasn't supposed to think about that, let alone talk about it. And this, this was real life. The present. Here and now. She turned away from Georgia's portrait of the old man in the wheelchair, and tucked Claire Novak's number into the breast pocket of her linen shirt, where it seemed to flutter a little, like a butterfly against her heart.

TESS FEELS FOR CLAIRE Novak's phone number in her pocket, steps on the gas, speeding a little now. The pink-and-purple chicken in front of the Seven Bridges Egg Farm glows in the final rays of sunset, seems to move as the light changes, inching toward the road in some barely discernible way.

She'll call Claire when she gets home. Or maybe tomorrow. She doesn't want to seem too eager. As she drives, she goes over what she'll say to Claire when asked about her education, her influences. More important, she thinks about all she'll leave out.

Tess spent four years studying art at Sexton, a small liberal arts school in the center of Vermont that had, at full capacity, no more than two hundred campus students. The dorms were cottages, complete with kitchen, lounge, and fireplace. There was the clothing-optional dorm, the vegan dorm, the women's dorm, the substance-free dorm, and of course the substance-friendly dorm.

Junior year, Suz appeared. Tess had seen her standing in line in the cafeteria at breakfast the first day—she got only coffee and dumped about eight sugar packets into it. She was a tall girl with straight, pale blond hair and amber eyes and was wearing combat boots, black leggings, and a flowing earth-tone silk tunic.

"She transferred from Bennington," one of the girls sitting at Tess's table said.

"Why the fuck would anyone leave Bennington to come to Sexton?" another asked.

"She got kicked out," the first girl said. "She set a fire in the dorm. Claimed it was an accident."

"No, that's not why," said yet a third girl, Dee, who had a face full of piercings. Her boyfriend Lucas was on the admissions committee, so Tess figured she should know. "She got kicked out for a prank. She painted the dean's house black, windows and all. Did it one night while everyone was sleeping."

"Impressive," said the first girl.

"Yeah," said the second. "If she did that here, she'd probably get independent-study credit for it!"

They all laughed, watched Suz take her coffee outside where she sat on the grass, took out a plastic pouch of Drum, and rolled a cigarette.

Suz took a sculpture-studio class with Tess and spent the first two months outside, constructing a fifteen-foot-tall man out of scraps of wood and tree limbs. She used a chain saw to cut pieces and worked from a stepladder. As a finishing touch, she gave him a gigantic, out-of-scale erection that nearly pulled him off balance, making him tilt slightly forward. Jon Berussi, their sculpture professor, clearly loved it.

"This," he said, shaking his arms at the sculpture, "is what you should all aspire to. Look at the lines! The symmetry. Look at the flow she's got going on here, people."

"Would you consider it modern primitive?" Spencer Styles asked. He had a pointed ferret face and wore black clothing that was a little too big on him. His family had tons of money, and here was Spencer rebelling with his Salvation Army wardrobe, the pockets of his trench coat full of books of poetry and existential philosophy. He was always trying to impress Berussi; to talk to him artist to artist.

Suz shook her head. "I'm not into categories. No artist should be put in a box."

Spencer's girlfriend, Val (who would one day become Winnie), smiled. She was a skinny girl who dressed in hippie clothes and had long, unkempt dark hair covering half her face. Val never spoke in class, but she would visibly cringe whenever Spencer opened his mouth, as if she just knew he was about to embarrass himself.

Berussi, a fifty-something bear of a man with wild gray hair and beard (both of which he kept confined in ponytails), said, "I'd consider it great art. That's what matters, people. Suz is right, in the end, all the categories, movements, and schools are bullshit." He put his hand on Suz's shoulder and Tess heard Spencer whisper to Val, "He's totally boning her." Val shivered.

Berussi took a photo of Suz's sculpture and brought it to admissions, suggesting it be put in the new catalog. The admissions director agreed only after cropping the photo off at the waist. So in the spring Sexton catalog, there was a photo of the giant wooden man with Suz next to him on her ladder, banging on his shoulder with a hammer.

When the sculpture was finished, she sent invitations to the whole school to view what she called an "Art Happening." Everyone gathered around the giant man after dinner, bundled up in the early November cold. Snow started to fall as they waited for Suz.

Tess zipped up her parka and shoved her bare hands, raw and red from the cold, deep into her pockets. All around her was the buzz of anticipation: *What,* people asked in hushed whispers, *is the kooky new girl up to?*

Spencer stood in his long black coat, doing his best to look bored, as if he was above all of this. Val was half a step behind him, head upturned, watching the snow fall through her chin-length shaggy bangs.

Suz came out of the sculpture building wearing a hooded cloak, carrying a lit torch.

"Maybe she's a witch or something," said Dee with the piercings. Dee took a swig of the bottle of schnapps she was holding and passed it to Tess, who had a tentative sip, her teeth aching from the sweetness; it was like a liquid candy cane.

The crowd parted to make way for Suz and she strode silently through the students and faculty, right up to her sculpture, where she paused, closing her eyes.

Tess held her breath.

In the silence, they could all hear Suz making a low buzzing sound. The noise got louder, turning into more of a groan, then she opened her eyes and touched the lit torch to the tip of his penis.

"No!" Berussi wailed, but it was too late. The flames spread down the penis, and onto the body. Within minutes, he was engulfed, the scraps of lumber and tree limbs cracking and popping—Tess had had no idea a fire could be so loud. The group moved back, away from the heat. The penis fell off, followed by the arms. Then the rest of his body collapsed in, leaving only a pile of burning wood that no one would guess had once been a sculpture.

"Okay, it's official—she's fuckin' crazy," Dee said, her teeth chattering as she moved closer to the heat of the fire and took another gulp of schnapps.

"Totally pagan," a hippie girl in a peasant skirt and poncho said.

"Brilliant," mumbled Henry, the brooding sculpture student Tess had had a serious crush on since freshman year.

Spencer shook his head disdainfully, pulled his coat around him tighter, grunted, "Come on," to Val, and started to walk away. But Val stayed, eyes fixed on the fire. "Suit yourself," he told her, heading off on his own.

Suz tossed the torch onto the flaming remains and pulled down the hood of her cloak.

Someone made a coyote howling noise.

A joint was passed around.

A guy in a floppy leather hat said, "Where're the marshmallows? There should totally be marshmallows."

Jon Berussi was near tears. "Why?" he whimpered, reaching out to clutch Suz's cloak. "All that effort . . . it's such a waste."

Suz smiled. "Don't you get it?" she asked. "It's the ultimate act of creativity. Destruction is transformation. In order to be reborn, you have to die."

"But your sculpture," Berussi said. "That will never be reborn. It's gone. Ruined."

"The energy behind it is stronger than ever," Suz said. "Can't you feel it, Jon? Can't you feel how this makes anything seem possible?"

He shook his head mournfully.

The smiled disappeared from Suz's face. "Then you have nothing to teach me anymore," she said, turning her back to him.

TESS TOSSES HER KEYS into the red ceramic bowl by the front door, on top of Henry's. His keys are on a ring with a silver horseshoe that Emma had picked out for him last Christmas. "For luck," Emma said.

"Home!" Tess calls. She hears the TV but no other signs of life.

The kitchen is tidy, the dishwasher running. The air smells tangy, acrid. Henry has barbecued. An empty bottle of merlot is in the recycling bin.

"Shit," Tess mumbles. It's not even seven o'clock.

She finds Emma on the couch, engrossed in a movie in which a group of very attractive people are shooting at each other and shouting obscenities. Emma's sitting with her legs tucked under her, a package of Oreos open on her lap.

"Where's your dad?" Tess asks, reaching for the remote and flipping until she finds a cartoon.

"On the phone," Emma answers, not taking her eyes off the TV, which now shows a cartoon octopus washing a leaning pile of dishes, pulling them from the bottom until the tower finally crashes down on him.

Tess finds Henry in her bedroom, the bedroom that used to be theirs, lying down with his eyes closed.

"Hey," she says. "Another headache?" She takes off her earrings, sets them on the dresser.

Henry sits up, his eyes red and glassy, and nods.

"Who were you talking to?" she asks.

"Was I talking?" Henry looks alarmed.

"I don't mean just now. Em said you were on the phone. Who was it?"

"The phone? No, I wasn't on the phone."

He's clearly lying. He has this way of looking just to the side of her face, somewhere over her shoulder, when he isn't telling the truth.

Was there even a time when they'd told each other everything? Isn't that what young lovers are supposed to do—stay up all night confessing each sordid detail of their lives? Not Henry and Tess. They had secrets from the start. Henry never talked about his feelings for Suz, which were obvious. And Tess never did tell Henry that she'd had a crush on him for three years before Suz finally pushed them together. Tess thinks that those first secrets were like seeds, and now a wild garden grew, the lies all tangled, untended. It's a dangerous place.

"So how was your evening with Em?" She leans down to unbuckle her shoe.

He looks pale but seems surprisingly sober.

"She told me Danner knows the lady who painted Francis."

Tess feels herself shiver involuntarily. The hairs all over her body rise, as if lightning has struck nearby.

"Emma loves that damn painting," is all she can manage to say.

"I think it's pretty fucking spooky. Yesterday, she's asking Danner how she died. Now today, Danner claims to know Suz." Henry tries to keep his voice calm, rational. He's just stating the facts. But Tess sees the panic in his red eyes. Hears the tremor in his voice.

"I think maybe you're overreacting," she tells him, sticking to her role as the rational skeptic. It's far safer that way.

That does it. Tess sees his face go from practiced calm to angry panic.

"Overreacting? You don't know how fucked up it was to hear her say that."

"Keep your voice down," she warns. "I think it's just a coincidence. Emma loves the painting. She doesn't know a thing about Suz, just that she's an old friend."

"A dead friend."

"We've never told her Suz was dead."

"No," Henry agrees. "No, we haven't. And that's my point. It's as if she knows."

Tess takes a deep breath, lets it out.

"Christ, Henry, I really wish you wouldn't drink so much. You're not thinking clearly. And it's no wonder you get so goddamn many migraines. Sometimes I think if you didn't drink so much, then maybe . . ."

"Maybe what?" Henry asks. His brown eyes are soft, expectant as a dog's.

"Nothing," Tess says. She turns her back to him, begins undressing, which she should probably be doing in the bathroom, but screw it, this is her bedroom. She unbuttons her shirt slowly, feeling his eyes on her.

Does some part of him still want her? If she turned now, would he come to her? She unzips her trousers and lets them fall to her ankles, then steps out of them and moves to the dresser in only panties and a bra. She's pulling out an old pair of paint-stained jeans when she feels Henry's hand on her lower back. Tess freezes, waits for the hand to move, for his other hand to join it.

Please, she thinks. She lets herself imagine how easy it would be to turn around; how that one small gesture could lead to an end to their separation. And things wouldn't be resolved—she would still feel second best, resentful that she wasn't with someone who would love her with his whole self—but at least it would put an end to the incessant loneliness.

And just when she's convinced herself that this is what she truly wants; just when she's sure she can't stand the heat of his hand on her skin any longer; just when she's about to turn and wrap him in her arms, she feels his fingers slip away. Listens to his footsteps cross the room, in full retreat.

Keeping her back to him, she slips on the jeans she's been holding in a tight knot in her hands. Finds a T-shirt.

"I'm going out to my studio," she announces, turning to face him. He's sitting on the edge of the bed, not meeting her eyes with his own. Ashamed.

"Don't you want dinner? I made shish kebabs."

"Not hungry," Tess says, walking past him, out into the safety of the hall. She pokes her head in on Emma, still glued to the TV, which has somehow ended up back on the shoot-em-up movie where every other word is *fuck.*

"Change the channel," she orders. Emma gives a dramatic moan, reaches for the remote, and flips back to the octopus cartoon.

"Bed in an hour, Em," Tess says. "I'll be back to tuck you in."

"Mo-om!" Emma says, rolling her eyes. "I can tuck myself in."

"But if I do it, then I know you're actually in bed and not watching some grisly movie where they seem to use every possible expletive for fornication."

"Forni-what?" Her brow is crinkled, her pale eyebrows raised.

"Never mind. Bed in an hour. And cartoons until then. Sitcoms. The Home Shopping Network."

Emma sinks down into the couch with a groan.

Tess stands, studies her for a few seconds. Nine years old and already so much her own person.

"Hey," Tess says, "I love you."

"Mmm-hmm," Emma says, not taking her eyes off the TV.

Out in the front hall, Tess stops at the painting of Francis, looks straight into his eye, which, tonight, looks troubled and stormy. It looks, she thinks, like Suz's eye.

"Coincidence," she mumbles, turning her back on the moose and feeling that electric buzz again, all of her tiny hairs raised.

Chapter 12

"DID YOU GIVE THIS to her?"

Tess is holding a box of frogs. Rotten, bloated frogs.

"Henry?"

He tries to speak, but can only manage a soft, disgusted moan.

His eyes flutter open. He's fallen asleep in her bed. The bed that was once theirs and now feels as strange to him as waking up in a hotel. The digital clock on the bedside table says it's a little after nine.

He'd stayed in her room, trying to call the mysterious number left in his mailbox, but there'd been no answer. Somehow, he'd drifted off.

Tess is standing over him and he moves to sit up, but is halted by the stabbing ice-pick pain in his left eye. She's waving a photo around. A Polaroid. He squints up at it. It's one Spencer took of all four Compassionate Dismantlers.

"Give it to who?" he asks.

"Emma, Henry. Did you give the photo to Emma?"

"No," he tells his wife. "Of course not."

"It was under her pillow. I was turning back the covers and I found it hidden there."

Henry shakes his head, mystified. "Under her pillow?"

"Do you know where it came from? Is it yours?"

"The barn," he explains, his voice sounding small. "I grabbed some photos that day we went back to the cabin, the day Emma was born. They're in the barn."

He rises, shuffles down the carpeted hallway, and looks in on his daughter, who is in her bed with the covers pulled over her head.

"Have you been out to the barn, Emma?" he asks. She doesn't answer. She's playing possum.

Henry turns, jogs down the stairs, out the front door, and across the yard, Tess following. He pulls open the sliding door of the barn, steps inside, and throws on the lights. They point at the canoe, light it up, make it glow, all holy, a tiny ark. The pain in his eye is pulsing like a living, breathing thing. He covers it with his palm, and steps forward.

Henry goes to the old metal toolbox, jerks open the lid. He pulls out the top tray full of screwdrivers and wrenches. The stack of photos is there, but they've been moved. And the photo of the four of them is missing.

"They've been moved. Someone's been through them," he calls to Tess.

Suz's journal is still there. The journal he hasn't been able to bring himself to ever open. Not once. Under it, he feels the small Magic 8 Ball key chain with a single key, wondering if Tess would even recognize it now, or understand its significance. It was the one thing he took with him the night Suz died, and it had been hidden in the toolbox ever since. Without thinking about what he's doing, he palms the key chain, balls it up tight in his fist, then slips his hand into the pocket of his pants.

"I don't get it. Emma doesn't play in here. She would never come in without me."

"Well, she found the photos somehow." Tess is suddenly behind him. He snaps the lid of the toolbox closed. Is he too late? Has she seen the journal that she has no idea he took? Did she notice what he just put in his pocket? He turns to face her, but she's already headed out of the barn, which surely means she didn't notice either.

Now it's Henry who follows Tess back out of the barn, across the wide expanse of lawn, motion-detecting floodlights picking up their movement and clicking on. Tess sometimes complains it's like living in a prison yard. Henry says he's just keeping them safe. That's his job, right?

"Safe from what?" Tess sometimes asks him and he never knows just how to answer.

They head back upstairs to Emma's bedroom, flip on the light.

"Emma, honey, have you been playing in your father's studio?"

"No." She doesn't look up. She pulls the covers up over her head and lays back down as if she's going to sleep.

Henry glances around the room. It's always so damn clean. Not a sock on the floor, or book out of order on the carefully alphabetized shelves. It smells of lemon furniture polish and fresh-off-the-line bedding.

"Okay," Tess says. "Can you tell me where you got this?" Tess pulls back the covers, shows Emma the photo.

Emma looks at it, then starts picking at a loose thread on her comforter. "The woods."

"Where?" Tess asks.

Henry digs his palm into his eye again, trying to press the pain away.

"The woods behind the garden," Emma says, looking up from the loose thread to Tess's face. "There are words on the trees."

"Can you show me?" asks Tess, reaching out for Emma's hand.

Emma nods, wraps her own small fingers tightly around her mother's.

It's dark out now, and they grab a flashlight from the hall closet. Henry is following them out the door when the phone starts to ring.

"Shit," he mumbles, and he doubles back, picks it up thinking it could be one of his crews working late on a beast of a job that they were way over budget on already—he'd told them they needed to stay until it was done and asked them to call if they ran into trouble.

"Hello?" There is no response at first from the other end.

"Anyone there?" Henry asks.

Great. He's about to hang up when he hears a man cough.

"Is this Henry? Henry DeForge?"

"Yes."

"This is Bill Lunde. I've been hired by the family of Spencer Styles to look into his death."

A lump forms in Henry's throat.

"Are you still there, Henry?"

"Of course. How can I help you, Mr. Lunde?"

"I've actually just arrived in Vermont. I was hoping to set up a meeting with you. I've got a couple of appointments at Sexton tomorrow afternoon, so how about getting together in the morning? Around ten? I can come to your house or your office, whichever is more convenient."

Henry swallows, trying to make the hard knob in his throat disappear. "That would be fine. The house is fine. I'll be here. We're out on Route 2 in Langley, about a mile past the center of town, on the right. Look for a white mailbox with pansies painted on it. It's number 313."

"Great, Henry. I look forward to it. If you have a moment, I wanted to ask you a couple of quick questions now?"

"Uh, sure. Of course."

"Spencer's sister told you about the postcard—do you have any idea who might have sent it?"

"Not a clue," Henry says, pleased to be telling the truth.

"You wouldn't happen to be in touch with a Valerie Delmarco or Suz Pierce, would you?"

Henry reaches into his pocket, pulls out the old key chain, gives it a shake. The white 8 is nearly worn off, and the liquid inside it has somehow darkened with time, making the plastic die inside nearly impossible to read.

"I'm afraid not. After graduation, Val went home to Boston. Suz was headed out to California."

He gives the Magic 8 Ball a shake, imagines he sees the words *Liar, Liar* through the murky water.

"And Spencer—he went home to Chicago?" Bill asks.

"Yes," Henry says. "I think so. I'm not sure, actually."

"And he and Valerie were a couple?"

Henry could barely remember. He hadn't really known them very well when they were a couple, only in the aftermath. He'd seen them on campus together, noticed that Spencer kept her on a tight leash. They were one of those couples where the guy does all the talking, all the decision making: *We're not going to that party. We think Cubism is totally overrated.*

"For a little while. They broke up senior year." *Around the time Val became Winnie.* "She got together with Suz."

"I see. All right. Thank you. I'll see you tomorrow."

"Great," Henry says, pleased to have gotten off the hook so easily this time. But he knows it won't last. If this guy is any good at all, he'll find something to prove Henry a liar. And what then?

The line goes dead. Henry's hand trembles as he places the phone back in its cradle. Henry stands for several minutes, trans-fixed, remembering Spencer's pointy face, the long black coat he always wore that seemed to have never-ending pockets. He's still standing by the phone in the front hall when he sees Tess and

Emma coming across the yard, up the walkway, flashlight bobbing in front of them.

"Nine," whispers Emma as she enters, a strange habit Henry doesn't understand. Is she speaking German? Saying *no* each time she enters their home? No. Like something's not right somehow.

Tess is pale, shaking. She looks like she's seen a—

"Henry," she gasps, "in the woods. Someone's painted the trees."

—ghost.

"Painted what?" he asks.

"Words on the trees."

"What words?"

"*The Compassionate Dismantlers Were Here.*"

Henry says nothing, just stands with one hand on the wall, holding himself up. He looks down at his daughter, who is concentrating very hard on the painting of the moose, staring it down.

"She used my vermilion paint," Tess says, her voice faint, so faint Henry wonders if he misheard her, if Tess really said *she*.

"Who?" he asks.

"Maybe it's the lady who painted Francis," says Emma, her eyes still fixed on the moose. "Maybe she's come back."

And then, just then, out of the corner of his eye, Henry thinks the moose has moved, blinked, given him a little mischievous wink.

"Did you see . . . ," he starts to ask, and his daughter just smiles up at him in a way that makes him sure she saw it too.

Chapter 13

TESS'S HAND IS TREMBLING so hard she can't get the key into the lock on her studio door. The red letters she saw in the trees are burning in her mind, their own neon sign: THE COMPASSIONATE DISMANTLERS WERE HERE. A confession. A warning.

"YOU HAVE A KEY to Berussi's house?" Henry asked.

Suz shrugged as she fit the key into the lock on the rough wooden door.

"Tell me you weren't fucking him," Val said.

Suz acted as if she hadn't heard. A low growl rumbled behind the soon-to-be unlocked door.

"That's Magellan," Suz told them. "A German shepherd. He's a real sweetie."

The hairs on Tess's arms rose. She didn't like this. Yes, Berussi would be occupied teaching Sculpture as an Evolutionary Process until at least four o'clock—there was no way they'd be caught. But it felt wrong. And what were they even looking for here? Suz said they were just going in to do a little spying. *Enemy infiltration,* she called it. *Reconnaissance.*

It was the spring of their senior year and Berussi was on the warpath, rallying to get the other professors and administrators behind him. Berussi was not a fan of the Dismantlers, and had done all he could to see that Suz not be given credit for her sculpture class last fall. Suz, true to form, persuaded the dean that this was ridiculous. As time went on, the battle between the two of them heated up, with Berussi leading a campaign to have Suz expelled. And now, he wasn't just after her, but the whole group. At a school the size of Sexton, it didn't take the administration long to figure out who the Compassionate Dismantlers were.

"It's a fucking witch hunt," Suz complained when all four were called into the dean's office where threats of expulsion were made.

The dean had rattled off a list of charges: taking apart tools in the sculpture building, breaking the Hobart dishwasher in the cafeteria, removing spark plugs from faculty cars.

"You have no evidence," Suz told the dean. "You expel us and we'll hire a lawyer and sue the whole fucking school."

"I'm not sure you'd have much of a case," the dean said.

"You might be surprised," Suz told him.

So maybe that was what they were doing here in Berussi's house. Looking for something that they could use as ammunition against Berussi; something that might take the spotlight off the Dismantlers and put it on their number one detractor.

They'd parked in a dirt pull-off down the road and walked to Berussi's so that there wasn't a chance of a friendly neighbor telling him about seeing an orange van in his driveway.

"And what's to stop Magellan the sweetie from ripping us to shreds?" Henry asked. In spite of the amazing sculptures he carved of them, animals made him nervous.

Suz smiled. "Don't worry. He's a vegetarian."

"Right." Val laughed.

"Seriously," Suz said. "Berussi cooks little meals for him—

eggs, carrots, whey protein. It's crazy. The guy is hard-core. It's one thing to not eat meat yourself, but to inflict it on your dog? I mean, hello! A dog is a carnivore. Just look at its teeth."

Suz unlocked the heavy door and stepped into the little house. Magellan leaped up on her, licking her face.

"Easy, boy, easy," she said. Suz reached into her bag and took out the plastic grocery sack inside it, unwrapped a piece of raw steak, and threw it to the dog. "There you go, big guy," she said, kissing the air in Magellan's direction. "Who loves you best of all?"

They watched the dog tear into the steak. "Tell me that's a dog who wants to be a vegetarian. I'm telling you, Berussi's got no respect for autonomy," Suz said. Magellan's teeth crunched down on bone.

The house was tiny. The front door opened into the living room, the kitchen was to the left and the bathroom beside it. At the back of the house was a bedroom barely large enough for a twin bed. The floors and walls were unfinished, knotty-pine boards. The place was surprisingly neat, considering the unkempt appearance of its owner. And there just wasn't much stuff. Shelves of art books, an old stereo system with a turntable, a collection of record albums, a futon couch, some framed prints. No television or computer.

Tess felt sorry for Berussi. She knew she shouldn't but she did. Seeing his house, hearing about how he cooked meals for his dog, it made him seem kind of lonely and pathetic. She wanted more than ever to jump in the van, head back to campus, and forget all about this.

"Look at all this vinyl. The guy loves his jazz," Henry said, holding up a Count Basie album. He thumbed through the rest. "Billie Holiday, John Coltrane, Charlie Parker. He's got some great old blues stuff too."

Suz rummaged through drawers in Berussi's tiny bedroom.

"Look," she called. "His high school ring. Isn't that sweet?" She held up a chunky gold ring with a burgundy stone. "It's got his initials and everything." Suz pocketed the ring.

"Won't he notice it's missing?" Henry asked. He'd left the records and joined Suz in the bedroom. Tess followed. The little room felt stuffy and airless. Tess sat down on the bed, which was covered in an old hand-stitched quilt with red and blue stars.

Suz shook her head. "Not right away. And besides, the guy's a total stoner. He'll probably just figure he misplaced it. Speaking of which," she said, reaching into the top drawer of his nightstand and pulling out a huge Baggie of pot that she dropped into her knapsack.

"Now that, he'll miss," Henry said.

Suz nodded. "But what's he gonna do? Call the cops? Say someone broke into his house, fed his dog a steak, and took his stash?"

There was a terrible wheezing squawk behind them. Val came dancing into the room with an accordion strapped to her chest. It was red and black with shiny mother-of-pearl-looking buttons and keys. "Look what I found in the professor's closet!" she said, playing a few drawn-out, wavering, off-key notes. She wrinkled her nose, leaned down, and sniffed. "This thing stinks!" she said.

Suz came forward and gave the bellows a sniff. "Oh my god," she chortled. "It totally smells like kielbasa!"

Henry and Tess had to agree. The thing reeked.

"I bet Mister Tree-hugging Vegetarian has secret kielbasa feeds here at midnight," Suz said. "I can see it now: a covert meeting with a sausage maker down in Massachusetts—someplace nobody knows him—then he drives home, locks the doors, and fries it up; has a big old heaping plate of it with sauerkraut and the world is good."

Val smiled at her, played a few notes. "Everyone has their secrets," Val said.

"Indeed they do, babycakes," Suz said. "Indeed they do."

GOD KNOWS TESS HAS her share. She stands in her studio now, the door locked behind her, as she holds the empty tube of vermilion paint.

The Compassionate Dismantlers Were Here.

There's a quick rapping on the door. Tess feels her heart trying to jump through the wall of her chest.

"Hello?" she calls, voice shaking as she presses against the already locked door with all her might, holding it closed. It's quiet for several seconds. The knob rattles as someone on the other side tries to turn it.

She can almost hear Suz's voice now: *Open up, babycakes.*

"It's me," calls Henry from behind the door.

Henry. Only Henry.

Tess lets herself breathe and opens the door. Henry squints in at her, one eye more closed than the other—he's still got his headache.

"Emma's asleep. I put on some coffee. I thought we could talk."

Tess nods. "I was just thinking about that old accordion we took from Berussi's. Do you remember?"

Henry stiffens.

"Remember how it smelled like kielbasa?" Tess asks, smiling in spite of herself.

"We shouldn't have taken it," Henry says. "Shouldn't have even been there."

"No," Tess agrees, "but we were just following Suz. And she made everything seem so . . . so justified. Didn't she?"

Henry bites his lip, nods.

"There's something I didn't tell you. Earlier, when you and Emma were out in the woods, that private investigator called. He's in Vermont, Tess. He's coming out here to see us tomorrow morning."

Tess feels it again: the blind panic of something just outside the door, rattling to get in.

"What'll we do?" she asks.

"He's not the police," Henry says. "He's just some midwestern PI who's only interested in what happened to Spencer. We'll practice our story, tell it to him, and he'll be on his way." He gives Tess a warm, reassuring smile. It's his best *everything-is-going-to-be-okay* look.

"Do you really think so?" she asks.

He nods.

Tess forces a smile, touches him gently on the arm. "Well then, let's go get our lies straight."

Chapter 14

THEY SIT IN THE kitchen drinking the coffee Henry made and going over their story again and again in preparation for Bill Lunde. Henry's never met a private detective before. He pictures a boxy-jawed guy in a fedora, some Philip Marlowe or Sam Spade wannabe.

"Suz packed her stuff and left at the end of the summer. She said she was going out west. California." Tess recites the carefully rehearsed lines as she clutches her coffee mug.

"Right," Henry says. "Good."

He keeps thinking about the message painted on the trees. How he pointed the beam of the flashlight from tree to tree, not believing what was illuminated there. As if the flashlight had somehow cut through the years, and there they were, peeking back through time at one of their own messages.

THE COMPASSIONATE DISMANTLERS WERE HERE

Henry stares down into his mug of coffee, wishes to god it was wine. *Later,* he promises himself. When he's done here, he'll head to the barn and pour himself a nice full cup. Then maybe things will start to make a little more sense. His headache will improve. The clouds will lift.

"I don't like that this Lunde guy is going out to Sexton," Tess says.

Henry sits up straight on his stool, sets his coffee down on the tiled counter. "There's not much to find. We got rid of all our records. He might run into some people who remember us, but what's that going to prove?"

Tess shakes her head. "I don't like it. What if he tracks down Berussi?"

Henry feels himself stiffen. The pain in his head is a many-tentacled monster, reaching, grabbing hold of the back of his eyeball and squeezing.

Berussi. Christ.

"DO ME A FAVOR, huh?" Suz whispered to Tess. "Keep Berussi busy in here for a few minutes, okay?"

They were in the sculpture studio and Berussi was over in the corner, fiddling with some welding gear. Henry was chiseling away at a large wolf sculpture.

Tess nodded. Called over to him, "Hey, Jon, could you give me a hand with something? I've got some tricky cuts to make on a piece of Plexiglas and I'm afraid I'll screw it up."

"Sure, Tess," he said. "I'd be happy to." He joined Tess over at the scroll saw.

Henry put down his mallet and chisel, and followed Suz out into the entryway where she picked up the campus phone and punched in some numbers.

"What's going on?" he asked.

She smiled, put her finger over her lips to shush him.

"Hey, Roz, this is Suz Pierce. Is the dean around? Yeah, I guess it's kind of urgent. I'm over here at the sculpture building—there's some kind of trouble in Berussi's office, and I think the dean better get over here. And maybe it would be a good idea to send campus security too—wait a sec. Wow, Roz, I'm hearing a lot of yelling. I think the more people you send, the better." Suz hung up.

"What is this?" Henry asked.

"Wait and see, babycakes," she said, leaning over to give him an excited little peck on the cheek.

Berussi was still helping Tess in the sculpture studio, the scroll saw screaming, the air stinking of melting plastic, when the dean arrived with campus security; Boris, the visiting poet in residence (who had become fast friends with Berussi); and one of the burlier maintenance men. They went straight for Berussi's office. Boris knocked once, then threw open the door.

Henry peered over the dean's shoulder through the doorway.

The men stood awkwardly, staring down at Winnie. She was sitting on the floor, a Mexican blanket wrapped around her. Her face was red, her eyes glassy with tears. Dangling from her neck on a thin, gold chain was Berussi's class ring. Boris spoke first.

"Are you all right, dear?"

"He says he loves me," Winnie said, voice cracking, her tone dramatic and profoundly wounded. "That he'll die without me. But I don't love him. I love Suz. I keep trying to break things off, but he . . . he gets so angry."

"Who? Who are you talking about, Valerie?" the dean asked.

"Jon." She sniffled for a moment, tugged at the ring on the chain around her neck. "I'm afraid of what he might do. The jealousy makes him so crazy. He made up this whole thing about the Compassionate Dismantlers, you know? Just to frame Suz and get her kicked out of school. Look," Winnie said, and stood up, still draped by the blanket. She went to Berussi's desk and opened the top drawer, pulling out a stack of photocopied notes that said *The Compassionate Dismantlers Were Here*. She thrust the papers toward the dean.

"Jon Berussi is the only Dismantler!" Winnie cried. "And he's got me so messed up. So confused. I can't stand myself anymore. I hate what he's made me become." And with this came the grand finale: Winnie dropped the blanket to the floor. She was wearing only a bra and panties, and the scars on her arms, legs, and stomach were painfully obvious. Even Henry, who knew about the cutting, who knew this was all an act, was shocked. "See what he's made me do!"

Boris the poet cried out. The campus security guy clapped his hands over his eyes. The burly maintenance man marched off in search of Berussi, clearly intending to wring his neck. The dean moved forward, picked up the blanket, wrapped Winnie back up, and promised, "Don't worry. We'll take care of this. We'll take care of you. Everything is going to be okay."

The next day, an emergency board meeting was called and Berussi was fired. When the meeting disbanded and Berussi finally stepped out—his face pale and puffy, his hair and beard disheveled and barely confined by their ponytail holders—a small parade marched by the administrative offices, then on through campus. Some of the students carried signs that said: JON BERUSSI IS A PREDATOR and KEEP SEXTON SAFE: ZERO TOLERANCE FOR HARASSMENT AND ABUSE.

Leading the parade of earnest, angry students was Suz, playing a dirge on a red and black accordion.

"EVEN IF LUNDE TRACKS Berussi down, what's he gonna say?" Henry asks, taking the last swallow of cold coffee.

Tess shakes her head. "You can bet Berussi remembers the Dismantlers pretty clearly—and they aren't fond memories."

"So what?" Henry asks, turning the empty coffee mug in his hands.

"So what? Christ, Henry. It ties us to Spencer—everyone knew how bad he wanted in, and the pranks we pulled on him.

Lunde's gonna make the connection between '*Dismantlement Equals Freedom*' on the postcards and the Compassionate Dismantlers in a heartbeat—which ties us to Spencer's suicide. And most of all, it ties us to Suz. If he figures out that she disappeared that summer, Spencer will be the least of our worries." Tess is looking at him as if he's an idiot.

"Okay, I get it," Henry sighs, pressing his palm against his eye.

Tess shakes her head. "When we meet with Lunde, we're not going to have any idea what he knows or doesn't know about the Dismantlers. And we can't afford to get caught in any lies."

Henry nods. Tess looks off into the distance.

"Even one little lie is a red flag, Henry. A warning that there are others—bigger, better lies just waiting to be dredged up."

Henry shivers.

Dredged up.

Why, of all words, did Tess have to use those?

Chapter 15

HENRY LEFT THE KITCHEN to go work on his canoe. Tess checked that Emma was sleeping soundly, and now heads for her own studio. She closes the front door behind her, makes her way down the steps, across the driveway and over the lawn to the small gravel path that winds through the sculpture garden, ending at her studio.

Jon Berussi. Fuck. Tess still bristles at the memory of what Suz and Winnie had done. It wasn't the first or last time Tess fought with Suz, but it was their biggest blowup.

"I thought we were supposed to be a group, a collaborative!" Tess snapped when she saw Suz later that day, after the so-called protest was over. They were alone in the dingy coffeehouse in the basement of the admin building. "How could you and Winnie just do something like that without any input from us?"

Suz smiled. "I'm sorry if you felt left out, Tess, but for certain missions, it's got to be on a need-to-know basis. Great art isn't made by committees."

"That's bullshit! You and I both know your *mission* was motivated by your personal grudge against Berussi, not art. And you have the balls to involve Henry and me in something like this without our knowledge? You realize that women actually *do* get sexually harassed, right? And that they are always accused of being lying, manipulating bitches, putting on a big act, just like Winnie's Oscar-worthy performance? Congratulations on confirming every sexist motherfucker's suspicions, Suz. Nice fucking job."

Suz had stopped smiling. Her eyes narrowed and her voice lowered to a hiss.

"Spare me the Feminism 101 lecture. I know more about how women are abused and hurt and treated like shit in this society than you could ever *dream* of. Berussi may not have been fucking Winnie, not individually, not specifically. But I guarantee you that he has violated someone—some girl, some woman—sometime, at some point. What man on earth hasn't? We gave her, or them— I bet there've been dozens—justice today."

"Justice? With you as judge, jury, and executioner? You seriously call that justice?"

Suz laughed now. She must have sensed that she was winning. She always won.

"It's not society's justice. It's not the machine's justice. It's justice Dismantler style, babycakes. And seriously, if you don't like the ride, you can get the fuck off. Makes no difference to me. Or to Henry."

Suz turned her back on Tess, and strolled up the stairs and out into the daylight, leaving Tess with her anger coiled in her guts.

MAKING HER WAY ALONG the gravel path, Tess stops, holding her breath. She sees a flickering light up ahead. A single candle is burning out at the grotto where she's lined up a row of small glass votive holders. But she hasn't been out there tonight— it's too close to the woods, to the message painted on the trees that Emma showed her only a couple of hours ago. THE COMPAS-

SIONATE DISMANTLERS WERE HERE. The words like bloody slashes done in vermilion paint.

No matter how hard she tries to rationalize things, to come up with plausible explanations, some part of her wonders if Suz is somehow responsible for the words in the trees.

Suz, who's been dead for ten years.

Our Lady of Compassionate Dismantling.

Has she found a way, Tess wonders, to dismantle death?

Is it possible that she didn't really die?

Tess closes her eyes. Remembers Henry gathering stones on the beach, stuffing them into Suz's clothing.

"Do you have to do that?" Winnie asked. She was on her knees in the sand.

"We've got to weight her down," Henry said. "So she won't float."

Winnie let out a howling moan, wrapped her head in her hands. "This isn't happening!" she screamed.

Weight her down.

TESS KNOWS HENRY WOULDN'T go near the grotto, afraid of Suz now, of his own memories of her.

So she won't float.

Tess sees clearly that a single candle is burning at the base of the grotto and slowly, on trembling legs, steps forward to investigate.

There's a warm breeze coming through the trees, toward her, teasing the hair back away from her face. She makes her way into the garden, through the trellised roses, past the small pond across which the mermaid and merman stare at each other longingly. The goldfish shimmer in the moonlight, working their way toward the edge of the pond, sensing her presence, expecting flakes of fish food to fall from the sky. She is God to these little fish, God of the pond, of the garden, creator of all. It is the only place she feels she fits these days, the only place (other than her boxing room in the basement) that makes any sense to her.

Her sneakers crunch on the gravel path as she nears the grotto, the lone candle beckoning like a light at the end of a pier. Behind the grotto, just beyond the edge of the garden, the woods begin, thick with hemlock, beech, and red maple. She hears footsteps in the leaf litter. Sees movement there—a flash of white floating through the trees. Hair. Blond hair. She blinks and it's gone.

"Wait!" she calls out, running toward the edge of woods, but by the time she gets there, the figure has disappeared. Was this just her mind playing tricks on her? Years of buried guilt making her crack, hallucinate?

Out on the road a motorcycle buzzes by.

She turns, walks back to the grotto.

Tess stands before the shrine, before Suz illuminated by the single flickering votive candle in a clear glass holder. Then she notices what's been left beside it.

"Impossible," she mumbles as she leans down, and from somewhere deep in the woods behind her, she's sure she hears a soft, breathy chuckle.

Tess stares down at the battered pocketknife resting in front of the row of votives. Something made for Boy Scouts, with a red handle, large blade, small blade, bottle opener, and spoon and fork that all fold together neatly. It is, Tess recognizes at once, the very knife Suz is using in the photograph in the plastic case, the knife that never left her pocket that summer. The knife Suz had taken from an unconscious Spencer Styles on the side of the highway in Nowhereville, Maine.

And now, ten years later, Spencer had been found dead, holding a postcard from Vermont with a Compassionate Dismantlers message. And here, laid out on the grotto, is his knife.

Nothing to worry about.

Right.

Tess kneels down, picks up the knife and turns it in her hands, her heart thudding in the small birdcage of her chest, her mind reeling. She's sure Suz had the knife in her pocket the night she died.

Knife in hand, Tess turns, her eyes searching the dark woods.

"Hello?" she calls. Then, in a near whisper, "Suz?"

Maybe Henry's right. Maybe there are ghosts after all. If Suz has found a way back somehow, Tess knows just what she's come for. She knows, but would never dare say.

Chapter 16

HENRY FINDS A ROLL of black plastic, cuts off a few squares, and staples them over the windows in the barn. He latches the sliding door knowing it's unnecessary—Emma and Tess never come in without knocking and calling out.

Henry takes four more aspirin, pours himself a mug of wine, and runs trembling fingers over the red nail polish on the cover of Suz's hardcover black journal.

DISMANTLEMENT = FREEDOM

All these years in his toolbox and he's never been able to open it, fearing, somehow, that cracking open the book would be like letting the genie out of the bottle. But now, he has this sense that it's too late: the genie is out. God help them.

He carries the mug and journal over to the canoe and climbs in, letting the rough-hewn sides cradle him.

Henry takes another sip of wine, thinking he should have brought the bottle, and flips through the journal on his lap, to a spot near the end.

Even now, after all this time, he can hear Suz's voice scolding him for daring to read her words, can almost hear her say, *What is it you hope to find?*

> *July 27—Cabin by the lake*
>
> *As I write this in the flickering light of the oil lamp, the prisoner is asleep. Winnie is watching him. Sometimes, when I see her with the gun, I get this rush that starts as a tingle at the top of my head, like a tickle, and moves down through me, growing warmer, then hot when it reaches my cunt. Who'd have guessed a string bean, sullen girl like Winnie could make me feel like that?*
>
> *Then again, who'd have guessed any of this?*
>
> *Now they want to know what to do next. I'd like to just slip away, let them figure things out for once. Maybe I'm not the fearless leader they believe me to be—the fucking cruise director who keeps everything going, big shiny grin, no crisis she can't handle.*
>
> *Yes, I brought us all together. I had the idea, wrote the manifesto. I identified the cause. We will change the world by taking it apart, dismantling it piece by piece. Break it down. Tear it up. Only then can we be truly free.*
>
> *Dismantlement = Freedom. Right? Right.*
>
> *But sometimes I'm scared that this thing we're doing is so much bigger and stronger than who we are that we may disappear inside it somehow, evaporate. Maybe it's happening already. Am I the Suz the others see*

or—steel yourself, it's cliché time—the girl behind the mask? The girl who's shaking in her fucking boots because somehow or other, everything's spiraled out of control?

We have a prisoner! We kidnapped a guy at gunpoint. Yep, we did. And we did it because I said it was the right thing to do. Shit. Who the fuck am I? I don't know who's to blame—me for starting it or them for blithely following.

Am I saving Winnie? Letting her point her gun (the gun I gave her) at the guy who put her in a box for months, made her totally hate herself. If ever an asshole deserved to be terrorized, this is that asshole.

And yet, is this really an act of dismantlement, or some fucked-up personal vendetta? Earlier today, Tess asked, "Where's the compassion here, Suz?" Tess can be a whiny little bitch sometimes—but she had a point.

Gotta admit, I'm afraid of where all this may take us. How it might end.

They're beginning to doubt me. Like maybe we went too far bringing Spencer here. Dissension in the ranks—ha! I don't know . . .

Do you hear that, Winnie, Tess, and Henry: I DON'T KNOW! News flash: I'm mortal. Not some James Bond mastermind who can always see twenty steps ahead.

Right, so what DO I know?

*This: It's more important than ever that we all stick
together now, whatever it takes. We can't afford to fall
apart. Though I wonder if maybe we're supposed to be
taken apart (we are the Dismantlers, after all!), reduced
to our bare parts, our individual selves?*

*Whatever happens—however this mess turns out—
we've done good work. I believe that. We committed
ourselves to something and we did it. We stripped
things down to their bare fucking bones. We have gotten
down to the marrow and sucked like hell. How many
people can actually say that? How many people have
ever been that brave?*

Henry closes the book, rises and gets the bottle of wine. Then
he settles himself back in the canoe and opens the journal to an
earlier entry.

June 26—Cabin by the lake
*We have these cats that come around. It started with
one huge orange tomcat, then he brought a friend.
Next thing we knew, there were five cats hanging out.
Then Winnie, she brings home a kitten from town.
She keeps bringing them. They don't look stray, but
she says they are. Lost, she tells me. They need a
home. Now we leave bowls of milk, tuna, and Friskies
all over the place. The cats come and go. And Winnie
keeps bringing more home. Giving them names none
of the rest of us can keep track of. Jasper, Yum-yum,
Iris, Wanton, Grover. Carrot, she calls that first cat,
the one that started it all. What kind of a cat name is*

*Carrot? is what I wonder, but I love Winnie, we all
love Winnie, so that's the cat's name.*

*Poor Henry's allergic, so he's stocked up on Benadryl
and walks around weeping and sniffling like someone
died. It's like me with the fucking pollen in the spring.
But I can't take the shit he does—I'd be out like a
fucking light.*

*Tess found an old aquarium at a yard sale, and she
and Winnie filled it with water from the lake then
threw in all these frogs' eggs they'd collected in a
peanut butter jar. We're watching the eggs every day,
waiting for them to hatch. Waiting for their little lives
to unfold right there, before our very eyes.*

*Metamorphosis. Is there any greater word in the English
language? And I can't help but ask, isn't that what's
happening to us? Don't the lives of the four of us mirror
those in the aquarium? Aren't we changing a little every
day, leaving our old selves so far behind that soon, we
won't even remember what we were like? And after the
metamorphosis is complete, it will be impossible to go
back. Though who would even want to?*

HENRY CLOSES THE BOOK. Closes his eyes.

Suz was right. There would be no going back.

Then he thinks about what finally became of those frogs: how
they died trapped in stagnant, brackish water.

The door to the barn flies open and Henry sits up drunkenly
in the canoe, turns, and sees Tess. He quickly slides the journal off
his lap and under his thighs.

"This was left at the grotto," she tells him. He squints at the object in her hand, bringing it into focus.

"Left?" Henry asks. Questions answered with questions.

"I saw something . . . *someone*. In the trees."

Henry just nods.

"Someone with blond hair."

"Oh," says Henry. He tries to come up with something else, and fails.

Henry and Tess both know Suz had the knife in her pocket the night she died. The night he swam her out to the middle of the lake, her clothes weighted with rocks, her head bleeding, her face placid, calm.

"So what the *fuck* is going on?" Tess demands. "I feel like I'm going crazy."

Don't we all? Henry thinks.

Questions with questions. But what's the answer?

"Metamorphosis," he mumbles under his breath, because it's the first word that pops into his head.

Chapter 17

SHE PICKS UP THE phone after the first ring.

"Yes?"

"This is Henry. Henry DeForge. Someone left this number in my mailbox."

It's nearly midnight. She was starting to think he wouldn't call. She lets out a soft, breathy chuckle.

"Who is this?" he asks.

"Haven't you guessed?"

"No—I mean, it's impossible," he mutters.

"Come for a swim, Henry. Right now. Our beach at the lake."

She hangs up before he can answer. But he'll come. She knows he'll come.

Chapter 18

EMMA OPENS HER EYES. Danner is standing above her, holding out her hand.

"What do you destroy when you speak its name?" Danner asks. She's wearing Emma's Disney World T-shirt.

"What?" Emma asks. She sits up, rubs the sleep out of her eyes, takes Danner's hand, which is always cold and fishy. Sometimes she expects to look down and see scales sparkling like tiny jewels on Danner's long fingers. She can't believe Danner woke her up in the middle of the night for one of her riddles.

"Silence," Danner says, then leads her to the window where she looks down onto the circular driveway and sees a man lurking near the cars. He's wearing a hooded jacket. Burglar. Prowler man. He fumbles with the door to Daddy's Blazer.

Emma understands. Danner woke her up because there's an intruder. Emma's about to say, "I'll go wake up Mom," when she sees the man drop something. Then he bends down and nearly falls over. When he regains his balance, he looks up at the house. Emma ducks out of sight. But she saw his face. This is no burglar. It's her dad.

She hears a car door shut, then the Blazer starts.

"Where's he going?" she asks.

Danner only smiles. "Why don't you ask him?" she says.

ONE TIME, DANNER SHOWED up at school, which was really weird because she'd never done that before. Emma went into the bathroom at the end of the hall near the gym, and there was Danner waiting for her in the stall.

"Don't go to Laura Pelsinger's house after school today," Danner told her.

"I wasn't going to," Emma whispered. "She's not even my friend. She's kind of weird."

"Laura's going to ask you to go with her and you have to say no. Promise?"

"Okay. But why? And how do you know Laura's even gonna ask?"

Outside the stall, Emma heard giggles.

"You talking to yourself again, DeForge?" a girl called. "Do you have to count when you take a piss too?"

There was more giggling, then another girl did an imitation of Emma's whispered counting, "*One* I'm-a-mental-case, *two* I'm-a-mental-case, *three* I'm-a-mental-case, all the way to *infinity* I'm-a-mental-case."

More laughter.

Frozen in the stall, Emma thought that was a stupid thing to say. No one can count to infinity. You'd never get there.

"Maybe she's not talking to herself," someone said. "Maybe she's got someone in there with her."

"Is that right, DeForge?" the first girl said, pressing up against the door, putting her eyeball right up to the crack. "Who've you got in there with you?"

"No one," Emma said, jumping back, bashing her calf on the toilet. She'd been so wrapped up in what Danner was telling her that she hadn't even heard the girls come in. How could she have been so careless?

Danner laughed. "I am too someone!" she yelled.

"Shut up," Emma hissed. Danner pinched her arm.

"I bet it's Chucky Hayden," the first girl said. "Are you in there with Chucky?"

Chucky was the fat boy who wore a blaze orange winter hat all year round. Emma's cheeks burned.

"I've got a riddle," Danner said. "What is coming, but will never arrive?"

Emma ignored the question; she couldn't even believe Danner had asked it—this was so not the time for riddles. Emma took a deep breath, pushed the door to the stall open, and found Erin LaBlanc and Vanessa Sanchez in front of the row of white porcelain sinks. They peered into the empty stall behind her.

"Tomorrow!" Danner called from behind the door of a stall farther down. "Got it?" Emma got it all right. And right then and there, as the snickering girls stared her down, she found herself wishing that tomorrow would never arrive.

By recess, everyone was talking about her invisible friend and saying she was a mental case for sure. Everyone but Laura Pelsinger, who got on the swing beside her.

"I don't think you're mental," Laura said.

"Thanks," Emma said.

"I know some people who really are. Like my aunt Lynn. She's a real nutcase."

"Oh," Emma said.

"My mom's picking me up after school. We're going to the Tastee-Freez. She said I could bring a friend. Wanna come? We can go to my house after. My dog just had puppies. You can pet them. They're real soft."

"No thanks," Emma said. Her heart was pounding. She wanted to go. She was so rarely invited anyplace and she loved dogs, had always wanted one. But she remembered what Danner had said.

The next day, there was a special assembly first thing in the morning. The whole school was there. The principal said there had been a terrible car accident out on Ridge Road, just past the Tastee-Freez, and Laura Pelsinger had been airlifted to the children's hospital in Boston. The principal said she wouldn't be in school for the rest of the year, and asked that each homeroom make their own card to send her.

HANDS BUNCHED INTO TIGHT, nervous fists at her sides, Emma puts her face back in the window, calls through the screen, "Daddy!"

But he's already pulling away. He's got the radio turned up loud to his rock-and-roll station. Emma hears the scream of a lone guitar, the boom of bass and drums behind it.

Emma's nose is pressed against the window screen; she imagines the marks it's leaving there, a tiny grid, as if her nose is a map with longitude and latitude lines. She opens her mouth to yell again, touches the screen with the tip of her tongue—the metallic taste is so sharp she jerks her tongue away, but then makes herself lick it again. Once, twice. Three more times. She watches the taillights of her dad's truck disappear down the driveway.

"Daddy!" she yells, louder this time, worried that maybe Danner somehow knows something terrible is going to happen. He's going to get into a wreck just like Laura and her mom. "Stop!"

The lights above her come on and she turns, blinking from the sudden brightness, to see her mother in the doorway.

"What's the matter, Em?" her mom asks.

"Where's Daddy going?"

"Going?"

Her mother comes to the window, looks out, and frowns at the empty parking space where the Blazer used to be.

"Where's he going, Mom?"

"I don't know, baby."

"I think something bad is going to happen. That's why Danner got me up. I think I was supposed to stop him," Emma says.

Her mom wraps her arms around Emma and rocks her as if she's little again. Her mom has just come from the shower. Her hair is still damp, her skin warm and moist.

"Would you like some hot cocoa, sweetie?"

"With whipped cream?" Emma asks, smiling into her mother's flowered nightgown. She smells like soap and sunshine, if sunshine had a smell.

"With whipped cream."

"Can Danner have some?"

"Absolutely. I was hoping she'd come. I think it's time Danner and I had a talk."

Chapter 19

DRIVING OUT TO THE lake, Henry remembers helping Suz stretch the canvases for the nine moose paintings. She was edgy, keyed up. She always got like this before a project. Once Suz started a new piece, she was transfixed. She could go days without sleep, living on cigarettes, black coffee, and peanut M&M's, which she claimed were the perfect food.

"You got your protein, you got your sugary carbohydrates, you got your red dye number forty, what else do you need?"

She was also on edge because of their most recent mission: the night before, they'd broken into the records office at Sexton to destroy any evidence of any of them ever having attended the college. Suz said it was important because their new lives had begun and it was time to destroy all proof of who they used to be.

"Shit. They've got Berussi's letters to the dean in my transcripts," Suz said, looking up from a thick folder. Winnie and Tess were struggling to delete any computer records, Suz and Henry were pulling the hard copies from the enormous bank of file cabinets.

"Listen to this," Suz said, clearing her throat. When she spoke again it was in a low, raspy voice, a tinge of Bronx accent: Professor Berussi's. "'Suz Pierce is obviously a girl in emotional distress, but more important, a person seemingly without a moral compass. She seems to have no remorse for the destructive acts she and her group have perpetrated upon the campus. Her delusions of grandeur and narcissism are clearly symptoms of some sort of personality disorder. I believe she is a danger to our community and recommend a full psychological evaluation, and ask that she be expelled if she does not comply.'"

"'Delusions of grandeur'?" Suz said in her own voice. "Can you believe that pompous motherfucker?" She threw the whole stack of papers down on the floor.

Winnie placed a hand on Suz's arm. "It doesn't matter."

"Damn right it doesn't," Suz said.

"We fixed him," Winnie said.

"Rat bastard," Suz mumbled, kicking at the papers on the floor.

HENRY HELPED HER HANG the nine canvases up on the wall behind the bed she and Winnie slept in. Every now and then, Suz would stop, mumble, "Delusions of grandeur" or "Personality disorder," shake her head angrily, then go back to what she was doing. She pushed back the mattress, threw down a drop cloth, and went to work, mixing paints on dinner plates, filling the cabin with the dizzying scent of turpentine. Only once she actually started work on the painting did she seem to forget her fury over Berussi's letters.

Suz stood on a chair to do the top row of paintings: the moose's head, neck, and broad back. She roughed it out with brown lines, circles, Xs and Os as if she was playing a giant game of tic-tac-toe.

Over the next three days and nights, the others watched as Suz created a moose on canvas, mixing hair, sand, and ash into the paints that she applied with brush, fingers, and a knife and fork. She wrote down words on a paper bag, then tore pieces off, chewed until they were pulp, and mixed this into the paint too.

"Alchemy," Winnie said.

What struck Henry most, what he could never truly reproduce in his memory years later, no matter how hard he tried, was the sound she made. When Suz was lost in it, completely caught up in the act of creation, she made this low, soft, droning buzz.

"The static noise," Winnie called it.

But there was more than static there. Sometimes, Henry would sit and listen and swear he heard words hidden inside the buzz, not just one voice, but many, all different pitches and tones; different accents and languages, all talking so fast over one another that it was impossible to make out what they were saying.

Chapter 20

TWO A.M. EMMA'S ASLEEP, her belly full of cocoa. Henry's god knows where. What a long, crazy day it's been: the meeting at the gallery with Julia, the words on the trees, the knife at the grotto, and now, to top it off, the strange conversation she's just had with Emma.

"Is Danner here?" Tess had asked.

"Yes." Emma was sitting with her elbows on the table, blowing into her hot chocolate. She was wearing her Minnie Mouse pajamas.

"Good." Tess smiled. "I'm glad she decided to join us."

Emma chewed her lip, stared down into her cocoa.

"Is something wrong, Em?" Tess asked.

Emma looked up, her face worried. "Danner says she doesn't really like you."

Tess bristled. She knew Danner had never really liked her, but had never heard Emma admit it. Over the years, Tess had been the victim of countless pranks blamed on Danner. Little things of hers went missing—lipstick, car keys, sunglasses—they all usually turned up later in Emma's bedroom. And there were more mischievous things too—Tess would get into her car and turn it on to find the radio blaring on some Christian station, the wipers and heater turned up to high; a load of dark laundry somehow ended up being washed with a cup of bleach. The answer, when Tess confronted Emma, was always the same: *Danner did it.*

Tess took a sip of her own cocoa. "Does she say why she doesn't like me?"

Emma was quiet a second, concentrating on her cocoa, and, apparently, on listening to Danner, who sat across from her with her own empty cup of imaginary hot chocolate with whipped cream.

"No."

"Does she know where your father went tonight?" God, she couldn't believe she was asking these questions. *Great,* she'd said to herself. *First you're talking to ghosts, now you're giving your daughter's imaginary friend the third degree. What's next? Channeling Elvis?*

Emma shook her head, ran her fingers through her sleep-tousled hair. "She knows, but can't tell."

"Why not?"

Emma shrugged. "She says she has a riddle for you."

Tess smiled. "Okay then. Go ahead and tell me. I love riddles."

A CRAZY DAY FOR sure. But it's not over yet.

Tess grabs a small metal-barreled flashlight, turns on the old baby monitor in Em's room, puts the other one in the pocket of her sweatshirt and heads for Henry's studio. The floodlights come on as she walks the path outside the house. Prison-break time.

She gets to his workshop and enters like a criminal. Tiptoeing carefully even though she knows it's foolish—Henry's gone, not sleeping in the room next door—she makes her way to the large metal toolbox. The latch is rusty, but opens easily. Holding the small flashlight between her teeth, the metal cold and sharp in her mouth, she lifts the lid, then the tray on top with its array of screwdrivers and wrenches. The photos are right where she saw them earlier tonight, and under them, just like she thought, is Suz's journal.

DISMANTLEMENT = FREEDOM

She flips through the photos: Suz and Winnie on the front steps of the cabin. Tess and Henry on their beach at the lake. All of them gathered around Henry's orange van.

Tess takes the journal and sits on the floor, holding the flashlight in her mouth, using both hands to flip through. Then, she decides to start at the beginning.

November 11—Sexton, Junior year
Last night, I had a revelation as I watched my wooden man burn: true art isn't just about creating. It's about taking a thing apart. Tearing it down. Watching the fucker burn. As I watched the flames, I had a waking dream. I saw a circle of artists, a small band of the devoted, dressed in black, completely committed to dismantlement. And I knew this was the future.

November 17—Sexton, Junior year
I think I've got the first one. I watch her day after day, and it gives me a secret thrill because she has no idea what's to come. That she's about to be chosen for something great, something so huge it's going to blow everything she's ever done, everything she's ever known, right the fuck out of the water.

Get ready, Val Delmarco.

*The girl I've been crushed out on all semester. She's
a poet. She's like the fucking walking wounded. You
know the kind . . . won't look you in the eye, always
looks like she's on the verge of tears. Now, I hate
weakness in all its forms, but see, I've seen the true
Val. I know she's a mouse with a lion hiding inside.
I know, because one night, I went to that godforsaken
coffeehouse and heard her read a poem. She stood up
there, head down, bangs covering her eyes, and she
ripped the face off of the whole motherfucking world.
She showed me the blood and skull and soul of every
living, breathing person. I've never felt more alive than
I did that night. It was this jolt, like cocaine, like speed,
like falling in love times a thousand. That's what
Val reading her poem did to me. And now, I see her
in the sculpture studio, making her little Cornell-like
assemblage boxes and I just want to put my tongue
in her ear, dig my nails into her back, make her mine,
mine, mine. I want to wake up the lion inside her and
hear it roar my name.*

*She's got this idiotic boyfriend named Spencer who
treats her like a six-year-old. He pussyfoots around
her, talks in this soft, condescending voice, and acts like
he is the greatest thing that ever happened to her. He's
such a jackass. And his art is shit. He makes huge
wind chimes, only he calls them spirit voices. Makes
me wanna puke. He's got to go. Val will see that soon
enough.*

November 25—Sexton, Junior year
I have the next two members picked out.

*Henry DeForge: Sweet, sweet Henry who is obviously
so infatuated with me he can barely speak in my
presence. He's funny. He's clever. And he's the best
fucking sculptor in the class. The morning after I
burned my sculpture, I went to my studio space and
found a small, typewritten note: I love you, Suz it
said. And I knew, I just knew, he left it.*

*Henry's got a van. We'll need that. And he'll be
dedicated. Sure, there might be some complications. But
what's life without a little drama, right?*

*Tess Kahle: She's the one who paints the carnivorous
plants. Huge canvases of these sexy as hell, pussy-
lipped, dripping Georgia O'Keeffe–style flowers
swallowing people whole, like fucking boa constrictors.
They give some guys instant hard-ons. I'd like to hang
one above my bed and fuck someone all night while
looking up at one of those paintings. Tess is building
a scaled-down sculpture of one of those plants in class.
She's using sheets of Plexiglas, PVC pipe, and plastic
soda bottles. Instead of one person, she's got the plant
swallowing a whole series of Ken dolls—the plastic is
a bitch to work with, but I admire her for trying it. She
knows how to stretch her limits.*

Tess closes the journal, turns off the flashlight, and sits in the
dark. Holding the book on her lap, she draws her knees to her
chest, wraps her arms around them, and begins to rock, Suz's
book at her very center.

She can't help but feel a twinge of pride to think that Suz had
watched her, handpicked her for the group. She had once been good
enough, intense enough, to catch the eye of someone like Suz.

How did she stray so far from who she once was? What happened to the girl who made those paintings? The girl with guts. The girl who knew what was sexy, how to push all the boundaries.

She wants so badly to be that girl again. To feel alive. She reaches down and touches the journal. DISMANTLEMENT = FREEDOM in raised nail polish letters. Then, she pushes the journal aside and touches herself. There. Fingers slipping under the waistband of her pants, under the boring old-lady panties she buys in four-packs at Wal-Mart. Closing her eyes, she pictures the flowers she used to paint. But it's no good. She tries something else. A dark, mysterious man. Still nothing. She switches fantasies like clicking through a child's plastic viewfinder. Then, she goes back to the flower paintings. She becomes the painting hung above Suz's bed, suspended from the watermarked ceiling of her Sexton dorm room, and she watches Suz watching her. She watches as Suz brings a girl into bed. A long-limbed, faceless girl. Winnie, maybe, before she was Winnie.

I'd like to hang one above my bed and fuck someone all night . . .

Suz and the girl move as if their bodies are liquid. *Symbiosis,* Tess thinks, though it doesn't make sense. But neither does being a painting. Symbiosis. Bodies entwined. It's all open mouths and sticky skin. Pistil and stamen. Pollen in the air. Moist nectar.

Suz is moaning, screaming, digging her nails into the other girl's back, but all the while, she keeps her eyes locked on the painting, on Tess, who moans right back, satisfied at last.

Chapter 21

HENRY STAGGERS DOWN THE path. Trips on tree roots. He brought a flashlight, but the batteries are dead. He's feeling his way. He used to know it by heart.

The path opens up on the beach, which is really just a tiny patch of sand and mud with a wide, flat rock in the center. *The sacrificial stone,* Suz used to call it. She'd lie across it naked sometimes, sunning herself like a stranded mermaid.

He sees her and his breath catches in his throat, filling it. When he opens his mouth, he lets out a croak like a bullfrog.

She's floating out in the water. Facedown. Dead-man's float.

"Suz!" he croak-shouts. His heart jackhammers in his chest, making his whole body vibrate.

What if time is not a linear thing? he wonders. What if it loops and circles; what if we can go back?

Is this what he has done—gone back to the night Suz died?

And now, will he be given the chance to save her?

He's standing at the water's edge, trying to will the courage to dive. She hasn't moved. She's just floating there, her pale blouse billowing in the water around her like a phosphorescent jellyfish.

Then, just as he's about to dive, she lifts her face, folds her body so that she's upright, treading water.

"Swim with me, Henry."

"You're dead."

"Am I?"

I checked you for a pulse. I filled your clothing with stones.

"They never found a body," she says.

Impossible, he thinks. He was there. He saw what happened.

"Come swim with me," she calls, and suddenly, it doesn't matter to him if she's dead or not. It doesn't matter that he's terrified of the water. He leaves his clothes on and walks out into the lake, toward her.

The lake envelops him. The water is warm, but still he shivers. Shivers like a man sure he is walking toward his own death. He should, he thinks, put up a fight. But what's the use?

Suz is laughing, teasing, calling his name. *Henry, Henry, Henry.* Siren song.

He's up to his chest now, ankle deep in muck, and she's swimming wide circles around him.

"You're dead," he repeats.

"Am I?" she asks. She swims in behind him, wraps her arms around his waist. Breaths on his neck. Hot dragon breath. He's trembling harder now.

"Do you still love me?" she whispers.

Love me. Love me not. Love me.

Should he answer her question with a question?

He remembers the night she burned her wooden man, how as he watched her face all lit up with flames, love hit him like a punch in the solar plexus. He stayed up all night writing her a letter to try to explain his feelings, but the next day, when he sneaked into her studio, he had the courage only to leave a simple, unsigned message: *I love you, Suz.*

"Yes," he gasps. He could never play games with Suz. She

was the one person he'd always been honest with. Too honest, maybe.

"Best of all?" she asks.

"Best of all." Yes, it's true. What a relief to say it out loud.

He starts to spin around, desperate to get his hands on her, and she stops him. "Close your eyes, Henry."

He does. He'll do anything she asks.

"Close them tight and make a wish, babycakes," she says.

A wish. But isn't this the one and only thing he would ever wish for? To have her back again?

He doesn't care that he watched her die ten years ago. He's swimming with a ghost and he doesn't care. If this means he's dead too, then he welcomes it. Dear God, yes. He opens his eyes, reaches for her, gets only her hair, which he tugs on gently, trying to turn her around. If he can just kiss her, put his lips against hers and taste her one more time . . .

"Suz," he breathes.

Her hair comes off in his hands. She turns to face him, her face no longer gentle and seductive, but mocking.

This is not Suz.

It's Winnie.

Chapter 22

THIS IS HOW IT began. A series of seemingly random events: a road trip, someone's alarm didn't go off, a lost set of car keys, some killer Thai weed pulled from a pack of Drum tobacco. But now, reading the journal here in Henry's studio, Tess wonders how random any of it really was.

It all started with a trip to Boston to see a modern-sculpture exhibit. Berussi's entire class was going. Henry offered to drive a group down in his orange Dodge van, which Suz called "the Love Machine."

"Bet you get a lot of action in the Love Machine, Henry! Try to tell me you haven't got some nasty old mattress back there!"

Suz said she'd ride with him. Then, under her name on the sign-up sheet, she added the names of Tess and Val. Spencer, Val's boyfriend, wrote down his own name.

But when they all met in the parking lot at six A.M., there was no Spencer. "I'll go get him," Val said.

"Nah, you stay here," Suz said, volunteering to run to the community center to call him.

"Dude who answered said he was sick and we should go on

without him," Suz reported when she got back to the van. Only later would they learn that Spencer wasn't sick. He simply overslept because someone had pulled all the insides out of his alarm clock.

But it didn't matter then. What mattered was that Spencer hadn't been there in the beginning. He wasn't one of the chosen.

It was a quiet ride at first. Suz sat in front, next to Henry, and kept flipping through the radio stations, looking for songs she could stand.

Tess closed her eyes in the backseat, trying to sleep. She kept squinting at the back of Henry's head, wondering what it would be like to touch him there, to run her fingers through his hair. Val sat beside her, hunched over her notebook, scribbling away, hiding behind her hair.

"What are you writing, babycakes?" Suz asked.

Val shrugged her shoulders. "Nothing much."

Suz laughed. "I really doubt that," she said.

Then, just before they were out of Vermont, Suz announced, "I have to pee," and asked Henry to get off at the next exit and look for a gas station. They found a tiny Texaco out in the middle of nowhere. The bathroom was out back and Suz had to get the key from the pimply-faced teenager behind the counter.

Henry and Tess went in for coffee and snacks: two stale crullers and a package of Gummi worms. Val stood outside smoking, insisting she didn't want anything to eat or drink.

"She seems a little lost without Spencer, huh?" Henry said to Tess when they were by the register. Tess shrugged. She thought Val seemed a little lost all the time, no matter who she was with.

When they all met back at the van, Henry couldn't find the keys.

"I coulda sworn I left them in the ignition," he said. He searched his pockets. The others looked all over the parking lot, in the store. No keys.

"It just doesn't make sense," Tess complained. "They couldn't have just disappeared into thin air."

"We could hot-wire it," Val suggested.

Henry laughed. "Right. And who knows how to do that?"

Val looked at Suz. "I figured Suz might."

Suz shook her head. "Sorry to disappoint, babycakes, but I guess my limitless talents have a limit after all."

"Do you have a spare set?" Tess asked.

"Back at the dorm," Henry answered.

It took them ten minutes to search for enough change to call Henry's roommate, Isaac, on the pay phone. Isaac wasn't there. He was off campus at his girlfriend's, whose phone had been turned off because she didn't pay the bill.

"Jesus!" Tess moaned as she stood next to Henry, listening to his end of the conversation.

Henry left a lengthy message at the dorm, giving the name of the gas station, the town they were in, the exit number, and the location of the spare keys. "Tell him I'll give him a hundred bucks. My firstborn. Whatever it takes for him to get those keys down here," Henry said to the kid who answered the phone.

"We could hitchhike," Val suggested after Henry hung up.

"No one's gonna pick four of us up," Tess said, already imagining the horror of being separated from the others, alone in some serial killer's car.

"Tess is right," Suz said. "I say we stay put and wait for Isaac to rescue us. Besides," she said, crossing the parking lot to the grassy slope behind the gas station, "It's kind of pretty here. We've got provisions. A bathroom. And this . . ." She pulled an enormous joint out of her pouch of Drum.

Henry, Gummi worms, and marijuana—Tess couldn't possibly ask for more. "I vote for staying," Tess said, plunking herself down on the hillside.

They formed a rough circle in the dead brown grass and Suz

lit the joint. It was early December, but freakishly warm. Tess's knee was pressed against Henry's, and from time to time, she reached over to take a Gummi worm from the open package on his lap. When they were good and high, weaving fallen brown oak leaves into their hair, whistling through grass blades, and all secretly hoping Isaac would never show up, Suz said, "Do you want to hear something that will change your lives forever?"

Tess held her breath expectantly, looked over at Henry, whose eyes were glistening, all lit up and locked on Suz.

"It's something I realized that night, when I burned my sculpture."

They each nodded, drawing in closer, as if Suz herself were the fire this time and they all wanted to get warm.

"Art, true art, isn't about putting marks on paper or canvas. It's not about building sculptures. It's about tearing it all the fuck down."

Suz had mastered this way of talking, this beautiful ebb and flow of words that drew Tess in, trapped her somehow, made her never want to leave.

"Think about it," she went on. "Destruction is the beginning of all creativity. Without it, there can be no transformation. No rebirth. It's the most powerful force there is."

Tess nodded vigorously. The whole thing made perfect sense. Tess felt as if her whole concept of not only art, but the world itself, was being cracked wide open right then and there by this girl in black leggings and combat boots.

Suz was beautiful, but not in a magazine-model kind of way. Her teeth were a little crooked, her nose a bit too small for her face, but these things made her more stunning somehow. The thing that drew them to her was the thing that had made all of them come to Sexton in the first place: they were all outsiders, people on the fringe. And no one, it seemed, understood this better than Suz. She turned her difference into a source of power,

power that radiated from her, humming, a live thing that sent sparks out to anyone who listened.

When Suz had finished describing her epiphany, her vision for a group of renegade artists, Compassionate Dismantlers, she had them all—hook, line, and sinker.

"So who would be in this group?" Henry asked.

Suz smiled, licked her lips, looked at each of them in turn. "You. All of you."

"Just us?" Tess asked, her heart beating a little fast at the thought that she was one of the chosen.

Suz nodded. "It needs to start small. Be people who are committed. People we can all trust. We're going to be doing some seriously crazy shit—breaking and entering, fucking stuff up. The group needs to be made up of people who can keep secrets."

Henry nodded. "I can keep a secret."

"So you're in, then?" Suz asked.

"I'm in."

"Me too," said Tess, looking at Henry when she said it.

They all looked at Val.

"Val here," Suz said, leaning over to brush the hair back away from Val's bloodshot eyes, which were focused on the brown grass, "she's a walking secret. A born Dismantler if I ever saw one."

Val looked up at Suz, smiled shyly.

"So what about it, babycakes? Are you ready to meet your destiny head-on? To set the whole motherfucking world on fire?"

Val nodded.

"Say it," Suz said. "Say you're going to set the motherfucking world on fire."

Val stood up, cupped her hands over her mouth, and shouted down the hill, to the valley below, "I, Valerie Delmarco, am going to set the motherfucking world on fire!"

Suz laughed. "Beautiful," she said. "Now we've got our first mission to plan."

Chapter 23

SHE LOWERED THE RAZOR blade, traced the surface of her skin gently, a soft, wanting caress, then, not being able to hold back another second, pushed the blade into her left forearm. Relief so sweet she let out a little moan.

The cut she made was short, not too deep. Just right. Perfect. She raised the blade, let herself do it again, another cut perpendicular to the first. No need to hurry. She could savor each luscious second. The others had gone swimming. She told them she was tired and needed a nap.

"What the fuck is this? What the fuck are you doing?" Suz swept back the makeshift curtain surrounding their bed. "Give me the razor!"

"Suz, I . . . What are you doing back?"

"Just hand me the fucking razor blade. Now!"

Mutely, Winnie passed the blade to her and watched as Suz left to throw it away. When Suz came back through the curtain, she was in tears.

"I thought we were done with all this shit," she said.

"I'm sorry," Winnie told her, thinking how like Suz it was

to say *we* instead of *you*. Was she really all that different from Spencer?

"Why?" Suz asked, but Winnie could not answer. Suz took hold of Winnie's arm, studying the cuts the way a doctor or scientist might. She kissed them lightly, then poked the tip of her tongue out and licked away the blood. "I love you," Suz said, and Winnie pulled Suz's face up to kiss her. Winnie tasted her own blood on Suz's lips, salty and metallic, like a lucky penny.

"THE WAY I SEE it, the cutting is all Spencer's fault," Suz said to Winnie later, as they sat naked in the little tent room they'd created with tapestry walls. Suz touched her lighter to the metal bowl of the bong she'd made from the plastic honey bear, took a hit from the pointed spout of his cap. "And the others. The whole string of fucked-up boys who treated you like a little-girl sex toy." She passed the bong to Winnie, then ran her fingers gently over Winnie's scars, which tingled with Suz's touch.

"Spencer put you in a box. Took away your very personhood. Invalidated your feelings. So of course you cut. You cut to feel something real."

Suz had part of it right. The part about cutting to feel. But she was wrong to blame Spencer or any of the other boys Winnie had been with. It wasn't about them.

After Suz was gone, Winnie started cutting again. Not often. Just when she needed to feel something. After Suz died, Winnie lived inside a void, a quiet vacuum in which no sound, no touch could penetrate. She felt nothing. Only when she took out the blade and drew it over her skin, forming neat little lines in rows along her arms and thighs, crisscrossing the old scars, only then did she remember what love was like.

Last Friday, her stepmother forwarded the postcard to her. *To understand the nature of a thing, it must be taken apart.*

Interesting. Very interesting.

Isn't it just, babycakes?

Winnie packed a bag and headed for the cabin in Vermont the day she got the card, thrilled and terrified to discover that it was in much the same shape as it had been when they'd left it.

What'd you expect, babycakes? Did you think the maid would have come? Some happy housekeeper doing her duty out in the woods?

Winnie immediately went to work cleaning up. She took two pickup loads of trash to the dump: old clothes chewed through by mice, shelf after shelf of ruined food, hardened tubes of acrylic paint. Some discoveries, like the unsent ransom note, she burned.

In the back corner of the kitchen, she found the aquarium they'd put the jar of frogs' eggs in. She covered her nose and mouth with a bandanna, held her breath, and carried the tank out of the cabin and into the woods behind it, eyes watering, throat closing instinctively as she gagged and retched from the smell. She dumped the thick, green scum and discovered that there, settled on the bottom of the tank, were frog bones—paper-thin skulls, a front foot so like a miniature human hand that Winnie had to count the digits to be sure.

She filled a big black Hefty bag with things that had belonged to Suz and drove it down to the beach. Winnie stripped off all her clothes, added some rocks to the bag, and swam it out to the middle of the lake.

Back at the cabin, Winnie swept and scrubbed until her back ached and her hands were rubbed raw. She washed all of the cups, bowls, plates, and silverware in hot water mixed with bleach. She put out tempting little piles of poison for the mice.

As she cleaned and brought things to some semblance of or-der, she collected artifacts from their long-ago summer: sketches on curled yellow-edged paper, Polaroids shoved in a drawer, a box of drawing charcoal. She tacked some of the old drawings to the wall, set a box of matches and some ancient, dried-up scraps of Drum tobacco next to an ashtray on the table. Sometimes, looking around, she could trick herself into believing that time had stood still here and Suz was just about to walk through the door.

Once the cabin was clean and in order, she began, like a paleontologist assembling old bones, to reconstruct Suz's moose, which lay in a collapsed heap out back.

Winnie branched out, leaving the cabin to watch Tess and Henry's house. She followed Tess to the farmers' market and art galleries. She tailed Henry to his office. DEFORGE PAINTING said the sign. Winnie remembered Henry going to meet his father there years before. Once, she came along and the old man took the two of them to lunch. Henry respected his father, but had, Winnie felt, a healthy sort of contempt for the life he'd chosen—the painting company, the old rambling farmhouse, the Chamber of Commerce dinners, meetings at the Elks Club. Now Henry had chosen the same thing. Or perhaps, thought Winnie, the life had chosen him, pulling him along like a strong current Henry had been unable to swim against.

She knew all about those currents. Wasn't that what had led her back home to Boston, to work in a series of crummy low-wage jobs: aide in a nursing home, night clerk at a 7-Eleven? Jobs her mother might have taken. Jobs her family expected her to fall into, in spite of the fancy BA from Sexton. Her life, after Sexton, after the Dismantlers, for the most part, had been shit. Shit jobs, shit relationships. She tried to write and couldn't. Poetry had left her. Or maybe she'd left it. Turned her back on that part of herself the night Suz died.

Winnie felt so alone after Suz died that she had tried to kill herself twice and had somehow been a failure at that too. The first time she just passed out and woke up sticky with blood that seeped pitifully from the all-too-shallow cuts on her wrists and groggy from the over-the-counter sleeping pills she'd swiped from the 7-Eleven. The second time was just pure idiocy. She was at home for Thanksgiving dinner and locked herself in the upstairs bathroom where she took everything she could find in the medicine cabinet. When she didn't come down for pie, her father broke down the door. Her stepmother, having watched one too many episodes of *ER,* began searching for a pulse. She pulled back Winnie's sleeve and caught sight of the scars. While they waited for the ambulance, her stepmother undressed her the rest of the way—Winnie could just see the scene in her mind's eye, her stupid, sturdy stepmother yanking the clothes off Winnie's seemingly lifeless body, getting angrier and angrier—and saw the extent of the damage. Winnie woke up in the psych ward, where she stayed for six weeks. Then she was deemed well enough to leave and given two prescriptions and a referral to a community mental health center, all of which went in the trash can at the T station.

YESTERDAY MORNING, HER STEPMOTHER called her on her cell to say a private investigator had phoned, looking for her—a man named Spencer Styles was dead, found holding in his own hand a postcard identical to the one that had come for Winnie.

Fueled by this bit of news, she'd finally gotten up the nerve to go pay an actual visit to Henry and Tess. She'd driven up the driveway to their house, sure she'd announce herself, have a cup of coffee, and reminisce while showing them the strange postcard she'd received, but no one was home. Winnie walked around the old brick farmhouse, peering in windows. She sat in a wooden chair beside the pool, even took off her tennis shoe and dragged her toes through the blue water. She made her way across the yard and discovered the sculpture garden. She stopped to watch the goldfish in the cement pond, then to study the statue of Tess and Henry as terrified half lions. It was clearly Tess's work.

Winnie continued on to the far corner of the garden and

found the grotto, the photo of Suz right at the center. Winnie knelt down so she was at eye level with her old lover, and it was as if she had caught Suz off guard, surprised. Winnie had looked through some window to the past, pried away all the years and found Suz startled to see her, as if Winnie herself were the ghost.

After seeing the grotto, she hurried back to her car and drove straight back to the old cabin, to the very place the photo had been taken, feeling like the line between past and present was too blurry to face Henry and Tess just then.

Then, this afternoon, she decided to try again, using a new approach. She left her number in the mailbox for Henry. It would be easier if he came to her. If she saw them one at a time.

BACK IN THE CABIN, Winnie peels off Suz's soaking-wet clothes and crawls into her sleeping bag, glad to be done with this beast of a day where nothing went as planned. She may have just blown any chance of reconnecting with Henry and Tess. She never did know how to reach out to people.

"Idiot," she mumbles to herself.

The moon plays with the shadows in the loft, stretching them out, making the building seem as if it has its own set of scars. And it does. Winnie knows. She can feel them. The cabin aches the way Winnie herself aches. She reaches under her pillow and takes out the stack of letters, flips on a flashlight, and reads the first:

January 1, 12:40 A.M.

Dear Val,

> *Happy Fucking New Year. I've just downed half a bottle of peppermint schnapps. No champagne in the house. Tsk-tsk. God, I miss you. Things here in cheery old New Jersey are just swell. I*

*divide my time between my days at the FRANKFOOTER—yes,
you read that right—slathering chili on foot-long dogs, and my
nights at my aunt's where I am making a collage to cover all the
walls in the dungeon that is my room. No word from my mother.
My aunt, who makes it clear that she's put out by my being here,
thinks maybe she's in jail again. Or rehab. But neither of us has
taken the incentive to call around.*

*I'm sorry you had such a lousy visit with Spencer. No, fuck
that, I'm not sorry. He's a pretentious piece of shit who treats you
like a little girl. You deserve better. You deserve true love, with all its
beautiful complications.*

*Thanks for the poems. I've pasted them to my wall, right above
my bed, and read them each night before falling drunkenly into sleep.
They're perfect, Val. You're perfect. If you were here, I'd kiss you.*

Here's hoping the New Year brings us all our truest desires.

Love and consequences,

Suz

*PS—Here's a copy of the Manifesto I've been working on. I
think it's a final draft but I wanted to show it to you before calling it
done. I ain't the writer in the group.*

Carefully, so as not to tear the worn pages, Winnie puts the
letter aside, finds the page below, and stares down at the words
scrawled in blue ink.

THE COMPASSIONATE DISMANTLER MANIFESTO

We, the Compassionate Dismantlers, hold five truths to be self-evident.

1. *To understand the nature of a thing, it must be taken apart.*

2.   *We oppose technology, hierarchy, rules and laws, and all forms of government.*

3.   *The universe was created in chaos, and the only true creative force is chaos.*

4.   *Dismantlement is an act of compassion as well as an act of revolution.*

5.   *Dismantlement = Freedom*

Winnie tucks the letter back into its tattered envelope, back under her pillow.

"We're going to stay here forever," Suz had promised one night, just weeks before her death. "Can't you feel it?"

Yes. Winnie could feel it. She'd felt it for years, a terrible aching tug at her chest, pulling her back to the old cabin. She felt it stronger than ever now that she'd returned, as she patched holes in the roof with a bucket of tar from the hardware store, or lay in her sleeping bag in the loft listening to the mice munching on poison.

Suz was here still. Waiting for Winnie to carry out one last act of Dismantling.

"I'm here, Suz," Winnie whispers to the shadows as she reaches down to run her fingers over the ridges of her scars. "I haven't forgotten."

Chapter 24

"WHERE THE HELL HAVE you been?"

It's a trap. Tess has been pacing in Henry's dark little apartment on the south side of the barn, lying in wait like a spider, and as soon as he comes in the door, she flips the kitchen light on, hoping that if she catches him off guard he'll be honest with her. She thinks she deserves that much at least.

"Out driving."

"You're soaking wet, Henry. You're dripping all over the goddamn floor."

"I went for a swim."

She laughs. "A swim. That's perfect. Fucking perfect."

He looks down at the puddle he's making on the linoleum floor. He looks so boyish, so guilty, that she almost feels sorry for him. Then she looks at the clock on the microwave: 3:30 in the morning. Where the hell does a man go at that hour?

"Are you seeing someone, Henry?"

"Jesus!"

"Are you?"

"No."

Is she jealous? Jesus. This is too much. *Get the fuck over it,* she tells herself.

She remembers the feel of his hand on her back this evening. The thrilling jolt it had given her. How close she'd been to turning around. Such an idiot!

"Well, maybe you should be," she tells him. She notices she's positioned herself in a boxing stance: her body turned so that her left shoulder is to him, chin down, fists clenched at her sides. "Maybe we both should. It's time we moved on. It isn't healthy to go on living like this. Not for us or for Emma. I think it's time you found someplace else to live."

"Someplace else?" Henry says, standing in his own little puddle, a leaking, melting man.

She thinks of the first time she laid eyes on him: both of them nineteen, standing awkwardly by the snack table at a new-student mixer their first week at Sexton. She was spooning hummus onto crackers and he was fiddling with the spout of the coffee urn.

His hair was buzzed like a marine and his face and arms were the kind of bronze you got working outside all summer. He was wearing brown canvas carpenter's pants and a black T-shirt that said ASK ME in big white letters on the front. He was exactly the type of boy Tess always found herself attracted to: well kempt, normal looking. But the trouble was, these normal-looking, handsome guys with their short hair and smooth golden skin were always a disappointment in the end. Duller than dull and sometimes just plain dim-witted. She wished she could be attracted to the artsy boys with piercings and purple-tinted hair who dressed in black from head to toe, guys she could actually have a conversation with, but for whatever reason, try as she might, there was just no spark.

Tess walked over to Henry, decided to take a chance.

"Ask you what?" Tess said.

His brown eyes met hers. "Huh?"

Dim-witted, for sure, she thought, sorry that she'd even approached him.

"Your T-shirt."

"Oh," he said, and turned so that she could read the back: ABOUT WILSON PAINTS AND STAINS.

Tess sighed. "And here I thought you were going to tell me the meaning of life, the origin of the universe."

He shrugged his shoulders. Smiled apologetically. "I could make something up," he told her. "Or how about I tell you the dream I had last night?"

"Okay." She took a step closer to him, listening intently.

"I was this cow in a field, you know, just hanging out, eating grass and clover. Happy and peaceful."

Tess nodded, waited for him to go on.

"Then I woke up," he said, scuffing at the linoleum floor with the toe of his work boot.

"That's it?" she asked. She'd outdone herself in the dim-witted department this time. She did a quick scan of the room, looking desperately for a reason to excuse herself.

Henry continued. "I woke up and thought, what if it's the other way around? You know, what if I really *am* a cow in some field and I'm having a dream that I'm a human, living this whole human life during one long bovine REM cycle? Wouldn't that be a trip?"

Tess focused her eyes back on Henry. "Descartes," she said.

"What's that?" Henry asked.

"It reminds me of Descartes. The French philosopher. We read him in high school. He had this whole theory about the separation of mind and body. Let me guess, you're not a philosophy major?"

Henry shook his head, smiled. "No. I'm an artist. A sculptor."

Tess laughed out loud. She couldn't believe her luck.

■ ■ ■

TESS WATCHES THE PUDDLE around Henry widen.

"You know what I want to know most, Henry? What I'm absolutely dying to know?" She thinks of the words in Suz's journal: *She knows how to stretch her limits.* Remembers Henry saying, *No. I'm an artist. A sculptor.* "When did we become the people we least wanted to be?"

Tess starts to cry and hates herself for it.

Enough. Get hold of yourself.

Henry comes to her, his shoes squishing. She steps away.

"Don't," she tells him. And it's that easy. He turns, head down, and makes his way through the little door that leads from the kitchen of his little apartment into his studio, leaving a wet trail, like a slug, to show where he's been, shoes making nasty wet sounds as he scuffles out, obscene sounds, like someone fucking an octopus.

PART THREE

THE UNIVERSE WAS CREATED IN CHAOS, AND THE ONLY TRUE CREATIVE FORCE IS CHAOS

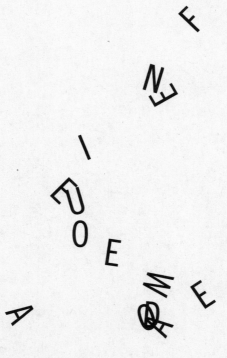

Chapter 25

"DADDY!" EMMA CRIES WHEN he enters the kitchen the next morning, as if he's been away for weeks, as if it's a miracle he's here at all.

He takes her in his arms, leans down, and breathes her in. Strawberry shampoo. Chlorine.

He could live on that smell. Be stranded forever on some small desert island, as long as he had a bottle of that smell to take out each day.

Someday soon, he thinks, Emma will be too big for this. She won't squeal *Daddy!* excitedly when he enters a room, won't jump into his arms or let him bury his face in her hair.

"Your shoes are leaking," Emma tells him.

"Indeed they are," he says, letting her go, then reaching for a cup, pouring himself some coffee. He woke up and put on the work boots beside his bed, just like he did each morning, forgetting somehow that he'd worn them into the lake last night. He'd just as soon forget the whole wretched thing.

Swim with me, Henry.

Maybe if he told himself it didn't happen, if he pretended and ignored the wet boots, then it would all just fade away, like a bad dream. Even the part where Tess told him it was time to find someplace else to live.

Where is he supposed to go? He belongs here, with his family. It's his house, for Christ's sake!

Tess puts toasted waffles on Emma's plate, lays down some sliced strawberries, tops it all with whipped cream from a can.

"Here you go, love," she says, kissing the top of Emma's head. "Just the way you like it."

Then Tess goes back to the counter and grabs a section of the newspaper, thrusting it at Henry. He glances down. The classified ads. She's circled apartment listings.

"Mom made me and Danner cocoa last night," Emma says, looking up from her waffles, traces of whipped cream around her mouth.

"Isn't that nice." He folds up the paper, tucks it under his arm.

"And Danner told her a riddle."

"Did she?" He stirs half-and-half into his coffee.

"Yup." She wipes her mouth with a napkin, sets down her fork. "Danner loves riddles. She's real good at them. Do you want to hear it, Dad?"

"Sure."

"You're in a cement room with no windows or doors. Just four walls. There's a mirror and a table. How do you get out?"

Henry feels himself grow pale. Of course he knows the answer, but he acts as if he's never heard it. He throws a desperate glance, like a lifeline, to Tess, but she won't hold his gaze.

So this is how it's going to be.

"How?" he asks. Some of the coffee sloshes over the edge of his cup and onto the floor. Maybe it's a different riddle. Something she heard at school.

But no.

"You look in the mirror to see what you saw. You use the saw to cut the table in half. You put the two halves together to make a whole. You crawl through the hole and escape." Emma's smiling, pleased with the riddle all over again.

Henry sets his coffee down on the counter and holds on with one hand, steadying himself. "Danner told you that, huh?"

"She told it to Mom. She said it was special, just for her."

"Lucky Mom," Henry says, chomping down hard on the inside of his left cheek.

"I have an appointment this morning," Tess says, seemingly oblivious to Emma's unexplainable connection to Suz.

Henry only nods, stunned. He wants to grab his wife by the throat and demand a rational explanation for the riddle Danner told them. He wants to say, *I told you so*. Then he remembers the private investigator.

"What about Bill Lunde?" Henry asks.

"There's a woman, here for the summer, she bought three paintings and wants to talk with me about doing a piece for her. She's renting a place out on County Road. She really wants me to come out this morning."

Henry only stares, still gripping the counter.

"So can you handle Bill on your own? And hang out with Em until I get home?" Tess asks, sounding slightly exasperated.

"Of course," he tells her in a voice barely above a whisper. "I thought I'd take the day off anyway."

"I shouldn't be long," she says.

He nods, but what he wants to do is get down on his knees and beg her not to go. Not to leave him alone with *them*.

Because for the first time, when he looks across the kitchen at his daughter diving into her too sweet waffles, he thinks he sees a shadow figure in the chair beside her. A dark girl with no eyes or nose, just a mouth, perfectly round, from which comes a damp, rotten laughter that only he seems to hear.

Chapter 26

"I'M GOING OUT TO the garden," she tells her dad. Emma's come downstairs from getting changed and caught him pouring vodka into his orange juice. He gives her a puzzled, nervous look.

"Fine, Em. I've got some things to do in here." He sits down at the breakfast bar with the newspaper open to the sports section. He's not really reading, she can tell. Just pretending.

Emma saw a Lifetime movie once about a girl who had an alcoholic mother who did awful stuff like make scenes in a department store and show up trashed for her daughter's graduation. Emma wonders if her dad is an alcoholic. Is it just a matter of time until he shows up drunk for a PTA meeting, giving everyone at school yet another reason to think Emma's a total freak?

Emma crosses the kitchen, heads out the sliding doors to the patio. She makes her way through the garden, stopping at the pond to say hello to the goldfish. They come up to the surface, mouths open, begging for food in their own fishy way. Kiss, kiss, kiss. Emma blows kisses down to them, imagines she's the Fish Queen, her skin covered in gold, shimmering scales.

She glances back at the house, sees the shadowy figure of her father through the kitchen window. He's still hunched over the paper. She waves to him, but he doesn't notice.

It's now or never.

She puts down her head, and speed-walks to the barn.

If she doesn't get the journal now, she might not get another chance. Mel's coming over after lunch, and fully expects that Emma will have the journal in hand. One way or another, she feels like she always disappoints Mel. It would be nice to do something right for a change.

Last night on the phone, Emma told Mel about her parents finally seeing the words in the trees.

"So what'd your mom and dad say?" Mel asked.

Emma bit her lip. "They kind of wigged out. It was weird. They acted like, like someone wrote *Satan, Satan, Satan* on the trees or something. Like it scared them."

There was silence. Emma could hear Mel puffing away on one of her stinky gum-wrapper cigarettes. Mel's room is in the basement and her parents never check on her. Plus, she burns incense all the time to cover the smell.

"Interesting," Mel said.

"What do you think it means?" Emma asked.

"I think it means we have to spend more time with that journal."

"But—"

"But what?" Mel interrupted.

It's not respectful.

"Just get the damn journal," Mel said.

"OKAY," EMMA TELLS HERSELF, her hand resting on the metal handle of the sliding barn door. "You can do this."

She takes a deep breath, pulls the door open.

The barn is dark and smells like damp cement, wood shavings, and old grease. She looks around and sees that the windows have been covered—her dad's stapled black plastic to them. Why? To keep the light out? To keep people from looking in?

She thinks about turning on the lights, then decides against it. If she hears her dad coming, she can hide. Jump into the canoe maybe. Or under one of the painting tarps.

She waits a few seconds for her eyes to adjust, pupils expanding after being out in the bright morning light. When she's able to make out the rough shapes of the canoe, shelves, and drill press, she moves forward, sliding along in her flip-flops as if she's ice-skating in slow motion, feeling her way. The toolbox is right ahead of her, she can just make out its shape.

Behind her, she hears the cat-sneeze noise, followed by a little chuckle.

"Danner?" Emma calls, turning. She doesn't see Danner anywhere. She hears a scuffling sound but can't tell where it's coming from.

"Why?" Danner asks.

"Why what?"

"That's the question you're not asking yourself, Emma. Why did your mom and dad freak when they saw the message in the trees? Why has your dad kept the photos and journal hidden all these years? And why is this guy here?"

"What guy?" Emma asks.

"Shhh," Danner says, a disembodied voice in the dark. "Turn around."

Emma turns back toward the toolbox and hears something in front of her, just to the left. The door that leads to her dad's kitchen is open and there's her dad, just a dark silhouette, watching her.

The lights come on and here she is, caught, caught, caught! She is such an idiot. Mel's going to kill her when she hears about this.

But when she looks up from the toolbox, with the lights blazing she sees that the figure who caught her isn't her father at all. It's a stranger—a man in tan pants and a button-down shirt, with a crew cut and a funny little sideways grin. She closes her eyes tight, thinking that maybe when she opens them, he'll be gone. Hoping that her parents are right and this is just her overactive imagination.

But no.

She opens her eyes and sees he's coming toward her, and Emma spins, takes off so fast that she loses one of her flip-flops. She jerks the barn door open, and runs into the garden, screaming "Daddy!" the whole way.

Chapter 27

AFTER TESS LEFT THIS morning, Henry found the Swedish vodka left over from a long ago Christmas party and made himself a screwdriver. He needed something to soothe his frayed nerves. To help him erase the image of the shadow girl he'd seen. The god-awful gaping mouth. There were teeth inside. Rows of teeth, like a fucking lamprey.

He's just fixed his second drink and is tossing away the empty orange juice carton when he looks out the window and sees Emma tearing across the yard, screaming for him.

He charges through the kitchen door to the patio, sure he'll see the shadow girl running behind Emma, chasing her down.

"There's a man!" she gasps as she falls against him, sweaty and clinging. He can feel her heart pounding against his own chest.

"What? Where?" Henry asks.

"In the barn."

Sure enough, a stranger is making his way across the yard, strolling briskly. Henry looks at his watch: 9:45. Shit. Bill Lunde.

"It's okay, Em. He's a . . . friend. I'm sorry he scared you."

Emma lets go of Henry, looks back over her shoulder at the man coming toward them.

"Why don't you go on up to your room, Em," Henry says.

She turns back to him. "But, Dad, who—"

"No buts," Henry says. "Go on up now." He gives her a gentle push toward the open kitchen door. She shuffles her way in, dragging her one flip-flop across the tile floor.

Only when she's out of sight does he realize that he didn't get a chance to ask Emma what she was doing in the barn to begin with.

Maybe her little friend told her to go poking around in there. Danner with the lamprey mouth.

"I thought we said ten o'clock," Henry says as Bill approaches. "And I don't think I agreed to any breaking and entering. Or having my home searched."

Bill Lunde shakes his head. His eyes are a clear blue, his skin bronze. No fedora, no cigarette.

"The door was open, Henry. I thought I heard someone in there, so I called out, then went in. I was early, and I'm sorry. I didn't mean to scare your daughter like that. I had no idea she was there. I was looking for you."

Henry doesn't buy it, but there's not much he can do. If he makes a scene, threatens to call the cops, it'll just make him look like he's got something to hide. So he puts on his best all-is-forgiven smile and says, "Well, we've found each other now. Why don't you come on in and have a cup of coffee?" What he's got to do is stick to the plan. Appear friendly and forthcoming. Tell Bill the story he and Tess practiced, then send him on his way.

"Indeed we have," Bill says.

Henry can't help but feel intimidated, despite the good-natured, guy-next-door demeanor Bill has. If Bill goes digging in the right places, if he discovers that Suz disappeared that summer and begins to suspect foul play, this smiling man with the clear blue eyes could ruin their lives forever.

The room is quiet, and Henry hears his own heart beating. He's waiting for the inquisition to begin.

"Tell me," Bill Lunde says at last, "who is Danner?"

"What?"

"Danner. Your daughter was talking to someone named Danner in the barn."

Henry sucks air through his teeth, making a little whistling sound.

"Imaginary friend," he says.

Bill Lunde nods, says, "I see."

Oh I really doubt that, Henry thinks and somewhere in the back of his brain, he hears Emma's voice asking, *How did you die?*

Silence again.

"So is there something I can help you with?" Henry asks, wanting to get this over with.

"Do you know where Valerie is?"

Henry hesitates, bites the inside of his cheek. Does he tell Bill about last night, how Winnie met him down at the lake, dressed as Suz?

Swim with me, Henry.

"Not a clue," Henry says. "Boston, maybe. She had family in Boston. That's where she was headed after college."

"So you haven't seen her since?" Bill asks, looking into his coffee mug.

"No."

"And you haven't seen or heard from Suz?"

"No."

"And your wife hasn't either?"

"No."

"I'm sorry Tess isn't here now. I'd like to talk with her too."

"She had a meeting," Henry says. "With a client. Someone she's doing a painting for." Even this comes out sounding like a lie. Henry wipes the back of his hand across his forehead and feels that he's beginning to sweat. He takes a big gulp of his screw-driver, the vodka and juice burning the holes he's gnawed inside his cheeks.

"Another time, then," Bill says, standing.

Henry stands with him. Is it possible that he's gotten off this easily? This was not the third degree he'd been expecting.

"So you're heading up to the college today?" Henry says.

"Yes," Bill tells him. "I've got a couple of appointments up there."

"Great," Henry says, forcing a smile. He'd been hoping for more—a few little details about who Bill was seeing, what leads he might be following.

"Thanks for your time, Henry," Bill says, extending his hand for a shake.

"No problem at all," Henry says, his cheeks aching from all this smiling. Bill's hand is dry and warm. Henry's is like a dead fish.

Henry walks Bill to the sliding glass doors that lead to the patio and opens them. Bill steps out, hesitates a moment on the patio, then turns toward Henry.

"So you didn't know she was back?" Bill asks.

Henry feels his throat constrict. "Who?" he croaks.

Suz. Suz is back.

"Valerie. She's here. In town."

"Oh," Henry says with a relieved little gasp. "No, I didn't know."

Bill smiles again, nodding, and Henry is positive that inside that smile, Bill is laughing at him for being such a piss-poor liar.

Chapter 28

"DO YOU MIND IF I smoke?"

Tess shakes her head. Watches Claire reach into a large embossed leather bag, retrieve a silver cigarette case and take one out. Inside the lid of the case is a tiny mirror.

Look in the mirror to see what you saw.

Clever riddle. One Tess hasn't heard in ages. She wonders where Em heard it, figures Henry must have told it to her one night when he was drunk. Told her and forgot, which is why he looked so freaked out hearing it again.

But what if he didn't tell her?

Tess shakes her head. He *must* have.

Claire lights her cigarette with a book of matches on the coffee table, inhales, then stares at Tess through the screen of smoke.

They are sitting in the living room of Claire's rented house. The floors are hardwood, polished to a shine. Everything else is white. The walls, the furniture. Even the tiny cups Claire has served the espresso in. The lack of color puts Tess on edge. It's like stepping into a blank canvas. Anything can happen next.

Outside the window, a hummingbird flits by, the shimmering ruby of its throat a surprising splash of color.

Just as Tess is about to point the bird out to Claire, it's gone.

"I'm sorry," Claire says, reaching back into her bag for the case and holding it out to Tess. "Would you like a cigarette?"

"I . . ." *Don't smoke. Haven't since college.* "I'd love one."

Anything can happen.

Claire lights it for her. She has the most amazing hands. All muscles and tendons. The hands of a sculptor. Tess would like to sketch those hands. She imagines the studies she'd do: page after page of Claire's hands shown from every possible angle—holding a cigarette, grinding coffee, cracking an egg. An egg in Claire's hand would be one of the most exquisite things Tess can imagine seeing.

Odd. This is something the old Tess, the Tess in Suz's notebook, might have thought once. The Tess who walked around, eyes wide in wonder at every little detail; the Tess who expected miracles in everyday life and found them simply because she knew they'd be there.

The cigarette is surprisingly sweet, like candied violets. Though she only had candied violets once, on a wedding cake. Not *her* wedding cake. Someone else's. She and Henry didn't have a cake, sharing a pint of ice cream instead as they stood, waiting to catch the train to Montreal for their weekend honeymoon. Mint chocolate chip, it was. Funny how romantic it seemed at the time— Henry still in the suit he'd borrowed from his father, feeding her ice cream from a plastic spoon, laughing when he got some on her nose, then leaning down to kiss the spot of ice cream away.

Tess tells herself she won't inhale, but she takes the smoke into her lungs and finds the sensation intoxicating. *Oh God.* How could she have given this up for so many years?

"Tell me about yourself," Claire says.

Tess laughs, letting the smoke seep out of her chest, which

now feels cleaned out and hollow. Empty. "Not much to tell," she says. She relaxes into the couch.

Anything can happen.

"Oh, I doubt that," Claire says. "I really do."

Claire's accent troubles Tess. It sounds vaguely European, but Tess can't quite place it. Claire has short coal black hair, bright green eyes, and alarmingly high cheekbones. She wears light makeup and smells like cardamom. She obviously works out, she's lean and muscled. Probably close to Tess in age.

Tess wishes she'd chosen something more elegant than the linen pants and black T-shirt she's wearing.

"What about you?" Tess says, turning the question around. "Where are you from?"

Claire smiles. "Here and there. I owned a gallery in Santa Fe but sold it last year. Now I'm in New York. Before all that, Prague."

"Prague," Tess echoes, thinking about how once, she and Henry were going to hike through Europe, see all those ancient cities. Other than the occasional weekend trip to Montreal, Tess has never been out of the country.

Tess studies the cigarette in her hand. There's a small brown picture of a tree inside a diamond near the filter. Obviously not American. If she had traveled through Europe, she might have smoked a cigarette like this. Might be able to show off now, calling it by name.

"Let me tell you why I asked you here," Claire says. "As I said on the phone, I'm very drawn to your work."

Tess smiles. Can't imagine what on earth her generic little paintings of flower gardens and watering cans could possibly offer this woman.

Her eyes wander back to Claire's hands. They're almost masculine, which seems incongruent with everything else about Claire.

A robin's egg would be particularly stunning in Claire's hand. Delicate and blue.

She finds herself wanting to touch Claire's hands, to run her fingers over the knobby knuckles and corded tendons. They remind Tess of a cat's paws; she thinks of the way a cat's paws stretch, knead at the air, claws extended.

How odd. To want to touch another woman's hands. It's something young, college Tess might have considered. But not *this* Tess—the practical mother who keeps the checkbook balanced, fills the pantry with jars of homemade strawberry jam, makes sure Emma has an umbrella when it's going to rain.

"But I feel there's something missing," Claire continues.

"Hmm?" Tess has gotten lost, forgotten the arc of the conversation.

"I look at your paintings, and feel something's missing." Her green eyes look right into Tess's.

"Missing?" Tess bites her lip. A remark like this would usually cause her to feel defensive, but somehow, coming from Claire right now, what it makes her feel is caught.

Claire nods, takes a sip of espresso. "I sense something just under the surface. Something untouched. This is what I want you to explore in the piece you will create for me."

"I'm sorry?" Tess murmurs.

Had she already agreed to do the piece? And what exactly was it this woman wanted?

Tess sits forward on the couch, ready to make polite excuses followed by a quick exit.

"Passion," Claire says, leaning forward to put her hand on Tess's arm, sending such a surprising jolt of electricity through Tess that Tess lets out a little gasp.

Claire smiles, keeps her hand where it is. Says, "That's what's missing."

Chapter 29

DRIFTING IN AND OUT. Clouds in the sky. Clouds in his head, on the back of his eyelids. Pretty pictures. Fluffy bunnies. A jack-o'-lantern. A moose. (Oh god, not a moose.)

Once upon a time, Henry, Tess, and Emma lay tucked inside a brightly colored hammock strung between two trees, watching the clouds, *cocooning*. The world felt so safe then. So perfect. They'd get up soon and build a campfire. Make some s'mores. Tell bad jokes.

Knock knock.

Who's there?

Boo.

Boo who?

Why are you crying?

Henry hears a splash, opens his eyes. The world spins. He's not in a hammock at all, but on a reclining plastic lounge chair beside the pool, a plastic tumbler of warm vodka in his hand. Emma has just done a cannonball. Henry watches his daughter surface, but he is unable to do the same. His eyes close. He's under the clouds. Under his own pool of water.

"Hey, Dad! Watch! I'm a frog!"

That's nice, sweetie. So nice. Nice to be a frog. Ribbet ribbet. Hop hop.

Henry thinks of the frogs in the aquarium. Bloated. Forgotten. And then he's gone. It's like someone's flipped a switch in his brain. The *you've been drinking since seven in the morning and got almost no sleep last night* switch. He's with the frogs. And they're splashing. Croaking. Trying to escape. His daughter the frog. His daughter. The frog. Croaking. Splashing. So much frantic splashing.

Henry can't open his eyes.

"She'll drown in that pool," Henry is saying to Tess somewhere in the back of his brain, in the land of the past. The voice of doom and gloom. The little black rain cloud. "You should have let me fill it in. We could have a tennis court. Green clay."

Henry rises to the surface, forces his eyes open. Emma is upside down in the pool. Henry only sees legs. Legs. Thin little legs scissoring in the air. Coming out of the rubber inner tube. Kicking. Head underwater, she's caught, struggling to right herself.

Oh God! Henry rolls off the lounge chair, tips the whole thing over. He gets to his feet, lurches forward. His baby is drowning, there, right before his eyes, like he always knew she would. Like he's seen in his dreams a thousand times.

I told you so, he hears himself say to Tess.

The legs are kicking furiously. Henry runs toward the pool. Trips on the white wooden deck chair he usually perches in at the water's edge. Tess calls it his lifeguard chair.

He goes down. Crash. Like a tree. The tree in the yard that became the canoe. One hundred and twelve rings. The ridiculous boat that will never see water.

His head hits the concrete and splits open. *There go my brains,* he thinks. *There goes my life.*

What if time is not a linear thing?

What if you can go back?

Put the two halves together to make a whole. Crawl through the hole.

Boo who?

Why are you crying?

Splash. Stroke. Stroke. Someone has jumped into the water with Emma. Splashing. Struggling. Emma coughs, gags, cries. Henry lifts his head—his bloated, two-ton head—blood seeping from the gash above his eyebrow and into his eyes.

Suz is carrying Em out of the pool. Only it's not Suz. It's himself in a blond wig. The wig falls off and he sees shaggy dark hair. White T-shirt.

He's sure he sees himself—his young, brave, college self—pulling his daughter from the pool. The Henry he was meant to be.

The figure comes closer, holding Emma in his arms. Henry closes his eyes, afraid to look up into his own face, sure that if he does, this Henry—the weak, pathetic, drunken Henry—will just disintegrate into a pile of useless atoms.

Emma is gasping, crying so hard and loud, calling, "Daddy, Daddy, Daddy!"

Henry holds his breath, counts to three, and opens his eyes.

"Hello, Henry," says the man, who Henry can see is not a man at all but a woman. A woman with the strongest, most beautiful arms Henry has ever seen. But then, looking carefully, Henry sees the pale cross-hatching in the skin, a pattern of scars covering her arms like sleeves.

"Winnie?" Henry gasps, finally looking up from the arms to the woman's face.

"Looks like you might need some stitches," Winnie says.

Henry lets all his breath out and everything fades to black.

Chapter 30

PASSION?

Fuck.

Tess puts on her sunglasses, pulls the shift lever toward her so that the car is in reverse, begins to back away from the salt-box covered in weathered gray shingles. Claire is standing on the porch, waving with the hand that holds a lit cigarette.

Tess sees the hummingbird return for a moment, zigzagging through the air above Claire. Claire looks up, smiles slyly, and points to the bird.

Tess nods, smiles back. Eases her car down the driveway in reverse, tires crunching gravel.

Claire asked her to think over the offer and call in the next couple of days. She mentioned that Tess would be "well compensated" for whatever work she produced.

"Even if you decline, it would be nice to see you again. Maybe we could have lunch," Claire said. Tess promised she'd call.

Tess's hands are shaking as she grips the Volvo's wheel tighter. Nicotine, she tells herself, but that's not it.

It's that Claire is right. This woman who hardly knows her saw through the crappy peonies stuffed in rusted watering cans; saw through to the carnivorous, dripping flowers with faces like gods who swallow men whole.

Tess's skin is still buzzing from Claire's touch.

It reminds her of . . . of what? Some long-forgotten feeling.

She's too pumped up to go home just yet; she knows that whatever magic happened just then at Claire's will be gone when she sees Henry and Emma. When she steps back into her regular peony-in-a-watering-can life. Up ahead, she spots a field of lupines and pulls over. Ordinarily, she'd pick some to take home for a painting. She sees herself doing this, like watching an actress in a movie. The artist in black T-shirt and crisp linen pants doing what she does best—getting a bucket and some water from the trunk and filling it, then racing home to arrange the found flowers, get an image down on canvas while their life force is strongest, before they begin to fade.

NO! she wants to scream at this image of her ghost self already out of the car, going through the motions of normal life. It's all wrong. Stop.

It's like those horror movies where the girl does something stupid—steps into the shower, opens the front door, goes down to the basement—and the whole audience is screaming *NO!*, feeling doom in the pit of their popcorn-full stomachs.

Stop.

"Passion," she whispers to herself, still gripping the steering wheel. "Shit."

IT WAS SUZ WHO finally got Tess and Henry together, at the beginning of senior year.

"It's obvious you're totally in love with him," Suz said to Tess.

"I don't think it's obvious to him," Tess said, picking at the lint on her sweater.

They were getting stoned in the tube that connected the

painting and sculpture buildings. It was one in the morning and Duane, the security guard, had already made his rounds on that side of campus. When you were in the Habitrail tube at night, you felt as if you were right up in the stars. Tess sometimes imagined that the two buildings and tube that connected them was a space station orbiting around the earth. The hardest part was always coming back down.

"So tell him," Suz said, exhaling smoke as she spoke.

"I can't," Tess told her. She'd tried a thousand times, dropped hints whenever she could. By now she figured it was pretty much a lost cause. And besides, if she actually came right out and told him and he didn't feel the same way (which she was pretty sure was the case), then that would probably screw up their friendship, which was the last thing she wanted.

"Life is too short for can'ts, babycakes," Suz said. She handed the joint to Tess and stood up. "Stay here," she said, heading toward the sculpture building, where Henry was working.

"What are you doing?" Tess asked, terrified by what Suz might do. "You're not going to say anything to him, are you?"

"Don't worry. Just stay here."

Tess waited for what seemed like forever.

She lay on her back and looked up at the stars, imagined she was out there, spinning through the universe, untethered.

Just when she was about to give up and head back to the painting building, Henry arrived in the tube.

"Hey," he said.

"Hey," Tess answered back. He sat down beside her, picking at a hole in his jeans. They were quiet a minute. Tess's heart felt as if it had dropped into her stomach. What had Suz said to Henry? What should she say now?

Life is too short for can'ts.

"Remember the dream you told me," Tess finally said, "when we first met? About being a cow in a field?"

Henry smiled. "Yeah. I think about it a lot. It's kind of an ex-istential conundrum. I mean, how do we know we're really who we think we are? I think I'm here sitting beside you, but what if I'm really a cow in a field, or a guy in a coma?"

"So all of life might be a dream," Tess said, the words trailing off as she looked out at the stars.

"Right," Henry said. "And how are we supposed to live our lives knowing that's a distinct possibility? It adds this whole other layer to things, don't you think?"

Tess smiled. "I think we just have to make sure we have the best dream we possibly can," she said.

And that's when he kissed her.

Later, when she asked him what Suz had said to him, he shook his head.

"Nothing," he told her, his eyes focused on the spot just over her shoulder—the look that she would, over the years, learn that meant he was lying. "She just said you were out there waiting for me."

Chapter 31

HENRY DOES NOT NEED stitches. Winnie was able to revive him by pressing her knuckles firmly into his sternum and rubbing; grinding her bones into his cartilage so hard that when he woke he felt like she was kneading his heart as if it were a piece of soft dough. Winnie stopped the bleeding above his eye and put on a butterfly bandage from the first-aid kit in the bathroom. Then she made a pot of coffee, and some hot chocolate for Emma.

"Danner would like some too," Emma says.

"Danner?" Winnie says.

"Invisible friend," Henry explains.

"She's not invisible. I can see her just fine, Dad."

Emma's sitting on a stool at the counter, her bare feet resting on the bottom rung. She looks to her left, at the stool beside her, where apparently Danner is waiting patiently for her own cup of cocoa.

Winnie smiles, gets down an extra cup and passes it to Emma, and says, "I gave her extra whipped cream," with a wink.

She looks right into Emma's eyes, and says in a low, conspiratorial voice, "You know, I used to have a friend no one else understood."

"Really?" Emmas asks. She's perched at the edge of her stool, leaning ever-so-slightly toward Winnie.

Winnie nods.

"Could other people see her?" Emma asks.

Winnie shakes her head. "Not really. Not the way I saw her."

Henry sits propped up in a kitchen chair and watches Winnie move through the kitchen as if he's peeking into some other dimension: some place and time where he married someone else. Maybe in this version of his life things worked out. Maybe their love for each other is somehow enough for both of them. Maybe she's not going to kick him out to live in the barn or hand him a newspaper with apartment listings circled in red pen.

Winnie has changed out of her wet things into a pair of sweatpants and T-shirt that belong to Tess. She's a good deal taller than Tess and has rolled the already short pants up into capris. Her own clothes and the drenched wig are draped over the shower curtain rod in the downstairs bathroom.

"Drink this," says Winnie, placing a cup of hot black coffee in front of him. "I'm going to make some sandwiches."

Tomato. Lettuce. Smoked turkey. Swiss cheese. Rye bread. Stone-ground mustard. Winnie seems to know where everything in the kitchen is. Some part of Henry's brain knows that this should puzzle him, worry him even, but instead, he's comforted. He smiles drunkenly at Winnie.

"You saved my daughter's life," he says.

Emma sets down her cocoa, looks from her father to Winnie, then back to the invisible girl beside her. Is it Henry's imagination or does Emma seem frightened when she glances at the blank space where Danner is supposed to be?

"Drink your coffee," says Winnie, slicing into a tomato, juice and seeds spilling out onto the cutting board. He watches her lick her fingers. Thinks that if they were married, this is one of those familiar gestures he would love, something he'd look forward to at the end of the day—Winnie, his Winnie, licking her fingers after slicing a tomato.

"Are you sure he doesn't have a concussion or something?" Emma asks. "He looks a little dopey."

Winnie glances up, still holding the knife. "Doesn't your father always look a little dopey? He did when I knew him."

Emma laughs.

"Seriously," Winnie says. "He's fine. A little food and some coffee and he'll be good as new."

When she's finished with the sandwiches, she hands Emma a plate and asks if she and Danner could go watch TV in the living room for a while. "Your dad and I have to talk." Emma nods and leaves them alone. Sometimes Emma seems like a grown-up in a girl's body. Intuitive and wise beyond her years. Such a serious kid, always counting, straightening, bringing things to order. He remembers the day the old tree fell in the yard, how frightened Emma had looked; how she'd said, *Maybe it's a sign.* She's a girl who believes in signs, who understands when the universe is sending you a warning.

"She would have drowned," says Henry, his eyes filling with tears. He's pathetic. He knows that. The most unworthy man on earth. The worst father. The most faithless husband. Maybe Tess was right. Maybe they'd all be better off if he found someplace else to live. But the thought of leaving his home, his family, splits him open. He's sure it would kill him.

"You don't know that," says Winnie.

Winnie begins stroking Henry's hair. Comforting him as if he were a little boy. Henry lets himself rest against her and stares at Winnie's arms. The beautiful patterns of scars that stop right at the wrist. Crisscrossing, like row after row of diamonds. Or fish scales. Maybe she's a mermaid, this wife in another dimension. Maybe she'll take him to live underwater.

Under. Water.

Down, down, down. Stones in her clothes.

He gets a cold chill, pulls away from Winnie.

"What were you even doing here?" asks Henry with the sudden realization of a drunk person.

"I came to see you. To apologize for that ridiculous stunt last night, and try to explain. See, a couple of weeks ago, I got this postcard—"

"But I didn't hear you. You didn't come in a car."

He feels cagey, sly.

"I parked by the road. I walked in through the woods. Through Tess's sculpture garden."

"Did you see the grotto?" Henry asks. He's slurring his words and grotto sounds like *rotten*.

"Yes, I saw it."

"Pretty unsettling, huh?" Henry asks.

"It's a beautiful tribute," Winnie tells him.

"You want to know a secret?" Henry asks, leaning toward her. He's still just drunk enough to be able to share secrets. To say anything.

"What is it?"

"Sometimes," he begins with a whisper, "I think Suz is here. I think she's found a way back."

Put the two halves together and make a whole. Crawl through the hole and escape.

"Lately," Henry continues, "I find myself wondering if she's behind everything that happens to us."

Winnie smiles. "Sometimes," she says, gently fingering the butterfly bandage over Henry's left eye, "I think so too."

They look at each other a moment. Henry remembers what he thought when he watched Winnie pull Emma out of the pool— that she was him somehow. He thinks, as he looks into Winnie's eyes, that Winnie can see everything that's happened to him in the past ten years: how one disappointment begot another; how he's never managed to make it to the happily-ever-after he was so determined to find for him and Tess. And Henry is sure that it's the same for Winnie. He sees the same emptiness in Winnie's eyes, and when Henry speaks, he says, "We deserve more than what we've had."

"Maybe," Winnie says, then she leans in and kisses Henry on his forehead, just above the butterfly bandage.

"Winnie," he whispers, the name itself a sort of life raft he's clinging to. But Winnie's not even her real name, is it? When he first met her, she was a girl with some other name who wrote poems thick with grief—suicide letter poems, lost-soul-at-the-end-of-her-rope poems. A twitchy, nervous girl who wouldn't look you in the eye. What was her name before? It was the name Bill Lunde had just called her by this morning, but the funny thing is, Henry can't think of it now.

All he remembers, all that matters, is that Suz turned her into someone else. She gave Winnie a gun, a haircut, and a new name. Henry wants to ask Winnie whatever became of that old Winchester rifle, but then, his drunk mind circles around again.

"Did you say something about a postcard?"

Winnie nods. "I got it a couple of weeks ago. From Vermont. There was a picture of a moose on the front. And on the back it said, '*Dismantlement Equals Freedom. To understand the nature of a thing, you have to take it apart.*'"

"Just like Spencer's," Henry says.

Winnie nods. "I know. My stepmother told me. She also said his father hired a detective. Anyway, when I got the postcard, I decided to come back and take a look around. It's a good thing I did too. I went to the cabin, and everything was the same, Henry. Just like we left it. It was a little eerie. Like entering the Land Where Time Stood Still. *Twilight Zone* shit. I've been staying there. Cleaning up."

Henry nods. "He's here, you know. The private detective. Have you seen him?"

Winnie shakes her head.

"He must have talked to your family or something, because he knew you were back. He came here today. When he left he was heading up to the college. It won't take him long to find out about the cabin if he doesn't already know."

"It's okay," Winnie says. "The place is clean. There's nothing for him to find but me."

"Which I think he'll find pretty interesting. Especially if you keep running around dressed like Suz," Henry can't help but add. "You didn't really expect to fool me again coming here dressed like that, did you?"

Winnie bristles. "God, no . . . that's not it. It's just that I was scared to come here. I didn't know if I'd have the guts to actually face you. Dressing up like Suz, it gives me strength. Makes me feel like I can do things I could never do as myself. And when I'm wearing her old clothes, I feel so close to her, Henry. Like she's right there with me again; like I'm whole again. I feel like these last ten years I've been half-alive, sleepwalking through life. When I first put on her clothes, I woke up. Does that make sense?"

Henry doesn't think it makes any sense at all, but doesn't say so. Maybe it makes as much sense as believing his daughter's invisible playmate may be a vengeful spirit.

"So where the hell did the postcards come from?" he asks.

Winnie shrugs. "Did you and Tess get postcards?"

"No."

She nods as if it's the answer she was expecting, then looks down into her coffee cup. "Don't you think that's odd?"

He doesn't like the way she's looking at him now. Suspicious.

"What, you think *I* sent them? Why the hell would I do that? Why would I want to risk my entire life like that?"

"I didn't say it was you."

"Who then? Tess? You think Tess did this?"

Winnie raises her eyebrows a fraction of an inch.

"Jesus!" Henry snorts hot, black coffee. Starts to laugh. "That's crazy, Winnie."

"The postcards were mailed from Vermont, Henry. You and Tess didn't get them. No one else—no one who's alive anyway—would be able to quote the manifesto like that. And there's the grotto . . ."

"The grotto?"

"When did she build it?"

He shrugs his shoulders. "She started a couple of weeks ago, I guess."

Winnie nods. "Around the same time the postcards were sent."

"Coincidence," Henry says.

Winnie blows air through clenched teeth. "Suz taught you better than that, Henry."

No. This is all wrong.

"Suz said we needed to take everything apart," Henry argues. "That the universe was created in chaos."

Winnie nods. "And in all that chaos there are patterns. There's no such thing as coincidence."

Henry lets this seep into his vodka-muddled brain. Is Winnie right? Is that the truth they were all trying so hard to prove by taking everything apart? That they could tear it all down, murder someone even, but like it or not, there were connections and patterns that couldn't be broken. Not by time or even death. Things all the wine and vodka in the world couldn't drive away.

Henry touches the Magic 8 Ball key chain in his pocket—just further evidence that Winnie's right.

Chapter 32

THERE WAS A FACE down there at the bottom of the pool. A face smiling up at her as she floated, trapped, upside down in the inner tube. It was Danner. Only different. A frightening sort of Danner with pale, wrinkled skin.

This is how dolphins die, thought Emma. Caught in fishing nets and pieces of plastic. That's why they cut apart the plastic circles six packs of soda came in. So animals wouldn't get trapped. She struggled to right herself, but her hips were wedged and she couldn't get leverage. She looked down at the face.

I have a secret, Danner whispered. Her blond hair was spread out around her face and glowed like a halo. Maybe she was an angel. Or a mermaid. Yes. A mermaid. There were green weeds in her hair. Pond scum. Duckweed. She'd been down there a long time. But this was a pool. Not a pond.

Come closer, she whispered, beckoning with her hands, the skin white, wrinkled and loose, coming off like gloves.

Emma couldn't move. She opened her mouth to scream, but only bubbles came out.

Everything you have is mine, the terrifying mermaid Danner said.

And just then, someone dove into the deep end of the pool and swam underwater to Emma, righting her at last.

"EARTH TO SUPER FREAK, come in!"

Emma opens her eyes, sees that Mel is standing in the doorway of her bedroom.

"Oh, hi," Emma says.

"God! You are such a space cadet! I'm gonna ask you one more time—who's the chick down there with your father?" Mel asks as she steps into Emma's room, closing the door behind her.

"Winnie."

"No shit? Compassionate Dismantler Winnie? The one we sent the postcard to?"

"She saved my life," Emma says.

"What? Were you guys in a car wreck or something? Your dad's face looks all messed up."

"I was stuck in the inner tube in the pool. Upside down. My dad fell down and cracked his head open trying to get to me. Then Winnie showed up."

"Showed up?"

"It was weird. Just when I couldn't hold my breath another second, there she was. She saved my life. It was kind of a miracle. There's something cool about her."

Mel furrows her brow. "Miracle, schmiracle. It was me who saved your life," she says.

"What do you mean?"

"I'm the one who had the idea to send the postcards, right? And if I hadn't, she wouldn't have just shown up out of the blue. So it's me you should be thanking."

Mel is over at Emma's bookcase, running her dirty fingers over the spines. She pulls out a book, flips through it, then shoves it back in totally the wrong place.

"You looking for something to read?" Emma asks. She

immediately hates that she's even suggested this. Mel's only bor-rowed one book from Emma—*The Complete Guide to Pet Ham-sters.* She brought it back with the cover torn and writing in the margins, not even in pencil but in green ink.

The kids at school call Mel Captain Smellville. They laugh at her baggy army fatigue pants and give her a special salute while holding their noses. Mel always acts as if she doesn't even see them. She just pulls out the little notebook she carries around in her back pocket and starts scribbling fast in one of her secret codes, as if she's writing them a ticket or something. She writes faster and faster, stopping now and then to lick her finger and rub at one of the words to try and erase it. She ends up with inky fingers and paper covered in illegible smudges, worn through in places. When she fills a page, she tears it off and folds it into a tiny triangle, then stuffs it into her front pocket. She says they all go into her files, but Emma's never seen any files.

"Where is it?" Mel asks.

"What?" Emma asks.

"Suz's journal. You got it, right?"

Emma bites her lip, looks at the book Mel shelved in the wrong place. *The Borrowers* by Mary Norton. It's now jammed in the Cs—next to *Alice in Wonderland.* Also, she's put it in upside down. It's all wrong and it's messed the whole shelf up. Maybe even the whole room. Emma feels a funny weight in her chest and it's almost like it's tied with an invisible wire to that out-of-place book. Like the book is tugging her toward it, pulling in this painful way that will only be relieved if she can just put *The Bor-rowers* back where it belongs.

Fastidious.

"Don't tell me you wimped out," Mel says.

"What? No, I was interrupted," Emma explains. "There was a man there. In the barn." She's leaning forward now. If she stretches out her left hand, she could reach the book. Put things back together the way they belong. She drums her fingers on her knee, counts to nine in her head.

Mel rolls her eyes. "Right. Sure there was. A friend of Danner's, right? Give me a break, Em." Mel stands up, heads to the door.

"Where are you going?" Emma asks, making herself take her eye off the bookcase to look at Mel.

"Home. Call me when you've got the journal."

"But—"

"But nothing, Em. Either you're going to take this seriously or not. Just get the freaking book. No more excuses."

Emma watches Mel head down the hall. She thinks of going after her, begging her to stay, saying she'll sneak over and get the journal right now. But instead, she goes right for the bookshelves, pulls out *The Borrowers,* gives it a quick wipe down with the bottom of her T-shirt, then puts it back in its place with the other *N*s. The weight in her chest lifts a little, she lets herself breathe. The world, at least this little piece of it, has been restored to order. She locks the door to her room, counts the number of books on each shelf (twenty-seven), and decides that she'll call Mel later to apologize and swear up and down that she'll get the journal tomorrow. She'll prove her commitment to Operation Reunite, and to Mel.

"Nine," she says, closing her eyes. "Eighteen. Twenty-seven." The numbers are swimming behind her eyelids. But they're not the only thing. There's a face there too.

She feels the pressure in her chest, all around it. She's back in the tire again, upside down, with her hips wedged, lungs screaming for air.

Everything you have is mine.

Chapter 33

"IT LOOKS WORSE THAN it is," Henry promises.

Tess has come into the kitchen and found Henry and Emma playing rummy at the table. Emma, as usual, is keeping score very methodically, in neat rows of carefully printed numbers.

Tess has missed Winnie by only about fifteen minutes.

"What on earth happened?" Tess asks, touching Henry's bandaged head gently, tenderly. She looks as though she's about to lean down and kiss it better. He shuts his eyes, waiting. Wishing.

"I almost drowned," Emma tells Tess. Henry opens his eyes and sees his daughter grinning from ear to ear.

"What?" Tess asks. She jerks her hand away from his head, draws back, the compassion in her eyes now clouded by fury. Henry looks away, reaches into his pocket for the bottle of aspirin.

"I was a frog and I tried to jump through a hole but I got stuck. Stuck like dolphins get stuck."

Put the two halves together to make a whole, Henry thinks. He smiles. Can't help himself. He dumps three aspirin into his palm, tosses them into his mouth.

"Do you mind telling me what is so goddamned funny?" Tess

asks him. "Come here, baby," she says to Emma, pulling Emma to her. "You okay?"

"Fine, Mom. The lady saved me."

"What lady?"

"The lady from the picture," Emma says.

Henry watches Tess hold her breath. It's almost painful. Poor Tess. Maybe she believes in ghosts after all.

"Winnie," Henry whispers.

"Where the fuck were *you*?" Tess asks.

Emma flinches at Tess's curse. She looks down at the rummy scores and starts adding and subtracting, then just penciling in a new column of numbers. Her lips move as she writes them. *Nine. Eighteen. Twenty-seven.*

"I fell down," Henry explains. "Emma flipped over in the inner tube. I was running to the pool and tripped over a chair." As if he can put some of the blame on the chair. The blame that rests, he knows, entirely on himself for getting too drunk to walk. Too drunk to watch their child. "I cracked my skull and I guess I blacked out for a second. Then Winnie appeared. She jumped in and pulled Em out."

He leaves out the part about how Winnie was dressed as Suz. Just like she was last night when he met her at the lake. There are details Tess is better off not knowing.

"It was a miracle," Emma says, looking up from her rows of numbers.

"But where did she come from?" Tess asks. Her voice sounds high and desperate. As if Winnie were the ghost.

"I don't know. The road. She said she parked by the road and walked through the woods. She wanted to surprise us," Henry says.

"Did she stay?"

"Only for a little while."

"What did she want?"

What was wrong with Tess? Her every question was an accusation. Winnie appears from nowhere, saves their daughter's life, and all Tess can think of to say is *What did she want?*

Henry bites the inside of his cheek.

"To visit, Tess. To see how we were."

Tess nods. Turns to Emma. "Sweetie, can you go up to your room for a few minutes? I want to talk to your dad alone."

"Are you going to yell?" Emma asks, looking up from her neat rows of numbers, gripping the pencil so hard her fingers turn white.

"No," Tess says, leaning down to tuck a strand of Emma's hair behind her ear. "Of course not."

Emma nods and leaves the kitchen, mumbling something to herself. Counting, Henry realizes. She's counting her steps. Maybe she's making a treasure map: ten paces to your right, five straight ahead, X marks the spot.

"You were drunk, weren't you?" Tess hisses once they're alone.

Henry starts to answer, but she cuts him off.

"I can smell it on you, Henry. Stale liquor oozing from your pores. It's inexcusable."

Henry stares down at his feet like a reprimanded little boy. He knows she's right.

"No more drinking. Not a drop. I catch you so much as having a glass of wine with dinner and you're out of here that minute. Do you understand? Next time, there won't be anyone lurking in the woods like a fucking stalker."

Henry nods, his eyes still on the floor.

"And I'm serious about you finding another place to live," she tells him. "I want you to start calling about some of those apartments tomorrow."

He nods again, knowing he's in no position to argue right now. But he'll be damned if he's moving out. This is his home.

This has always been his home. Emma sleeps in the room that was once his, hung with model planes and Red Sox pennants. There is a handprint on the wall of the basement stairway, right next to the emergency switch for the furnace, that he made when he was ten, when his dad was painting shelves and Henry touched them when they were still wet.

"What I still don't understand is what Winnie was even doing here. Why would she come back now, after all this time?" Tess asks.

Henry looks up, relieved that the spotlight of accusation is off of him for the time being.

"She got a postcard. Just like Spencer. She's staying at the cabin. Cleaning it up. Getting rid of anything incriminating, which is a good thing. Bill Lunde isn't a stupid man, Tess. He knows a lot already. It's only a matter of time until he finds his way to the cabin."

Tess walks over to the coffeepot and pours herself a cup. It's the coffee Winnie made. Black as tar and strong. Tess takes a sip and scowls.

"I thought you'd taken care of things at the cabin," she says.

"I hadn't gotten around to it yet."

"So you haven't been out there at all?" she asks.

Henry shakes his head. Watches Tess swirl the thick, brackish coffee around in her mug.

"Why," Henry asks Tess, "do you think Winnie and Spencer got postcards when we didn't? I'd think of all the Dismantlers, we'd be the easiest to find. We're the ones who never really went away."

Tess shrugs her shoulders, turns so that her back is to him and dumps the coffee from her mug into the sink.

"I'm going to my studio," she says, her back still to him.

And for the first time, Henry starts to wonder if maybe there's something to Winnie's crazy theory about Tess, the postcards, and the grotto. If maybe there are things about his wife he does not know.

Chapter 34

WINNIE'S NEARLY TO THE cabin when she realizes she left the Suz outfit and wig behind, drying in Henry's bathroom. Shit. Here she is, stuck in Tess's too-small clothes, imagining what it might be like to be Tess, trapped inside a too-small life.

Hadn't she been trapped once, too?

And then Suz showed her the way out.

"I'M SICK TO FUCKING death of you hiding behind your hair," Suz said, and in just two snips of the scissors, the long bangs Val had since she was ten were gone. She felt her body stiffen reflexively. It was as if someone had severed a limb.

"Relax, already," Suz said, placing her hands firmly on Val's shoulders, like she was afraid Val might stand up and run off. "Trust me."

They were in Suz's dorm room. The walls were covered with sketches, paintings, and photographs. Clothes, books, and art supplies lay in scattered piles on the floor. The desk was covered in clumps of melted candle wax. It was two months before graduation and she and Suz had just started sleeping together. Val had broken up with Spencer, and he hadn't taken it well. She'd spent an entire night held captive in his dorm room. He stood blocking the door, promising to let her go if she could give him just one valid reason why she'd chose Suz over him.

"I love her," Val had told him and he'd laughed, said only, "You've gotta be kidding." He didn't move from the door. Over the next eight hours, he tried reasoning with her, begging her, and even threatened to end his own life if she left him.

"I'm sorry," she told him over and over. She wept, but would not change her mind.

At five in the morning, Spencer stepped aside and let her pass through the door.

"I'm sorry," she whispered one final time.

He said nothing, and stared at the floor.

VAL HAD DECIDED TO let Suz cut her hair not just at Suz's insistence, but because she knew how much it would piss Spencer off—he always said her hair was her best feature and made up for her skinny ass and flat chest.

Suz went to work around her ears, then moved to the back of the head. Val held her breath and closed her eyes. *It will grow back,* she told herself. Her chest clenched and her breathing was fast and shallow. The scissors were moving quickly, singing almost. Val opened her eyes to see her hair fall in great clumps to the floor.

"Who's behind all this raggedy-ass hair?" Suz asked, her voice lilting, teasing.

Who indeed? If Suz saw, would she stay? She'd already seen the scars. She knew about the cutting and hadn't been scared away. She'd listened to Val's poems, even the ones Val had never shown another living soul. Maybe, just maybe, Val had finally found another human being who might understand her, who might love her for who she truly was, not what she pretended so hard to be.

Val bit her tongue, not sure if Suz was waiting for an answer.

Sometimes, with Suz, you couldn't tell what was an actual question and what was just a springboard for one of her monologues. And you didn't want to make the mistake of jumping in and interrupting her before she was ready.

"And while we're at it, babycakes—what's up with the hippie clothes?" Suz stopped cutting, plucked at Val's baggy peasant blouse. The bells on the neckstrings jingled. "You wear them because that's what half the people at Sexton wear, right? You want to fit in, to blend, so no one will notice you. Just another long-haired girl in Birkenstocks, right?" Val didn't respond.

"Am I right?" Suz repeated.

Val shrugged.

"Is that who you are, Val? Are you just a mousy little hippie girl? Thinking her limp organic broccoli thoughts?"

Val held her breath.

"Or are you something more?"

Val looked down at the clumps of hair scattered across the gray linoleum floor.

Suz went back to work with the scissors, said, "It's time to show the world who you really are."

"So who am I?" Val asked, her voice a papery whisper. Wind through cornstalks.

Suz stopped cutting, leaned down and put her mouth right against Val's ear, and asked, "Who do you want to be?" Val shivered as Suz ran her tongue lightly over the folds of her ear, gave the lobe a startling nibble. "You can be whoever, whatever you want, babycakes. Be the lion or the mouse. You choose. But I've gotta say, the lion is a lot more sexy."

When she was finished, Suz guided Val over to the mirror, her hands covering her eyes.

"Behold the new you," she said, taking her hands away.

Val gasped. She hardly recognized herself. "I look like a boy," she said.

"You look hot," Suz said, kissing her on the back of her newly exposed neck.

"I've got something for you," Suz said and went over to the bed. She got down on her knees, reaching for something underneath. Val stood in front of the mirror studying the shape of her closely cropped head, the squareness of her jaw, her thick eyebrows. She was wearing an old black T-shirt Suz had told her to put on for the haircut and baggy jeans. She looked . . . tougher. She stood up straight and scowled at herself, practiced her evil eye.

"Surprise!" Suz was holding a gun. A deer rifle.

"What's that for?" Val asked, taking a step back.

"It's a gift. I picked it up at that flea market last weekend. I thought it would come in handy for our missions. I even got bullets. After dinner we'll go down to the lower field, and you can try it out."

"I don't think I can," Val said.

"Don't give me this pacifist bullshit," Suz snarled, shoving the rifle at Val, who reached out and took it with trembling hands. It felt solid—the wood smooth and dark, the metal barrel somewhat sticky and covered in greasy fingerprints. Val imagined the men who might have held the rifle: men in red wool hunting jackets, hats with earflaps; men whose breath reeked of stale beer and cigarettes; men with huge leather boots who took up space just because they could. Men who knew what it was like to kill, who had a taste for it, a burning need.

Suz ran her fingers though Val's freshly shorn hair and said, "I'm not asking you to go on any killing sprees or anything. The rifle's just a prop, Val. The gun, the haircut, they're about letting go. Deconstructing yourself. Becoming someone else. Someone with more power who no one would ever dream of putting in a box. I say enjoy the fucking ride. See what it's like on the other side for once."

Val took in a breath, raised the rifle up with the butt end

against her shoulder and used the sight to look down the barrel. *Just a prop.* Her own small fingers mingled with the greasy fingerprints, covering them, as she aimed right at her reflection in the mirror, and didn't recognize the figure she saw there. Someone stronger, braver, scowled back at her. Someone who refused to back down or take any shit. Suddenly, this whole thing felt like one of their missions, only this time, it was Val herself who had been dismantled. And peeking over her shoulder with an I-told-you-so grin, was Suz. She wrapped her arms around Val from behind, her hands working their way under Val's T-shirt, up to her breasts.

"Who do you want to be?" Suz asked, the words hot against Val's neck.

Val felt her body turn to liquid beneath Suz's hands, and the unspoken answer echoed through her head, driving everything else away:

Whoever you want me to be.

Chapter 35

TESS CAN STILL TASTE the sweet floral smoke of Claire Novak's cigarette on her tongue. Violets, but not violets. Someone else's wedding cake. She longs for another cigarette as she locks the door to her studio.

She finds herself unsettled by the idea of Winnie being back in town. Winnie, at least the Winnie of ten years ago, was not to be trusted.

"HAS SHE FUCKED HIM yet?" Winnie asked.

The two of them were on the beach at the lake, moon bathing. Henry and Suz were having one of their races out to the rocks at the other side.

"What?"

It wasn't just the words that caught Tess off guard, but Winnie's tone. It seemed, to Tess, like these past few weeks since school ended, Winnie had been trying out different voices—varying her tone and rhythm, even experimenting with slight accents, struggling to find something that would fit with her new name and the haircut Suz had given her. The voice that seemed to have the most staying power, the one she'd just used, was dark and gravelly, bubbling with quiet rage.

"Suz and Henry. Do you think they've fucked yet?"

Tess flushed and immediately felt stupid. "Henry's with me. And Suz is with you."

"Don't be an idiot, Tess," Winnie said. "If they haven't done it yet, it's just a matter of time, right? He thinks he's in love with her. You've seen the way he looks at her. The way she teases him."

"And what about Suz?" Tess asked. "Is she in love with him?"

Winnie laughed, rolled over onto her side to look at Tess. Her short hair made her eyes seem huge. Henry said the new haircut gave her a sexy androgynous look. Tess thought it made her look sick in some way, like someone with cancer, or a mental patient.

"Suz is in love with being loved," Winnie said. She scooped up a handful of sand, watched it run through her fingers.

Tess sat up, tried to spot Henry and Suz out on the water. They were just two pale dots in black water at the other side of the lake.

Winnie lit a cigarette, held it out to Tess who took a drag. The filter was squished from Winnie clamping it tightly between her teeth.

"You love Henry, right?" Winnie asked.

Tess exhaled smoke, nodded.

"Like I love Suz," Winnie said, laying her head back down in the sand.

They were silent a minute. Tess watched Winnie smoking on her back, her eyes fixed on the stars.

"I don't think it's too late," Winnie said. "You could hold on to him. You could find a way."

"I don't know . . ." Tess's voice trailed off. The two white specks out on the lake were gone. Underwater? Or had they made it to the rocks already?

"Henry's a good guy. One of the few. If you got into trouble, like say you got, you know, knocked-up or something, he'd do the right thing. He'd stand by you."

Tess turned back to Winnie. "Are you suggesting I get pregnant on purpose to get him to stay with me? To choose me over her?"

Winnie sat up, shrugged her shoulders.

"That's a little fucking archaic, isn't it? Not to mention pathetic. If Henry wants to be with me, I want it to be his choice. I'm not using a baby to tip the scales."

Winnie nodded, stubbed out her cigarette, stood up and headed for the path back to the cabin. "It was just a suggestion," she called back. "A way to fix both our problems. To make sure everyone ends up where they're meant to be."

LATER THAT SUMMER, WHEN Tess first began to think she might be pregnant, she studied the condoms Henry kept in the milk crate next to their futon in the loft. Did condoms have an expiration date? She picked a foil package up by the corner and held it to the window to check. Light shone through a dozen tiny holes. Pinpricks.

One by one, she checked the rest of the box. They were all the same.

She gathered them up, threw them into the trash. Later, she borrowed Henry's van and drove to the drugstore for an identical box, which she replaced without him ever knowing, and a home pregnancy test, which she used in the ladies' room at the Green Mountain Diner, confirming what she already knew.

TESS SHAKES THE MEMORY from her head, looks over the work scattered around her studio. She sighs, realizes Claire is right. All these paintings are empty. Meaningless. Technically accomplished, but so what? A flower is a flower is a flower.

"Knows how to stretch her limits, my ass," she mumbles, sitting herself at the drafting table and reaching for a new sketchbook. She picks up a pencil, places the tip of it on the paper, and waits.

White space. Blank canvas. Intimidating, but thrilling beyond belief. *Anything can happen*.

When was the last time her art mattered?

When was a flower not just a flower?

"YOU NEVER MENTIONED SETTING anything on fire," Tess said as she watched Suz lug a gas can from the back of the van. They were at the construction site for the new Green Hills Savings Bank. Earlier that afternoon, Tess had discovered the holes in the condoms and learned she was pregnant. She hadn't said a word about it to Henry or confronted Winnie. When she returned from town with the van, she was swept up in a flurry of activity getting ready for the evening's Dismantling mission. Suz's plan had been to tear down whatever they could at the construction site and maybe take some lumber to use for art projects. But now, it seemed plans had changed.

Tearing things down and taking a few pieces of plywood was one thing, arson was another. If they were caught, they'd be arrested. Tess wondered if you could have a baby in jail.

Suz began dumping gas on the neatly bundled piles of framing lumber and plywood.

"Won't people from the highway be able to see the flames?" Henry asked. He shifted from one foot to the other, nervously watching the headlights going by on the hill off to their left.

"That's the point," Suz said, emptying the last of the gas. "Fire is cathartic. Cleansing. It burns away anything transient and imperfect. I think that people get that—fire speaks to them on this kind of primitive level. Fire is life. And death. And rebirth."

Tess touched her belly, trying to imagine the baby inside. Winnie watched, grinning, the rifle cradled in her arms. If Tess had any doubts about how the holes got put in the condoms,

they disappeared when Winnie smiled at her knowingly, con-
spiratorially.

Suz took out a book of matches, lit one, and held it to her face,
smiling. "Fire is a wake-up call," she said, dropping the match. The
gas caught with a whooshing sound and the flames raced over the
wood. Tess felt as if all the air around them was being sucked into
it and replaced with thick smoke. Suz lit the second pile, then
the third. She grabbed the empty gas can and danced around the
flames, screaming, "Dismantlement equals freedom!" She pulled
Winnie to her, kissed her so ferociously that Tess was sure when
they pulled apart, Winnie would be bleeding.

"Banks are all just part of the trap," Suz said as they made their
getaway in Henry's van. "Part of the machine. They keep the rich
rich and the poor poor. Think what a different place the world
would be if we could just go back to using barter. If I could walk
into the market with one of my paintings and trade it for a week's
worth of groceries."

Tess believed that barter might be better, but knew it would
never happen. Not on the large scale Suz dreamed of. And the
truth was, Tess thought as she watched all that lumber go up in
flames in the rearview mirror, she kind of hated the waste. She
would rather steal than destroy—take the wood from the bank
construction and use it for a sculpture, or give it to some home-
less guy to build a shack under a bridge. But that's not what it was
about for Suz. For her, it was about tearing it down, burning it
up. That's what got her off—made her eyes light up, all wild and
surprised, like she'd just won the fucking lottery.

WITHOUT EVEN REALIZING IT, Tess has begun to
draw, her hand moving freely across the paper, seeming to have
a memory and will of its own. And it's a flower she sketches; not
a common sweet pea, but some hothouse beauty growing from
a vine with tendrils like arms and legs reaching, grasping, trying

to pop through the two-dimensional trap of paper and actually touch her. Wrap its sticky limbs around her, threatening to never let her go.

Tess draws in a trance, remembers that this is what it's supposed to be like: the goal is to lose yourself in the work, to give yourself over entirely.

As she draws, she feels everything else slipping away: Henry's drinking, Emma's near drowning, Winnie's arrival in town, even Claire Novak vanishes from her mind.

It's not until she's finished, ready to flip the page and start another, that she sees that there, in the dark folds of petals curled like flames at the flower's center, is a face. Hard eyes, a mischievous grin showing crooked teeth.

Suz.

The only true creative force is chaos, babycakes. Don't you forget it.

Chapter 36

It's nearly midnight. The main house is dark and Henry's sure Tess is asleep. He makes his way through the garden, around the fish pond and to the grotto, navigating by moonlight. Once there, he pockets the little photo of Suz in its plastic case, then hurries back to his barn.

Henry tucks the photo from the grotto into a bag of rags on a shelf in his workshop, then settles himself into the canoe with a fresh bottle of wine. He flips through Suz's journal, knowing full well that this is evidence too, but at least he has the good sense to keep it hidden.

> *July 4—Cabin by the lake*
> *Happy birthday, America, you cocksucking, bloodthirsty*
> *wasteland of corporate greed and power.*
>
> *Yesterday, we did something wonderful. Our best act of*
> *compassionate dismantling yet. We dismantled Spencer!*
> *Left him out cold in the middle of nowhere. Can't say*

*he wasn't warned. He knew he wasn't welcome here.
I mean, Winnie dumped his ass months ago, before
graduation even. But the stupid fucker was too proud
to let her go. Too arrogant to think that anyone in her
right mind might not want the great and powerful heir
to the Styles fortune as her very own boy toy. And
what does Styles Industries make? Security systems.*
SECURE YOUR WORLD *is their ridiculous slogan.
Cameras, alarm systems with keypads and secret codes.
Secure your world. Ha! Perfect! But Winnie chose to
dismantle her world, which included, first and foremost,
breaking up with the great Spencer. Her hooking up
with me should have been the final slap in the face, the
grand fuck off and farewell, but the idiot didn't give up.*

*He is the worst person in the world for her. Maybe the
worst person in the world, period. Did he even notice
that she was slicing and dicing herself? Think it was
odd? Did he give a flying fuck?*

*For weeks, Spencer has been hassling us—he wanted
to join us, move to the cabin, be a Dismantler.*

*"So prove it," I finally said. And I asked him to
perform a simple act of sabotage. To show Papa's
company just how insecure their world really is. Lo
and behold: he did it! Broke into Styles Industries
and smashed up hundreds of thousands of dollars of
equipment. A fire was set in the office of the CEO.
It was on the news—police were investigating. When
Spencer came back here yesterday, he had his knapsack
with him. "A deal's a deal," I said. "Welcome."
Without missing a beat, he starts creeping around after*

*Winnie, calling her Val. Then he gives her this note all
secretive like. Of course Winnie showed it to me.*

*"Come back to me, Val," it says. "Suz doesn't love
you. She doesn't love anyone but herself."*

*I don't love anyone but myself? Spencer Styles is the
most pretentious, egotistical, self-centered, pompous fuck
I have ever met. And it was high time for someone to
teach him a lesson.*

"I NEED FOUR OF your Benadryl," Suz whispered, leaning
in so close that her hair tickled his face.

Tess, who was on the other side of the room with her sketchbook, gave them a warning glance.

"What for?" Henry asked.

"You'll see," she promised.

They could hear Winnie and Spencer outside, gathering wood
for a bonfire.

Henry handed over four of his Benadryl and he and Tess
watched Suz grind them into powder and dump it into a shot of
tequila.

Winnie and Spencer came in laughing, said the fire was good
to go. Spencer said something about porcupines that Henry didn't
catch, but it made Winnie start laughing again.

"Celebration time!" Suz announced, a sickly sweet grin pasted
on her face. "Let's drink a toast to the newest member of the
Compassionate Dismantlers." Suz handed Spencer the first shot
she'd poured and gave him a hearty thump on the back.

"To Spencer," she said, and they all clicked their glasses together. When Spencer finished his shot, Suz poured him another.
Then another. She filled her own glass too.

Henry and Tess threw cautious, worried glances at each other. Where was Suz going with this?

"Not gonna let a girl outdrink you, are you, Spencer?" Suz asked. He shook his head, held his glass out for another shot. In half an hour, he was slouched in the chair, slurring his words, barely able to move.

"Give me a hand," Suz said to Henry as she looped Spencer's left arm around her shoulder and started to stand him up. Henry got the other side, figuring maybe they were just going to carry him off to bed. He should have known better. With Suz, things were never that simple.

"Wherewegoin?" Spencer moaned.

"For a ride," Suz said. "Grab the keys to the van, Henry."

"Keys?" Henry repeated, more worried than ever.

Winnie touched Spencer's face, pried open one of his eyes. "What the fuck did you do to him?" she hissed at Suz.

"Relax, babe," Suz said. "It's all part of the plan. Now let's get him to the Love Machine."

"Where are we taking him?" Tess asked, once they'd all settled into the van. Henry was behind the wheel, a lit cigarette between his lips. He liked to smoke when he was nervous. It gave him something to do with his hands.

"East," Suz said. Then she turned to Henry and said, "Get on Route 2 and drive, babycakes. I'll tell you when to stop."

On and on they drove, past farms, lakes, and campgrounds. Through St. Johnsbury and across the bridge into New Hampshire where they stopped at a McDonald's drive-through for coffee and milk shakes. The road twisted and turned. Suz rolled cigarettes, played with the radio dial, never letting a song finish before searching impatiently for something better.

Three hours after leaving the cabin, Suz told him to pull over.

"Where?" Henry asked. They had just crossed into Maine and

were on a two-lane highway without a house or streetlight in sight. The last town they went through had a paper mill, and the air was still heavy with the thick, sulfuric stink of it.

"Right there," Suz said, pointing to a dirt pull-off about ten yards ahead. Spencer was out cold.

"Now what?" Tess asked.

Suz smiled. "We dump him. Come on, help me get his clothes off. And grab his wallet too."

"Jesus!" Tess said. "This is going too far, Suz. You can't leave him out here in the middle of nowhere, naked, with no money or ID."

Suz thought a moment. "You're right. Let's leave his underwear on. What do you think, is he a boxer or briefs guy?" Suz unbuttoned his black jeans and started pulling them down. "Tightywhities! I knew it. But then again, it's no surprise to you, Winnie, is it?" Winnie looked away as Suz pulled the jeans the rest of the way off, then rifled through the pockets. She pulled out his wallet, a book of poetry, and a jackknife.

"I am *so* keeping this," Suz said, turning the knife over in her hand.

"Are you sure it's a good idea?" Tess asked. "I mean, it's evidence, right?"

"Evidence of what, exactly?" Suz asked.

"That we were here. That we did this to him," Tess said. "What if he doesn't make it back?"

Suz laughed. Shook her head.

"It's fine, Tess," Henry told her.

Spencer was on his back on the floor of Henry's van, wearing only white briefs.

"Are you sure he's okay?" Tess asked. "He hasn't moved at all."

Henry leaned down, found Spencer's pulse, which seemed strong enough, nodded. "Nothing to worry about," he whispered to Tess.

They got Spencer out of the van and laid him down in the

dirt. Suz took a Sharpie and wrote, I TRASHED STYLES INDUSTRIES across his forehead. "How's that for a finishing touch? Fucking brilliant, isn't it?"

Later that night, back at the cabin, everyone was quiet. Suz sat carving her initials into the table with Spencer's knife. At last, she looked up and addressed the group.

"I know you're all thinking we crossed a line tonight. But that's the nature of compassion," she explained. "Think about it: sometimes, the most compassionate thing to do is the hardest. Like when you have to put an animal down, or cut off someone's leg to save them."

Tess shook her head. "Spencer's not an animal. And he didn't have gangrene or whatever the fuck in his leg."

"You're missing the point," Suz said. "People who think they know everything need to be shown that they don't have a fucking clue," she told them. "That's the true path to enlightenment. Sometimes, the most compassionate thing is to be the wrecking ball that changes someone's life forever."

BE THE WRECKING BALL.

Jesus.

Henry rises out of the canoe, goes over to the phone and picks it up. He's got to get out of his own head for a while. Talk to someone who might understand.

He's surprised to hear Tess in the middle of a call. Henry covers the mouthpiece of the phone with his palm and listens. "I'll do it," he hears her tell someone.

"I knew you would," a woman's voice says. The woman has a thick accent. This is clearly not anyone Henry knows.

Who would Tess be making deals with in the middle of the night?

Henry hangs up quietly, waits a few minutes, then calls Winnie at the cabin.

"I can't sleep," he tells her. "I think something's going on with Tess."

"Henry," Winnie says, her voice lulling, almost seductive. "Can you come out here? To the cabin."

"What? Now?" Henry looks at his watch—nearly one in the morning.

"Yes. There's something I want to talk to you about, but not over the phone."

Val. That was her name before.

Before they were the Dismantlers, what were they? And after?

Isn't the reality that everything else, for better or worse, pales in comparison to the lives they lived that summer?

"I'll be there in an hour," he says.

Chapter 37

SHE'S COLD. SCARED. EMMA'S been watching her father's barn all night from her bedroom window. As soon as she saw him turn out the lights, she raced down to the Blazer and climbed into the backseat.

When Emma called Mel earlier to promise to get Suz's journal tomorrow, Mel said, "I've been thinking. Maybe your dad's got a girlfriend."

Emma let out a snorting laugh.

"Think about it," Mel said. "It would explain why your mom kicked him out of the house. And where he goes so late at night. Maybe he's playing hide-the-salami with some other lady!"

"Eew!" Emma shrieked. "No way."

But she needs to make sure. To prove it to herself.

And if it's not a girlfriend (which she knows it isn't, thank you very much, bigmouthed, smarty-pants Mel), what is it that he's doing so late at night? Where does he go?

If she has any hope of getting her parents back together again, she has to do more than what she's been doing. She needs to understand what they're really up to.

The truth is, Emma's worried that her plans are backfiring. Her mom and dad seemed oddly frightened by the message she and Mel painted on the trees. And the riddle! She'd read it in Suz's journal when Danner convinced her to go back in and take another quick look. Hearing the riddle again would surely take her parents back, give them a little thrill; they'd share a look, a gesture, and be on their way to reconciliation. What really happened was that they both looked horrified. As if Emma had opened her mouth and spit out shards of glass.

Emma's in her favorite pajamas, the ones with little red moose all over them. She's crouched down behind the driver's seat, the blanket from the backseat covering her. She's a worm underground. Wriggling. Writhing. But worms are dirty things. Full of germs. Bacteria. Microbes. Some worms are parasites and there's nothing more repulsive than a parasite. Emma knows that if she starts to really let herself think about parasites, she'll get itchy all over and need to take a scalding bath, scrub her skin until it's raw. It's starting already—that creepy, wiggly feeling just under her skin.

"Hold still," Danner says.

Emma hadn't even realized Danner was with her. But at the same time, she knows that in some way, Danner is always with her. She wants to push away the blanket, look around and see where Danner is hiding, but instead, she holds still. Listens to her own breath.

Now she's a worm asleep. A worm who has rolled over and is playing dead.

Stop the worm thoughts, already! she tells herself.

She starts counting by nines. Nine. Eighteen. Twenty-seven.

She listens. Hears nothing.

"Danner?"

"Yeah?"

"Was that you earlier. At the bottom of the pool?"

The blanket is scratchy against Emma's face and she wonders if it's possible to suffocate under it. She hears a gurgling sound—a wet, rasping choke. She goes to lift the blanket, to peek and see if Danner is okay, but she's afraid. What if it's not Danner? Or what if it is and she looks like she did at the bottom of the pool, skin sloughing off?

Stop it, she tells herself, then she goes back to counting. *Thirty-six. Forty-five. Fifty-four.*

She feels as if she's playing hide-and-seek, but what is it she's hiding from?

Ready or not, here I come.

Through the blanket, she smells something wet and rotten— an animal that's fallen into a well; a fish left in a plastic bag in the sun.

"Danner?" she says, the word little more than a gasp caught in the back of her throat.

She covers her nose and mouth with her hand to protect herself from the smell that's growing stronger each second. She hears the gurgling sound again, someone sucking air through a wet straw. But there are words behind it; voices piled on top of each other, straining, screaming, panicked. She thinks she hears her father's voice among them, saying something about stones.

No stone unturned.

Sticks and stones can break your bones.

Emma reaches out from under the blanket and gropes for the door handle. At last, she's got it and she's about to pull it open, to throw herself out of the car, blanket still covering her, when she hears her father open the driver's-side door, climb in, and start the engine.

All at once, the wet sucking noise stops. The smell disappears. She lets go of the door handle.

They ride a long time. Swerving, bumping along like maybe they're in a boat, not a car. She smells cigarette smoke. She didn't know her father even smoked. Weird. Maybe it's not him. Maybe someone has stolen his car. Maybe she's been kidnapped.

She thinks of the face at the bottom of the pool.

I've got a secret.

Her feet are full of pins and needles. Gone to sleep. Or maybe it's the parasites under her skin. She starts to scratch.

"Don't move," Danner whispers. "Stay where you are and don't make a sound." She sounds so serious. A lump forms in Emma's throat.

Everything you have is mine.

In movies sometimes people jump out of moving cars. The trick is to roll. She thinks maybe she should do this. But where would she be? And how would she find her way home with a broken arm or leg? And what if she landed in something gross like a pile of dog poop or a swamp full of skunk cabbage?

The Blazer is going up a steep hill now. Rough and bumpy. They've slowed to a crawl. Emma feels as if she's on a carnival ride. It's that the-ground-is-not-the-way-it-should-be, sick-to-her-stomach feeling she gets. Then, all at once, it's over. The Blazer stops. Her father (or whoever the driver is) gets out.

Then he shouts something. He's calling a name that sounds like *Give me. Give me.*

A woman calls back.

Give you what? Emma imagines her saying back.

Emma pulls the blanket off and sits up, looking out the windshield. The Blazer's headlights are on and focused on the building in front of them: an old cabin. On the steps is Winnie and she's still wearing Emma's mother's clothes. Her father is standing in the yard, talking to Winnie. Emma can't make out the words, but her father looks sheepish, worried. His hands are dug deep into his pockets and he's scuffing at the pine-needle-covered ground with the toe of his boot.

And there, just to the left of her father, stands a figure Emma recognizes at once. There he is, real and life size, just like she always imagined. Like she's always wished for. And if this wish has come true, doesn't that mean others might as well?

"Francis!" Emma cries, slamming open the car door and rushing to him. "Francis! Nine! Nine! Nine!"

Chapter 38

TESS HEARS HENRY DRIVE off, and slips out of the house and across the yard in her pajamas and robe.

She can't picture Henry having an affair at all. He's just not the type for clandestine meetings in the middle of the night.

She slides open the door to Henry's workshop and flicks on the tiny Maglite she brought. She doesn't know how long he'll be gone. (Maybe he just ran out to an all-night supermarket for something; maybe he's off for another moonlight swim. Ha! Right.) Wherever he's gone, she may not have much time.

Tess makes her way across the concrete floor, past the enormous dugout canoe, which sits in the dark like some giant, pale monster lurking. Trotting now, she goes straight for the toolbox.

After drawing the flower with Suz's face this afternoon, Tess filled page after page with images she recalled from the summer of the Dismantlers. She drew the wooden moose, Winnie and her gun, Henry with a beard and wistful expression, and sketch after sketch of Suz. Suz writing in her journal. Suz holding a bottle of tequila. And the final drawing: Suz in the lake.

But no matter how hard she worked on Suz's face, she felt she wasn't getting it quite right. The rigid jaw. The crooked teeth. Little, sharp nose. Stormy, amber eyes.

Then she remembered the photos stashed in Henry's studio and thought maybe they'd help. She'll just borrow them for a few days. He'll never notice they're missing.

Tess opens the toolbox, the rusty hinges letting out a little squeal of alarm. Removing the top tray full of tools, she reaches in and grabs the photos: Suz, Winnie, Henry, and a younger, smoother, surer version of herself smile up at her. There's the moose. Henry and Suz clowning around on the beach. The photos are just what Tess needs to give her sketches new life, accurate detail. She looks down at an image of Winnie with the gun pulled up against her shoulder, her finger on the trigger, left eye closed, right eye sighting her target down the barrel.

"I KNOW WHAT YOU did to the condoms," Tess said. They were alone, outside the cabin. Suz and Henry had gone on a beer and cigarette run. Winnie was polishing her gun.

"What'd I do?"

"You can't play with people's lives like that," Tess said. This got no reaction from Winnie, who just kept polishing the metal barrel of her gun with an old bandanna. "You think it'll help you hold on to Suz, but it won't. Just like it won't help me hold on to Henry. They're going to do what they're going to do, Winnie. Baby or no baby."

Winnie continued polishing the gun, a little harder and faster now.

"Maybe I should tell Suz about it," Tess said.

Winnie looked up. "Tell her what, Tess? That you were so desperate to hold on to Henry you poked holes in the condoms, then tried to blame someone else for it?" She smiled with amusement and went back to polishing her gun.

Tess clenched her hand into a fist, then opened it again.

She stood up and climbed the steps up to the front door of the cabin.

"So it worked then?" Winnie called after her.

"What?"

"You're pregnant?"

"Fuck you!" Tess said, slamming the door behind her.

TESS TUCKS THE PICTURES into the pocket of her robe, then lifts out the journal, flipping through it until she comes to a place near the middle.

> *June 21—Cabin by the lake*
>
> *Winnie is actually a pretty good shot—who knew the gun would be such a perfect gift? When I gave it to her I was just thinking that here was this thing I could hand over that would make her feel strong and powerful. I bought it from some old-timer at a flea market. At first I thought we'd just use it as a prop in our missions . . . you know, something to carry around and flaunt. Then I thought that it would be good for Val to learn how to shoot. She was scared at first. But now, she's hardly ever without it. It's so naturally a part of her that I started calling her Winnie. It was just a joke, but it stuck. Now none of us ever call her Val. We hear someone call her by that and we're like, "Who?"*
>
> *Winnie rides in the passenger seat of the Love Machine, hanging her gun out the window on our midnight runs. Hence the term "riding shotgun." She's taken out mailboxes, satellite dishes, transformers on telephone poles. She puts holes in aboveground swimming pools and water towers. Tonight, we drove out past Sexton and down a little dirt road to the*

*Green Mountain Power substation. It was all fenced
in, razor wire on top. Henry pointed the headlights of
the van at it and Winnie just started shooting—she
turned the big boxy transformer into Swiss cheese, blew
the tops right off the two towers. It was beautiful!*

*After, we drove around screaming, passing the tequila,
all of us shouting, "Yee-haw!" like a posse of cowboys.
Every house we passed was dark, not a single
streetlight was working in town. Even the college was
lost in the black night.*

*"Look, Suz," Winnie said, smiling. "I made the rest of
the world go away."*

I'm so fucking proud of Winnie. Of all of us.

*I'm so in love with each and every one of these people.
I don't want any of this to ever end.*

Tess closes the journal, places it back in the toolbox and shuts
the lid. Then she hurries past the great hulking monster of a canoe, out of Henry's barn, and into the garden.

She never told Henry about the condoms. About Winnie. It
felt pointless. It would have clouded the real issue, which was that
she was pregnant, and they needed to hurry up and make some
decisions.

Tess's heart is pounding as she crosses the yard, making the
motion-detecting floodlights click on. Taking the photos has
given her a little thrill, reminded her of what their Dismantling
missions had been like. Things were always tinged with danger,
acrid as the smell of gunpowder when Winnie fired the rifle. The
fear they might be caught was a living, breathing, palpable thing.

It filled their bellies, left them feeling buzzed and satisfied, but always wanting more.

The moon is just a thin sliver in the sky. The stars, millions of tiny pinpricks.

Which makes her think of the condoms again.

Winnie's casual act of treachery had brought Emma into the world and changed the course of Tess's life, given it color and shape. For a moment Tess tries to imagine an alternative reality, one in which Winnie thought better of sabotaging the condoms, and therefore one in which Emma—her beautiful, bright, and quirky girl—had never come to be. Tess is sure she would feel the ache of her missing child, like a phantom limb.

Chapter 39

HENRY TAKES A STEP toward her, staggers a little. He's been drinking again. Winnie imagines him getting through the sad repetition of his days—running the painting company, paying the bills, shuttling his daughter around—by getting good and smashed every evening. We all need something to look forward to. Something to take the edge off. Winnie rubs her fingers over the scars on her arms.

"I'm glad you came," she says to him. She's standing on the steps, still in Tess's clothes.

"I brought your things," he says, handing over a plastic grocery bag. She peers inside. Her Suz outfit is there, dry now. Mud brown tunic, black leggings.

But something's missing.

"Where's the wig?"

Henry shrugs. "I figured you must have grabbed it. It wasn't with the clothes in the bathroom."

Winnie feels a moment of panic. It doesn't make sense. She left it to dry with the clothes in the bathroom. How can the wig be gone?

"Francis!" a little voice calls in the darkness beyond Henry. Winnie squints and sees the girl leaping out of the Blazer. Emma—the girl she pulled squirming and choking from the pool this afternoon.

But who the hell is Francis?

Emma runs to Suz's moose, which Winnie is close to finishing. She throws her arms around the creature's neck. "Francis! Nine, nine, nine!"

Henry turns, stares at the girl, blinking. "Emma?"

Winnie watches as his whole demeanor changes. He goes into a slouch. His voice becomes tender.

"Look, Daddy—kitties!"

Henry stares at his daughter, who is down on her knees in a growing sea of cats.

"How did you get here?" he asks.

"I stole away. In the backseat."

"Stowed away? Jesus, Em. Do you have any idea how dangerous that is?"

Emma's face, beaming with amazement just seconds ago, darkens. Her chin starts to quiver.

Winnie puts her hand on Henry's arm. He flinches a little, but doesn't pull away. "I'm sure she won't do it again, right, Emma?" she says.

Emma nods.

"The cats are hungry," Winnie says. "Would you like to feed them, Emma?"

Emma's face cracks into an excited grin as her head bobs. Winnie goes inside, gets three cans of tuna and some bowls.

"How can the cats still be here?" Henry asks Winnie when she comes back out.

"I guess they didn't have anywhere else to go," she says.

"But how could they have survived all this time?"

"Instinct," she tells him, passing a bowl of tuna to Emma.

"Can we take one home, Dad? Please?" Emma pleads as she places the bowl down in the sea of hungry, screaming cats.

"They're strays, honey. They probably have fleas. They might bite."

A little orange cat is purring while she strokes its ears.

"Let her have a cat, Henry. Hell, take two. One for Danner."

He gives her a furious glance and she laughs. Poor Henry. He still takes everything so seriously. He needs to lighten up. Learn to play a little.

"Emma?" Winnie calls. "Do you know the moose has a secret?"

Emma shakes her head.

Henry's shaking his, too. *NO*, he mouths the word to Winnie, but she pretends not to see.

"He's hollow inside. There's a little door on his chest. You can climb in if you want."

"That's not a good idea," Henry says.

Winnie stands and opens the door on the side of the moose. The new hinges she picked up at the hardware store work perfectly.

"Please, Dad," Emma says.

Defeated, Henry boosts Emma up so she can climb in.

"Why on earth did you rebuild this thing?" Henry asks.

"I can't say exactly," Winnie says. "I guess I just wanted to see if I could."

She's proud of the job she's done, glad someone can finally appreciate it. Someone who knew the moose in another life, who knew the work that went into it. She couldn't find all the original pieces and had to make some new ones out of branches. She's not done gluing the canvas over him yet, but it's getting there.

"I'm standing where his heart would go!" Emma cries with delight, her voice muffled.

"When I began the moose, Henry, things got weird." Winnie has lowered her voice so that Emma won't hear.

"What things?"

"If I tell you, you'll think I'm crazy."

"Try me," he says. "I know a thing or two about crazy."

Winnie smiles.

I just bet you do.

"Okay," she begins. "When I got here, I took all of Suz's clothes, sealed them up in a big trash bag and sank it out in the middle of the lake. Getting rid of evidence, you know?"

Henry nods.

"The morning after I started working on the moose, I woke up and found one of the outfits I'd sunk laid out beside me. Silk tunic, leggings, boots. Like Suz had been there in the night, and evaporated, leaving just her clothes."

"Jesus!" Henry yelps.

"Dad," Emma calls from inside the moose, "I can see through his eyes."

Winnie continues, whispering hurriedly. "I was pretty freaked. I balled the clothes up and put them at the bottom of the trash barrel outside. Then, the next morning, I woke up and there they were again, right beside me. This time there was a blond wig on top."

Henry shivers.

"So I go downstairs with the stuff, thinking maybe I'll burn it this time, then I see my journal laying open on the table. There's writing in it that I didn't do. Handwriting I recognize. Suz's writing."

Henry shakes his head in a this-can't-be-happening kind of way. "What did it say?"

"It said: *Put the clothes on, Winnie.*"

"And you did?"

Winnie nods. "I was terrified at first. But then, I slipped on the wig and looked in the mirror. Something happened. I felt her presence, Henry. It was as if she was right there with me, filling me with confidence, whispering in my ear. It was as if I actually *became* her."

Henry is quiet, looking away from her now. She's gone too far. She shouldn't have confessed so much, not all at once like this.

Take it slow, babycakes.

"It's been so hard," Winnie says. "Even after all these years, I think of her every day. I miss her so much. She was the one person who got me. The one who told me I could be anyone, anything I wanted. But all I ever wanted was to be with her, to be what she wanted me to be. So yeah, I put the clothes on. Maybe I shouldn't have. Maybe—" She doesn't let herself finish. Henry reaches out, puts a hand on her arm and gives it a gentle squeeze.

"I can hear what the moose thinks!" shouts Emma.

"She's an amazing kid, Henry," Winnie whispers. "You're a lucky man."

"I know," he tells her, but she can tell he doesn't. He doesn't feel lucky at all. She smiles. This is the Henry she thought she might find, dismantled as the moose. He fumbles in his shirt pocket for a pack of cigarettes.

"Still smoking, huh?" she asks.

"I gave it up. Quit the day we left the cabin that summer. But I picked up a pack last week."

"Mind if I have one?" He shakes a cigarette out and lights it for her. They stand smoking a minute, listening to Emma commune with Francis the moose.

Winnie thinks about how Suz was right—everything is a prop, really: the cigarette, the lost wig, the reconstructed moose. All just little pieces to set the scene, to help us move from one act to the next. Things to hide behind, to give us courage, propel us along.

"So you don't have any plans for it?" Henry asks.

"For what?"

"The moose."

She laughs. "Like am I going to use it to kidnap some poor

lovesick boy or some other crazy Suz scheme? No way. I was thinking of putting it in the lake."

"The lake?"

"You know? Have a sort of Viking funeral for it. A final tribute. I'd like to float him out there and set him on fire. I thought it would be ... cathartic or something."

She looks straight at Henry, sure she sees him start to smile, then stop himself.

From inside the moose, a small voice yells, "I can see what Francis sees! I know what he knows!"

And Henry shares a panicked sort of look with Winnie, a look that says, *I sure as hell hope not.* They're coconspirators now—bound.

"Come on out of there, sweetie," Henry calls.

"Now I just have to figure out how to get him out on the lake. I'll have to build a raft or something," Winnie says, dropping the cigarette butt and grinding it out with her boot.

Henry smiles as he helps Emma out of the moose. "I have a canoe," he tells her.

Winnie laughs out loud. She can't help herself. It's all too perfect for words.

Chapter 40

"I WAS ABOUT TO call the police," Tess says as they enter the kitchen. "I went into Emma's room and she wasn't there. I tried to get you on your cell, but you didn't answer." He can see Tess has been crying. Henry wants to go to her, put his arms around her, but instead, he gently guides Emma over to her. Emma hesitates, looking down at the floor, scared she's in trouble.

"Baby! I was so worried," Tess says, crossing the kitchen, brushing the hair out of Emma's eyes, kissing her forehead.

"She's fine," Henry says in a soft voice. "She's right here. I'm so sorry."

"I stowed away," Emma says. She's stroking the little orange kitten clamped firmly to her chest.

"What?" Tess asks. "Who is this?" she asks, petting the kitten on the head.

"I went out to the old cabin," Henry explains. "Just to see the work Winnie had done. I'm sorry I didn't answer my phone— you know how shitty the service is way out there. I was standing talking to Winnie when Em came rolling out of the car. She and Danner had hidden themselves in the backseat."

Tess takes her hand away from the cat. Looks sternly at Emma. "Don't you *ever* do that again. Do you know how dangerous that is?"

Emma nods, looks down at the kitten.

"She knows," Henry says. "She's promised never to do it again."

Henry bites the inside of his cheek, wonders if he should tell Tess about the truck he saw parked along the road, near the driveway to the cabin when they finally left. There was a figure inside, hunched over the wheel. The truck followed them nearly the whole way home.

Henry's sure it was Bill Lunde. Which means he knows about the cabin.

"I saw Francis, Mom!" Emma squeals. "The real Francis. I crawled inside him."

Tess turns to Henry, her face twisted in confusion. "Winnie rebuilt the moose?"

Henry nods.

"Do you think that's a good idea?" Tess asks.

Henry shrugs. *No worse than building the grotto.* "I'm not the one putting it back together. What I think doesn't matter so much."

The understatement of the year.

Tess used to care what he thought. She'd ask his opinion, include him in on every decision, from what they'd have for supper to whether or not they could afford the new Volvo. Now everything he thought seemed to be a joke to her.

How do these things happen? Was it a gradual change he hadn't noticed, or did she just wake up one day and decide all his ideas and opinions were complete and utter shit?

"Why wouldn't rebuilding Francis be a good idea, Mom?"

Tess's face softens as she turns back to Emma and the kitten. "Let's get you and your little friend to bed," she says. "In the morning, we'll go out and get him some bowls, food, collar, and litter box."

"And he'll need to go see the vet," Henry says. "He's probably got fleas. And worms."

Emma shivers, hugs the cat tighter. "Disgusting," she says.

"Cats are full of parasites," Henry says. "Especially a stray like that."

"Don't listen to your father," Tess says. "He doesn't know a thing about cats. Never did." Tess gives him an icy glare. *Keep your cat-hating thoughts to yourself, mister.*

"Mom, there were so many of them!" Emma says, voice bubbly and bright. "There's this really old one, named Carrot. Winnie says he's been around since forever."

Tess glances at Henry, eyes huge. "Carrot? Some of those same cats are still around?"

Henry nods, though he couldn't say for sure. He could never keep track. The naming of the cats was always Winnie's job. But Tess loved them just as much, got all caught up in their little idiosyncrasies.

Since forever.

Henry's eyes begin to itch and water. He'll have to start taking allergy medicine again. Fucking cats.

Tess reaches out and puts a hand on his arm. He's surprised at first, then realizes she must think he's crying. Like the cats got to him on some emotional level. He doesn't correct her. He puts his hand on top of hers. Maybe it's not too late for them after all.

He watches his wife, Emma, and the stray kitten go up the stairs to bed and thinks that maybe, just maybe, everything will be all right. There's still a chance that he'll be invited back into the house, into normal life. Maybe what he needs to do is bring back more cats, a whole fucking herd of them, little mangy offerings. Carrot definitely, if he can just figure out which one it is.

He rubs his burning eyes, glances out the window toward the barn just in time to see a shadow move across the yard.

A dog? A coyote maybe?

No.

What he sees is clearly a person running, clothes flowing be-hind, blond hair glowing under the security lights, which have just clicked on. Henry races out the door, yells, "Stop!" but the figure is gone.

Heart pounding, Henry crosses the yard at a sprint, stands at the edge of the woods, looking, listening.

"Hello?"

Nothing.

He doubles back to the house, grabs the phone in the kitchen, and punches in Winnie's number. She picks up on the second ring.

"You're at the cabin?" he asks.

"It's nearly three in the morning, Henry," she says sleepily. "Where else would I be?"

"I just saw . . ."

"What?"

"Nothing," he tells her. "Go back to sleep."

PART FOUR

DISMANTLEMENT IS AN ACT OF COMPASSION AS WELL AS AN ACT OF REVOLUTION

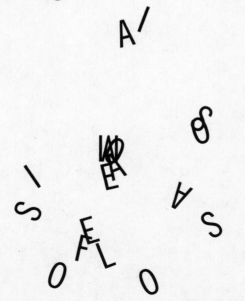

Chapter 41

SUZ IS KISSING HER.

Kissing. Sucking. Biting. Chewing her lips. Scratching her skin with ragged fingernails.

Winnie, Winnie, Winnie.

We're going to stay here forever. Can't you feel it?

Then Suz clamps down, her teeth ripping through the flesh of Winnie's lips, biting them off, like the bright red wax-candy lips kids chew on Halloween. Winnie screams, her mouth a fleshy, bleeding hole, while Suz goes back in for the tongue.

Winnie opens her eyes, touches her lips, dry and chapped, but whole, and the dream is gone.

"Fuck!" she yelps, rolling over.

We're going to stay here forever. Can't you feel it?

"Suz?" Winnie calls. She sits up, listening. Holding her breath. "Are you there?"

But there's nothing. Just a few early morning birds. Mice rustling in the walls. The drum of a far-off woodpecker hunting for breakfast.

Winnie licks her lips, so dry and cracked they've begun to bleed.

She gets up, throws a sweater on to ward off the early morning chill, and heads down the ladder to make herself coffee. The cabin is neat and tidy. The faded old Indian tapestries with their concentric, mandalalike designs that once formed the walls around the bed she shared with Suz are gone. Taken to the dump with a dozen other trash bags full of relics: old sneakers, rusted cans of pork and beans, the honey-bear bong, the aquarium.

She thinks of the tiny frog skeletons, the stench of rot and ruin.

Metamorphosis, babycakes. It's a beautiful thing.

Yeah. Fucking lovely.

Winnie shivers. Walks past the table with four chairs spaced carefully around it, set up as if they're just waiting to be filled, for another meeting of the Compassionate Dismantlers to take place. *Break out the tequila! We've got a new mission to plan!*

On the table are some wildflowers she picked and put in a canning jar. A candle in an old wine bottle. Four gallon jugs of water. And the notebook she uses as her journal, pen left on top. To the left of the notebook, a paper grocery bag, the top folded closed. She walks toward it, then changes her mind, steps back.

"Not yet," she tells herself. Later. She'll open it up later. After coffee. After she's cleared the cobwebs and nightmares from her brain.

She stumbles into the kitchen, puts water to boil in a little aluminum pan on the propane camp stove. Measures grounds into the single-serving coffee filter.

Open the bag, Winnie. Take a look.

Winnie gives in, sets down the coffee filter, goes over to the bag, opens it with trembling hands.

Good girl.

Chapter 42

HE'S SWIMMING OUT TO the center of the lake, his arm around Suz's limp body. He's on his back, looking up at the stars, wondering about heaven, about time and space, if he's really a cow in a field having a dream that he's human.

He kisses her hair, lets her go. He's stuffed her clothing full of rocks so she won't float back up.

Down she goes, the lake taking her into its deepest, darkest place.

Her hands are the last to go under, floating like white starfish. Under the surface, he can still make out her face.

She opens her eyes, smiles, says something to him underwater.

His body goes rigid.

He's made a terrible mistake.

This is not Suz at all.

It's Emma.

The one word, "Daddy," floats to the surface, a bubble of sound.

He dives, trying to reach her, but she's gone.

■ ■ ■

HE WAKES SOAKED IN sweat (lake water), lungs screaming for air. The phone is ringing. Rolling over, he grabs it, makes
a choking sound.

"Henry, you okay?" Winnie asks.

"Mmm," he mumbles. "Just getting up."

"Can you come out here today? There's something I need to
show you. Something I just found this morning."

"What is it?" he asks, closing his eyes, imagining his daughter's
body floating to shore.

Stop, he tells himself. Enough.

"It's better if I show you in person," Winnie says.

"Tess has stuff going on, so I've got Emma all day."

"Bring her. We'll have a picnic. She can help with the moose
sculpture. Maybe we can go swimming."

Henry stiffens, chomps down hard on the inside of his cheek.
"No. No swimming. I don't want her to go anywhere near the
lake. But we'll come out. Around lunchtime. I'll pack a picnic."

"Perfect," she says. "See you then."

Henry hangs up, and slides out of bed. The dream is still fresh
in his mind.

Daddy.

"DO YOU THINK YOU'LL ever have kids?" Henry asked
Suz. They were swimming to the rocks on the other side of the
lake. Henry thought the tops of the rocks poking out of the water
looked like the backbones of a dragon, curled and waiting.

Suz laughed. "I'm not exactly mommy material," she said.
"And I didn't have the greatest role model. Not like you—born
and raised in a quaint little Vermont town with Mr. and Mrs.
Apple Pie."

Henry splashed her. He hated her vision of his life. That she saw him as being so very ordinary. So predictable. He hated the condescending tone she took; the implied judgment that she was somehow better than he was, that he could never really understand her because her family was fucked up and his wasn't. "It wasn't like that," he said.

"Oh, sure it was," Suz said, rolling over to float on her back, staring up at the sky as she spoke. "And you'll appreciate it one day, when you settle down with your own little bundles of joy." She studied the clouds as if his future was laid out up there, unfolding as the breeze blew in from the north.

"What makes you so sure I'm going to have kids?" Henry asked her, getting pissed off now. One of these days, he'd find a way to show her that he wasn't nearly as simple and predictable as she thought. "Maybe I don't even want them."

Suz smiled. "I think . . . I think there are a lot of things you want that you don't even know you want. And there are things you think you want that you wouldn't really be all that happy with." She was treading water now, looking straight at him.

"That's not true," Henry said, shaking his head, frustrated.

I'd be happy with you. He thought the words, opened his mouth to say them, but they didn't come.

Suz laughed. "You'll have kids, Henry. Trust me. And just think, babycakes—think how fucking lucky they'll be. I wish I had a time machine and could jump into the future right now. I'd pat those buggers right on the head. I'd say, 'God dealt you a good hand making this guy your daddy. You watch him, listen to him, and everything'll turn out just fine.'"

Henry watched as Suz held her breath and went under. She surfaced almost two minutes later, nearly at the rocks. Suz could hold her breath forever and swam faster underwater than she did on top.

"Face it, Henry," she said when he'd finally caught up with her and they were resting on the rocks. "I swim like a fucking submarine."

"What about me?"

"You? You're something slow and steady. Dependable. An aircraft carrier maybe."

Henry shook his head. "You've got it all figured out, haven't you?"

"Pretty much, babycakes," she said, leaning in so that her lips were resting on his neck, the words buzzing against his skin, her breath this hot liquid thing that made him forget he'd ever been mad at her. "Pretty much," she said.

Chapter 43

"IT MAY BE TIME to call off Operation Reunite," Mel says, pushing the thick Velma glasses back up to the bridge of her nose.

"What?" Emma protests. "Why?"

Emma collapses against the wooden moose. She can't believe she brought Mel here. Not when Mel is so obviously clueless.

All Mel's done since they got here is complain: *I thought it was gonna be a log cabin; the moose looks more like a deformed horse; we're going to get malaria or West Nile virus if we stay out here much longer.*

It's only midafternoon and already the mosquitoes are starting to come out in force. She and Emma have covered themselves in some herbal bug repellent Winnie gave them. It doesn't really work to keep the mosquitoes away; it just makes them smell like cough drops.

"If we stopped breathing, they'd leave us alone," Mel says. "That's how they find us, you know. Each time we breathe out, it's like we're ringing a big old dinner bell."

Winnie called Emma's dad this morning to invite them out

for a picnic. Emma asked if she could bring Mel and her dad said it was fine.

"Why don't you come with us today, Mom?" Emma asked once she got off the phone with Mel. "You can meet the new cats! We're taking a picnic. We can get that cheese you like—the one that's all moldy outside."

Emma's mom shook her head.

"Not today, love. I have to meet with a client I'm doing a painting for."

"But it's Saturday," Emma whined. "You never work on Saturday. We usually go to the farmers' market together."

Her mom just shook her head. "Sorry. You go have a special day with your dad and Mel. You and I can do something together tomorrow."

Even when tempted with moldy cheese, she had an excuse.

Emma doesn't get it: if Winnie and her mom used to be friends, why isn't her mom jumping at the chance to go see her? You'd think she'd be eager to go out to the cabin again, to visit Winnie and see all the old cats for herself.

They've named the cat Emma brought home last night Thor because he has a white mark, shaped like a hammer, on his chest. It was Emma's mom's suggestion. When Emma got up this morning, she found her mom in the kitchen with bags from an early Price Chopper run—cat food, litter box, flea collar, and brightly colored felt mice stuffed full of catnip.

THE EIGHT REMAINING PAINTINGS of Francis are hanging inside the cabin. Emma stood before the wall earlier counting under her breath; counting to nine over and over again as she studied the details of his chest, legs, back, hooves, and tail. He has texture, the moose. Fur that actually looks like fur, coarse and matted.

But even better is the sculpture, which Emma and Mel are

helping to finish. Winnie showed them how to spread glue from the little pot across strips of canvas, then wrap the frame of nailed-together branches that make up his body. It's like bandaging. Making a mummy.

Emma loves it. She's figured out how to apply the canvas strips carefully, neatly, with just the right amount of glue. If she uses too much, if some drips out the edges, she tears off the canvas, cleans up the glue, and has to start over. Francis deserves perfection.

"You're a natural artist," Winnie told Emma.

Mel snorted, said, "Nah, she's just fastidious."

"BUT WE CAN'T GIVE up!" Emma tells Mel. "Winnie being back, my dad coming out here to help with the moose, with the cabin, it's progress. Any day now, I'm going to get my mom out here and this place—it's magic, I think. They'll totally get back together if I can just get them both to the cabin."

Winnie and Emma's dad have gone inside and left the girls alone with the strips of canvas and pot of glue.

"This glue stinks," Mel complains. "And I think I just found a horse hair in it. It's totally the product of some rendering factory." She smears more of it onto the moose, says, "From one ungulate to another."

Show-off, Emma thinks.

"Why do you think we should give up?" Emma asks.

"Sorry to be the one to tell you this, Em, but your dad totally has a thing for Winnie," Mel says, dropping her glue-covered brush into the pot and standing up to stretch.

"What? No way! They're old friends. She's gonna help get him and my mom back together!"

Mel shakes her head, makes a buzzing sound like when someone gets the wrong answer on a game show. "In your dreams, Em. The truth is, Winnie's going to be the thing that finally drives your parents apart once and for all. Believe me."

"You're wrong." Emma's voice is shaking now. "You don't know her at all."

"Yeah, well, neither do you," Mel says.

Mel's just jealous because Winnie hadn't told Mel she was a natural artist or offered to teach her to do a perfect butterfly stroke. Emma knows all she needs to about Winnie: Winnie understands about Danner, which is way more than she can say for Mel.

But Emma's trying not to think about Danner today. Danner's been freaking her out—first, the weird thing she said at the bottom of the pool: *Everything you have is mine.* Was it some kind of riddle? Then there was the trick she played in the car last night, making that horrible sound and smell. Later, when they got home, her dad said the new kitten had peed all over the backseat. "Did not," Emma told him. She'd been snuggling the kitten on her lap the whole time. But Emma's dad was right, the seat beside her was all wet.

"Come on," Mel says, taking Emma's hand, dragging her toward the cabin. "I bet they're making out right now."

"You are so *sick*. They're just friends." Emma jerks away from Mel, goes back to the safety of the moose. She wants to open the little door in his chest and crawl inside. Count the sticks that make up his rib cage. Breathe in his sweet, gluey smell. Emma knows, just knows, that if she were to count every stick that made up his body, it would be a multiple of nine.

"If I'm wrong, then what are you so scared of?" Mel asks. "Come look."

Mel's at the window now, standing just to the side and peering in.

"Come away from there!" Emma hisses. "They'll see you!" *It's not respectful.*

Mel doesn't turn. Her eyes are focused on whatever's going on behind the darkened glass, like a girl looking into a tank of sharks at an aquarium.

And it's just to spite Mel that Emma finally gives in and joins her. Just to prove how wrong she is. Because if Emma doesn't come and see for herself, Mel could make up anything about what's going on in there. Mel could say all kinds of gross and terrible things about her dad and Winnie.

"I should never have brought you here," Emma whispers when she gets to the window.

Mel just grunts in response.

Emma turns away from her and makes herself look in the window, where at first, all she sees is the reflection of Francis behind her, so large he takes up half the window and she has to look into him to see the figures inside.

Chapter 44

CLAIRE HAS LOADED HER mesh shoulder bag with sourdough bread, maple syrup, breakfast radishes, arugula. Tess just introduced Claire to Lisa, who makes goat cheese at Second Chance Farm.

"Delighted to meet you," Claire says, holding out her hand. Claire is wearing loose linen capris, an olive green silk blouse, leather sandals, and a cowrie shell necklace. A wide-brimmed straw hat keeps the early afternoon sun off her face.

"Enjoying the market?" Lisa asks. Lisa left a big corporate job in New York ten years ago after being diagnosed with MS. The disease hadn't progressed much, and Lisa told people that she believed this was because she'd followed her bliss. She bought the land, the goats, went to France for a summer to study cheese making, and now was living the life of her dreams.

"Very much," Claire tells her. While Claire peruses the cheeses, Tess scans the crowded farmers' market. She sees her dentist, one of the men who works for Henry, and the holistic practitioner she saw two years ago when she was exhausted all the time. She was advised to give up dairy, white flour, and sugar—a regimen that lasted approximately one week and left her feeling more tired and grumpy than ever.

"A life without ice cream and pizza is a life half lived," Henry told her. In the end, Tess agreed and didn't go back.

Across the market, over by the heavily tattooed woman selling eggs, a man is watching her. He's wearing a green polo shirt, khakis, and sunglasses.

Don't be paranoid, she tells herself. But is it paranoia? The man has had his eye on her since she and Claire arrived. She tries to think back to when she first noticed him. It may have been back in the parking lot by the courthouse. Had he followed them here?

She feels Claire's hand on her elbow. "I chose the chèvre encrusted with fresh herbs," Claire says.

"Excellent," Tess says, her eyes still on the man, who has his back to them now and is talking with the tattooed woman.

Tess and Claire say their good-byes to Lisa and wander away from the goat cheese, meandering between umbrellaed tables laid out with free-range chicken, the first of the season hothouse tomatoes, cinnamon buns, and potted sunflowers. Claire is still holding on to Tess's elbow. Tess nods and says hellos to all the people she knows, glowing and giddy because she's here with this exquisite woman on her arm.

At the center of the market, on a little makeshift stage under a canopy, a woman with a shaved head and a pink guitar does a version of Dylan's "Tangled Up in Blue."

"I am absolutely enchanted with this place," Claire says, leaning in so that Tess will hear her as they walk past the singing girl's amplifier. "I may never leave."

Claire's breath in Tess's ear is as warm and silky as her blouse. Tess feels her heart jump-start. Lets herself imagine what life might be like if Claire took up permanent residence here: the Saturday trips to the farmers' market, the galleries she'd take

Claire to, sharing popcorn at the foreign film festival that she could never get Henry interested in.

"I see you two found each other!"

Tess turns. Julia from the Golden Apple is coming up behind them, a flat of dianthus in her arms.

"We certainly did," Claire says, giving Tess's elbow a little squeeze.

"No Emma today?" Julia asks. Emma is usually the one to accompany Tess on these Saturday trips. After the market, they go to Ben & Jerry's for waffle cones.

Tess shakes her head. "She's off on an adventure with Henry." Tess looks over at the tattooed egg woman and sees there's no sign of the man who'd been watching her.

"How *is* Henry?" Julia asks. "I haven't seen him in ages."

Tess feels herself stiffen a bit. "Fine. It's his busy season and he's working too hard, as usual."

Julia nods, shifts the tray of plants in her arms. "What you all need is a vacation. Robert and I really enjoyed Tuscany last fall. When we came back, we were just so *invigorated*. It did wonders for our marriage—we were like newlyweds."

Tess smiles. Is it painfully obvious that her marriage is on the rocks and needs to be *invigorated*?

"We're not big travelers," Tess says, almost apologetically.

She feels the gentle, comforting pressure of Claire's fingers on her elbow. "When you live in a place as magical as this," Claire says, "why would you *ever* want to leave?"

Chapter 45

"IT LOOKS LIKE THE same wig," Henry tells her. He can see the disappointment on Winnie's face. She probably picked it up and brought it back to the cabin yesterday without even thinking about it. He tries to remember seeing it in her hand as he watched her leave his house and walk down the driveway and out to the road where she'd left her car.

Being in the cabin again puts him on edge. Everything is the same, but different. The place is neat and tidy now, everything in order. The mouse smell is still there, but hidden behind the stronger scents of pine cleaner and coffee. What did the cabin smell like when they were all there that summer? Cigarette and pot smoke. Oil paint and turpentine. The curry powder Suz dumped into practically everything she cooked.

He sees the place where Suz carved her initials in the heavy wooden table and runs his fingers over the pale letters: SP.

Why'd you come back, babycakes? What was it you were hoping to find?

Winnie claims the new wig appeared this morning. She woke up and found it sitting in a paper bag on the table, beside her journal.

"It's not the same wig. It's new. And it's too big. I lost the first one and she gave me another."

"She?" Henry asks. He bites the inside of his cheek.

"She's come back, Henry. She left me another message in my journal too! Look."

Henry watches her open up the notebook on the table, flip through the pages.

He's worried. Not that Suz has come back. But that being here is just too much for Winnie. She's breaking down in some crucial way.

Already she looks older, more worn than she did just twenty-four hours ago, when she pulled Emma from the pool. There are dark circles under her eyes. Her face seems gaunt. Henry finds himself scanning the cabin, making sure she's got food. He sees a can of coffee, some instant oatmeal, a large bag of cat crunchies.

"Here. Look." She thrusts the notebook at him.

He reads the lines on the page:

Use the saw to cut the table in half. Put the two halves together to make a whole. Crawl through the hole and escape.

His breath catches in his throat.

Of all the crazy coincidences.

But then, maybe Suz was right: there's no such thing as coincidence.

Henry flips to earlier pages in the journal, then back to the last page.

"It looks kind of like your writing, Winnie," he tells her.

She shakes her head. "No, Henry. No. It's impossible."

He lays his hand gently on top of hers, gives it a comforting squeeze. "Maybe you're sleepwalking. Maybe you don't remember."

But what if she isn't? What if someone really is leaving clothes and wigs laid out for her, scrawling messages in her journal?

"It's her!" Winnie says. "I know it is. She's come back." Winnie starts to tremble. Henry pulls her gently to him, takes her in his arms, and whispers, "Shhh," into her hair.

A horrible popping sound fills the cabin and he jerks away from her, turning to the front window, which has cracked in a starburst pattern. And there's Emma looking in at him, her face twisted in pain, her right hand dripping blood.

Chapter 46

"I'VE NEVER TOLD ANYONE this before," Tess says, her face flushed from wine and the thrill of confession. "My friends and I in college—we formed a sort of outlaw art group. The Compassionate Dismantlers."

Claire's green eyes widen with interest. Tess has never seen eyes the color of Claire's. Emerald eyes that draw you in, make you think you're the only one in the world who matters right now, at this moment, because those eyes, those beautiful eyes, are focused only on you. You have said something interesting. Something to hold her attention. You don't want this moment to ever end. You want it to be one of those rubber-band moments that stretch on and on, and only later, when everything is snapped back into place, does the world seem small and lacking.

They've spent the afternoon in town and are now having an early dinner at a little café with outdoor tables on a deck that overlooks the river. Claire ordered them a bottle of wine, and the waitress brought a sliced baguette, olive oil with garlic, and a peppery tapenade.

Claire had been asking Tess about college.

"You went to Sexton, right? And isn't that quite close to here?"

Tess nodded. "About forty-five minutes away. It's small. Funky. Alternative. The classes were taught in circles. We called the professors by their first names. No grades. No exams. The dorms were tiny houses—there was even a clothing-optional dorm, and a vegan dorm—you had to take off any leather products and ditch your coffee with cream before entering." Tess rolled her eyes in a can-you-believe-it kind of way.

Claire refilled Tess's wineglass. They ordered dinner, both choosing the pan-seared sea scallops with roasted red pepper sauce. Claire got out her cigarettes, prompted Tess to continue.

Tess's sketchbook is out on the round wrought-iron table and she's showing her new drawings to Claire, giving the people in them names: Henry, Winnie, Spencer, Suz. Real names. Nothing invented or withheld. She's a teacher giving a lesson, naming the parts of a thing, diagramming it, telling all its secrets.

Claire offers her a cigarette and lights it for her. Tess inhales the perfumed smoke hungrily.

"I'm sorry," the waitress calls from the doorway into the restaurant. "But you'll have to put those out. State law."

Claire groans, rolls her eyes as she stubs her cigarette out on the rail of the deck. Tess does the same, then lets herself continue.

"We believed that in order to truly understand something, you had to take it apart. That art, real art, was more about destruction than creation."

Claire smiles. It's an aha-moment smile. A please-go-on-you've-got-me-on-the-edge-of-my-seat smile.

"We did all kinds of crazy stuff—destroyed our records at Sexton, set fire to a construction site, shot up a power substation, we even kidnapped this guy once."

Tess knows she shouldn't be saying the words. But she can't stop herself. She's caught up in the dizzy momentum of their day together. She pulls her wrought-iron chair around, moves closer to Claire so that their thighs are touching as they study the sketchbook.

"It was silly, really," Tess says. "How seriously we took ourselves back then. How earnest we were."

Tess remembers back to third grade when she first learned to write in cursive, the first assignment she did for Miss Ferris after weeks spent practicing letters and words. Tess filled an entire page with words, all attached to one another, no spaces, no periods or commas; a run-on, breathless word that told an entire story.

This moment is like that sentence, she thinks now.

"I find this drawing the most interesting," Claire says, her hand tracing the edge of the first sketch Tess did of Suz's face inside the carnivorous flower. "Tell me about this girl in the flower."

I didn't mean to put her there. She just appeared. She keeps appearing. In my yard. My studio.

Tell me.

"She died," Tess says, reaching for the wine. How many glasses has she had? Three? Four? She's sure Claire is still on her first glass. Other than the occasional paper cup half full of wine at gallery events, Tess rarely drinks. Now here she is, good and drunk and suddenly terrified that she's going to make a fool of herself.

She glances at Claire, who is clearly waiting for her to say something more. "Drowned," Tess says. "The summer after college. We were all living together."

Tess tells herself she will not have any more wine. She will shut her mouth and not say any more. But it feels so good, such a release. To finally be telling the truth, or some part of it at least. She mustn't tell the whole truth, she knows that, but it's okay to skirt around the edges, isn't it? To flirt with it. Tease it by telling these little half-truths.

"How horrible for you," Claire says, reaching out to put a hand on Tess's knee, making it feel warm and cool all at once.

Tess nods. "It was. I think"—she hesitates—"I think that's when my paintings stopped mattering so much. When I lost the . . ." Tess bites her tongue.

Shut up. Just shut your mouth before you say any more.

"Passion," Claire says, pushing her leg ever so slightly into Tess's, keeping her hand on Tess's knee.

Tess's heart is a moth fluttering toward light.

"Yes." Tess doesn't pull away. She loves the closeness. The feel of this woman next to her, the dangerous temptation to open her mouth and tell Claire everything. How easy it would be.

"But now you're ready to get it back?" Claire asks.

"I don't know."

"I think what you need to do is paint something completely different," Claire says, looking right into Tess's eyes with such intensity that Tess has to fight the urge to turn away. "Something you're both compelled by and afraid of."

Tess lets this sink in as Claire empties the last of the bottle into Tess's glass. Tess takes a sip, holding the wine in her mouth, tasting oak, cherries, and something vaguely metallic. It's blood she tastes. From the cut her teeth made on her own tongue.

She's been silent so long. Afraid for so long. She's studied boxing. Made her body lean and strong. Getting ready for a fight with some imagined enemy. But all along, her biggest enemy has been her own self. And she has this deep and true sense that this woman beside her in the restaurant can somehow help her raise the flag of surrender, maybe even set her free.

She spots the waitress coming through the open door onto the deck with two plates of food.

"I know what I want my subject to be," she says as the waitress approaches. Tess looks right into Claire's eyes, green as the canopy in a tropical forest, as the waitress sets the plates down in front of them.

"Can I get you ladies anything else right now?"

"No, thank you," Claire says. "Everything looks perfect."

The waitress walks away in quick, gliding steps. The delicate white Christmas lights that line the porch come on.

Claire turns back to Tess. "You were saying?"

"You," Tess tells Claire, the pungent, charred scent of the food hitting her suddenly, making her realize how truly ravenous she is. "I want to paint *you*."

Chapter 47

"I DON'T BELIEVE THIS," Tess says. "Twice in one week she gets hurt on your watch."

Is it Henry's imagination, or does Tess seem a little drunk? Her words sound slightly slurred and she sways ever so slightly, like a snake ready to strike.

They're all standing in the kitchen, having arrived home within five minutes of each other.

"Mom," Emma protests, cradling her bandaged hand, "it wasn't Dad's fault. I—"

Henry jumps in. "She cut her hand working on the moose. I was right there with her. We put peroxide on it and wrapped it up. It's not a very deep cut."

The lie comes easily. He shoots Emma a warning glance: *Don't tell the truth. This needs to be one of our secrets.*

Emma lets out a little hissing sound, leans back against the counter, studying her wrapped hand.

Henry keeps thinking about the incident with the window: how when he and Winnie got to Emma outside, they could see the cut wasn't bad, just a thin slice across her knuckles. But something else was wrong. Emma was staring down at her hand, perplexed. When, at last, she looked up at Henry, Winnie, and Mel, she asked, "What happened?" as if she had no recollection of punching the window. As if it had been someone else.

"Maybe Danner made her do it," Mel had said, disgusted, rolling her eyes.

"I don't want you taking Emma to the cabin anymore," Tess says.

"Mom!"

"I think you're overreacting," Henry tells her. It's a line he's so used to hearing from her, it feels strange to be parroting it back. But here he is, perfectly sober, and she's the one slurring her words, not being rational.

Tess shakes her head. "It's not a safe place. I should never have agreed to it to begin with. Emma, go up to your room. I need a moment alone with your father."

Emma stamps her foot, rolls her eyes, and groans. "You're always sending me to my room. I'm the one who cut my dumb hand. And you can't keep me away from the cabin! It's not fair!"

Tess doesn't engage Emma in the argument, just silently nods her head in the direction of the stairs. When Emma doesn't budge, Tess lets out an exasperated breath and says, "Please, Em?"

"Fine," Emma spits out. They hear her creep into the front hall, whisper something to the moose painting before heading upstairs.

"Do you want to tell me what's going on up at the cabin?" she asks him once they're alone.

"What? Nothing. I took Emma and Mel. They worked on the moose. Played with the cats. I think it's good for Emma to be out there in the woods. If she spends more time there, she might really take an interest in art." He feels himself stammering, as if he's telling lies. "You should come with us. See the work Winnie has done."

Tess shivers. "I think all of us should stay away from that place," she says. "Emma most of all. I don't know what's going on between you and Winnie, and I'm not sure I want to know, but leave Emma out of it."

"But Emma loves Winnie," Henry says.

Winnie represents their past, the truth. He likes that when he's with her, he remembers who he used to be. The brave Henry. The strong Henry. The artist and dreamer. And when he's with Winnie, they talk openly about that summer, about Suz.

"Are you even listening to me?" Tess asks, then steps forward, staggering a little.

No. He wasn't. He missed her last words.

"The picture of Suz at the grotto—did you take it?"

"No," he says, not at all sure how the subject switched.

"Don't you think it's a little suspicious that Winnie showed up in town and these strange things began happening: the message in the trees, the knife being left, now the photo being taken from the grotto?"

Henry shakes his head. "She saved Emma's life, Tess."

"Yeah, I remember. No thanks to you. But what was she doing here? She just happened to be strolling by our pool—on private property—when Emma flipped over?"

Her face is twisted into a cartoonish scowl. Her nose looks sunburned.

"I think if you went out to the cabin with us, if you sat down and talked with Winnie—"

Tess shakes her head. "It's not open for debate. No taking Emma to the cabin. If she's so damned attached to Winnie, then Winnie can come here. But only when I'm around."

"Winnie's not a criminal," Henry says.

Tess bites her lip, sucks in a breath. "Yes, she is. We're all criminals, Henry. Or have you forgotten?"

Chapter 48

SHE BOBS AND WEAVES. Practices her footwork. Side step, side step, back to center. Right. Left. Forward. Back.

She hears Joe, the trainer's, voice in her head: *You have to learn the footwork first. It's the foundation you're going to base everything else on. If you don't have a solid stance, you're through.*

Her fists assail the bag. She steps back, hands raised in defensive posture, then moves forward to attack again, targeting the yellow Everlast logo.

Everlast. Everlasting.

Does anything last forever? Go on and on?

Tess steps back, trying to clear her head.

Focus, damn it.

Her mind goes back to the feel of Claire's hand on her thigh. How it made her feel heated and chilled all at once.

"I would love for you to paint me," Claire had said. "I'm honored. I think we should get started right away! I'll sit for you at the house. The lighting in the front room, where we drank our coffee yesterday, is perfect, don't you think?"

Tess nodded, her mouth full of scallop. Yes, perfect. It was all perfect.

She imagined the two of them in the front room, by the windows, hummingbirds flitting outside while they sipped wine, and Tess worked at the easel, her eye moving from Claire to the canvas.

"I could pose nude if you'd like," Claire suggested. Tess felt her face redden.

She'd sketched hundreds of naked bodies over the years—first in college, then in the weekly life-drawing sessions the art guild organized.

But this was different, wasn't it?

Don't think about why. Focus: the bag; the punches; the footwork.

If you don't have a solid stance, you're through.

Forward again, left fist raised, chin down, she goes in with a right hook. Once. Twice. Three times.

And those eyes. Those green eyes.

"Stop it," she tells herself out loud, stepping back from the swinging bag.

What the hell is wrong with her?

She hears Claire's voice in her head: *Passion.*

Left. Right. Left. Jab. Hook.

The sweat is dripping down her face, neck, and shoulder blades. Her hands are wet inside the giant gloves. Her arms are shaking and her knuckles and wrists are beginning to ache.

She can't believe she told Claire so much tonight. Revealing so many secrets to a woman who is practically a stranger. But that's just the problem, isn't it? When she's with Claire, Claire doesn't feel like a stranger. She feels like someone Tess has known all along. A soul mate.

Everlast. Everlasting.

"Idiot," Tess says, pounding the bag again, feeling what's left of the wine leave her body through her skin. She's purging herself.

How could she have lost control like that? Especially now,

when things are getting dangerous: Spencer's suicide, Winnie's arrival in town, the private investigator sniffing around. At a time when she should be the most guarded, here she is spilling her guts.

Jab. Jab. Uppercut. The bag swings, the chains above it rattling.

Tomorrow she'll be clearer. She'll phone Claire first thing to say that the portrait is a bad idea. That she's content to stick to safe little flower paintings. They sell well enough and that's what matters to her now, at this stage of her life. It's not about stretching herself as an artist or finding passion. It's about being a grown-up. Making a living. Keeping herself and her daughter safe and provided for.

This is what she'll tell Claire. Thanks, but no thanks. A neat, tidy ending. Then she'll just go back to life as normal. Compressed life. No rubber-band moments that you wish would stretch on forever.

She lunges at the bag again, stopped only by a searing pain in her thigh, right where Claire's hand rested.

She's pulled a muscle. She should have warmed up. Stretched. "Fuck!"

Then, she does something she hasn't let herself do in ages: she drops down on her knees and cries, sobbing and gasping as quietly as she can, her face buried in the warm leather of her boxing gloves.

Chapter 49

"I'm sorry about the window," Emma whispers into the phone. She's in her room with the door closed, sitting on the edge of her bed. Out the window she sees her dad walking away from the house to his barn. His hands are deep in his pockets, his head hanging down. Her mom yelled at him again. Emma can tell. And this time it was all Emma's fault.

"It's okay," Winnie says. "I taped some plastic sheeting over it. I'll pick up a new piece of glass Monday when the hardware store opens. It's an easy fix, really. How's your hand?"

Emma flexes her fist inside the wrap of gauze. "Okay."

"You really don't remember doing it?" Winnie asks.

"No."

The last thing Emma remembers is seeing the reflection of Francis in the window. Then everything went black.

Mel thinks maybe she got possessed. Emma laughed at this. Mel said, "Seriously, maybe it was Danner or something. Maybe Danner's the devil."

Emma shakes her head at the memory. Right. Danner's the devil.

Still, it scares her. Not remembering. What if the kids at school are right and she really is a mental case? Danner could be just another symptom; maybe she has multiple personalities, like Bernice at D.J.'s General Store.

Everything you have is mine.

Maybe what that means is: I am you, and you are me.

She hears the line of a song in her head: *And we are all together.* Lyrics from some CD her dad listens to. A song about being a walrus that makes no sense at all.

"Dissociative episode," Mel said earlier when they were riding home in the backseat of the Blazer. "A sure sign of possession."

"Right," Emma said, thinking that maybe it's time for her to take a little break from Mel, who has been getting on her nerves big time these last few days.

Emma presses the phone against her ear. "You still there?" she asks.

"Yeah," says Winnie. "You know, there's this ancient Chinese proverb that says that once you save a person's life, you're responsible for it."

Emma lets this sink in and smiles. "So what? Does that mean you're always going to be looking out for me?"

It seems backward to Emma. Like she's the one who owes Winnie something, not the other way around.

"It means I'll try. It means I'm here for you. If you ever want to talk."

Emma twirls the phone cord with her finger. Maybe Winnie thinks she's crazy now. Troubled. That she's a girl who *needs to talk.* At least she doesn't think Emma's possessed by the devil. Not yet anyway.

"My mom doesn't want me coming out to the cabin anymore."

There's silence. She can hear Winnie breathe. "Did she say why?" Winnie asks.

"She says she thinks it's dangerous."

"Maybe she'll change her mind," Winnie says.

Right. If there is one thing Emma knows about her mother it's that once she's made a decision, it's pretty much set in stone.

"Was my mom always so stubborn? Back when you knew her, I mean?"

Winnie chuckles. "She was always strong willed," she says. "And she and your dad, they were both such terrific artists."

Emma thinks of the photo she found: her dad's arm around her mom, both of them young and happy. A Long Time Ago.

"And they loved each other, right?" Emma asks, her voice shaking a little.

"Of course," Winnie says.

"I think they could again," Emma tells her. "I mean, I think they still do, they just need to remember. To be reminded."

"Emma," Winnie says, "sometimes when two people split up, it's for the best. I'm not saying that's the case with your parents, I'm just saying it's not going to do any good to make yourself crazy hoping for something that might not ever happen. Do you understand what I'm getting at?"

"Sure," Emma says, her voice thick. She bites her lip.

"One thing I'm sure of," Winnie says. "They love you very much. Nothing's going to change that."

Emma wonders how much they'll love her if she turns out to be a total mental case. The fights they might have, arguing about who's to blame. She's supposed to be bringing them together, not giving them new stuff to argue over.

"You know," Emma says, "working on Francis today got me thinking. Maybe I should try to make my own sculpture."

"I think that's a fantastic idea, Emma!"

It *is* a good idea, an idea she didn't even realize she had until the words were out of her mouth, which, she guesses, is just what it means to be artistically inspired.

She'll follow in her parents' footsteps. Maybe if she works on a sculpture, it will help draw her parents back together. It will give them all something to talk about. A family of artists. The only problem is, Emma's never felt very artistic. She's more the math and science type. Art has always seemed so . . . so messy.

"But I don't know the first thing about it. I mean, how do I even start? I don't have clay or tools or anything."

"You use what you have," Winnie tells her. "People make sculptures from cloth, old telephones and garbage. Look around the house with an artist's eye."

Emma likes this: the idea that she has an artist's eye. Something that ties her to her parents.

"No one sees the world like you do, Emma. Creating art is about sharing your own personal vision with the world. Taking something no one else can see and bringing it to life."

After getting a few more pointers from Winnie, Emma hangs up and walks through the house gathering things: plastic trash bags, stray socks, rubber bands, an old dress of her mother's from the box of things to go to Goodwill.

She hears her mom attacking the Everlast bag in the basement. The thud of leather gloves on the bag, the rattle of chains making angry ghost sounds. The floor shakes below her feet.

"I live in a haunted house," she says to no one.

On the kitchen table, Emma spots the digital camera her dad gave her for her birthday. A little voice tells her, *You'll need that too.*

Mixed media, it's called. Bringing all these elements together into a single work of art. She's spent her whole life hearing about art from her parents. Passively absorbing the meaning of the color wheel, phrases like "mixed media." Now it's time to put all that sponged-up information to use. She'll create something that will make them proud.

Emma goes into her room and lays the stuff out on her bed, and, at first, it seems like this random assortment of junk.

"Great going, super freak," she says to herself, understanding the truth: there's no way she could ever be an artist. She can't believe she even thought she could pull this off. A girl who is good at numbers and being fastidious, but not much else. She's about to stuff everything into the back of her closet when she hears a voice say, *Not so fast.*

She rearranges the things on her bed, walks around it counting by nines, moving objects from here to there, squinting so that she can barely see, like an artist's eye is a blind eye. Then, as if by magic, the sculpture starts to take shape.

And she feels it, she truly feels it: this connection to her parents, to Winnie, to all the artists who have come before her. It's as if she's plugged into this art-powered party line, and now she's being guided, inspired by some force so much bigger than herself. A force that whispers in her ear, says, *Get the scissors. Get a bucket of sand. Don't be afraid. I'll show you what to do.*

All her life she's heard that art is done in a trance, and when she looks up at the clock two hours later, she finally gets what it means. The sculpture is laid out on the bed, nearly complete, and here she is, covered in sand and glue, pinpricks in her fingers from numerous mishaps with a sewing needle. Emma the artist.

"Dissociative episode," she says out loud, trembling a little as she wipes the sand from her clothes, eyeing her creation with wonder, her skin prickly, a strange new hum in her ears.

Chapter 50

TESS IS STANDING IN line at the supermarket, casting an eye over the tabloids and fat Sunday papers, when she spots the irises over in the floral department. She came out to the store for bread and tea and has been throwing a random assortment of things into her cart: cat treats, a tin of cookies, low-fat balsamic dressing. She didn't really need bread and tea, but she had to get out of the house before she drove herself crazy. All day, she's been putting off calling Claire to tell her she can't do the portrait. She kept herself busy with one distraction after another: cleaning the oven, working out with the heavy bag until her knuckles screamed, organizing her desk. She began each task promising herself that when she was done, she'd pick up the phone and call Claire. After dinner, she announced to Emma and Henry that she was running to the market. She even asked Emma if she wanted to come along, but Emma declined.

"I'm working on something in my room," she said. "A project."

"We can get ice cream after," Tess said, thinking a little bribery just might work.

"No thanks," Emma told her. "I really want to finish this. I can't wait for you guys to see."

Henry tousled Emma's hair, said, "We can't wait either, sweetie."

Now, as Tess makes her way from the checkout line with the racks of magazines and candy bars to the deep purple flowers, she knows just what she'll do. She'll buy two bouquets, and drop by Claire's place with one of them, tell her face-to-face. She owes her that much. Tess imagines bringing her own bunch of flowers home, setting them right out there on the table in her white vase, right out in the open. Every time she sees them, she'll think of Claire and how brave she was to end things before they became . . . unmanageable.

She carries the red plastic basket with her oat-bran bread, Earl Grey tea, cookies, dressing, cat treats, and two bunches of cellophane-wrapped flowers to the checkout line, feeling purposeful. Almost giddy.

SHE PARKS IN THE gravel driveway and creeps up the railroad-tie steps to the rented house with its weathered gray shingles, clutching the irises to her, wondering if this was a good idea after all. She hesitates at the front door, considers leaving the flowers there and running.

What is wrong with you?

Her palms are sweating, greasy and slippery against the clear cellophane covering the bouquet.

What are you doing here? What are you really doing here?

But then, before she can knock or plan her next move, Claire surprises her by swinging the door open, smiling.

"I was hoping you'd come," Claire says.

"I . . . ," Tess stammers. *Focus. Say what you came to say and get the hell out.* "I have something to tell you."

Claire is wearing a light muslin dress. Sleeveless. Her arms are tan.

"Well, come in then. Are the flowers for me?"

Tess nods, follows Claire inside then holds the bouquet of irises out.

Named for Iris, the messenger of the gods, who, some stories say, used a rainbow to transmit messages between heaven and earth. Tess opens her mouth to tell Claire this, but stops.

Claire steps toward her, reaching for the flowers, but instead of taking the irises, she lays her hand on Tess's, which is clinging to the damp cellophane wrapping the flowers. Claire strokes Tess's wrist with her index finger, right at the pulse point.

And Tess knows, at this moment, that it's all over. This woman has her. Has her in a way no one person has ever had her.

Her whole body is humming, glowing like an electric filament.

"What was it you wanted to tell me?" Claire asks, her accent thick, her voice husky.

Iris. Messenger. Rainbow.

Tess steps forward until her body is pressed against Claire's, and she lets out a little sigh, a little "oh" sound she hadn't meant to make, then turns her face up and kisses Claire on the mouth, tasting lipstick, flowery cigarettes, and a sweet spice she cannot name.

Chapter 51

July 14—Cabin by the lake
Spencer found his way back from the wilds of Maine.
He hasn't shown his face here at the cabin but he's
been around for the past week.

He's been sending letters to Winnie at her P.O. box
in town. Letters and chocolates. Good, expensive
chocolates, not the waxy kind in heart-shaped boxes
from the drugstore. The letters are angry and arrogant,
but also pleading and pathetic. He's even asked her to
marry him, of all delusional things!

Winnie laughed when she read this out loud to all of
us, but it was this weird, strangled-sounding laughter.

Winnie disappeared one afternoon last week. She said
she was out walking. Only later, I saw that Spencer's
wallet was gone. So I asked Winnie, "Did you see
anyone on this walk of yours?" She said no, she didn't.

*Spencer still has this asinine radio show on WSXT
and every week, he dedicates a song to her, "This
is for Val," he says. And it's always some sappy-ass
love song. We all listen in the cabin and groan. This
week, he played Elvis Costello's "Don't Let Me Be
Misunderstood" and I thought we would die laughing.*

*When he's not playing songs, he's reading poetry or
rambling about nature. Sometimes he treats his listeners
to some of his spirit chimes. Jesus God.*

*This week's topic was moose. He'd read an article
about them in some wildlife magazine and decided
to dedicate a show to their "magnificent beauty and
strength." Talk about making a person want to puke!
Spencer read most of the article on the air, recited all
these totally dull moose facts, and asked people to call
in with their moose stories and that's when I got my
idea. True inspiration really is like a bolt of fucking
lightning sometimes!*

*I had Henry go down to the pay phone at the general
store and call in. He can do this real thick Vermont
accent, sounds just like his grandpa. So Henry tells this
story about driving out on Route 2 real late a few weeks
back and damned if he doesn't almost run smack into
this young bull moose. He gets out of the car to take a
look—this old duffer, he's lived in Vermont his whole life
and has never seen one up close before. And the fucking
thing talks. Henry gets to this part in the story and
Spencer starts laughing, like the old guy's telling a joke,
and Henry's like, "No, sir. You listen to me. I'm deadly
serious. That moose opened its jaws and spoke."*

*"Well, what did the moose say?" asked DJ Spencer,
live, on the air. We were all listening in the cabin,
laughing our asses off.*

"It asked me a riddle."

"What was the riddle?" Spencer wanted to know.

*"You're in a cement room with no doors or windows.
All you have is a table and a mirror. How do you get
out?"*

*Spencer was silent. Dead air. "What's the answer?" he
asked.*

*"Can't tell you that," said Henry-the-old-timer.
"What if one day you meet the moose? Wouldn't he
be disappointed if you already knew the answer to his
riddle?" Then Henry hung up. And I started work on
phase two of What to Do About Spencer.*

Henry closes the book, looks at his watch: 10:30. And still, Tess is not home from her trip to the market three hours ago. He's tried her cell phone, but she doesn't answer. He doesn't even know why she has the phone—it's always either turned off or dead because she forgets to charge it.

Henry has Emma's old baby monitor so he can listen to his daughter sleeping back in her room. He hid the other half under her bed. He knows she's too old for this, that she'd be horrified if she discovered he was listening to her sleep, but she's been acting so strange today: staying in her room behind a locked door on which she's hung a DO NOT DISTURB sign; coming out only for an odd assortment of things: a needle and thread, to use the printer in the office, a bucket of sand from her old plastic turtle sandbox.

He climbs out of the canoe, pours himself a coffee cup of merlot and wonders what's going on with Tess. First, the grotto. The strange phone conversation he overheard. And now she's gone missing. Should he be worried? A normal husband might have called the police by now. The wine stings the raw places where he's been biting the insides of his cheeks.

"Screw it," he says, rising from the canoe, shoving the baby monitor into the pocket of his jacket and heading to the main house. He grabs the key to Tess's studio from the bowl in the entryway and heads back outside, across the lawn, floodlights blaring. He skirts the edge of the little pond, goldfish rising to kiss the surface as the mermaid taunts him: *Where are you going? What are you doing?*

Through the crackly receiver in his pocket, he hears Emma groan, roll over in her bed. The cement owls leer, eyes huge; the dodos chuckle. Behind him, the floodlights click off.

He hurries to Tess's studio, fits the key into the lock by feel, opens the door and flips on the light. Safe. But feeling like a criminal. He hasn't been in her studio in over a year, not since they were "together." It's an unspoken rule that this place is off-limits. It's a Henry-free zone. Her own private clubhouse. He wishes he'd remembered the wine.

On the desk, he finds an empty tube of vermilion paint. And a brush, stained red.

Beside those is the red camping knife Tess claimed she found at the grotto. Henry picks it up. Large blade, small blade, bottle opener, spoon, and fork. Battered red handle. Suz's. Or one exactly like hers. But originally, it was Spencer's, wasn't it? Taken from him when they emptied his pockets back on the side of the highway in Maine.

Henry picks up a sketchbook. Under it, the stack of Polaroids he'd been hiding in the metal toolbox. So she's been sneaking around his studio too. Which means she knows about Suz's journal. Maybe she's even been reading it. Eyes still on the photos, Henry absentmindedly flips open the sketchbook. What he sees astounds him.

Suz.

Suz's face at the center of a flower. Not one of the tame, farmers'-market-style flowers that Tess usually paints these days, but one of the old flowers. The carnivorous, toothy, dripping flowers. On the next page is a drawing of himself from that summer, bearded, young and smiling. Others of Winnie. The moose. Suz. The final drawing in the book is the most haunting: Suz in the lake. Eyes closed, sinking into the dark water.

"Jesus," he mumbles. Outside, he hears something. A popping sound. Then another. He freezes, eyes still on the drawing.

Suz. It's Suz.

Now a dog is barking, far off in the hills.

Is that a car door closing? Shit. That's all he needs now, for Tess to come home and catch him here. He snaps the sketchbook closed, throws it on top of the photos, and flips off the light. He stands at the door for a moment, listening. Nothing. Or almost nothing. There's the faintest sound of footsteps on the gravel path that weaves through the garden. And they're coming his way.

In his pocket, Emma sleeps on through the static.

Looking around the dark studio frantically, he sees there's no place to hide. His only hope is to open the door and make a break for it, hope she isn't close enough to see him.

Slowly, he opens the door, heart leaping, mouth salty with blood from where his teeth have been clamped down on the insides of his cheeks. He crouches down and sneaks along the edge of the building like a burglar. When he gets to the back side, he stops and listens. Nothing. Had he imagined the footsteps?

Still crouched down, running like a soldier in battle, Henry hurries around the edge of the sculpture garden, to the driveway where he stands up straight at last. No sign of Tess or the Volvo. And no motion lights. It's pitch black. He gets close to the one angled down from above the front door of the main house, jumps up and down to try to get it to come on. Nothing.

"Must have blown a circuit," he says out loud, thinking that the sound of his own voice will help keep things rational.

He makes his way to the barn and checks the breaker, which is fine. He flips it off, then on. Henry pulls back the stapled-on black plastic and looks out the window. Still no lights.

He chomps down on the inside of his cheek, tells himself he should get back out there and check the lights more carefully. But somehow, the very thought of it makes his guts go cold. So much for being rational.

"Coward," he says.

What is it that's supposed to be out there?

In his mind, he sees the sketch of Suz in the lake, going under.

He steps toward the sliding barn door, then stops, hears Winnie's voice in his head: *In all that chaos, there are patterns. There's no such thing as coincidence.*

His fingers are on the door, but instead of opening it, he finds himself pushing the latch closed, bolting himself safely in.

He's just had too much to drink. That's what Tess would say. The wine's making him jump to conclusions rather than think things through. Maybe Tess is right. Maybe it's time to give up the drink once and for all.

He looks out the window again. It's dark. Too damn dark. He'll probably trip over shit if he goes out there. Break an ankle or something. It's best to stay inside. He'll check the lights tomorrow when he can actually see what he's doing.

Content with this plan, he refills his coffee mug with wine, settles back into the canoe with Suz's journal.

July 18—Cabin by the lake

Beautiful day today. We went skinny-dipping. Henry and I had a contest to see who could swim farthest underwater. I made it all the way to the rocks and won. Scared the shit out of poor Winnie. She thought I'd drowned. Henry and I sat on the rocks and talked about the model rockets he used to build when he was a kid. I told him I thought model rockets were sexy. He said, "Everything is sexy to you," and kissed me on the cheek, then he slid back into the water before I could say the thing I was gonna say next. Which I guess is for the best.

I have been working hard on the sketches for my new sculpture. But it'll be more than a sculpture—it's a key piece in the new plan I've been working on, our next mission, the biggest yet. What it is is a blind. A Trojan horse of a sort. I showed the drawings to Henry and he thinks it'll work. Then I showed them to Tess and Winnie.

"A moose?" Tess asked. "A fucking moose?"

"I think it kicks ass," Winnie said, leaning in and kissing me hard on the mouth.

It's eleven at night now. I worked all evening sorting wood, cutting pieces for the frame. In my mind, the moose is beginning to take shape. I'm thinking I might take a break from the sculpture part and do a huge, life-size painting of the moose, a sort of moose study. I can work out the dimensions, get the details right before tackling it in 3-D. I want the final product to be as realistic as possible.

*This is my favorite part of a project: the beginning.
Everything seems possible. The art lives in the mind's
eye, beautiful and shimmering, some kind of holy
grail you have to get to. And the act of creation is
the quest. But I haven't set out yet. I'm still just
gathering supplies, visualizing the end result, all golden
and perfect, infused with this kind of light that lives
only in my mind. I pity anyone who is not an artist.
Who doesn't know what this feels like. This beautiful
gestation.*

Henry sits up, closing the book. He hears a sound on the baby
monitor. He fumbles in the pocket of his jacket, turns the volume
all the way up.

Emma's awake. Talking. Whispering. Having a conversation.

She's not alone.

Henry holds his breath. Puts the receiver to his ear, trying to
make out words in the static.

They'll burn, he hears a voice say.

But this isn't just any voice.

It's Suz. Crackly, faint, but Suz. He's sure of it.

Henry stands on shaky legs, coffee cup in one hand, monitor
in the other. Dropping the cup of wine, he bolts out the door,
monitor in hand, heading for Emma's room, terrified of what he
might see when he gets there.

But he stops dead in his tracks, arms pinwheeling like a cartoon character who has just found himself at the edge of a cliff.

Across the yard, the little shed Tess uses as her studio, the building where he was just a trespasser, is in flames.

Chapter 52

TESS WAKES UP DISORIENTED and in complete darkness. She's naked. Hot under a thick comforter, the sweat making the cotton stick to her like loosely wrapped bandages.

Then she remembers.

"Claire?"

She reaches over to the left side of the bed. Feels a warm pillow, but other than that, only empty space.

Tess rolls out of bed, gropes around on the floor for her things, and dresses quickly in the dark. Her body feels liquid, mercurial. Tangled in her shirt is her digital watch. She pushes the light. It's 12:13 A.M. Shit! She can't believe she fell asleep. How could she? What will she say to Henry and Emma?

Guilt floods over her. What has she done?

It was all so easy—the kiss, the way she let Claire lead her up the stairs to the bedroom. It felt so . . . inevitable. Unstoppable.

But maybe she should have stopped. Thought things through a little more.

She's not the sort to just jump into bed with someone she

hardly knows. The truth is, other than Henry, the only other person she's slept with was her high school boyfriend.

And now here she is, slinking around in some other woman's house, feeling more like a character in an art house movie than herself.

Stumbling her way through the dark, Tess heads out of the bedroom and down the carpeted hall on tiptoe, reaching the doors to the bathroom and office, which are both closed. She pauses a second, listening.

"Claire?" Her voice is barely above a whisper.

There's no response. Tess puts her hand on the bathroom doorknob, starts to turn it, then is overcome by the need to get home. She needs to get away, think things through on her own before facing Claire again.

She gently releases the doorknob, and pads down the stairs. The living room and kitchen are dark.

Fumbling in her purse, Tess pulls out her keys and hurries out the front door, down the steps and to her car, where she backs down the driveway with her headlights off, feeling like a criminal who's just barely gotten away.

TESS IS PASSING THE woods that line the road on the north side of their property when she sees it: red lights circling, flashing.

A rush of adrenaline quickens her heart even as she holds her breath, all her senses on overdrive.

The tires of the Volvo squeal as she guns it down the road to the driveway, where she loses control on the turn, nearly ramming one of the fire trucks.

Whatever has happened, I am to blame, she thinks. When you have an affair, you leave your family wide open to danger.

She makes a quick deal with God right then and there: If everyone is all right, she will break things off with Claire. She will be a better mother. She won't leave her child unguarded. She's not going to run off again like some hormone-crazed, love-struck teenager.

Who does she think she is? How could she forget her responsibilities, her own daughter, like that?

"Emma," she says without even knowing she's saying it. Her daughter's name is like a breath. That much a part of her.

Please, God, let her be all right.

Right away, she sees her prayers are answered. Emma's standing in her moose pajamas next to Henry in the yard, holding his hand. They're watching the volunteer firefighters douse what's left of her painting studio with their hoses.

"What happened?" Tess asks, running up to them over the grass. She hugs Emma fiercely.

Henry looks at her with sadness. He doesn't seem angry or suspicious. He doesn't ask where she's been until after midnight.

"They think it started with a candle," he says.

"But I wasn't even in there today. I never lit any candle."

"Maybe it was your daughter," one of the firefighters suggests. He's joined them in their little semicircle.

"She never goes near the studio," says Tess. "She knows better. Don't you, Em?"

Emma nods.

Tess hugs her again, pulling Emma tight against her own body, holding her there.

"You'd be surprised how long a candle can burn," the man says. "You could have lit it yesterday."

"I'm always careful," Tess says.

I will be careful. From now on. My daughter is safe and I will keep my promise and be a better mother. No wild affairs or great search for all the passion missing in my life. I will not see Claire again.

"I'm kind of suffocating here, Mom," Emma says, her voice muffled. Tess lets her go.

"Sorry." She gives Emma an apologetic smile, watches the fireman leave them, go back over to one of the trucks.

"Pretty flowers, Mom," Emma says, and it's only then that Tess realizes she's clutching the bouquet of irises, now crumpled, ruined.

"I bought them earlier today," she says, as if Emma has asked for an explanation. "I thought it would be nice to put them on the table. Paint them maybe."

She thinks of the matching bouquet she took Claire, how it was dropped on the floor in the front hall, forgotten once their kissing began.

Tess blushes, self-consciously raises her hand to cover her right shoulder where she knows Claire left tooth marks in her skin. She won't be able to wear a bathing suit for a while.

"It's okay," she tells Henry. "It's not as if anyone was hurt. And there weren't many paintings in there. Just a lot of supplies. A few new sketches. It can all be replaced."

She feels a stab of pain at the thought of the new sketches being gone. Then, she remembers the Polaroids she'd taken from Henry's studio. Shit.

"Danner says it will be worse next time," Emma tells them. Her arms are crossed tightly against her chest.

"What?" asks Tess.

"She says something bad is going to happen."

"Bad in what way?" Tess asks.

Emma bites her lip, shrugs.

"Emma, before I called the fire department, I heard you talking in your room," Henry says. "Who were you talking to?"

"Danner."

"Is Danner ever a . . . real lady? That other people could see?" he asks.

Emma smiles. "She's real now," Emma says. "Come see."

Chapter 53

HENRY FREEZES IN THE doorway of Emma's room. Emma and Tess have stepped inside, Emma's voice babbling, bright with excitement.

"It's my sculpture," she tells them.

Tess makes a strange gurgling sound.

Henry tries to speak, but feels like he's been gut-punched, there's no air left. He reaches toward Emma as if to save her, but as usual, he can save no one. He can't even gather up the courage to step through the doorway.

There, reclining on Emma's bed, is Suz.

Suz in rag doll form.

Her face is made from an old pillowcase, her mouth stitched up with thin red yarn. On top of her head is a blond wig: Winnie's wig, Henry's sure. The one she left in the bathroom to dry and could never find.

But the most disturbing thing by far is the doll's eyes. Emma has taken close-up photos of the eye of the moose painting in the hall, blown them up, cut them out, and stitched them onto the plain white face. They're so like Suz's eyes: flickering amber and golden brown. Henry can almost see them move.

Emma has clothed the doll in an old sundress of Tess's—pale gray wrinkly rayon. Underneath are leggings. And—can he be seeing this right?—his own beat-up boots tied onto its stuffed sock feet. The boots Danner was named for.

He shivers.

None of them speaks.

Emma's rocking back and forth, from her heels to the balls of her feet, excitedly waiting for their response.

Finally, Tess, in a voice so meek it sounds completely unfamiliar, almost foreign to Henry, asks, "Is it . . . supposed to be anyone in particular?"

Henry holds his breath as he waits for the answer.

Emma smiles so wide her teeth glow. "It's Danner."

Chapter 54

"I'm not sure they liked you," Emma whispers, curling up against Danner, nuzzling her bunched pillowcase neck. Danner smells fresh and clean, like cedar from the little sachets her mom keeps in the linen closet. But underneath that sweet woodsy smell, there's something damp. The slight scent of decay.

"Does it matter?" Danner asks, her voice louder, clearer than ever before.

"I wanted them to. That was kind of the whole point."

But the truth is, now that she's made the sculpture—turned Danner into this solid, real-life thing—Emma feels as if her project has taken on a much deeper meaning than just trying to impress her parents. She's discovered what true art can be, and that it's so much more important than everything else.

Emma studies her handiwork in the low red glow of the clock radio. She strokes Danner's hair, the blond wig Emma found in the bathroom the day Winnie pulled her from the pool. Emma remembers the guilt she felt at taking the wig—how Danner was the one who insisted Emma stuff it under her shirt, carry it up to her room and hide it under the bed.

"What for?" Emma had asked, the damp wig pressed against the skin of her stomach.

"You'll see," Danner had promised.

Now Emma understands. Danner, whether she's a part of Emma or not, has a way of knowing what's going to happen next.

"You're real now," Emma says, holding the doll tight.

"I was always real," Danner says.

"Yeah, but now everyone can see you."

Emma thinks she sees Danner's stitched mouth twitch into a grin.

She leans in and gives Danner a kiss on the cheek, which feels cool, moist, not like a pillowcase at all.

Chapter 55

"WHERE THE HELL DID she get that wig?" Tess asks.

They're alone in the kitchen, having tried their best to convince Emma that they were genuinely pleased with her sculpture and that it was time to go to bed. They tucked her in and turned out the lights, the Danner doll nestled under the covers beside her. The Danner doll, who, Tess has to admit, looks an awful lot like Suz.

Coincidence?

There's no such thing as coincidence, babycakes.

"It's Winnie's. She left it here to dry after she jumped into the pool that day."

"Winnie's? You mean she was wearing the wig when she jumped into the pool?"

Henry nods. "When she first came back . . . she thought it would be easier, safer, if she wore a disguise."

Tess can't believe what she's hearing.

"So, what, are you telling me she was dressed like Suz?"

Henry nods again.

"Jesus! Is she crazy?"

Is Winnie the ghost she's been so afraid of? The one who painted the trees and left the knife? Who's been watching, spying, from the woods? It made perfect sense in a sickening sort of way.

And hadn't Emma just told them that Winnie knew about her sculpture project? She'd been giving Emma advice over the phone.

"I heard them on the monitor, Tess."

"Them?"

"Emma was talking to someone. It was Suz," he said. "It sounded just like her."

Tess shakes her head. "It was ten years ago, Henry. How can you be sure it was her voice?"

"I remember. I'd know it anywhere."

Of course. Of course you would.

Tess turns away.

"And what did it say? This voice that sounded like Suz?" she asks.

"It said: *They'll burn.*"

A chill overtakes Tess. "Henry, do you think—"

"Yes!" he interrupts. "That's what I've been saying all along. I think Suz has found a way back. I think that maybe . . . maybe Danner is Suz."

Tess lets out a breath of disappointed air. "That's not what I was going to ask, Henry. What I want to know is if it's possible that Emma had something to do with the fire."

Tess hates to suggest it, hates herself for thinking it, but they've got to look at the evidence. The fire didn't start itself.

"Emma? Of course not! She was asleep in her bed."

"But she wasn't asleep. She was awake, talking about burning something."

Henry shakes his head. "No! I told you—that wasn't her. It wasn't her voice, Tess. There was someone else in the room." His voice is desperate. Frantic.

"Were you drinking tonight, Henry?" she asks, pretending she can't smell the wine on him.

"No. Of course not." He's looking over her shoulder as he says it.

They're quiet for a minute.

"It's been a helluva day," Henry finally says. "I'm going to turn in." Tess watches him leave the kitchen, walk across the driveway to the barn. The motion lights in the yard don't come on, which is odd. She'll have to ask him about it in the morning.

In the chaos of the fire, no one thought to ask her where she'd been until after midnight; how it was possible that a trip to the store for bread and tea had taken nearly six hours. She picks up the phone to call Claire, then remembers her promise and stops herself. No more.

She turns to straighten the kitchen instead. Busywork. She'll be a good mother. Keep a neat and tidy house. Bake bread. Collect strawberries and rhubarb from the garden and make jam. A pie maybe. Emma loves pie.

In the morning, when she's thinking clearly, she'll try to put the pieces together: Emma and the Danner doll; Winnie; the voices in Emma's room; the fire. She remembers the voice of the fireman: *Maybe it was your daughter.* Could it have been? Or is it possible that Henry is right: that there was someone else in the room with Emma? But who? Winnie? Had Winnie started the fire?

The one thing Tess is sure of is that she needs to keep more of an eye on Emma. Tess knows her separation from Henry has been hard on their daughter, but maybe it's affected her more deeply than they realize. Maybe it's time to think about sending Emma to see someone; to admit that her quirky little compulsions and imaginary friend may be signs of trouble.

Tomorrow. She'll think about it all tomorrow. For now, she'll straighten the kitchen, then head up to bed.

Henry's left his jacket draped over the back of one of the chairs at the table. She picks it up to move it to the coat rack beside the front door. It smells strongly of smoke. And it's humming. She reaches into the right pocket. The first thing she finds is a pack of cigarettes and a lighter. When had Henry started smoking again?

Next, she discovers the source of the hum: the old baby monitor is in his pocket, turned on. She smiles at the idea of Henry the responsible father, worrying over his nine-year-old daughter while she slept. The smile fades as she recalls Henry's insistence that he heard Emma talking to Suz on the monitor.

Then, she reaches in again, feels a key. A key on a piece of red ribbon.

It's the key to the locked door of Tess's painting studio. The painting studio that just burned to the ground.

Be calm. Don't jump to conclusions.

Was it possible he got the key so the firefighters could get into the studio?

No. Henry said that by the time he called them, the building was fully engulfed. The roof had collapsed just before the first truck arrived.

"No such thing as coincidence," she says, running her fingers along the jagged teeth of the key, then placing the key in her own pocket.

Chapter 56

July 21—Cabin by the lake
The moose is almost finished. He's beautiful, really.
Lifelike. He's ten feet long, a good six feet high at the
shoulder. I started with a small platform built from
lumber that became his legs and the bottom of his torso.
Then I added a framework of curved branches to shape
the rest of his body. It was kind of like building a giant
cage on a table; a cage that happened to have a head
with a rack of antlers.

Today, we put on the canvas skin. I was thinking some
fake fur would be a good idea, but then decided it
wasn't necessary. We'll be using him in the dark and
fur won't matter. So instead, Henry picked up a gallon
of brown paint at the hardware store. There's a door
on the left side of his body that swings open and we
made his belly wide enough so that there's room for one
person to crouch inside. I've left slits in his neck to see
through.

*We know Spencer rides his bike down Route 2 every
week after his radio show. He's got a camp set up in
the woods a mile or so from the main campus. We've
been watching him. Spying from the trees, watching
him cook cans of baked beans over his pathetic little
campfire.*

*So, the plan is that we'll put the moose along the side
of the road tomorrow at midnight. He'll ride right by.
I'll be inside and I'll ask him the riddle.*

*I almost feel sorry for the asshole. He's going to shit a
brick.*

Henry closes the journal. Goes to the phone and dials Winnie's number.

"Hello?" she says sleepily. Clearly, he woke her. He tells her
about the fire. About the Danner doll.

"I think it's Suz," he says. "And I heard it speak earlier tonight."
He knows she'll understand. That she's the one person who might
believe him. Regardless of what Tess thinks, Henry knows what
he heard. He's not crazy. And it wasn't, like Tess suggested, just
Emma talking to herself. There was someone else in the room.
And that someone had a voice just like Suz's.

"Emma took your wig, Winnie. She must have found it in the
bathroom that day. She's got it on the damn doll. It's just a rag doll
stitched together by a kid, but it's so much like Suz."

She listens. Says, "Mmm-hmm," to show she hears and understands.

"There's more. Before the fire, I went out to Tess's studio. She
took the photos I'd saved from the cabin, the Polaroids of all of
us. And she's been drawing images from that summer. There was
a picture of Suz in the lake, going under."

There's silence on the other end of the line. Henry wonders if Winnie's still there. If she's drifted off to sleep. He bites the inside of his cheek.

"I don't know what I'd do if you hadn't come back," Henry tells her, almost whispering now. "You're the one person who understands. The only one I can talk to. And I wonder if maybe—"

"Henry," Winnie cuts him off, suddenly sounding wide awake. "I've been thinking. I hate to say this, but if Suz really has found a way back, she may not have the best of intentions. Think about what really happened to her that night. What if it's revenge she wants? You remember how vicious she could be when she was alive, think about what she might be capable of now that she's really got nothing to lose. I loved Suz more than life itself, you know that. But I think that if she's back, then we're all in terrible danger. We've got to find a way to stop her."

Chapter 57

TWO A.M. AND TESS lies in bed, tossing and turning, thinking over the day: Claire, the fire, the key in Henry's pocket. And the Danner doll that Henry swears is Suz somehow. Jesus. What next?

Emma said she got the idea to do her own sculpture after working on the moose yesterday. Damn moose. Tess still can't believe Winnie's putting it back together—what is she up to? Weren't they better off forgetting all about it? Leaving the poor thing to rest in peace in a pile of sticks and rotted canvas behind the cabin?

Tess remembers how he stood once, carefully erected, wooden joints aching to move, canvas skin stretched and painted, brought to life under their careful hands. *A magnificent beast,* Suz called him, echoing Spencer's own words.

Now that he is back together again, a new skin on, does his body remember, in bits and snatches, like pieces of a dream, his previous incarnation?

This is something the old Tess, the Compassionate Dismantler Tess, might have believed—that the objects we create have souls, memories.

Does the moose remember Suz inside him that night, beating like a heart? They were by the side of the road. He'd ridden in a van and was lifted carefully out by the group. Tess got her fingers pinched between his back leg and the door of the van. "Bugger!" she said, letting go of the leg, making the whole moose shift.

"We're losing him!" Henry yelped. He was beside Tess, holding the other leg, the butt of the moose resting against his chest.

"Everything okay out there?" Suz called. She and Winnie were inside the van, guiding the moose's head and front legs.

"We've got it," said Tess as she grabbed the leg again, fingers throbbing. Together they backed him out and down.

A logging truck roared by as they were unloading him, barely slowing. As if it wasn't so strange to see a group of four people lifting a stiff moose from the back of a van and putting him by the side of the road like a mile marker or a sign warning drivers about a dangerous curve or saying FOOD AHEAD, 2 MILES.

Henry pulled the van onto the edge of a small field farther down the road. Suz opened the door in the moose's chest and climbed inside. Quietly, they waited. Crickets chirped. Mosquitoes buzzed, landed on the moose's back, then flew away, confused by his lack of flesh.

Then, there was word.

"He's coming!" a shouted whisper from Henry, who was on lookout up the road. Tess ducked behind a tree as she saw Spencer rounding the bend on his bicycle, the one small headlight on the handlebars glowing dimly.

Suz shifted inside the moose. Began to call his name.

"Spen-cer," she called, her voice low and growling. "Spencer."

Then, Spencer slowed and finally stopped, still straddling his mountain bike. He had a black helmet on with a little rearview mirror clipped to it that made him look like a beetle with antennae. He looked utterly flabbergasted.

Tess watched, peeping from behind the tree, biting her lip to keep from laughing. Weeks of planning and here they were at last, pulling it off. She imagined the celebration they'd have later at the cabin, patting each other on the back, saying, *Did you see his face?*

"I have a riddle for you," Suz said, her voice muffled and strange inside the moose. "You're in a cement room with no door or windows. All you have in the room is a mirror and a table. How do you escape?"

Spencer clung to his bicycle and stared in disbelief. He was being asked a riddle by a moose. These things don't happen every day.

Tess thought that the moose, as beautiful as he was, surely couldn't have looked that realistic to Spencer, even in the dark. But maybe it didn't matter. He was held there, transfixed by the absurdity of the sight before him.

A mosquito landed on Tess's arm. Not wanting to move, she let it stay there, fattening itself on her blood.

"Answer the riddle, Spencer!" bellowed the moose.

He stood in silence for a few seconds, then jumped back on his bicycle.

"Wrong answer!" the moose told him. "Winnie!" Suz called and out of the woods stepped Winnie with the gun.

Spencer seemed almost relieved to see her, and then, as it slowly dawned on him that there was a gun pointed at his head, he looked worried. Suz swung open the door in the moose's chest and climbed out.

Tess came out from her hiding place. What the fuck was this? This was not part of the prank they'd planned. They were just supposed to let him ride off, confused and maybe a little terrified. She rubbed at the bite on her arm that itched like mad.

"Henry, go get the van," Suz ordered. "When he gets back, we shove Spencer and the bike in."

No one moved.

"What are you going to do to me?" Spencer asked.

"You couldn't answer the riddle, so you're being kidnapped," she said. "And held for ransom."

"You've gotta be kidding," Spencer said.

"Shut up!" Winnie said, putting the barrel of the rifle right against his head.

"This wasn't part of the plan," Tess argued. She looked at Suz, said, "We weren't supposed to kidnap him! We were just going to scare him, that's what you said."

"Great art is all about improvisation," said Suz.

Tess rolled her eyes, then looked to Henry, who was standing frozen, keys in his hand. "Tell her, Henry. Tell her this is too fucking much."

Stand up to her for once. Choose me this time.

Henry sucked in his cheeks, studied the ground, then walked down the road toward the van.

She had her answer.

Shit. Here she was, pregnant, in love with a man who clearly loved someone else. Fucking hopeless.

Tess made up her mind then to pack up and go. Not tell Henry about the pregnancy, just sneak off and get an abortion, see if she could still get into grad school at the Rhode Island School of Design. She was sick and fucking tired of playing second fiddle to the almighty Suz. It was time to get a clue and move on.

Henry backed the van up the road, the reverse lights coming at them like angry eyes.

"Now," Suz ordered, "let's get the moose and prisoner into the van and get the fuck out of here before someone comes along."

The moose was lifted again, into the back of the Love Machine. Spencer sat beside him, worriedly picking at a small tear in the moose's leg. Winnie was crouched, gun across her lap, watching over them, daring either Spencer or the moose to try to escape.

"Val, this is stupid," Spencer said.

"Her name is Winnie, asshole!" Suz snapped.

Henry started the van. Tess sat in the passenger seat beside him, turned so that she could see the others in the back.

"You should have answered the fucking riddle," Winnie said, and for a second, she looked almost sorry. Then she raised the gun to Spencer's head and smiled. Tess held her breath. Suz kissed Winnie on the mouth, slipped a hand down into her shirt and fondled her breast, watching Spencer, laughing.

Chapter 58

THE CLOCK ON THE dashboard says 10:21 A.M. as Winnie downshifts to get up the hill, navigates her way over the rocks and ruts in four-wheel drive. The pickup can handle a rough ride, but the sheet of window glass she's got wrapped up in the bed cannot.

She's thinking about everything Henry told her on the phone last night: the fire in Tess's studio, the Danner doll that looks just like Suz. In the back of her mind, she hears Suz say, *There's no such thing as coincidence.*

Winnie pulls up next to the cabin, turns off the truck, brushes the hair from the blond wig out of her face, and hops out of the cab. She begins unwrapping the glass and sees that it made the trip from the hardware store in one piece. Good news. She'll have the window fixed by lunchtime.

"I've got a riddle for you." The voice, muffled but firm, coming from just behind her.

Winnie turns toward the moose sculpture, every hair on her body raised.

"Four college friends form a subversive art group ten years

ago." Winnie stands frozen as a man steps out from behind the moose. He's wearing khaki trousers, a blue polo shirt, and hiking boots. His hair is short, more gray than brown.

"The funny thing is," he continues, "all of their records disappear. There's no history of them ever having attended Sexton College. But it wasn't that long ago. People remember. Other students. Faculty. They remember a group called the Compassionate Dismantlers. I talked to one man, a Professor Berussi, who remembered the group quite well. He's down in Florida now, teaching at a community college. He told me an interesting story about how he got fired from Sexton."

Winnie holds her breath.

"But what's even more interesting to me at this point is what happened to these four students after they left Sexton. Their leader seems to have dropped off the face of the earth after graduation. And the ex-boyfriend of one of the members kills himself ten years later after getting a postcard that seems to be from someone in the group. So what's going on, Val? Or should I call you Winnie?"

"Winnie's fine," she says.

"I'm Bill Lunde," he tells her, holding out his hand to shake.

Winnie takes his hand, shakes. Her own hand trembles a little and she prays he doesn't notice.

"I was hired to look into the death of Spencer Styles," Bill says. "Which, in a suicide, really means looking into his life. His family wants answers. Closure."

Winnie nods.

"What's with the disguise?" he asks.

Shit.

"It's an interesting choice. Going around town dressed as your ex-lover." Bill pulls out the old Sexton catalog with the photo of Suz and her giant wooden man on the cover.

There's a little whistling sound as Winnie has a sharp intake of air. She feels a stabbing pain in her chest. Panic in its purest form. Certain animals die from panic. Little rodents. Shrews. Voles.

She says nothing.

"It's my job to find these things out," Bill says. He doesn't sound especially proud of himself, just as if he's stating a simple fact. "I know about you and Suz. In fact, I know everything you've done since you left Vermont that summer. I know you got fired from your job at the 7-Eleven for stealing over-the-counter medications. And I know about the hospitalizations."

He says this last word slowly, emphasizing each syllable. He's talking to her, she realizes, like she's a crazy person. A little dim-witted from meds, not in touch with reality.

"What I don't know is why you came back here."

He stares at her, waiting.

"Not that it's any of your business, but I got a postcard," she tells him, her voice as level as she can make it. "Sent from Vermont. My stepmother forwarded it to me." She reaches into her purse and pulls out the tattered card, handing it over. Bill Lunde studies it, nodding.

"I decided to come back here. To try to figure out what was going on. Who might have sent the postcard. When I heard about Spencer, getting to the bottom of all this seemed even more important."

"And what did you learn?" Bill asks.

Winnie shakes her head. "Not much. Henry and Tess didn't get postcards, which I thought was strange."

Bill nods again, apparently agreeing. "So where's Suz?" he asks.

The stabbing panic pain in her chest moves up into her throat, constricting her vocal chords.

"I don't know. We all stayed here for a while after graduation, then went our separate ways. Suz said she was heading out to California. San Francisco, I think."

"And you never heard from her again? Never tried to find her?"

Winnie shakes her head. No. She didn't.

Bill pulls out his wallet, removes a card, and scribbles something on the back before handing it over.

BILL LUNDE, PRIVATE INVESTIGATOR. Then a cell phone number. On the back, he's written *Alpine Motor Court, room* 7 and the phone number there.

"Call me if you decide there's anything else you'd like to share. I'll be in town for the next few days. I've got more digging to do."

She forces a smile. "Sure. If I think of anything," she tells him, dropping the card into her purse and watching him navigate his way back down the driveway on foot.

He'll be back, babycakes.

"I know," Winnie whispers. "I'll be ready."

Chapter 59

"WHAT HAPPENED TO YOUR hand?" Erin LaBlanc asks.
Vanessa Sanchez is standing beside her and they're behind Mel
and Emma, in line for the early matinee. It seems like half their
class decided to come to the movies today, which is making Emma
squirm in her skin. Mel's already gotten the Captain Smellville
salute half a dozen times and she's got her little notebook out,
filling pages with dashes, dots, Xs and Os.

"Let's just go," Emma whispers to Mel.

Mel ignores her, keeps on scribbling in her ratty little notebook.

"Are you deaf now too, DeForge?" Erin asks, leaning so that
her face is right next to Emma's. Her breath smells like grape
bubble gum.

"I'd be more careful if I were you," Mel warns, still not looking
up from her notebook. "Emma here's kind of like a mad dog—
you never know what she'll do next."

Vanessa snorts. "Right," she says.

"Really," Mel goes on. "She went nuts and put her hand
through a window. You should have seen it. Blood everywhere!"

Emma's body stiffens.

"Really?" Vanessa asks, staring at the bandages wrapped around the knuckles of Emma's right hand.

"It was an accident," Emma says, wishing the line would move a little faster. She wants to get into the air-conditioned darkness, slouched in a padded folding seat with her Twizzlers and popcorn. She has a special way of eating each Twizzler in nine bites. And she sits with her feet tucked under her so they don't touch the floor that's sticky with god-knows-what.

"Demon possession," Mel says. Emma cranes her neck, looks at the concession stand in the next room as if she's seriously focused on the price of popcorn. Everything ends with the number 9. $1.59. $4.89.

"What are you talking about, Smellville?" Vanessa asks.

"I'm just saying it happens sometimes. Like in *The Exorcist*. One minute, you're innocently playing with a Ouija board you find in the attic, the next you're speaking ancient languages and puking green slime everywhere."

"Gross!" Erin gives a visible shiver.

"Tell me about it," Mel says.

"So, Emma, are you supposed to be possessed by the devil now?" Erin asks.

Emma's up next at the counter, so she ignores the question. "One, please," she says, passing a crinkled five-dollar bill under the Plexiglas window.

"For what movie, dear?" the old woman behind the plastic ticket window asks. Emma's mind goes blank. She stares up at the movie titles, but the letters are jumbled. Only the numbers seem clear.

"The one o'clock," Emma says, squinting at the sign. "The animal movie."

"Nah, it's not the devil," Mel tells the other girls behind her. "She's possessed by Danner."

"What's a danner?" Erin asks.

Emma's skin gets all prickly, as if there are bugs under it. Little microscopic ones crawling in and out of her pores.

Emma walks over to the concession stand, orders a Coke, Twizzlers, and a small popcorn, no butter. Behind her, the three girls are snickering together. *Mental,* she hears one of them say.

How could Mel, of all people, betray her? Captain Smellville herself, who wears fake glasses, cuts her own hair, and never takes showers. It's not as if she's got other girls busting down her door, begging her to hang out with them. She and Emma have always been best friends—the two odd girls out, destined to stick to-gether, no matter what.

Emma heads down the carpeted hallway, past the bathrooms and through the double doors into theater 2. It's crowded with kids, laughing, throwing popcorn. She sees a lot of faces she knows from the elementary and middle school. Dicky Jarvis is there—his mom is the accountant for DeForge Painting.

Emma likes to sit in the very back row, but all the seats are taken. She finds three open ones toward the middle and darts into one of them, not sure if Mel will be able to find her, secretly hoping she won't. She tucks her feet under her and puts her head down, studying the ingredients listed on the Twizzler package: corn syrup, wheat flour, sugar, cornstarch, artificial flavors and colors. *A low-fat candy,* it says. She opens the wrapper, takes out the first one and puts it in her pocket. There are ten in a package and she never eats the first one. Bad luck.

The lights go down. The sound comes on, crackly and too loud, giving a message about turning off cell phones, not talking during the movie. *Be considerate,* says a man's voice, booming in her ears. *Be considerate.*

"There you are," Mel says, plopping into the seat beside her. Emma doesn't answer. She keeps her eyes focused on the screen. Previews. Some robot movie that looks like it might be okay, if you like robots, which Emma really doesn't. Emma feels for the single Twizzler in the pocket of her jeans, thinks of giving it to Mel, but begins to pick it apart instead. Mel's shoving handfuls of popcorn into her mouth, letting kernels fall onto the floor. It's gross. Definitely not considerate.

"I know what you're thinking," Mel whispers, her mouth full of half-chewed popcorn. Emma keeps her eyes on the screen. "You're wishing it was her here instead of me."

"What?" Emma asks. "Who?"

The movie's begun now. Someone behind her says, "Shhh!"

"Your stupid doll," Mel says. "Maybe you two should go out on a date. Make out or something." Mel shoves another handful of popcorn in.

So that's what this is about. Danner. Emma should have guessed. Mel's been acting strange since Emma showed the sculpture to her just before they left for the movies.

"What the hell is this supposed to be?" Mel had asked.

"It's art. A sculpture."

"It's creepy as shit, Em. Who's it supposed to be?"

Emma bit her lip.

Mel shook her head. "No way. You did *not* go and turn your invisible friend into a giant-ass voodoo doll."

Emma shrugged. They went downstairs, got into Emma's mom's car, and headed to the movies without speaking another word.

Emma rips at the Twizzler in her pocket, which is now in sticky shreds.

"Excuse us," Vanessa says as she squeezes by, toward the two empty seats at the end of the row.

Great. Just great. Emma looks down at the red exit signs to the right and left of the screen, wondering if it's possible to make an escape.

Emma can't focus. The movie is stupid anyway. Animals doing

martial arts. Right. The panda bear gets hit in the crotch and the theater explodes into laughter. Emma closes her eyes.

Someone pinches her arm. "Ow!" she yelps.

"Shh!" hisses the woman behind her.

The skin on Emma's arm is twisted this time, what everyone calls an Indian burn when there aren't adults around, and she doesn't need to look to see who's doing it. Danner. Emma looks anyway, shakes her head. *No.*

"Go away," she whispers.

"You go away! It was your idea to come to the stupid movies anyway!" Mel says.

"Not you," Emma whispers.

"If you can't be quiet, I'm going to get the manager to kick you out," says the woman behind them.

Danner laughs. She's wearing Emma's lime green bathing suit, swimming goggles, and Emma's mom's white rubber bathing cap with flowers on it.

Emma thinks that maybe if she doesn't look at her for long enough, Danner will go away. She focuses her eyes on the screen, but can't tell what's going on. It's all just colors and shapes, none of it making sense. Maybe she needs glasses. She sinks down into her seat, closes her eyes.

Beside her, Danner makes a wet, sucking sound. Slime through a straw. Mucus in the back of a throat. There's a rasping gurgle and Emma closes her eyes tighter, starts rocking in her seat.

This is not happening. Not here.

It's your imagination, she tells herself.

She remembers Danner's words: *Everything you have is mine.*

"If we're the same, then I created you and I can make you go away," she whispers.

Then the smell hits her. Rot. Stagnant water. Something long dead pulled from the bottom of a well: a lost kitten, a baby no one wanted.

Stop it, she tells herself. *Enough.*

"Go away," she whispers to Danner. "This isn't funny anymore."

"Damn right it isn't," Mel says.

"Shh!" scolds the woman behind them.

Emma covers her nose and mouth with her hand. Feels her stomach churn, the Twizzlers and popcorn dangerously close to coming back up. She opens her eyes a little, squints at the warm glow of the exit signs, imagines pushing through one of them into the cool, brick alley behind the theater. But in order to get there, she'd have to go past Danner.

Her arm is being pinched again, the skin just below the wrist bone grabbed and twisted. She looks down. Sees a pale hand, whiter than white, skin loose and sticking to the skin of her own arm, which Emma jerks away. Danner's skin is still stuck to Emma's arm, flapping like tiny, pale flags. Danner reaches for Emma again with her hand, which is just raw, oozing flesh.

Emma screams and lunges out of her seat. She trips on Mel's legs and goes down, hitting her face on the seat in the row in front of them, landing on the floor, tacky with spilled soda, butter-flavored oil, and grime. She screams again. The hand reaches for her, doesn't let go this time. Emma clamps her eyes shut tight—it's pulling her up, toward its body. She kicks, claws, lashes out at the creature grabbing hold of her. This is not Danner, this thing. This cannot be Danner.

She's stuck upside down in the inner tube again, her head underwater.

Everything you have is mine.

She hears voices coming at her in waves and ripples, a steady hum of words: *parents, doctor, hurt, friend.* Then she hears someone say, *Danner.* She opens her eyes. It's Mel's face above her; Mel's hand on her arm. Vanessa and Erin are there, and a movie theater employee with a flashlight.

It's not until they've led her into the bright sunlit lobby, framed posters of coming attractions looking on, that she notices Mel's face. It's all scratched up. So is her arm. One of the girls from the concession stand is handing Mel a cold cloth.

The old woman who sells the tickets is there, along with a portly guy in a tight blue suit who is asking for Emma's name and phone number. Emma feels as if she's still stuck underwater, and everyone else is way up at the surface, looking down. The words take a long time to reach her. If she opens her mouth, she's sure all that will come out will be sad little bubbles, no sound.

"Emma DeForge," Erin says. "I don't know her number, but she lives in Langley on Route 2. She's a total mental case. For real."

"Oh my god," Vanessa cries. "Look. She peed herself!"

No, Emma wants to explain. *I'm just wet from the water. From being under the water.*

The manager guy in the suit pats Emma's arm lightly, barely touching it. "Do you have a history of seizures, hon?"

Emma shakes her head.

"Don't worry. I'm going to call your parents," he tells her, departing to an office in the back. She wants to ask him not to, to follow him into the office and say, *See, my parents are splitting up and if you call them, if they hear about this, then that'll be the final straw, so please don't, they don't need a crazy daughter right now.* But the guy is gone, the office door closed. The old woman and the concession girl are staring at her with pity on their faces. Erin and Vanessa are whispering, shaking their heads. Vanessa takes a cell phone out of her purse, punches in a number, and says into it, "Hey, I'm at the movies and you are not going to believe what just happened . . ."

Emma looks at Mel, at the ragged red scratches covering her face and arm. Then she looks down at the tips of her own fingers, sees blood there under her neatly trimmed nails.

"Let me guess," Mel says, taking a step back, away from Emma, her face twisted with fear and disgust. "Danner made you do it."

Chapter 60

"WHAT WAS SPENCER'S ROLE in the group?" Bill asks.

They're sitting at the kitchen table. Tess has made them coffee. Put out some fancy European cookies from a blue tin, cookies she picked up at the market yesterday, just before seeing the flowers. Just before her decision to go see Claire.

Stop. Don't think about that. Focus.

The trick, she thought, was not to treat Bill as an inquisitor, but as a guest.

"Cream?" she asks, holding the little ceramic pitcher. He shakes his head.

When Bill showed up unexpectedly just after Tess dropped the girls off at the movies, Tess instantly recognized him as the man who'd been watching her at the farmers' market Saturday. If he'd been furtively following her around town he must think she had something to hide. And if he's been up to the college, there's no telling how much he knows already. He's calling them a group, but hasn't actually mentioned the Compassionate Dismantlers yet, which Tess takes as a good sign.

"Spencer wasn't ever really a part of the group," Tess says, remembering Suz's own words: *A lie works best if there's a piece of truth woven into it.* "He was kind of in the background. Not a key player."

"Not. A. Key. Player." Bill writes the quote down in his little notebook, nodding.

Tess glances at her watch—1:15. She adds a spoonful of sugar to her coffee even though she doesn't take sugar. Her nervous hands need something to do. She stirs a little too long, the spoon chinking against the heavy ceramic mug.

"I understand you had a little fire here last night," Bill says, looking up from his notes. His eyes are pure pale blue, like the sky.

His question throws her off. This is not something she practiced for.

"My studio was destroyed," Tess says. "The firemen think it started from a candle I left burning."

"So they don't suspect arson?"

"Arson! No. Not at all. It was an accident."

Bill nods. "Do you know all of your motion lights are broken?"

"I'm sorry?" Tess is outmaneuvered. Just like that.

"Shattered. Shot out maybe. Or they could have been broken by someone throwing rocks. Someone with excellent aim." He gazes at her, waiting.

Sweat forms at her hairline and on her upper lip.

Shot out maybe. Someone with excellent aim.

Tess closes her eyes, sees Suz going under. Henry diving in after her. When she opens them again two seconds later, Henry is there, in the kitchen, not dripping wet from the lake, but dressed in painting clothes. Good, dependable Henry who has been out with a crew.

"Henry," Tess all but gasps. "This is Bill. Bill Lunde. The private investigator Spencer's family hired."

Henry nods. "We've met." Henry gives Bill his hand to shake.

"Oh, sorry," Tess says, flustered. "Of course you have."

"What would you say Spencer Styles's role in the Compassionate Dismantlers was?" Bill asks.

Tess takes in a sharp, panicked breath. Okay, she tells herself. So he knows about the Dismantlers. It's not the end of the world.

Not yet.

Henry stands back against the counter, bracing himself.

"Spencer was not a key player," Henry tells him.

Bill just stares at him, then moves his eyes to Tess. He makes a show of writing the words in his little notebook: "Not. A. Key. Player."

"It wasn't much of a *group,* really," Henry adds.

"What's that?" Bill asks.

"The Compassionate Dismantlers. Suz came up with the name. But what we really were was a group of friends making art together. Nothing formal. Nothing too organized."

Bill nods, closes his notebook, stands up. "Thank you both for your time. I can see myself out," he tells them.

"Jesus," Tess hisses in an angry whisper once Bill's gone. "He didn't believe a fucking word we said! We're screwed!"

"You don't know that," Henry says.

"Damn. Damn!" Tess says. "We should have been more prepared."

Henry looks down at his shoes.

"Did you know the lights are broken?" she asks.

"What lights?"

"The security lights. Outside. Bill says they've all been shot out. Or broken with rocks."

Henry's face grows pale.

The phone rings and they both jump.

"I'll get it," Tess says. As she's reaching for it, she watches as Henry opens the sliding door in the kitchen and steps out onto the patio.

"Hello?" she says.

"Mrs. DeForge?" A man's voice.

"Yes."

"My name is David Macallister. I'm the manager of the Star Theater."

Tess watches Henry moving around the yard, looking up at the lights, bending down to study the ground, looking more frightened by the second.

"I'm afraid there's been some trouble with your daughter."

Chapter 61

HE'S FINGERING THE THICK shards of broken lightbulb on the walkway, looking up at the light mounted above the front door, when he sees it. There, up in Emma's bedroom window, a figure with blond hair looks down at him. Smiles and waves.

His heart comes up into his throat, making his breath wet and whistley, his lungs desperate for air.

He looks down at his hand, sees he's gripped the shards of glass so tightly that they've cut open his palm. Dropping the glass, he goes through the front door, past Tess, who has her bag slung over her shoulder.

"I have to go get Em," she says. "The manager of the movie theater just called. He said she had some sort of . . . episode."

"Episode?" Henry repeats, stopping. He's at the foot of the stairs, hand on the railing.

"I don't know much. He insists she's fine now, but I'm going to go get her."

"Okay," he tells her, starting up the stairs.

"Henry, your hand is bleeding," she calls after him.

He grunts a "Nothing serious" back to her and takes the stairs two at a time. The front door closes behind him. He reaches the carpeted hallway. Hears Tess start the Volvo in the driveway. Taking a left into the bathroom, he unrolls a few feet of toilet paper and quickly wraps up his bleeding hand. Good enough for now.

Stepping back into the hallway, he sees that the door to Emma's bedroom is closed. The DO NOT DISTURB sign is up again.

Maybe he should heed the warning.

DO NOT DISTURB.

"Fuck that," Henry mumbles, trying the doorknob. If it's locked, he'll break it down. But the knob turns easily in his toilet-paper-wrapped hand. He bites down on the inside of his left cheek and swings the door open, into the room.

He lets go of the doorknob, sees he's left it sticky with blood. The toilet paper is soaked through, beginning to disintegrate.

"Hello?" he calls from the doorway, leaning in but not yet stepping across the threshold.

Nothing. The room is empty.

The computer at Emma's desk is on, bright little creatures bounce and scamper across the glowing screen. Fragments of tinkly, happy music are playing in a loop. One of Emma's damn games.

Henry holds his breath, steps into the room. Turning to the right, he glances into the open closet. Nothing but clothes on hooks and hangers, a pile of shoes, a milk crate of abandoned stuffed animals and toys. Everything in perfect order. A little too perfect.

The endless music on the computer game is torturous and Henry steps over to the desk and uses the mouse to close the game. She's got another program open behind it. It's an online health-information site—an article about hallucinations. He scans it, his eyes falling on the lines: *Patients suffering from psychotic disorders such as schizophrenia frequently experience hallucinations. Hallucinations can also occur in patients as the result of stress or exhaustion.*

Does Emma think she's seeing things? And more important, what is it she thinks she's seeing?

Stepping away from the computer, Henry moves into the center of the room, studies the empty bed, neatly made. There, on the far side of it, as if she'd just tumbled off the bed, is the Danner doll, facedown on the floor, under the window.

"Jesus," he gasps, frozen in place.

A drop of blood falls from his hand onto the carpet.

Just a doll. Only a doll.

Bullshit. It's a doll that speaks. Can get up and wave.

He hears Tess's voice in his head, her constant refrain: *You're overreacting, Henry.*

"Right," he tells this imaginary Tess. "I'm sure it's just stress and exhaustion."

Every muscle in his body is flooded with the urge to run. Get the fuck out of there. Forget all about the wave from the window. Go back into the bathroom and clean up his hand, get some real bandages on, leaving the door to Emma's room shut tightly behind him.

DO NOT DISTURB.

But no. Henry forces himself to step forward. He nudges the doll's torso with his foot. Solid. Unmoving.

Or almost unmoving.

He's sure her right arm twitches a little. The hands are a pair of Tess's old canvas gardening gloves stained green. He steps back, kicks the doll harder this time. No movement. But damn, the thing is solid.

Just a doll, Henry tells himself.

He takes in a breath, drops down to his knees, and places a hand on its shoulder and feels the slightest quiver, a thrum, like electricity.

He snatches his fingers away.

"Fuck!"

He bends down again, forcing himself to touch the thing, to roll it over. It's solid. Like an actual flesh-and-blood person. Only heavier somehow. Like dead weight. At last, the doll flips, its neck twisting, head following along so that the eyes are looking up at last. But the eyes do not seem to gaze blankly at the ceiling. The eyes are looking straight at Henry.

He jumps back, letting out a little yelp.

"Daddy?"

Emma has come into the room behind him.

Henry backs slowly away from the Danner doll thing, turns to face his daughter. Her face is red and puffy, the bandages on her hand are coming unraveled.

"What are you doing here?" he asks, his voice sharp, accusatory. Emma takes a step back, frightened. He softens his voice. "Mom just left to pick you up."

"I got a ride. From Winnie."

"Winnie? What was she doing there?"

"I called her. From the movie theater. She was in town doing errands anyway, so it wasn't a big deal."

"Well, your mom's gonna freak when she realizes you're not there. The manager from the movie theater called here."

Emma's chin starts to quiver. "I was hoping he wouldn't get through. I didn't want to bug you guys. It was nothing, really. And Winnie . . . she'd told me to call her anytime, if I ever needed anything."

Henry nods. "I'll handle your mother," he promises, trying to make his voice as level as he can. "So what happened at the movies?" he asks.

"I guess I kind of fainted or something," she says. "Um, Dad?"

"Yeah?" his eyes shift nervously toward the doll.

"You're kind of bleeding all over my room."

"Sorry," he says, looking down at his hand, scraps of bloody toilet paper hanging from it. "I had a little accident outside."

"Twins," she says, holding up her own bandaged hand, giving him a weak smile.

"Your doll," Henry says, "why is it so heavy?" His mouth is sticky, making it hard to talk.

"Sand," Emma tells him. "I filled her with Ziploc bags of sand. From my old sandbox."

Everything in Emma's room gets dark and wavy. Henry hears himself speak in some other dimension: *We've got to weight her down. So she won't float.*

"Dad, are you all right?"

He can't answer. He's underwater again. And this time, the Danner doll is down there with him.

Chapter 62

EMMA IS ON HER hands and knees, dabbing a Q-tip soaked in hydrogen peroxide onto the spots of blood her dad left on her carpet. What had he even been doing in her room anyway? And how did Danner get on the floor?

"He didn't hurt you, did he?" she asks Danner, who's back up on the bed now.

The doll is silent.

Emma goes back to cleaning the rug. When the hydrogen peroxide hits the blood, it bubbles and takes the stain away. Then she scrubs the spot with a clean, damp cloth.

Her head is pounding. Even now that she's showered and changed her clothes, she still feels dirty. Her parents' voices in the kitchen come up through the floor, muffled, but clear enough for her to get the gist of what they're arguing about. She hears her name again and again.

Leaving Danner, the Q-tips, peroxide, and drops of blood, she sneaks out into the hall and makes her way to the top of the stairs where she crouches, listening.

"I'm not talking about shock treatments or anything, Henry," her mom says. "I'm just saying she needs to be evaluated. We can't ignore her behaviors any longer. Especially not now that they've become . . . dangerous."

"Emma's not dangerous," her dad says.

"She attacked Mel, Henry. They said she was hysterical. Screaming. Rolling around on the floor. She wet her pants, for God's sake. Think how humiliated she must have been! Maybe it's not psychiatric. Maybe there's something neurological going on, seizures or something. You're the one who's been fixated for years on her obsession with Danner—what if Danner is some kind of, I don't know, *symptom*?"

"It's not a doctor she needs," her dad says.

"Well, what do you propose? A shaman? An exorcist maybe? Jesus, Henry. Our little girl is sick! If she had a broken arm, you'd be rushing her to the ER. This is no different. You need to start taking this seriously."

"I *am* taking it seriously," her dad says.

"We're not just talking about an imaginary friend anymore. We're talking violent behavior, the possibility that she set the fire . . ."

"Emma didn't start the fire."

"I know you want to protect her, Henry. I know you do, God knows I do too. But if she needs help, it's just going to make things worse."

"That's not it." Her dad sighs.

"Mel told me what really happened out at the cabin. How could you lie to me like that? Is there anything else you're not telling me?"

"There's nothing else."

"Doesn't the fact that Emma put her fist through a window and claimed to have no memory of doing it concern you? Jesus! How could you not share that with me? I'm her mother, for Christ sakes!"

Emma hears the sound of a chair scraping on the tiled floor.

"It was an accident," her dad says.

"Mel told me Emma was watching you through the window. You and Winnie. What did Em see, Henry? What did Emma see that would make her so angry she'd punch through a window?"

"Nothing," her father says, his voice high and tight, like a little boy's.

"And why the hell would Emma call Winnie, not us, from the theater? Worse than that—why would Winnie pick her up without checking in with us?"

"I don't know any more about it than you do, Tess. I'm sorry."

There's silence, then more sounds of chairs being moved, cups being put in the sink. Sometimes, when her mom gets mad, she starts cleaning and doing dishes. When her mom puts on her rubber gloves and gets out the Comet, Emma knows it's time to duck and run.

Emma retreats back down the hall to her room. Behind her, she hears her mom say she's going out. The front door slams. The Volvo starts in the driveway.

"My mom thinks I'm going crazy," she tells Danner. "She thinks I set the fire in her studio."

"Did you?" Danner asks.

Emma shakes her head. "Of course not."

"Are you sure?" Danner asks.

Emma bites her lip and thinks. If her hand hadn't been cut, she would have been sure that she couldn't have really put her hand through the window. And until seeing Mel's face and arm all scratched up today, she would never have believed that she would ever do anything to hurt her best friend.

"I don't know what to think anymore," Emma confesses.

Danner smiles. "Now we're getting somewhere."

Chapter 63

TESS ISN'T SURE THE Volvo will make it up the logging road, so she parks at the bottom and hikes up. It's steeper and farther than she remembers, but she takes pleasure in her aching legs and labored breathing.

When she gets back home, she'll call the pediatrician and make an appointment to take Emma in. He'll know what sort of tests to do; what evaluations might be needed. They've got to get a handle on this thing before it gets any worse.

And maybe Henry's right—maybe Emma didn't have anything to do with the fire.

She remembers what Bill said about the broken lights: *someone with excellent aim.* In her mind, she sees Winnie leaning out of the window of Henry's old van with her gun, taking aim, firing at some impossibly far-off target, which she hit every time. *The world's only poet sniper!* Suz would say.

When Tess crests the hill and catches sight of the old cabin, sees the moose standing guard, she thinks maybe the journey was not just upward, but backward, through time. She's twenty-two all over again. In love with her life, with the possibilities it holds.

She'll swing open the door to the cabin and find Henry with shaggy hair and beard, Winnie with her rifle, and Suz throttling a bottle of tequila, laughing but sincere, promising them that the only way to really love a thing is to undo it, unwind it, break it down, tear it the fuck up.

The cats encircle her as she gets to the door; a living, mewing, purring moat she must cross. She bends down to touch them: little Tasha, Carrot, so many others whose names she doesn't know. It was a miracle they had survived, and if this miracle had occurred, why not another?

She stands. Keeps moving while the cats rub against her ankles, the low drone of their purrs reminding her of the sound Suz used to make when she was painting or sculpting: the static noise.

Tess jogs up the steps and doesn't knock, just pushes the door open and walks inside, half thinking she might catch up with the past if she hurries.

What she sees makes her gasp, believe in the impossible. Suz is sitting at the table, writing in a journal. Blond hair, silk tunic, combat boots. She looks up, startled. Then she gives a wink.

"I've been wondering when you were going to show up, Tess," she says.

And Tess wants to run, screaming, but she's held to the spot by the idea that it's somehow more frightening to leave. Like the cats are guarding the door, vicious beasts with foaming mouths and fangs.

Everything in the cabin is eerily the same. The four chairs are set up around the table, the white ceramic dishes stolen from the Sexton cafeteria are stacked on the shelves. There's even a pack of Drum tobacco on the table, next to an ashtray.

Tess's eyes search the back corner of the kitchen for the dreaded aquarium, but it's gone. Thank god.

She hears the static noise again, this time in her own head: a radio tuned to a place between stations.

Neither here nor there.

Not present. Not past.

Tess steps forward, closer to Suz, thinking that if she moves, the sound in her head will go away.

Up close, she sees that this is not Suz at all. Just the idea of Suz. Winnie in disguise.

"I want you to leave my family alone," Tess tells Winnie, remembering at last why she came. Her voice sounds strong and even, which surprises her. "If I catch you trespassing on my land, going anywhere near my little girl, I'll shoot you myself. Do you understand?"

Winnie nods. The blond wig slips a little.

"You're pathetic," Tess tells her. "I don't know what you could have been thinking, sending those postcards, coming back here to the cabin. What did you possibly have to gain?"

Winnie shakes her head. "You've got it wrong."

"If I find out you had anything to do with the fire in my studio, or that you snuck into my daughter's room that night—"

"No! I wasn't anywhere near your house, Tess. I would never do anything like that to you or Emma. I adore Emma!"

Tess takes in a breath, tries to see through the bright white glare of rage. Her hands are clenched into aching fists, her fingernails clawing her palms.

"You come near Emma again and I will kill you."

"Tess, if you'll just sit down a minute and listen. Something's going on. I think . . . I think maybe Suz has found a way back. Henry thinks so too. And I'm starting to wonder if Emma's relationship with Danner has something to do with Suz."

The buzzing sound intensifies.

Tess gives a disgusted laugh. "Right, Winnie. You know what? You and Henry can play whatever sick little game of make-believe you want, but leave me and my daughter out of it. I'm not playing anymore. Understand?"

"But, Tess, I'm telling you, she's back! You've got to listen. If not for your sake, then for Emma's."

Tess moves without thinking. She lunges forward, rotates her hips, puts all of her power into a right hook that hits Winnie square on the jaw, sends her toppling off the chair.

Tess stands, clutching her aching fist, shocked by what she's done. The buzzing sound in her ears turns to laughter.

Tear it up, babycakes.

Winnie is lying crumpled on the floor, hands covering her face. The wig has come off and lays beside her like a stunned animal.

Tess stands, frozen, muscles quivering.

You can tear it up, knock it down, bury it deep in the lake, but it comes back. You can't fight the past.

Winnie moans at Tess's feet.

Tess hurries out the cabin door, through the cats who seem to be calling to her as she runs back down the hill. *How could you forget us,* they screech. She covers her ears with her hands and runs harder, faster, until at last, she reaches the safety of her car.

Chapter 64

"WHAT?" MEL SNAPS INTO the phone.

"I'll get the book. Tonight."

Mel laughs. "I don't care about the stupid book. Do whatever you want."

"I'm sorry," Emma says. "For what happened in the movie theater today. I thought . . ."

"You thought what, Em?"

"You didn't see anything weird?" Emma asks. "Smell anything?"

Mel gives a disgusted snort. "Right! The only thing I saw was you falling out of your seat and rolling around on the ground screaming like a mental case. I tried to pull you up and you attacked me. What I smelled was a huge load of bullshit—you're no more crazy than I am. You just want attention and you think that somehow these little stunts are gonna help get your parents back together."

"What? No . . . I—"

"News flash, DeForge: your parents are not getting back together. They can't stand each other. And if you're not careful, they'll end up not being able to stand *you!*"

Mel slams the phone down, sending a screech through the wires that goes straight into Emma's ear; an electronic viper that jumps around in her head, chasing everything else in there away.

"Nine," she says weakly, hanging up her phone. "Eighteen. Twenty-seven. Thirty-six."

"Quit counting!" the voice behind her says. Emma turns, sees the Danner sculpture lounging on her bed. "No wonder your parents think you're nuts. I thought you wanted to help them. I thought you were ready to find out the truth."

"My parents think I'm nuts thanks to you! What were you *doing* at the movies? You scared me so bad, Danner. I thought you were going to . . ." She can't say it: *kill me.* "To hurt me. I hope I *am* crazy and you're nothing but a hallucination! They'll give me some medicine and you'll go away forever; how would you like that?"

Danner laughs—a sound that fills the room, makes the air vibrate, causes each and every hair on Emma's body to stand on end. "I'm as real as you are," Danner says. "And soon everyone will know it."

Chapter 65

June 17—Cabin by the lake
Bumper sticker in the post office parking lot today: If you
love something, set it free. I took out my trusty Sharpie,
crossed out "set it free" and wrote "tear it apart."

Just tear it the fuck apart.

Henry snaps the journal closed and goes to answer the phone.

"Henry, it's Winnie. Tess was just here."

"Jesus." The wine in Henry's coffee mug sloshes over the side. "When she left here, she was really pissed about you picking up Emma at the movies. Why would you do that without calling us?"

"Emma called me on my cell, crying and desperate. She just wanted to get out of there. Sounds like it was a horrible scene for her. I was only two blocks away. I just wanted to help, Henry. Anyway, she attacked me, Henry."

"Emma?"

"No! Tess. She nearly knocked me out."

"Oh my god, are you okay?" He's seen Tess hit the bag. Knows the power behind those punches. The unleashed fury she's capable of.

"Fine. Bruised and swollen, but nothing's broken. Henry, she threatened to shoot me if I come near Emma again. She thinks I sent the postcards. She also thinks I burned down her studio last night."

"Jesus," he says again without thinking.

Tess thinks Winnie sent the cards. Winnie thinks it's Tess.

Henry's head is spinning too much to know what to think. He's just doing his best to keep up with everyone else.

"And that detective was here earlier," Winnie says. "I think he knows more than he's letting on. It's just a matter of time until he figures everything out."

"I know. He was here. Tess and I stuck to our stories, but it's as if he knew we were lying."

"Look, I've gotta get away from here. Go back to Boston or something. It's getting too crazy. Before I leave, I want to float the moose out on the lake and burn it. Put in the wig and the clothes of Suz's I've been wearing. Everything left from that summer. Maybe . . . I know this might sound crazy, but maybe we should put Emma's doll in there too."

Henry takes a deep breath, lets it out slowly. Remembers the face he's sure he saw in Emma's window. The blond woman who gave him a smile and a wave.

Hallucinations can also occur in patients as the result of stress or exhaustion.

"Emma's so damned attached to that doll," he says.

"I know . . . I just thought that since it looks so much like Suz, since you think you heard it speak in her voice . . ."

If Emma ever found out, she'd never forgive him.

He remembers the weight of the doll. How solid she was.

Sand. I filled her with Ziploc bags of sand.

"I've got Suz's journal," Henry tells Winnie. "We should throw that in too. Maybe that's even better than the doll."

"You've got her journal?"

"Yeah. I took it when Tess and I went back to the cabin just before Emma was born."

There's a long pause. Henry holds his breath. Does Winnie think of him as a criminal now?

We're all criminals, Tess has said.

"Okay," Winnie says. "Tomorrow night. We'll take the canoe and the moose down in the afternoon and get it all set up. Then meet back at the lake after dark. I'll head home to Boston right after."

Henry feels a pinprick of pain start behind his left eye.

"Are you sure?" he asks her.

"About burning the moose? Of course. I think it's what we need to do. If Suz really has come back then I think this may help her to move on."

"No." Henry palms his eye, trying to squelch the growing pain there. "Are you sure you have to leave?"

Conspiring with Winnie—sharing secrets, planning to burn the moose out on the lake—has brought him right back to those days with Suz, plotting and planning their next dismantling mission. It's reminded him of who he used to be, made him feel alive in a way he hasn't in a long, long time. He's not ready to let it all go again.

"Henry . . . I've been thinking about what you said. How the messages from Suz look like they're in my handwriting. What if it *is* me? What if I'm—I don't know—channeling Suz in some way, blacking out whenever I'm her. I could be doing anything. Going anywhere. This morning, I got up and couldn't find my keys. I had to go to town to buy glass to fix the window. I finally found them in the truck. In the ignition."

"So you left them there and forgot," Henry says.

"No. I would never leave keys in the car. Anyway, almost half a tank of gas was gone. And there were cigarette butts in the ashtray. Except for the one you gave me the other night, I haven't smoked since college."

Henry considers this. "Are you taking any medications?" he asks. "I've heard stories about people on Ambien doing stuff like this."

"No, Henry. I'm not taking anything. I don't even drink anymore."

"So, what, you think maybe you're driving around in some kind of fugue state?"

"I don't know. But whatever's happening, it's scary as hell. And I think the best thing is for me to get out of town."

"This doesn't sound like you, Winnie. Turning and running."

He pictures her Compassionate Dismantler self, strong and brave, gun in hand, not afraid of anything. Refusing to back down.

"Sometimes," Winnie says, her voice breaking a little, "the thing you're up against is too big. The bravest thing left to do is surrender."

Chapter 66

NEARLY MIDNIGHT. TESS HAS worked out, showered, watched the evening news; now she lies alone in her bed, tossing and turning. Her hand throbs from hitting Winnie. Since returning from the cabin, Henry's been avoiding her. She's sure Winnie called and told him what happened. Now Henry's acting afraid of her, as if she's supposed to be the enemy. Shit.

She called the pediatrician and made an appointment for Emma tomorrow afternoon. She's decided not to tell Henry—she'll just take Em herself. Once there's a plan in place, she'll let Henry know and he'll have to accept it, whatever the outcome.

The worst thing is that in spite of all these distractions, Tess cannot get Claire out of her mind. She imagines she now knows what addicts must feel like. She needs a fix. Her whole body is screaming for it.

Claire. She needs Claire.

"Get over it," she tells herself. Remember the promise you made.

She rises from the bed slowly, looks out the window at Henry's barn where she sees cracks of light leaking from around the windows covered in black plastic. She should explain things to him. Tell him why she went to the cabin, why she hit Winnie. Make him see that it's Winnie who's behind all this—it's got to be Winnie.

Once upon a time, Tess and Henry were allies. It was the two of them against the world. And she believed, she truly believed, that somehow they were safe.

Daddy makes all the bad things go away.

She pads softly down the hall, down the steps and into the kitchen thinking she'll make some tea and call Henry at the barn. Maybe once he's settled in at the table, she'll say, *Do you remember the dream you told me about the day we met—about being a cow in a field? Do you still think about it? Wonder if maybe there's some other life than this that we're a part of?*

But that's not what she does. Instead, she grabs the cordless phone off the wall and punches in Claire's number.

"Hello?" Claire says.

Tess wants to speak, but she has promised to give up her lover. Promised God. But does Tess even believe in God? Would He forgive all the terrible things she's done?

She breathes into the phone, wraps her aching hand around it.

It's not God's forgiveness she wants.

"Tess? Is that you?" Claire asks.

"I . . . I can't do this," Tess says.

"I miss you," Claire says. "My whole body misses you. Do you know what I mean, Tess?"

"What am I supposed to do?" Tess asks, gripping the phone tighter.

"What do you want, Tess?"

"You," Tess answers simply. "I want you."

"Sometimes I think," Claire says, "that everything happens for a reason. From the hummingbird that catches your eye first thing in the morning to the way the two most unlikely people in the world are thrown together because they're the only two who can save each other. Do you know what I'm saying, Tess?"

"Yes," she mumbles back. A tear runs down her cheek, seems to fall in slow motion, then splatters on the tile floor.

"Do you want to be saved, Tess?"

"Yes." The word is a gasped intake of air. Another tear falls to the ground.

"Come see me. Right now."

"But Emma . . ."

"I'll be waiting, Tess." Then she hangs up.

Tess holds the phone in her hand a minute, listening to the dial tone. Then she calls the barn.

"It's me," she says when Henry picks up. "Look, I need to go out. I'll be back by breakfast. Can you come sleep on the couch, just be here with Em?"

"Of course."

She expects a barrage of questions, but all Henry says is, "I'll be over in ten minutes."

Chapter 67

THE HOUSE IS TOO quiet. He settles in on the couch, turns on the TV. The Weather Channel, volume low so he doesn't wake Emma. There's a chill in the room. He gets up, climbs the stairs, and grabs a blanket from the linen closet, then pads down the hall to check on Emma. He gently pushes open the door, peeks in at his sleeping daughter. She's alone in her bed, no sign of the Danner doll. Thank God. Her eyes move behind pale lids, her lips purse together, then relax. She kicks the covers off, sighs. Henry leans over, kisses her damp forehead, then steps back out of the room, pulling the door closed behind him.

Back down on the couch, he can't get to sleep. He keeps hearing things: rustling, creaking. Just the old house settling. Mice. Emma's kitten maybe. Thor. What the hell kind of name is that for a little flea-bitten kitten?

Henry finds the remote and turns it up, catches only some of the words: frontal system, cyclonic.

He should have asked Tess where she was going. And where was she last night when her studio burned to the ground? He should have demanded answers. Is she having an affair? Or is it something more sinister?

We're all criminals, Henry. Or have you forgotten?

He hears a floorboard creak. The sound of shoes scuffling across a hard surface.

Footsteps. Definite footsteps. A shuffle-drag, quiet tiptoeing walk coming from the kitchen.

He closes his eyes tight, firmly instructs his brain to shut up and go to sleep already.

More sounds from the kitchen: a rustle and scrape.

Emma's upstairs. He remembers what she told them the night of the fire: *Danner says it will be worse next time. She says something bad is going to happen.*

Henry rolls off the couch in slow motion, blanket tangling his legs like a man trapped in a cocoon. He frees himself, then crawls along the floor toward the kitchen.

He's crouched, there in the dark, fingers on the Mexican tile floor, cool and rough. He waits. No sound. He has a clear view of the sink, stove, and fridge. No one's there. The other half of the kitchen, the table and pantry, are blocked from view by the breakfast bar.

Behind him, a man murmurs about a tropical front.

Henry reaches up, feels along the wall behind him, fingers finding the switch. In one swift movement, he stands, flipping it.

The kitchen explodes with light.

Henry screams.

There, at the table, tucked neatly into a chair, is the Danner doll, staring at him, smiling with her stitched red mouth, ugly as a scar.

"Daddy?" Emma calls down from the top of the stairs. Shit. He woke her.

"Sorry, hon," Henry yells up, not taking his eyes off the doll. "It's just me. I stubbed my toe. Go on back to bed."

He waits a minute, hears the upstairs toilet flush. The water runs, then the sound of Emma's bedroom door being closed.

He and Danner have locked eyes, both holding statue still.

"I've had about enough of you," he tells it.

He pulls back the chair and lifts the doll, reaching under its armpits so that his arms circle its chest. It's heavy as a bag of cement, a good eighty or ninety pounds at least. Damn sand. What kind of crazy idea was that?

He drags the doll to the broom closet and dumps her there next to the empty buckets, mops, and brooms. Pushing her legs in with his foot, he closes the door. Then, knowing it's foolish, he grabs a ladder-back kitchen chair and wedges it against the door, under the knob.

"That should hold you," he says to the closed door.

Inside, something shifts. A broom falls over, maybe, and there's one loud knock against the inside of the door, then nothing.

Chapter 68

"TELL ME YOUR BIGGEST secret," Claire says. "The one thing you've never told anyone."

They're naked on the bed and Claire is running her fingers over Tess's taut stomach, tracing the faint stretch marks like lines on a map.

Skin is a map, Tess is thinking, *bodies remember.* Not just the marks of pregnancy, but endless scars, freckles, moles, wrinkles. Laugh lines. Frown lines. The tiny hairs that pop up in places they shouldn't.

Tess has been telling Claire about everything that's happened over the last weeks: Spencer's suicide, the words on the trees, Winnie saving Emma in the pool, her studio burning, Emma's disturbing behaviors, the Danner doll who Henry thinks is possessed by the spirit of Suz. She told Claire about how she's been reading the old journal of Suz's Henry keeps locked in his toolbox.

"I'll tell you how the Compassionate Dismantlers ended," Tess says, drawing in a breath.

Does she mean it? How far is she willing to go?

Tess lets herself imagine what it might be like to tell Claire everything. To be unburdened. To finally name the terrible thing she did ten summers ago, the one action that changed her life forever.

"It was the night I told Henry I was pregnant. I wasn't going to—I was just going to take off without telling him, go get an abortion, try to get into grad school. He caught me packing my bags and I told him the truth—I figured he deserved to know. He asked me to marry him. We were in the loft of the cabin. Below us, Winnie was holding Spencer at gunpoint."

Claire nods. She knows the names of the key players and has already heard about how Suz decided to kidnap Spencer as a joke, just to scare him. But then suddenly, it wasn't a joke anymore.

"And Henry and I were really getting into it, having this knock-down, drag-out fight, when all of a sudden, from down below, Suz yells that she's had enough. We looked down and she was crumpling up the ransom note. She told Winnie to untie Spencer. And Winnie had trouble with the knots and had to use Suz's knife to cut him loose."

Suz's knife. How had she not remembered this before? Suz gave the red camping knife to Winnie that last night. It must have been Winnie who had it all this time. Which would explain how it happened to appear at the grotto just when Winnie showed up in town.

"Once he was free," Tess continues, "we were all so relieved. Until we found out we weren't letting him go. No. Suz said we were taking him down to the lake. We were going to drown him."

Claire nods, looking neither surprised nor shocked. Only expectant. "Go on," she whispers.

"Everyone thought she was joking, at first," Tess says. "That it was just one more way to terrorize poor Spencer. This funeral march to the lake.

"But I wasn't sure she was joking. She'd been drinking, and

Suz was unpredictable when she was drunk. And she had this thing against Spencer. I think Suz felt threatened, worried that Winnie was going to go back to him or something. She really loved Winnie. I don't think Winnie ever realized how much."

Claire nods.

"Henry had some Vicodin he'd swiped from the medicine cabinet at his parents'. His father had had surgery for a slipped disk or something. We thought it would be fun to take the pills sometime and watch the shooting stars out on the lake.

"So I grabbed four pills from his stash and suggested that before we go, we each have a shot of tequila."

It was a play right out of Suz's book: the very same thing she'd done to Spencer.

Tess shivers at the memory. How often, over the years, has she wondered what might have happened if she hadn't given Suz the Vicodin, used her own trick against her?

"I just wanted to slow her down," she explains. "You know, to our own speed. Back to our planet."

"Did Henry know you'd dosed her drink?" Claire asks.

"Are you kidding? No way. No one knew. No one saw. I volunteered to pour the shots and went into the kitchen and crushed the pills with the side of a tuna can. Everyone was shouting and laughing. Even Spencer was getting into it—laughing about how we were going to drown him.

"We drank the shots, then poured more. We'd had most of the bottle by the time we headed out. It was just getting dark and we were all shit-faced, even Spencer, because Suz said no one should have to die sober. The others thought that was really funny. Like it was all a big joke."

"But you didn't?" Claire asks.

Tess shakes her head. "I didn't think so. Suz was kind of crazy, you know? Way too intense for her own good. And we all went along with her, never reined her in."

"So you drugged her tequila. Then what?"

"Suz went first, staggering down the path, reciting the damn manifesto she'd come up with: *Dismantlement equals freedom; to understand the nature of a thing, it must be taken apart.*

"Behind Suz was Spencer, then Winnie, the barrel of her rifle jabbed into his back. Henry and I were trailing along at the end, and we were still fighting about whether or not we should get married."

"What was the hesitation?" Claire asks. "Didn't you love him?"

"He didn't really love me," Tess says, wincing a little at the pain of it even now, after all the years she's had to accept it. "Not like he loved *her*."

"Suz?"

Tess nods. They were all a little in love with Suz. Even Tess herself, who was sick with envy. Maybe that was its own form of love.

"The shit hit the fan once we got to the lake," Tess remembers. "Suz was serious. She was really fucking serious. All the joking and holding forth was done. She told Winnie to shoot him. And when she wouldn't, Suz took the gun to do it herself," Tess says. "She had her finger on the trigger. If Henry hadn't tackled her . . ." The words fade away. She can't go on. She can't tell how it ends.

"Tell me the rest of the story," Claire says, lying back and closing her eyes, like a child at bedtime.

"I can't."

"It'll be like confession. At the end, I'll absolve you of your sins."

Tess bites her lip. "I don't think I can."

Claire strokes Tess's hair, rolls over, whispers in her ear, "Yes, you can. Whisper it to me, Tess. Tell me what happened next."

If she tells, it will be over. There's no way Claire could absolve her, but maybe, just maybe, the weight of what she's done will lessen.

"The gun went off. It was so loud. I turned to see if Spencer had been shot, and he was crouched down, covering his head with his hands. But he was fine. She'd missed. She and Henry started struggling for the gun. He got it away from her, but then she grabbed his shirt and ripped it, clawed the shit out of his arm. She just went nuts and he hit her across the face with the butt end of the gun, then turned it on her. Aimed at her chest. That's when she told us. 'You don't want to shoot a pregnant woman, do you?' she said. 'You'd be killing your own child.' And I was so confused because I thought she was talking about me. Like he had the gun pointed at me.

"Henry threw down the gun and lunged at her. He grabbed her by the hair and dragged her into the lake."

Tess's voice breaks. "He was so drunk. We were all so drunk."

"Go on," Claire whispers.

"I can't."

What if it's too much? How could Claire ever look at her in the same way again?

"Wait here," Claire whispers. She rolls over, gets out of bed, and goes into the hall. Tess hears her padding around downstairs.

If only Tess hadn't given Suz the Vicodin. If only Henry hadn't dragged her into the lake.

Claire comes back. "Have a little of this," she says, handing Tess a glass of wine. "It'll help you finish."

Tess puts the glass to her lips and drinks; not little sips, but desperate gulping swallows, burning her mouth, tasting of regret, of failure, of unspeakable loss.

If only . . .

Claire is running her fingers over Tess's body, whispering, "Go on, tell me . . ."

Tess drains the glass, asks for a refill, stalling until she comes up with either a plausible excuse for stopping or another ending altogether. A lie.

"Be right back," Claire takes the glass, kisses Tess on the ear, running her tongue along the inside folds. Tess shivers, lets her eyes close.

She's so tired. So very tired. Her tongue feels thick in her mouth. She keeps her eyes closed, lets herself drift. She hears something downstairs, a crash, and tries to surface, to sit up, but finds she can't. She opens her eyes, but her vision is blurred. The world is fuzzy, as if she's looking at it through a thick layer of Vaseline.

Where's Claire? How long has she been gone?

"Cclrrr . . ." The name comes out a drunken slur.

There's movement in the hall. Tess tries to focus, to keep her eyes open and make sense of what she's seeing, but it's no use. She gives in and lets them flutter closed.

The last thing she sees is a blond woman in a flowing tunic, moving toward her.

"Hello, babycakes," she says.

Chapter 69

HE WAKES UP GASPING, drenched in sweat, his heart thudding in his chest. His face is pressed into the back cushion of the couch. He rolls over, lets himself get a breath.

He's had the dream again.

The TV is still on. Satellite imagery. The East Coast viewed from space.

He reaches for the remote on the table, turning a little, and that's when he sees it: the Danner doll.

Sitting up in the rocking chair in the corner, arms and legs crossed, just watching him.

"Fuck!"

Henry falls off the couch, tangled in the covers again.

Sucking in air through clenched teeth, he moves to her, kicks her out of the chair. She slides to the floor, her body crumpled in an impossible way, a way only someone without bones could land.

Once more, he bends, slips his hands under her armpits (is she warm there? moist?), encircles her chest, and lifts.

Can she have gotten heavier?

Henry grunts, and walking backward, drags her out of the living room, through the front hall, out the door and to his truck, in the driveway. It's a slow-going shuffle-walk across the gravel, over the shards of broken glass from the motion light.

He knows what he has to do. How to finish this once and for all. He'll put the doll in the moose, float her out on the lake, and burn the bitch. Let her remains settle on the floor of that already haunted lake: scorched clothing and play sand right beside the bones of the real Suz. Rest in peace, you creepy, fucking thing.

He opens the back of the Blazer, dumps her in. Then he locks the car doors, pushes the child-lock safety button. He tucks the keys into his pocket and turns back toward the house.

The sky in the east is swirled with pink.

Red sky in the morning, sailor take warning.

PART FIVE

DISMANTLEMENT = FREEDOM

O

M

N

E

T

A

Chapter 70

HENRY GLANCES OUT THE window toward the Blazer as he downs his third cup of coffee, stirs strawberries and brown sugar into the oatmeal.

"I still can't find her," Emma whines, trudging back into the kitchen. She's been all over the house looking for the damn doll. When she first woke up, the searching was frantic, and Emma was bordering on hysterical. Now it seems she's exhausted herself.

"I'm sorry, sweetie," he says, handing her the bowl, watching as she adds spoonful after spoonful of brown sugar to her already sweetened oatmeal, turning it to sticky glue. "Maybe your mom put her somewhere."

"Where *is* Mom?"

"A friend of hers is sick. She had to go help out." Henry bites his cheek. He hates having to lie and is sure she'll see right through it.

"Not Winnie, right?" Now Emma looks extra worried. Her big brown eyes search Henry's face.

"No, sweetie. Winnie's fine. It's some other friend. Someone from the art guild."

"When will she be back?"

"I don't know. Soon, I hope."

Emma frowns into her oatmeal. "She was in my room last night. I know she was."

"Your mother?"

Emma rolls her eyes. "No, Dad! My sculpture. Danner. She was in bed next to me when I fell asleep. Maybe I can call Mom and ask her."

Henry shakes his head. "Her phone's turned off. You know your mom. She never remembers to keep it on."

How could Tess do this? Just leave in the middle of the night and not come back. Leaving him was fine. He understood that. But Emma? Did she deserve to wake up to lousy oatmeal and a bunch of piss-poor lies?

"I thought you could spend the day at Mel's. I called her mom and she said it's okay."

She looks away, picks at the bandages across her knuckles.

Henry leans in, puts a hand on her arm. "I'm sorry, Em. I know you and Mel had some trouble at the movies yesterday, but I'm sure whatever the problem is, you two can work it out, right?"

Emma shrugs, still won't look at him.

"Would it be okay to just spend today with her? Just so I can go to work if I promise to get out early?"

Emma shrugs again, looking forlorn.

"After breakfast you can get your things together. Mel's mom will be here in another hour. I'll pick you up when I leave work around four. We can do something special together then. Go out to the Tastee-Freez maybe. Would you like that?"

"Do you have to work today, Dad? Can't you just stay home?"

"Sorry. No can do." Another lie. He's not going in to work at all. He's spending the day moving the canoe to the lake, strapping the moose to it. And tonight . . . tonight he'll put the possessed doll inside and watch it burn. Good-bye, Suz.

Tess will be home by then. If not, he'll have to call Laura from down the road and see if she can come babysit. He doesn't trust Laura, is convinced she smoked pot the last time she watched Emma, but Tess likes her, says she's a good girl.

"Can't I just stay here, Dad? I'm old enough. I'll wait for Mom. I'll just watch TV and read. I won't even go near the pool. I promise."

A chill washes over Henry. He shakes his head. "Sorry, Emma."

"Maybe I can go to the cabin! Hang out with Winnie. I can call her right now and ask."

"Not today," Henry says.

"Is it because of Mom?" Emma asks. "She doesn't have to know. It can be our secret." She gives him a weak, pleading smile.

"No," he says. "No more secrets. You're going to Mel's. It's all arranged."

MEL'S MOM HAS JUST pulled away, Mel and Emma tucked safely into the backseat, not talking or even acknowledging each other, which is troubling, but Henry's got bigger concerns right now. He hustles over to the Blazer, checking his watch. The guys from the painting company are coming in forty-five minutes to help him load the canoe. He's got to have the doll hidden in the half-ton pickup before they get here.

He approaches the Blazer slowly, worried that he might see a desperate hand in a worn gardening glove reach up and pound at the rear windshield. The windows are slightly fogged with condensation. Like someone's been breathing inside.

He pushes the button on his key chain to unlock the truck. The lights flash. The truck beeps its mechanical hello. The locks open. Henry takes a deep breath, reaches for the handle on the rear door, pulls and yanks it open. He draws back the tarp.

Nothing.

No, not quite nothing.

Under the tarp is a small mound of sand.

The doll is gone.

"Fuck!"

He slams the door closed, goes back to the house and searches. Nothing. No doll. He looks around the yard. In Tess's sculpture garden and the charred remains of her studio. Then, he heads into the barn. The Danner doll is just plain gone.

Henry checks his watch. Ten minutes until the two guys arrive. He's got to focus. He grabs ropes, chains, a come-along, and his toolbox. Once he drives the canoe to the lake, he and Winnie have to be able to get it out, slide it into the water, and attach the moose to it. A Herculean effort. He throws two two-by-tens into the bed of the half-ton DeForge Painting pickup truck to build a ramp from the truck to the water's edge.

He's trying not to think about the doll, but she's there, in the back of his mind, grinning her scarlike grin.

He hears tires on the gravel of the driveway, then remembers the journal and jogs over to the toolbox to retrieve it. If he can't burn the doll, he can at least torch the notebook.

But it's not there. Left in its place at the rust-flecked bottom of the box is a dusting of fine white sand.

Chapter 71

EMMA HAS MADE A sculpture of herself this time, a dummy, scarecrow girl out of pillows piled under her comforter. She rummaged around in the closet and found an old dolly that pees and put it up at the head, with just a tuft of its hair sticking out, the same light blond color as Emma's. She knows that dumb babysitter, Laura, won't even check. She'll just stay downstairs all night flipping through channels on the satellite TV and smoking cigarettes. In between each cigarette, she sprays perfume into the air. Emma knows. She's seen her. She also knows that Laura will pick her toes all night. Sometimes, she'll lift a foot to her mouth and chew her toenails. She's very flexible, Laura is. She can wrap her leg around the back of her neck. Her mother is a yoga instructor and Laura has been taking classes since she was two. She's like a human pretzel.

Why does Emma even need a babysitter, anyway? Mel's parents leave her alone all the time.

"Well, your mother and I aren't Mel's parents," her dad said earlier when she tried to persuade him to forget about calling Laura.

Being at Mel's today was a total disaster. When they got there, she followed Mel down into her basement bedroom and watched her light candles and incense, then smoke a gum-wrapper cigarette. Mel acted like Emma wasn't even there.

"What do you want to do today?" Emma asked.

Mel just stared at the smoke she blew out of her mouth. When she finished her cigarette, she climbed up on a milk crate, opened one of the little rectangular basement windows, pulled herself up, and wriggled through it. Emma got up on the milk crate to follow, but Mel slammed the window closed and disappeared into the woods at the edge of her yard.

Emma stayed down in the basement all day, sneaking up around lunchtime to make a sandwich in the kitchen.

"Isn't Mel hungry?" Mel's mom asked when she found Emma spreading mustard on rye bread.

"She asked me to bring her down a sandwich," Emma said. "She's working on a new invention."

Mel's mom winked. "Let me guess . . . it's top secret, right?" Emma nodded. Mel's mom made a ham-and-Swiss sandwich, threw it on a plate with some chips. Then she got two cans of root beer from the fridge. "Even a mad scientist has to eat," she said, handing Emma the plate.

Emma left Mel's lunch on the table next to her bed, thinking Mel might show up any minute. She didn't. Emma stayed alone in the basement until her dad came to pick her up at four.

EMMA ADJUSTS THE COVERS over the dummy in her bed. She knows she doesn't have much time. Her dad is talking with Laura in the kitchen. He's already tucked Emma in and said his good nights. Now he's telling Laura to help herself to the chicken shish kebabs in the fridge.

Emma sneaks down the stairs and through the front hall, past the painting of Francis.

"Nine," she whispers, then opens the front door gently, quietly, careful not to let it squeak, and pads out to the big company pickup her dad has been driving all day. She climbs up on the bumper and lifts herself over the gate, into the bed of the truck, where she scuttles all the way back against the cab and hides under an old painting tarp that smells of mildew and turpentine.

Earlier tonight, she picked up the phone to try her mom again (her cell's been off all day), and caught her dad and Winnie. Her dad was saying, "Are you sure we should be doing this?" and Winnie said, "It's too late to back out now."

Emma couldn't believe it: Mel was right. Her dad and Winnie were having an affair! It was all so obvious. And her mother must have found out and left him. Left them both.

The worst part of it is, it's all Emma's fault. She sent the stupid moose postcard to Winnie. It was Emma who brought Winnie back here. If she hadn't been trying so hard to get her parents back together, she wouldn't have done the thing that would tear them apart.

There's only one thing left to do—stop them.

And that's just what she's on her way to do: to crash her father and Winnie's little rendezvous and find a way to make them see that this thing between them is a horrible mistake. That it throws everything out of balance. And how that lady Suz was all wrong: art is not all about chaos, about taking things apart. True art, Emma will tell them, is about finding a way to make what's broken whole.

Chapter 72

RUNNING LATE, HENRY HEADS for his workshop to grab the gas can. As he approaches the barn, he realizes the lights are on, which is odd—he hasn't been out there since this morning, and he's sure he turned them off then. He slides the door open slowly, stepping inside. The bright white halogen bulbs illuminate the empty wooden frame where the canoe had rested for over a year.

But the frame is not empty.

Lying there, faceup in the middle, like she's been caught taking an innocent little nap of the damned, is the Danner doll.

Henry makes a strangled sort of gasping sound.

He circles around the doll to the workbench, walking on tiptoe, as if he might actually wake her. There, he finds rope. Bright yellow, thick-braided nylon. Knowing it makes no sense, it's a ridiculous waste of time, but still unable to stop himself, he ties her. Henry lifts her arms, crosses her wrists and wraps the rope around tight.

Tighter, Henry. Tie it tighter.

Then, he does her ankles.

For the sheer fuck of it, he uses all hundred feet of rope, wrapping up her entire body, from his old Danner boots to the top of the blond wig, until she resembles a bright yellow chrysalis.

"Henry?" A voice in the dark outside. A man's voice. "You in there?"

Shit. Bill fucking Lunde.

Henry grabs a painting tarp from the floor, hurriedly tosses it over the doll just as Bill slides the barn door open.

"Hey, Bill," Henry says. He's leaning casually against the frame that once held the canoe, smiling so hard his cheeks ache.

"The babysitter said you'd gone, but I saw your truck and the light on in here."

"I'm just about to take off. I'm helping a crew finish a late job," Henry says, lying without meaning to. But it's too late to back out now.

Bill's eying the black plastic stapled to the windows. "Not a fan of daylight, huh?" he says.

"Guess not," Henry says.

"I was hoping to see Tess actually," Bill says.

"Tess?"

"Yeah, I spoke with Julia at the Golden Apple gallery. I wanted to ask Tess about the woman who bought her paintings. Any idea where I can find your wife?"

Henry stiffens. "No," he says. "Actually, I have no idea at all."

"And you're not worried?" Bill asks.

"Should I be?" Henry snaps. "She's a grown woman."

He takes in a breath, tries again. "Look, my wife and I . . . we're sort of separated. I'm sure you figured that part out when you saw our living arrangement."

Bill nods.

"I assume she's dating someone. She's probably off with him."

"Well, when you hear from her, can you ask her to give me a call?"

"Sure," says Henry. "Will do." He looks at his watch—a not-so-gentle hint that he's running late.

"So you got her out on the water, then?" Bill says.

"Huh?" Henry chomps down on the inside of his cheek.

Have to weight her down. So she won't float.

"The canoe. How'd she handle?"

Henry lets out a breath, smiles. "Like a dream," he says.

HENRY STANDS IN THE driveway, watches the taillights of Bill's rented SUV disappear as he takes a left onto the main road, back toward town.

Henry checks his watch. Shit. He grabs the cell phone from his pants pocket, punches in Winnie's number.

"What's up?" she asks.

"I'm running a little late," he tells her. "Lunde was here. Tess never showed up, so I had to get a sitter."

"That's fucked up," Winnie says. "For her to leave you and Emma like that."

"Yeah," Henry says. "Look, I'm leaving in about five minutes."

"Great. Don't forget the gas can."

"I won't. And I've got the doll." *Tied up. I tied the fucking bitch right up.*

"Perfect," Winnie tells him. "I'll see you at the lake in an hour. And wait till you see the latest present someone left for me."

"What is it?" he asks.

"Suz's old journal. It was here on the table when I came back from meeting you at the lake earlier. I'll bring it with me and we'll toss it in the moose."

"One hour then," Henry says, hanging up.

How the hell did the journal get from his workshop to the cabin? An absurd thought hits him: it was the doll. She took it there.

Jesus.

"Get a grip, Henry," he tells himself.

He hustles back into the barn, grabs a corner of the tarp, and hesitates before pulling it back. What if she's not there?

He chomps down on his cheeks, counts to three, and yanks up the tarp, feeling like a magician: now you see it, now you don't.

But there she is, still wrapped in yellow rope.

And for my next trick . . .

When he finally lifts her, carries her fireman style over his shoulder to the truck, he's once again amazed by the weight and heft. And he thinks, for an instant, that maybe he feels her move; her body going rigid, then limp again as he tosses her into the bed of the truck. His heart is hammering in his chest, his breath is wet and whistley. And that's when he hears it, coming from the doll, a low, throaty hum: the static noise.

Chapter 73

WINNIE'S SITTING AT THE table in the cabin, wearing the Suz outfit one last time. She's exhausted, but the whole thing is nearly over. Earlier, she and Henry wrestled the canoe out of the truck and into the water, driving a huge eye hook into the front and running a rope from the hook to a nearby tree so the boat wouldn't drift away from shore. Then, with great effort, they maneuvered the moose into the back of Henry's truck, carrying it up a board ramp, then tying it down for the rough trip to the lake. At the beach, they performed the whole procedure backward to get him out of the truck and onto the canoe where they used boards to brace him upright. He was too tall, and made the canoe tip, so they cut off his legs from the knees down to give him a lower center of gravity. Even then it was a trick, balancing him just so; they had to put rocks in his belly, over on his left side, to keep the canoe from tipping.

Now, Winnie's sitting at the table with Suz's journal, which is laid out right next to hers on the table in the cabin.

She checks her watch: nearly 11 P.M., minutes before she's due to meet Henry. Fingers trembling slightly, she opens the journal to the last entry—Suz's final written words.

July 29—Cabin by the lake

*Everything's going to hell. It seems that, at last, the
Dismantlers are coming apart. And if you want to
know the truth—I'm actually a little relieved.*

*Spencer's tied and gagged, sweaty and pathetic.
Winnie's pacing around with the gun. She whispered
to me earlier that we've gone far enough. We should
just let him go.*

How far is far enough?

*This is the end and I think we all know it. Everyone's
looking to me to make sure we go out with a bang, not
a whimper. They're all expecting something great. A
show worthy of Suz the Magnificent. Christ.*

*Tess and Henry are up in the loft arguing. They think
we can't hear them, but I've heard every word. Tess is
pregnant. And noble, sweet Henry is swearing he'll
marry her, get a job and settle down. Poor Henry.
Everyone knows it's not Tess he's in love with.*

*What they don't know is how one night back in June,
Henry and I swam way out to the other side of the
lake. We floated on our backs and saw shooting stars,
one after the other, like the whole sky was coming
apart. Magical. Truly, it was. When we got to the little
beach at the other end of the lake, we did it there in
the sand. It was stupid, but it happened. Sometimes
I think I get so caught up in being the Suz everyone
believes I am that I lose track of what's right. The
romance of the idea of Suz the outlaw artist, Suz the*

revolutionary, Suz the red-hot lover. Or maybe that's just bullshit. I've always known this wasn't going to last forever. The summer will end. We'll all drift apart, forget the Dismantlers. The others are living this shared delusion that we can go on and on, but I know the truth. And maybe, just maybe, that night on the beach with Henry, I wanted to milk it for all it was worth. Cause I was sure that I was gonna go back to fucking Trenton and get some shit job and date some idiot and maybe get married and join the whole fucking rat race and no one, no one will ever look at me the way the other Dismantlers have looked at me this summer. The way Henry looked at me that night on the beach.

After, Henry got all maudlin on me, told me how he's been in love with me since the second our eyes met and all that. "I know," I told him. "I've known all along." And then, I did the thing I've been meaning to do since we got to the cabin.

"I have something for you. A present." I pulled the Magic 8 Ball key ring out of my pocket and handed it over, pressing it into his palm.

"My van key! But I lost it that day at the gas station ..." Henry trailed off and I watched as the truth hit him.

"You had it all along," he said, grinning.

I nodded.

He asked what I wanted him to do now, and I told him to stick with Tess, how she would never let him

down. "She loves you more than you know," I told
him and he just cried.

"But what about us?" he asked.

"Part of you will always be with me," I told him.
"When you're eighty years old, drooling into your
oatmeal, part of you will still be back here at the lake,
watching the sky fall with me."

That's really how I feel about this whole summer.
No matter what happens now, part of us will always
remain here. And I think it's the best part. The purest
part of our souls. We'll haunt this place like ghosts
while we live our "real" lives in cities far away, get
married, have 2.5 kids, work our meaningless jobs.

Part of me feels gone already, a living ghost.

Winnie closes the journal, sure she's a living ghost herself. The
veil between the past and the present is so thin in this place, so tenuous.

Outside, headlights come up the driveway. It could be Henry
in his old orange van, coming back from town with Tess and Suz
and a cardboard box full of supplies: tequila, drawing charcoal,
oatmeal, coffee, and sugar.

She hears footsteps, stands and looks out the window, but before she
can get a look, whoever it is is at the door, opening it. Coming inside.

Maybe, Winnie thinks, time is a layered thing and the past is
always there, hidden right beneath the present, but somehow, they
both exist in each moment. Maybe that's what ghosts really are.

"You," Winnie says.

The visitor smiles, says, "Who were you expecting? The goddamn queen of England?"

Chapter 74

PARKED ON THE BEACH, Henry stares out at the water and gnaws the insides of his cheeks. Feels his heart jumping around in his chest like some caged wild thing that thinks it's about to be set free.

He understands now. There never was a Danner. It was Suz all along, coming to their daughter before she was even old enough to speak, befriending her, watching her, winning her over. What better way to haunt them? To make them pay for what they'd done.

Stomach acid churns, rises up, burning his esophagus, pushing its way to his throat. He swallows it back down, opens the door, and climbs out of the truck.

And now Suz has been given life, a body, by Emma, fed by the power of their fears, not unlike Frankenstein's monster. And like that monster, she must be destroyed. Henry knows it's up to him to do it, because he's the only one who understands. He's got to send her back where she belongs, to a grave at the bottom of the lake so her spirit can join her bones.

First thing this morning, he called Winnie to tell her he'd decided to follow her suggestion and put the doll in the moose.

"You really think it's alive in some way? That Suz is inside it?" Winnie asked.

"There's no doubt in my mind," he said, then went on to tell her about his adventures with the doll in the night.

"Jesus!" Winnie yelped into the phone. "I say let's burn it. Soak it in gas and torch the fucker."

But then he'd gone out to the Blazer and discovered the doll had made another miraculous escape.

"But I got you now," he mumbles, thinking he should walk around to the back of the truck to check, but he can't bring himself to. Not yet. In his mind, he hears the static noise.

Henry leans against the front of the pickup and lights a cigarette. Just killing time.

Killing. Time.

He shivers, takes a deep drag of his cigarette. It tastes horrible, dank and rotten.

It's dark. Too dark. The moon hasn't risen yet. Or maybe it's a new moon. He should have paid attention to the goddamn Weather Channel last night. Maybe then he'd know.

He pushes the button on his watch, lighting up the face: 11:10. Where the hell is Winnie? Tossing his cigarette down without finishing it, he moves to the back of the truck and opens the tailgate, half expecting to find the doll gone, having jumped from the truck bed when he slowed at a stop sign.

But even in the dim light he can see that it's there. Jesus, yes, it's there.

And thankfully, it's quiet. No buzz. No hundred voices coming from its sand-filled throat.

Henry dances from one foot to the other, scared to touch it, but finally, he tells himself, *Fuck it,* and lifts the Danner doll from the bed, throws her over his shoulder and staggers toward the canoe. The trick is to keep moving. To not stop to think about what he's carrying.

His feet sink in the sand, his ankles twist on rocks. He remembers carrying Suz into the lake once before, her clothes full of rocks, Tess and Winnie sobbing behind him.

We have to weight her down. So she won't float.

He remembers how he swam out on his back with Suz resting against his chest, one final embrace. How he saw Tess on the shore and thought of the baby inside her. He made a decision then, as he neared the middle of the lake—he would protect and defend Tess and the baby, no matter what. It was too late for Suz.

"She loves you more than you know," Suz had told him, and now, he would do his best to honor that. To cherish it. To love Tess back.

He reached the middle of the lake and let Suz go, the rocks carrying her down into the darkest part of the water.

NOW, AS THEN, HE'S a man on autopilot, doing just what needs to be done. He's protecting his family the only way he knows how.

He doesn't stop to kick off his shoes or roll up his khaki work pants, just wades out so that he's knee deep in water, opens the door in the moose's chest and dumps her in, with a triumphant "Arghh!" like some comic book action hero.

But he hasn't won yet.

He reaches for the can of gas, raises it up high, and soaks the whole moose, from his antlers to the tip of his tail, fuel raining down, some new kind of baptism.

Chapter 75

EMMA CRAWLS OUT FROM under the tarp, lowers herself over the opened back gate of the pickup and down to the ground. Behind her are woods, thick and shadowy. Off to the left, the rough old logging road they must have taken in, her father creeping along in low gear, Emma bouncing in the back, needing to pee so bad that each bump was agony. In front of them, a lake, probably the lake from *A Long Time Ago*. The water's black and smells of whatever it is that lakes smell of: fish, algae, bugs, and bacteria. Do bacteria have a smell? she wonders. Mel would know. She suddenly finds herself wishing like crazy that Mel was here, which is dumb because Mel would just be ignoring her, no help at all. She wouldn't be alone if Danner was here, but Danner hasn't made an appearance since their argument the day before—in fact, the Danner doll itself seems to have taken off too. What Emma really wishes is that she was back home now, in her warm bed with a bathroom just down the hall. Laura would be downstairs, sneaking cigarettes, chewing on her toes, and watching one of those reality TV shows.

Crouching behind the left-rear bumper of the truck, looking desperately around for the best place to pee, Emma sees her father at the edge of the water.

He's carrying something. Whatever it was he put in the back of the truck. Emma had been too scared to look and had ridden the whole way with the tarp covering her head, making her dizzy with the smell of turpentine. She'd probably killed some brain cells. It was supposed to make you high, sniffing turpentine, but it just gave her a headache and made her nostrils burn. Why would anyone do that for fun?

Now, as her eyes adjust in the darkness, she sees that this some-thing her father had transported is actually a someone. A woman. Unconscious.

Oh. My. God. This was way worse than her dad having an affair! What if he turned out to be a serial killer or something? Would she still love him? Would she go to the police and tell?

Emma holds her breath, watching.

Soon, she sees that this is not really an unconscious woman.

"No," Emma mouths the word, her mouth making a little O shape in the dark.

He's got her sculpture! It's Danner, she can see from the boots, the tuft of her blond wig. He's got Danner all wrapped up in shiny yellow rope.

But that's not even the worst part.

There, at the water's edge, is the huge canoe Daddy made, and strapped to it, like a prisoner, is Francis, down on his knees. A moose begging for mercy.

"No," Emma mouths again, a cry without a sound.

Her dad wades out into shallow water, heaves Danner inside Francis through the door on his chest.

What is he doing?

A magic trick, Emma thinks. Like putting the lady in the box before sawing her in half.

Then, she sees her father pull something square and red from the front of the canoe.

Emma can smell the gasoline even from her hiding place behind the truck. He's pouring it on Francis and the canoe. She hears the liquid rush out of the spout, spatter on whatever it hits.

She has *got* to pee. Now.

She gets down on her hands and knees, crawls into the woods behind the truck, her bladder a hard, painful clenched fist inside her. She finds a tree to hide behind where she still has a view of the beach, pulls her shorts and underwear down. Emma hates peeing outside. You never know what bugs are hiding there in the leaves. Or snakes. She heard a story once about a girl who went to pee when she was camping and a snake crawled up inside her. Then, she had all these snake babies. Mel said it wasn't a true story, because snakes lay eggs. "Maybe the eggs hatched inside the girl," Emma said. Whether or not it really happened, it just went to show that when you pee outside, you're vulnerable to all sorts of terrible things.

Just as Emma starts to go, squatting in leaf litter, holding on to a skinny white birch tree to keep from tipping over, and praying for no snakes or poison ivy, she hears someone coming through the woods. But it's too late now, she can't stop midstream to hide, so she hunkers down as low as she can, keeps right on peeing as a figure moves down a path just to her left. Emma watches, holding her breath, shorts down around her ankles as Winnie passes not ten feet to the side of her.

Winnie's wearing the same outfit she had on the day she jumped into the pool; the day she saved Emma's life. The wig an exact copy of the one Danner wears, like she and Danner are sisters or something.

Maybe it's all part of the trick.

Emma is still peeing, it's the pee that goes on forever, when Winnie steps out of the woods, making her way to the beach.

"You're late," Emma's dad calls.

Winnie approaches the canoe but keeps her head down, as if she's studying the ground.

In a low voice, she asks about the doll.

"I got it. It's in the moose," Emma's dad tells her.

The betrayal takes Emma's breath away. How could her father have taken Danner, how could he and Winnie be doing this terrible, unspeakable thing?

Winnie nods, unties the rope from the tree, and pushes the canoe out, then climbs in the front. Emma's dad gets in the back, behind Francis. They each pick up an oar and begin to row.

Emma rises, pulls up her shorts, waits for them to get a ways out, then slips into the water silently, determined to stop them, to do whatever it takes.

Chapter 76

PUSHING OFF IS EASIER than he thought it would be. And the canoe stays upright. There's room enough for Winnie up front, and Henry tucked in back, behind the moose, which reeks of gasoline. They row in silence toward the middle of the lake, going right to the spot where he swam out with Suz, and let her sink, clothing full of rocks. Where she went under and was never seen again. He remembers how he treaded water there, watching her sink, following the white ghost of her hair down, down, down until it was a tiny speck, like the reflection of a star.

His paddle slices the water. Henry looks at the ripples it leaves, thinks he sees a face underneath. Suz looking back at him, her face framed in starlight.

He believes that somehow, Suz has become the lake. Her spirit is all around them, lapping at the sides of the canoe, teasing, taunting, telling them she's got them right where she wants them.

"I thought you were going to burn the clothes and wig," he says to Winnie. If he peers around the left side of the moose, he can see her back. The blond wig glowing like a beacon. He closes his eyes. Listens to the sounds the water makes.

"And where's the journal? I thought you were going to put it in the moose."

She doesn't answer.

"Winnie?"

She doesn't respond. Just keeps on paddling, a little harder now.

Henry feels his throat constricting around the gasoline fumes. He glances back toward shore. It's a long way. He's not sure he'll make it. Too much of a swim for a man who is so afraid of water. He wishes he had worn a life jacket. Or never let Winnie talk him into this to begin with.

He thinks he sees something in the water. A duck or a loon maybe. Moving slowly toward them.

Suz, he thinks, some irrational part of his brain taking over. It's Suz.

He makes himself look away, paddling harder, faster, his eyes fixed on the hind legs of the moose, amputated at the knees. He thinks he hears a muffled moan from inside it.

A muffled voice. No, voic*es*. Definite voices.

The static noise.

But they're not coming from the moose. There are voices calling from shore, from the beach behind them.

Henry's paddle cuts into the water. He turns and looks back toward the beach. It's still coming at them, the thing in the water.

And what Henry thinks of now is not a loon, or a duck, or even Suz. What he imagines is the frogs left in the aquarium—a tank full of pale, bloated bodies. Somehow, in his mind, it's those frogs who are chasing him—swollen, stinking, and vengeful.

Metamorphosis, babycakes.

There, beyond the frogs, back on the beach, are two figures, jumping up and down, flapping their arms, calling out. They look like puppets: far away and unreal. A woman with blond hair in flowing clothes. And a man waving a flashlight through the air.

The blond woman looks like Winnie, which is all wrong—Winnie is in front of him, rowing. The man, Henry thinks, might be Bill Lunde.

They're calling his name desperately.

And they're saying something else.

Something about Suz.

"It's *Suz*," they're yelling.

But they've got it wrong—this is just Winnie dressed as Suz. Even though she said she was going to burn the clothes and wig. Just Winnie.

"Winnie?"

Henry peeks around the moose at Winnie, who has turned to face him, smiling. Only now, she looks straight at him so that he can see her face, and he realizes this is not Winnie at all.

"Oh my god," he stammers.

It can't be. It isn't.

But some part of him knows the truth.

"Surprised?" she asks. "You haven't seen anything yet, baby-cakes. I've saved the best for last."

Chapter 77

THERE WAS A LOUD rapping at the cabin door, and Winnie screamed against the duct tape over her mouth, thrashed against the ropes so that her chair rocked on the floor. Bill Lunde burst in. Winnie was almost satisfied to see Bill looking shocked for once, seemingly unsure of the next move. He froze for two or three seconds, strode over to Winnie, pulled the duct tape from her mouth.

"Suz," she gasped. "Suz is here! She looks totally different, but it's her. She's here! She's alive!"

"I know," Bill said. "But where is she now?"

"Out on the lake with Henry. Oh my god, what's she going to do to Henry?"

"I followed Henry from his house. I must have missed the turnoff for the lake. I just assumed he was coming here," Bill explained as he cut Winnie loose. He pulled her up from the chair, out the door and toward his truck. "Come on!" he told her.

"No!" Winnie said. "It's faster if we go on foot. We'll get there in half the time. There's a path just over here."

She led the way, going fast at first, slapping branches out of the way. Soon she was hesitating, losing sight of the trail. Bill had a flashlight, but everything was so overgrown it was impossible to make out a path.

"Goddamnit," she hissed. "It's been ten years since I've come down here at night."

She remembered their last march down to the water in the dark, Suz in the lead. Winnie was pressing her gun into Spencer's back, but, in between barked commands, they were laughing. It was a joke. Nothing bad was going to happen. It was just Suz kicking things up a notch, giving them a night to remember.

Winnie and Bill scrambled and stumbled through the dense undergrowth.

"We'll be too late!" Winnie said, her voice high and squeaky.

Bill found the path.

"This way," he said.

A flashlight in one hand, gun in the other, he led them down through the woods to the beach. The trees thinned and the packed dirt under their feet turned to sand. Henry's truck was there, pulled up to the edge of the water, tailgate down. The lake lay in front of them—not the shimmering quicksilver water Winnie remembered from that summer, but something black and bottomless that gave no reflection, just absorbed the light of the stars, swallowed it down deep.

And they were too late.

Henry and Suz were out in the middle of the lake, just reaching the place where they'd watched him let her go ten years before, her clothing stuffed full of rocks.

There was nothing to do but start screaming.

"It's Suz!" Winnie called, her voice cracking, near hysteria.

Chapter 78

WHEN TESS WAKES UP, the first thing she thinks is that she never finished her story for Claire. She never got the chance to say how things ended. How they watched Henry drag Suz, snarling and twisting, into the lake that night and how, when he let go of her, he started to cry.

"What, aren't you going to drown me?" she said, treading water as he swam away, back toward shore. "What's the matter, Henry? Did you really believe I was pregnant? No such luck, babycakes. Poor, poor Henry. In love with the wrong girl. But it's okay. We've gone beyond that, haven't we? We've dismantled relationships. Love and sex. We've moved above it. Beyond it. Don't you see? We can leave here now and go off and lead our pathetic little lives changing diapers and being married to the wrong person, but we'll always have this summer to remember. To come back to. Part of us will always be here."

And that's when Tess threw the rock. She'd picked it up when Suz and Henry were struggling for the gun and had been holding it tightly in her hand. She hadn't intended to throw it. It wasn't a premeditated act, as they say in all those television courtroom dramas. She felt as if she was throwing the rock straight into the future that Suz was describing; that the future was this horrible, senseless world encased in a delicate glass globe and all she wanted was to shatter it before it ever had a chance of coming to be.

The rock was the size of a grapefruit and smooth. It flew from her hand like a perfect pitch in the final inning, right into the strike zone. She never knew she had such a good aim.

Tess watched in what felt like slow motion as it sailed out over the water and caught Suz on the left temple. There was a loud cracking sound, then Suz slipped under, silently.

Tess stood frozen, arm extended, fingers open, as if she was expecting the rock to come back.

Winnie screamed. Spencer said, "Jesus!"

Henry, who had reached the beach by then, ran back into the water and dove in. It took him several long minutes to find her and when he did, he grabbed her, swam back, and carried her in his arms to the beach where he laid her down in the sand. Her face was covered in blood from the deep gash on her temple.

"I don't think she's breathing," Henry said.

"Do something!" Winnie wailed.

"Does anyone know CPR?" Spencer asked.

Henry crouched down, pounded Suz on the chest, and gave her three quick breaths on the mouth. It didn't look quite right to Tess, but what did she know? Just what she'd seen in movies. Henry did it again—pound-breathe-breathe-breathe, pound-breathe-breathe-breathe—and again for what seemed like a long time. Tess looked on expectantly, waiting for the part where Suz's chest would convulse, and she would puke up lake water, look around, dazed, maybe even say, "What happened?" But the minutes passed and Suz lay limp and pale in the moonlight. Henry felt both wrists for a pulse.

"I think she's dead," he pronounced. He said it so calmly, so matter-of-factly that Tess didn't believe he could possibly be serious.

Winnie wailed. Spencer wrapped his arms around her, and held her tight while she fought against him. Spencer, who should have been gone, who should have taken off running after the shot was fired, but for some reason hadn't.

"We have to get help," Tess said. She was sure that if she could just get to a phone, someone would come, some miracle man with medicine, bandages, and electric paddles would bring Suz back to them and they'd all laugh later about what a close call it had been. They'd say Suz had dismantled death.

Tess started walking back toward the path. She would go to the cabin, get in the van, and go to the store. There was a phone there. She'd dial 911. Tell them there'd been an accident.

"Tess," Henry was holding her arm, gripping it so tightly she'd be black and blue for a week, pulling her back to the beach. "Stop. We have to think this through." His breath was fiery and tequila scented. He looked at her as if she was a stranger.

"You killed her!" Winnie screamed, and Spencer held tight to her, whispered *Shhh* into her hair as if she was a child who'd just woken up from a terrible nightmare.

"I . . . ," Tess began, "I didn't mean to."

This was not happening. It could not be happening. Her arm was hurting where Henry's hand clenched it, and she tried to break away.

"I didn't mean it," Tess said again quietly. She didn't know who she was talking to.

"This is totally fucked up," Spencer said.

"Everyone just *shut up* and let me think!" Henry barked. He let go of Tess and went to sit on the big flat rock in the center of the beach. The sacrificial stone, Suz always called it. Tess stood over Suz's body, watching for a sign of life, some inkling that Henry had been wrong. She kneeled down in the sand, put her ear against Suz's chest, listening for a heartbeat. All she heard was Spencer behind her, trying to get his lighter to work, flicking it with his thumb over and over without getting a spark. Tess moved her head up, put her cheek above Suz's mouth, feeling for breath. Suz's lips were cold, bluish in the moonlight.

"The way I see it, we have two choices," Henry said at last, sounding altogether too sober. "We can go call the police and explain what happened. In this scenario, Tess would probably go to jail and maybe the rest of us too. Once they started their investigation and found out about some of the stuff we've done, we'd all be in some pretty deep shit. The Compassionate Dismantlers would be put under a microscope and I don't think any of us want that. Suz wouldn't have wanted that.

"Choice number two is that we put her in the lake. We weight her down and swim her out to the middle."

"We can't just sink her in the lake!" Winnie shrieked. "People will ask where she went. You can't just make someone disappear like that! We can't do that to her!"

"No one will come looking," Henry said. "Shit, all she's got is that one aunt who couldn't even bother coming to graduation. It's not like Suz kept in touch with anyone. We're the only family she's got. If anyone ever asks, we say she took off hitchhiking to California. Besides, I think this is what she would want. Think of how much she loves this place. Now she'll be a part of it forever."

Henry began picking up stones from the beach, filling Suz's clothes with them, and since no one stopped him, he continued.

"Do you have to do that?" Winnie asked, sobbing.

"We've got to weight her down. So she won't float."

Tess fell to her knees then, twisting her right hand with her left, feeling the sand and grit the rock had left on her palm.

Slowly, Henry carried Suz into the water, then swam on his back, her body resting on his chest and belly, out to the middle of the lake. They looked like two lovers doing the backstroke on a moonlit night. Suz's head bobbed on Henry's shoulder. It looked to Tess, squinting out at them, as if when Henry let Suz go, she went down smiling.

THE FIRST THING TESS thinks of when she wakes up is the story she never finished. The next thing she thinks is that she smells gasoline. And she can't breathe. Slowly it dawns on her that her mouth is taped closed. Arms and legs tied. It's dark. She's wrapped up tight in some sort of shroudlike sheet. And she's on the water. Floating. Bobbing up and down in some kind of boat. She's just cargo.

She remembers drinking the wine Claire gave her. And then Suz stepped into the room. Or someone dressed as Suz.

She has a very fuzzy memory of waking up again in a different room, hearing voices. Or one voice. The voice getting louder.

"She's waking up," it had said. Tess had forced her eyes open and saw Suz leaning down with a needle, felt a stinging in her arm.

Tess hears voices again now. They are muffled but recognizable. It's Henry and a woman. What are they saying? Something about dismantling love? But no, that was a conversation years ago. A conversation with Suz.

Tess starts to scream against the tape, but it only comes out as a sad little moan. And she thinks of that stupid riddle the moose told Spencer all those years ago. The riddle her daughter just re-told her. You're in a cement room with no windows or door. All you have is a table and mirror. How do you get out?

She wonders where her table and mirror are. How she's going to make a hole to crawl through.

Chapter 79

"SUZ?" HE'S SQUINTING AT her, not quite believing. This isn't the Suz he remembers: the one in the photos, the one Winnie has been running all over town dressed as. Her face is different, cheekbones more pronounced, nose slightly smaller.

"The new and improved, babycakes!" she says.

And yes, it *is* her. He'd know that voice anywhere, lilting, teasing.

"But I don't . . . I mean, I can't . . . ," he stammers.

She laughs. It's that throaty, seductive Suz laugh he's remembered each night in his dreams. His nightmares.

"My greatest accomplishment—I dismantled myself. Let Suz Pierce die that night and started over. It's amazing what a little cosmetic surgery can do, isn't it? Colored contacts, some hair dye, capped teeth."

"How?" Henry gasps. "You were dead."

She shakes her head. "No, Henry. Just unconscious. A little sluggish from the Vicodin Tess dumped in my drink. Mix that shit with booze and it's pretty much roll over and play dead—slows your heart and breathing way the fuck down. I came to as I was sinking, and started swimming underwater, pulling these fucking rocks out of my clothes—nice touch, Henry—as I went. When I couldn't hold my breath another second, I surfaced and was clear on the other side of the lake, away from you idiots."

Henry stares at her in disbelief, remembering how he had searched for a pulse on her wrist, her neck. Her skin was damp and cold. Frog skin. Her chest did not rise and fall.

"I thought I was all done with this place, but a couple weeks back, I got this postcard. My cousin Nancy forwarded it to me from my aunt's. She called me a week later to tell me about Spencer. Icing on the fucking cake, right?"

"You didn't send the postcards?" Henry asks.

Suz shakes her head.

"Well, who did?" he asks.

She shrugs. "You got me, babycakes. I thought maybe it was you. But it doesn't matter now. The way I see it, whoever sent them did me a favor. They gave me the perfect opportunity to come back for one final act of dismantling."

Henry's head is spinning. He's trying to focus on her words, to connect the dots to see the full picture at last.

"*You* left the notes for Winnie in her journal. Gave her the clothes and wig. You wanted us all to think it was her."

She nods. "Now you're catching on. And playing Claire Novak was just too much fun."

"Who?" Henry asks.

"The woman your wife's been having an affair with. Or didn't you know?" She laughs.

Henry remembers the conversation he overheard on the phone: Tess saying, "I'll do it," and a woman with an accent answering, "I knew you would." It was Suz.

Of course she'd target Tess. Tess would have been the first person she went after.

But where *is* Tess?

Frantic voices float across the lake. *It's Suz!*

"Care to do the honors?" Suz asks, pulling a book of matches from her pocket, holding it out to him. He shakes his head.

"Suit yourself," she says. "Maybe you're still too spooked after that fire burned down poor Tess's studio. A terrible thing, wasn't it? Funny how much damage a single candle and a few cans of turpentine can do." She strikes a match, her face glowing like an orange demon behind it, eyes glistening as she holds the match to the antlers of the gas-soaked wooden moose.

"It was you," Henry said, deflated.

The flames jump over the moose's ears, down his head and neck.

Suz stands, perching at the bow of the canoe, says, "Henry, you poor fool, it's always been me," then dives into the water, smooth and graceful, as if she and the lake are one.

Chapter 80

EMMA'S MOVING FAST THROUGH the water, her cadence perfect. She's almost to them, though she doesn't know what she'll do when she gets there.

She knows only that she has to save Danner and Francis.

Back on the shore, a man and woman are screaming something about Suz.

It's Suz!

What is?

Maybe Daddy and Winnie know.

Emma remembers the photo of the four of them: her parents young and in love; the girl giving the finger; the other, dark-haired girl holding the gun. The Compassionate Dismantlers.

Emma wishes she could loop back in time to the morning she and Mel searched her dad's studio. She'd put that photo back in the toolbox with the heavy black journal, lock it all up tight. Tell Mel to forget all about Operation Reunite.

Some things are better left alone.

Emma's almost to the canoe when Winnie rises, lights a match, holds it to her face.

But this is all wrong. The woman in the boat doesn't look like Winnie. Not now that her face is lit up.

Emma's skin prickles.

They'll burn.

The match hits Francis's antlers, and the flames race over his head, following a trail down his great neck, over his shoulders, spreading across his wide back.

Winnie (or the person dressed up like Winnie) dives from the front of the canoe, making the whole thing rock; Francis the moose sways, dancing in the flames. Emma's father clings to the sides, then lowers himself carefully into the water, like a stiff old man, one leg at a time. Her father, who never swims, who is petrified of bathtubs even, is soon kicking, thrashing his arms in a blind panic. He's like a man who's never learned to swim.

"Emma?" her dad says, then, just as she's about to answer—to say, *Yes, Daddy, it's me*—he goes under.

Chapter 81

WHEN SUZ DIVES OFF the front, it makes the canoe rock, nearly tipping. Henry drops the paddle, grips both sides of the canoe in a desperate attempt to stay upright.

What are his options? Swim or be burned alive.

He feels the heat as the moose's head is engulfed in flames. The smoke blows back, hitting him like a wall, choking him, making his eyes burn. Slowly, carefully, he lifts himself out the canoe and slips into the inky water.

The panic he feels is incredible. He's fighting with the water, flailing uselessly, exhausting himself. Then, he sees her.

There, just in front of him, is his daughter, exactly as she appears in his dreams. Emma, his Emma, is sinking down, her hair and clothing full of pondweed—a little girl playing dress up, with a necklace, boa, and tiara of slimy green stems, brown algae-covered leaves.

"Emma," he calls, the word a desperate sigh.

He holds his breath and goes after her.

He swims blindly down, reaching out with his hands, not seeing anything.

Down, down, down he swims, sure he'll touch bottom at any minute. He's holding his breath, but his eyes are open. He sees his own arms, glowing and pale, moving in front of him; disembodied, creatures all their own.

Hands are grabbing the back of his shirt. He's being pulled up.

No! he wants to scream. *My little girl is down here!*

He struggles against the hands, but he needs a breath, just one sucking gulp of precious air, then he can go under again.

He fights his way to the top, his rescuer still holding tight to his shirt. He surfaces, gasping for air, and hears Emma's voice.

"Daddy!"

He turns, sees that it's Emma clutching his shirt.

"But you went under," he says, coughing and sputtering, reaching out to take her in his shaking arms.

"I thought you were drowning," she says, gasping herself.

No. It was you. You were drowning.

He holds her against him, both of them treading water and shivering. Emma's in shorts and a T-shirt. No flowing clothing. No long fronds of pondweed draped around her neck and woven through her hair.

Is it possible, Henry wonders, that your fears can take on a life of their own? Is this what ghosts are—things worried into existence, frantic energy manifesting itself in an almost physical way?

Suz, like a buoyant otter, is swimming playful circles around Henry and Emma.

"Thought we lost you there," Suz says. "What happened, Henry? You used to be a great swimmer. Pretty sad. Having to be rescued by a little girl."

Behind them the moose crackles and snaps as the flames spread.

But beyond the noise of the fire, there is another sound, a low howl, as if the moose is crying out in pain.

It's almost human—buzzing and frantic: the static noise.

Treading water, Henry remembers the weight and heft of the Danner doll. The way she was laid out in his studio, waiting for him like some kind of sacrifice.

"Daddy!" Emma cries, nearly to him now. "You've got to put out Francis! Hurry! You've got to save Danner."

Another humming groan from inside the moose.

Tess was the one who threw the rock that night. The one who'd drugged Suz's drink. It was Henry who stuffed her clothing full of rocks and dragged her out into the middle of the lake, but it had been Tess who killed her.

He begins paddling madly toward the blazing moose carcass. Henry's battling with the water, struggling to stay afloat and move forward. His face keeps bobbing under. He swallows great gulps of lake water, coughs and sputters.

"Danner!" Emma screams, swimming toward the burning moose at a steady clip.

Henry's swimming muscles are stiff and out of practice, but soon he hits his stride, stops taking gulps of water. His body remembers and takes over, overpowering the crushing fear in his mind. He was always a strong swimmer. The strongest and fastest of the bunch.

"You're too late, Henry," Suz calls. She's treading water behind him. "You're fucking pathetic!"

The moose is throwing off too much heat. Its antlers have collapsed; its head is teetering forward, hanging by a thread. Flames have covered its back. The tail is nothing but crisp carbon and ash.

"A crime of passion," Suz says. "You discovered your wife was having an affair with another woman and you snapped. So tragic! So sick and titillating and tragic! Gonna be on Court TV for sure!"

Henry swims closer to the moose, the truth moving through

him like its own sort of fire. He turns back to Suz. "What have you done?"

Suz laughs. "Oh, Henry. The question is, what have *you* done?"

Emma is beside him now. "Danner, Daddy!" she squeals.

"Stay back!" he yells at Emma. And then, he holds his breath and goes under.

Eyes open. Black water. He dives down and forward, reaches ahead and up, grasping blindly until he feels the wooden hull. He's under the boat now, and brings his hands up, grabs the edge of the canoe, fingers screaming from the heat, and yanks down with all his might. The canoe teeters, then flips. He slides through the water and comes up for air on the other side.

His lungs clog with the thick smoke. Pieces of burning moose have floated away from the smoldering carcass and sail like a tiny flaming regatta. The body of the moose, what's left of it, is quickly sinking.

"Hurry, Daddy!" Emma yelps. She's treading water near the sinking moose. He scans the wreckage, sees the moose is door side down. He grabs hold of it, the charred wood is hot but the flames are out. He's trying to flip it over, to keep it from going down. With his left hand, he finds the door underwater. He takes a scorching breath and dives under, pulling at it. Then Emma is beside him, reaching for the door in the moose's chest. The door that has jammed, won't open. They're both feeling along the edges, scrabbling and pounding. Henry has to rise to the surface for a breath, but Emma, Emma can stay underwater forever, she's got gills, their daughter, and by the time Henry takes a stabbing breath and dives back under, he finds that Em's got the door open. Now it's her turn to go up for air.

The figure wrapped in rope is thrashing, fighting against him as he pulls it out of the skeletal wreckage of the moose. He loses his grip, the body slips away, sinking down. He dives deeper, groping in the dark water and grabs it again, yellow rope looped around his hands as they struggle to the surface where his lungs scream for air.

With Emma helping him, treading water, they awkwardly unravel the waterlogged rope mummy to reveal Emma's doll. Henry rips at the cloth face, the terrible eyes stitched on, ink running like tears down the pillowcase face.

"Dad! No!" Emma shouts, but then she sees what's underneath.

Tess is inside, her own eyes wide with panic, mouth duct-taped closed.

"Mom?" Emma says. "You're Danner?"

Henry and Emma free her from the remaining rope and Danner doll suit, pull the tape from her mouth. She gulps at the air, coughing and retching.

"Henry," she whispers at last. She's naked against him. Shivering, but okay. She's going to be okay.

She gives a little shriek.

"Shhh," he says. "You're okay. It's okay now."

"Suz," Tess gasps as she looks out across the water. "She went under. She's gone."

And they all look to the place where Suz just was, scan the surface of the water for bubbles, ripples, anything, but she's slipped away. All that's left is the blond wig, floating.

Chapter 82

"I WAS SO CLOSE to piecing everything together," Bill Lunde tells them. They're huddled around Henry's pickup, on the beach, waiting for the police to arrive. Tess has wrapped herself in a paint-splattered canvas tarp from the back of the truck. She's shivering. Can't seem to get warm. Henry is standing beside her, their bodies not quite touching. Every now and then, when she lets out a hacking cough, he reaches over and gives her shoulder a tentative little pat, something an old-maid aunt might do. Emma is sitting cross-legged on the big rock in the center of the beach. She's holding a soaking-wet canvas gardening glove—all that remains of the Danner doll.

"I'd followed Tess out to Claire Novak's and seen Claire sneaking around at the cabin," Bill tells them. "I suspected she might be Suz, but didn't have any hard evidence. And of course I had no idea that you all thought she was dead."

Henry's already explained that ten years ago, there'd been . . . an accident. "I swam her body out into the middle of the lake," he told Bill. "I watched her go under."

Tess still can't believe it.

Suz. Alive.

Claire was Suz. It doesn't seem possible.

Passion. That's what's missing.

She pictures Claire's hands. Tries hard to go back in her mind and see Suz's. Could they really be the same? Yes, she may have changed the shape of her face, the color of her hair and eyes—but shouldn't Tess have known? Isn't it possible to recognize someone by their hands, the small gestures it's impossible to hide?

Was Tess that desperate for love, for someone to come along and actually understand her, that she was blind to the warning signs?

Pathetic.

"She's the one who left the wig and clothes for me. Who'd been writing in my journal," Winnie says. "It *was* Suz. Only not the ghost version."

Bill nods.

"I can't believe she's been alive all this time," Winnie says.

"Alive and harboring one hell of a grudge," Bill adds.

Tess touches her bruised shoulder—the faint bite marks Suz left there.

Do you want to be saved, Tess?

"Did she say anything to you?" Henry asks Winnie. "When she came out to the cabin and tied you up like that?"

Winnie's chin quivers. Her eyes fill. "She said we'd disappointed her. She couldn't believe how easy it had all been. To set us up like this. To fool us."

Henry turns to look at Tess, who has said nothing so far. What is there to say? What can she possibly add to all of this? She had been the one most fooled. The joke was on her.

Tell me your biggest secret. The one thing you've never told anyone.

"I think she was the one who sent the postcards," Bill tells them. "Though I can't figure out why she waited ten years."

It'll be like confession . . . I'll absolve you of your sins.

Henry shakes his head. "When we were out on the canoe, she said it wasn't her. But that whoever did send them had done her a favor."

"It was me." A weak voice from the edge of the group. "I sent the postcards," Emma says. She looks so small, hunched there in her soaking-wet shorts and T-shirt. The little girl brought into existence by holes Winnie poked in a condom. The one good thing that had come out of that long-ago summer.

"Mel and I found the pictures and old journal in Dad's studio." She looks at her parents. "I thought that if I could get your college friends back . . ." Her chin starts to quiver and she looks down at the ground.

Tess steps forward, takes Emma in her arms, enfolding her inside the paint-splattered tarp, like a mother moth.

Flashing lights come bouncing down the old logging road. Bill insisted on calling the police, but Tess knows it won't make a difference. They can search the woods around the lake all night—they'll never find her. As always, she's about ten steps ahead of everyone else.

Suz is gone.

PART SIX

LOOK IN THE MIRROR TO SEE WHAT YOU SAW

Chapter 83

HENRY'S ON THE FLOOR of his workshop, amid the sawdust and shavings: all that's left of the canoe.

He's got Suz's journal on his lap. Winnie handed it to him yesterday just before she got in her pickup to head back to Boston.

"Suz left it for me that last day," Winnie told him. "She must have taken it from your studio when she grabbed Emma's doll out of the Blazer."

Henry nodded. Over the past week, they'd put everything together. It had been Suz dressed up in the wig and old clothes, sneaking around. She'd burned Tess's studio. She'd learned about the doll from Tess, knew how Henry hated it. Winnie told them that Suz seemed to know all about their plan to float the moose out on the lake with all her things inside and set it on fire.

"She must have been spying on us all the time. Listening to our phone conversations. She knew everything," Winnie said. "I think she snuck into your house that night and moved the doll around, knowing it would freak you out to the point of wanting to burn it up in the moose. Then she stole the doll and returned it with Tess stuck inside."

Tess, they'd learned from blood tests at the hospital, had been injected with walloping doses of tranquilizers to keep her knocked out, hidden inside the Danner doll.

"Veterinary drugs," the emergency room doctor told Henry. "It's a lucky thing your wife is in such excellent shape—her heart could take it. Another person might not have been so lucky."

Henry still didn't understand how Suz had pulled it all off—it wasn't possible that she'd planned for things to go the way they had. She had no way of knowing about the canoe or the doll when she'd first gotten to town.

"You know what Suz used to say," Winnie told him. "Great art is all about improvisation."

Henry had one hand on the door of Winnie's pickup, in the other was the journal. He remembered Suz taunting them from the lake just before Tess hit her with the rock.

We'll always have this summer to remember. To come back to. Part of us will always be here.

"Do you think we'll ever see her again?" Henry asked Winnie just before she pulled away.

Winnie shrugged. "It depends," Winnie said. "On whether or not she thinks she's through with us."

HENRY FLIPS THROUGH THE journal. Reads about the formation of the Dismantlers—how Suz pocketed the keys to the van so they'd be stranded at the gas station that long-ago December. As he turns the pages, he watches Suz falling in love with Winnie, determined to save Winnie from the boys and the cutting, even from herself. He reads about Suz's plot to get him and Tess together, how she talked him into going out to the Habitrail tube to meet Tess that night by saying, "If you want to prove your allegiance to me, Henry, then go out there and hook up with Tess. It's not forever. It's just what works best for now."

Last night, after checking on Emma, Henry stuck his head in

to say good night to Tess. She was sitting on the edge of the bed, staring at a sketch she'd done of Suz, crying.

Without a word, he sat down beside her, put his hand gently on her shoulder. She leaned into him, let him hold her. They stayed like that for a long time, not speaking, but together. Finally, too exhausted to sit any longer, they lay down together on top of the quilt covering the bed. He held her all night, listened to her fall asleep, breathed in the smell of her hair, felt her chest rise and fall.

And in the morning, when he woke, she was down in the kitchen, the smell of coffee drifting up the stairs. He lay there a long time, savoring the moment, tricking himself into believing that it had never been any other way—he had always been there, waking on his side of the bed, her pillow still warm.

Part of him was twenty again, waking up in her dorm room at Sexton, waiting for her to bring in a cup of thick, sweet Turkish coffee, in love with his life because it was so full of possibility.

Sometimes I think we're just conduits.

Then he sat up looked down at the floor and saw Tess's sketch looking back at him.

Suz.

Suz the creator. Suz the destroyer. Suz the shaman, who put hair and blood and dirt and little pieces of other people's souls into every work of art she ever created, making the static noise, speaking in tongues.

Suz. His Suz. Their Suz.

Part of you will always be with me.

He bent and turned the drawing over, facedown, then joined his wife and daughter downstairs for breakfast.

HENRY'S DECIDED TO BURN the journal today. He'll look at it one last time, then have his own little bonfire out behind the barn. Time to put the past to rest once and for all so he can concentrate on rebuilding his life in the here and now.

Henry flips to an entry he hasn't read before. Dated one week before Suz's supposed death, before the end of everything.

>*July 20—Cabin at the lake*
>*I told Winnie the truth today. I expected her to be*
>*furious, but she wasn't. She said that when this*
>*thing with Spencer is over, this final mission of the*
>*Compassionate Dismantlers, she and I can leave here,*
>*make a new start someplace else.*
>
>*I laughed a little. "But what about the baby?" I asked.*
>
>*"We have it. We go out to San Francisco and have the*
>*baby. Our own little family."*
>
>*"What about Henry and Tess?"*
>
>*"We don't tell them. They never have to know."*
>
>*"But Henry's the kid's father," I argued.*
>
>*"No," Winnie said. "One drunken fuck in the sand*
>*doesn't make you a father."*
>
>*"Neither of us was drunk," I told her. "And Henry*
>*used a condom. I don't get how it happened. We were*
>*careful."*
>
>*I watched Winnie cringe. "These things happen," she*
>*said. "It doesn't matter how it happened, but we've*
>*gotta believe it happened for a reason, right? We're*
>*meant to have this baby—you and me. We're the only*
>*parents she'll need."*

I kissed her.

*I don't know what's really gonna happen—the whole
thing scares the shit out of me, to be honest.*

*I know it doesn't make any sense, and it's not really
possible, but sometimes . . . sometimes I think I feel
her in there, swimming around like a little tadpole; the
tiniest secret with a heart all her own.*

Henry closes the journal, his head beginning to throb.
Part of you will always be here with me.

Did Suz have a child? His child? Does he have a son or daughter out there somewhere, walking around in the world?

The child would be about Emma's age.

He tosses the journal aside, pulls the cell phone from his pocket, and punches in Winnie's number. He gets her voice mail.

"Why didn't you tell me?" he says into the phone. "Suz really was pregnant. That baby was mine! What happened to it? If you know, if she said anything to you about it when she found you at the cabin, you've got to tell me. Please call me back."

As he's hanging up, his landline rings. He pulls himself up off the floor and hurries to grab the phone mounted on the wall beside his tool bench. Maybe it's Winnie! Or even Suz—he lets himself imagine it for half a second—Suz calling to say, *Would you like to meet your child? The one you never knew about?*

"Hello," Henry says, nearly breathless with expectation.

"Henry? Bill Lunde here."

"Hey, Bill." Henry sighs, dusting wood chips from his pants.

"Henry . . . I wanted to give you a heads-up. The police, when they couldn't find any trace of Suz in the immediate area, they dragged Number Ten Lake. The divers found something."

Henry presses the phone harder against his ear. "Something?"

"First, they pulled up a trash bag full of clothes and personal effects." Bill pauses, Henry nods into the phone, remembers Winnie telling the story of swimming the clothes out when she first got back to the cabin. Bill clears his throat, continuing, "Then they discovered human remains. Out in the middle of the lake."

"Oh my god! Did Suz not make it back to shore? Did she get caught up on the moose somehow?"

"No. The bones they pulled from the bottom of the lake had been there awhile. A decade or so. Female, trauma to her skull."

Henry feels the little pinprick of pain in his left eye that says a headache is coming. His breath is fast and shallow. His skin cool and clammy.

"I don't understand," Henry tells him.

"Suz's old dental records were faxed over this morning. They're a positive match, Henry. I think you're going to want to get a lawyer."

Henry remembers the feel of Suz against him, on top of him, as he swam on his back out into the middle of the lake. How cold her body felt. How still.

"But that's not possible. Suz is alive. She came back," Henry says. "You saw her. She told me things in the canoe—things only Suz would know."

"We were wrong, Henry. I don't know who Claire Novak is—I can't find a trace of her anywhere—but she's definitely not Suz Pierce."

Henry feels all the air leave him.

He's underwater again, trying to save his drowning daughter. Only this time, at last, he understands it's not Emma. It's the unborn child Suz was carrying when he swam her out to the middle of Number 10 Lake, her clothing full of rocks.

Chapter 84

TESS'S EYES ARE MOVING from wall to canvas as she tries to capture . . . what? Surely not passion.

Answers. That's what she wants: answers.

She's been working on the portrait for three days now. With no studio to work in, she's set herself up in the bedroom. The wall opposite her is covered with the sketches she'd done of Claire Novak: pair after pair of Claire's green eyes follow her everywhere she goes, each version of her face forming the same unspoken question: how could you let yourself be fooled?

As she's worked from the sketches, filling in details from memory, she's studied the painting for some sign. She's recalled each conversation, each meeting, replaying words and phrases, searching for clues. Surely, Suz must have dropped clues. That would have been part of the game.

She's found herself talking to the portrait, begging for answers. And now, as she adds the finishing touches—the little highlights in Claire's eyes—she steps back to look and sees that what she's captured on the canvas isn't really Claire. Yet it isn't Suz either. It's a strange amalgamation of the two: a mythical creature with startling green eyes, blond hair, and a cigarette in her mouth.

"Tess." Henry's stumbled into the room, looking pale. He's holding a hand over one eye the way he does when he has a bad headache. She goes to him, gently moves his hand away and places her fingers on his forehead, her thumb hooked under the ridge of his eyebrow, and begins to rub in slow circles. She knows what to do. How to make this go away.

When Tess woke up this morning with Henry's arm wrapped around her, she had the feeling for the first time in days, weeks, months even, that things might be all right. Maybe, now that she wasn't a murderer, now that Henry wasn't her accomplice, they could start their lives over in some way. Maybe the past would let them go.

She wasn't an idiot. She didn't expect that they'd get together again and live happily ever after. But maybe now that things didn't feel so trapped and stagnant, they could try again. Go out for dinner and a movie: best friends who might, one day, become something more. They could even take that silly gallery owner's advice and go on a trip: see Europe. Go wine tasting in Provence. Get to know each other all over again.

Tess smiles at the thought as she holds his head cradled in her hands, rubs the pain away with her magic-finger circles.

"It wasn't her, Tess," he says. He's crying now, but trying not to. His whole body heaves and trembles with the effort of holding it all back.

"Wasn't who?" she asks, her voice calm as a lullaby, her fingers and thumb still doing their slow, steady circles.

"They found . . . remains. At the bottom of the lake. A female. Trauma to the skull. They've been there ten years. All this time."

"No," Tess says, the word little more than a weak sigh.

"They faxed over her dental records this morning, Tess. Lunde says it was a positive match. It's Suz."

Her fingers slip away from his face.

"But she—" Tess hears herself say, reaching up to touch her shoulder, where her shirt hides a gold-colored bruise marking the place Claire's teeth met her skin.

"They've been down there the whole time," Henry repeats, as if what remains of Suz is somehow more than she ever was in life.

Tess turns to look back at her portrait. If Claire wasn't Suz, who was she?

Behind her, Henry slips away saying something about finding a lawyer. "And you should call your parents," he says. "See if they can drive up and help with Em for a while."

Tess nods, her eyes still on the portrait.

Tell me your biggest secret. The one thing you've never told anyone.

The police will come. And she knows what she'll tell them, no matter what any lawyer advises: the truth. It's time for the truth.

She held a rock in her hand. It was the size of a grapefruit. She didn't realize she was going to throw it until it was in the air. Even then, she never thought she had a chance of hitting Suz. She was so far out. And Tess had such lousy aim. She was just angry. Wanting to scare Suz, shut her up for once, just for one minute.

Tess closes her eyes. Sees Suz on a hillside of brown grass, a crown of oak leaves in her hair. Behind her, the parking lot with Henry's van, keys lost; the Texaco sign—a bright white star shining down, marking their place on earth, in the universe. And Suz leans toward them, and in a fevered whisper says, "Do you want to hear something that will change your lives forever?"

Chapter 85

WINNIE ROLLS OVER. THE train is rattling along on
its tracks, rocking her, lulling her back to a dreamless sleep. For
once, the nightmares are gone. She lifts her head from the pillow,
pulls back the curtain to see a brilliant sunrise lighting fields and
mountain. They could be anywhere. The truth is, she's lost track.
Isn't sure which borders they've crossed.

Over the intercom, the conductor makes an announcement
she doesn't understand.

"You awake, love?" Amber asks.

Winnie turns, sees Amber's got the wig on. God, she loves it when
Amber wears the wig. It gives her a little jolt, makes her scars tingle.

When they met in the hospital two years ago, Winnie knew
that her luck was about to change. Here was a person who understood everything Winnie said, everything she had to offer. A mysterious woman with deep green eyes and the highest cheekbones
Winnie had ever seen. *Nefertiti,* Winnie called her.

Now that she knows her better, she calls her *My Little Chame-
leon,* because Amber has this uncanny ability to change her look,
her voice, to turn into someone else.

In the beginning, Winnie started with the story of her scars. And to tell the story of her scars, she had to tell the story of Suz. The story of the Dismantlers. Amber wanted to know everything. Every detail. She became enraptured with Suz, even secondhand.

And everything they'd done together had all started with Amber's idea: "You know," she said, "we should really find a way to make the others pay for what they did to Suz. And the baby."

When the postcards arrived it was an unbelievable stroke of luck. A miracle.

They hadn't started out with much of a plan. Just that Amber would play Claire Novak—Suz in disguise—and somehow, they'd pull off an act of revenge worthy of the Dismantlers, of Suz. And things had fallen into place so perfectly: the moose, the canoe, Emma's doll, Tess's seduction; it was as if Suz herself was guiding them, pulling everyone on invisible puppet strings.

Winnie loves to imagine the look poor Tess must have had on her face when Amber came into the bedroom dressed as Suz, syringe in hand. She wishes she could have been there to see it instead of hiding out at Henry's, moving the damn doll around. She joined Amber as soon as she and Henry finished putting the moose on the canoe; got there in time to see Amber give Tess the final dose of tranquilizers before stitching her up inside Emma's doll. For an instant, Tess seemed to come to, opening her eyes to see them both standing there in their matching blond wigs and silk tunics. Tess had the oddest look of being both puzzled and suddenly understanding everything.

"What if she recognized me?" Winnie had asked Amber once Tess was out again.

Amber had shaken her head. "If she even remembers, all she'll think is that she had double vision, and instead of one Suz, she saw two. Besides, it's not as if it matters now. Once she's in the moose, it's all over. Now come on, we've gotta hurry up and get her over to Henry's barn."

■ ■ ■

"I'M GLAD YOU BROUGHT the wig," Winnie says, running her fingers up the bumps of Amber's spine, a train track all its own. Bumpity, bump.

Amber turns to face Winnie. They kiss. Amber's kisses are all tongue; hungry dog kisses.

"What wig?" Amber says, breaking away from the kiss and using the mysterious Claire Novak accent.

And Winnie thinks it again: Suz would have loved this. She'd love Amber. Wherever she is right now, she's pleased.

Winnie reaches for what's left of the bottle of champagne and refills their glasses.

"To Suz," Amber says, as if reading Winnie's mind.

"And to the new Compassionate Dismantlers," Winnie says.

"Tear it up, babycakes," Amber whispers, so like Suz it gives Winnie shivers. "Let's tear it the fuck up."

Chapter 86

IN ORDER TO TRULY understand something, you have to take it apart.

This is what the moose tells her.

"No," Emma argues. "You have to put things together. That's the only way to make sense of the world."

Francis the moose is whole now, all nine paintings hung in the entryway of their house, taking up the entire wall.

"Nine," Emma whispers again, smiling as she stands in the front hall, dwarfed by Francis in his entirety.

He gives a little shuffle. A happy whole-moose grunt.

Sometimes, like now, Emma's sure she can even smell him—his thick, musky scent of fur and dung; wild, far-off places. Places like *A Long Time Ago*.

Yesterday, she watched a fly land on the painting, crawl along the entire length of his body, moving carefully, prodding with its proboscis, apparently unsure whether it was tasting actual moose or paint-covered canvas.

It makes her dizzy to think of it.

Emma has heard the hushed conversations her parents have

been having this morning. She knows about the skeleton pulled from the lake. She understands what it means.

Emma goes upstairs to her room, locks the door, then lays down on her bed with her eyes closed tight.

"Danner?" she calls. "What if they take my parents away?"

Emma's skin gets prickly and she opens her eyes. There, in the chair by the computer, is Danner. The real Danner—the one she's known her whole life, has grown up alongside, not some stupid doll.

"Don't worry," Danner tells her. The light coming through the window seems to shine through her, make her glow and sparkle. "We're sisters, after all. We'll always have each other."

BOOKS BY
Jennifer McMahon

DISMANTLED
A Novel
ISBN 978-0-06-168934-5 (paperback)

"[A]n eerie and gripping tale of suspense....
It's rare that I find an author who can so
compellingly convey a child's point of view."
—*Boston Globe*

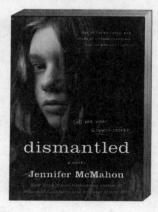

ISLAND OF LOST GIRLS
A Novel
ISBN 978-0-06-144588-0 (paperback)

"McMahon never flinches, but her readers will at
every dark secret." —Keith Donohue, author of
The Stolen Child

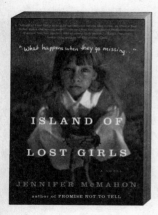

PROMISE NOT TO TELL
A Novel
ISBN 978-0-06-114331-1 (paperback)

"This taut novel is above all a reflection on the
haunting power of memory."
—*Entertainment Weekly*

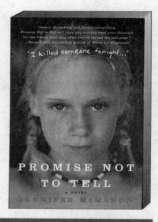